LUNA'S

CALIFORNIA POPPIES

Bilingual Press/Editorial Bilingüe

Address:
Bilingual Press
Hispanic Research Center
Arizona State University
P.O. Box 872702
Tempe, Arizona 85287-2702
(480) 965-3867

LUNA'S
CALIFORNIA POPPIES

Alma Luz Villanueva

Bilingual Press/Editorial Bilingüe
TEMPE, ARIZONA

Library of Congress Cataloging-in-Publication Data

Villanueva, Alma, 1944-
Luna's California poppies / Alma Luz Villanueva.
p. cm.
ISBN 0-927534-98-3 (alk. paper) — ISBN 0-927534-99-1 (pbk. : alk. paper)
1. Girls—Fiction. 2. Mexican American women—Fiction. 3. Ethnic relations—Fiction. 4. Toleration—Fiction. 5. California—Fiction. I. Title.

PS3572.I354 L86 2000
813'.54—dc21 00-062174

PRINTED IN THE UNITED STATES OF AMERICA

Cover art, *Wolf Dream,* by Carmen León
Photo of art by Wilfredo Q. Castaño
Back cover photo by Leon Camerot
Cover and interior design by Aerocraft Charter Art Service

Acknowledgments

Partial funding provided by the Arizona Commission on the Arts through appropriations from the Arizona State Legislature and grants from the National Endowment for the Arts.

Acknowledgments continue on p. 238.

"Mexicans they's supposed to be the cosmic race . . . And then I started thinking it must be nice to be a people that looks at each other and sees they own gods and ain't have to look at other people's gods."

GAYL JONES, *MOSQUITO*

(AUGUST PHONEY SUMMER FOGGY SAN FRANCISCO)

NOTICE TO BURGLERS AND SNOOPS—THIS IS A PRIVATE DIARY, AND IF YOU READ THIS WITHOUT MY (LUNA LUZ VILLALOBOS) PERMISSION I WILL PUT A HEX ON YOU LIKE THE PYRAMIDS, LIKE YOU WILL DIE A SLOW DEATH, I MEAN REALLY SLOW AND EVERY THING YOU EAT WILL TASTE LIKE DOG SHIT, BOOGERS, CAT PUKE, HAMSTER TURDS, LEFT OVER SNAKE AND THE SUN WILL MAKE YOUR EYES POP OUT, AND IF YOUR A GUY YOUR DICK WILL FALL OFF AND IF YOUR A GIRL YOUR BOOBS WILL FALL OFF, SO BEWARE—BEWARE AND CLOSE THIS NOW! CLOSE THIS DIARY NOW! THIS DIARYS NONE OF YOUR BEES WAX!!!!

HA HA HA HA

END OF THE CURSE—NO MANS LAND—END OF THE CURSE—NO MANS LAND—

LAND OF LUNA LUZ VILLALOBOS—END OF THE CURSE NOW (LAND OF LA VIRGEN)

AND A HA!!!! HA!!!!

Dear La Virgen,

Can you keep a secret or two like every thing I write to you cause theres no one else to write to or talk to but you. About how I feel I mean. How I really feel and all the weird stuff that happens in my life. Like don't tell God or any thing cause its none of his bees wax. OK? I figure if I don't pray to him he'll kinda leave me alone and not punish me for the stupid things I have to do some times like steal stuff to eat like the phoney ham with El Diablo on it kinda a joke of mine, like El Diablo doesn't scare me on the front of the pham, like hes kinda telling me You hungry kid? Well go to Hell with me and hes sort of danceing, kinda haveing a good time, well hes not hungry. Hes on the pham can right? (phoney ham = PHAM, my new word cool!) And it tastes delisious fryed and better with eggs and bread. Its harder to steal eggs and bread cause there fat but the pham cans fit right in my pockets and I can hear him laughing and danceing as I walk out of the store with an icy cold Coca Cola in my hand to go with it. OK I stole a hamster one time in the Pet Store, put him right on my stomach and felt its scratchy little paws trying to get out, then I think it liked how warm my stomach was and it fell asleep and it was mine all mine to keep. I fed it lettice, bread, peanuts, stuff like that and it scared the shit out of my mother Carmen.

Thats her name. Carmen. She called it a RAT. She doesn't know a rat from her Big But and I said Its a HAMSTER not a RAT, but she hated it any way. Then one day it was gone from the bath tub where I kept it cause it couldn't climb out cause the sides were to slippery for its scratchy paws. I used to sleep with it all night and put it on my stomach. Then Carmen went to stay with her old husband Jake whos a REAL PSYCHO (I spell pretty good don't I?) I'm a Spelling Bee Champion and my teacher says I could be a writer some day cause I write good stories some times. I make them up and its like lieing which I'm pretty good at, Virgen, but you already know that right? I promise to never ever lie to you—not ever. Here I'll always tell the truth and if I spell some thing wrong let me know OK? (THE LAND OF LUNA LUZ VILLALOBOS Y LA VIRGEN OKAY?) Maybe you can tell I'm learning where to put my commas and stuff—any way just don't tell GOD any thing I tell you, you know all those storys in the Baptist Church about how he'll smite thee and thou and all of Creation, I mean I just don't pray to him ever, not any more. I used to pray to the Baby Jesus cause I figured at least he was a kid and would probably know what I was talking about right? Mi Mamacita used to laugh at me when I told her I was praying to the Baby Jesus not to God cause he wasn't my father. I don't have a father and if I did would he SMITE me like Jake my psycho step step step father tryed to hit me once, like just one time he hit the side of my head like my ears and called me Rabbit Ears (And it really hurt but I didn't cry cause I know thats what he wanted me to do The Psycho.) You know Virgen I got him back but good, so hes scared of me now and calls me THE WITCH and I just stare at him harder trying to make my eyes look like The Witch Power to kill him cause I almost did. I'll tell you about that some time, like one time I knocked out his front tooth with my fist as he came flying through our front door after he broke it down and Carmen was screaming her stupid head off and my baby brother Jake Junior was screaming his baby head off, well it was up to me so I stood on a chair next to the door and as It (The Psycho) appeared I swooped with my Killer Fist (The one I use on boys). Right on the MOUTH and I swear I'm not lying the tooth hit the wall. OK I was scared and he was drunk and crazy as usual but when I saw the blood cover his hand, My tooth, my tooth he kept saying. I felt better—I felt HAPPY cause I stopped him from wrecking our place or throwing the Christmas Tree out the window or strangling Carmen almost to death as usual and so I ran down the steps and called the cops and when he told the cops I knocked out his tooth the cops looked at me and laughed.

Probably cause I'm 11 years old and pretty skinny and all, I know that, but I'm pretty strong for a girl probably cause I play foot ball and fight boys all the time. I've never fought a girl cause they just like to call each other names and make a circle around you and say WHOS THE PRETTYEST? I always point to the ugly girl cause it makes her happy and the pretty girls get mad and confused and I say YEAH SHES THE PRETTYEST GIRL I'VE EVER SEEN! HA HA Pendejas! as Mamacita used to say when some one was being dumber than dumb but thought they were being so COOL. You know Mamacita always prayed to you cause I think she knew you can really keep a TRILLION secrets even from God In Heaven and besides Heavens far away right? She always told me she saw you in her dreams telling her what to do about her problems and some times I was the problem right? She told me she saw you some times when she woke up at night to go to the bath room and every time she saw you there was a big lake between you and her and you were always dressed in blue. So peaceful she told me and her eyes were happy and sad and full of water, but I never ever saw Mamacita cry.

So I figure your here not far away in Heaven and that feels better especially now that Mamacita is dead (You know that right?) Yeah she died like one more breath in her mouth and that was it. Some times I hear it in the wind like when I climb to the top of a building thats just being built like way up there I'll hear that last breath sound she made and I won't lie to you Virgen, it scares the SHIT out of me and I climb down so fast my hands are some times bleeding. I hope you don't mind but I'm going to swear some times cause thats how I really really talk, so if I'm going to tell you the whole truth well I figure its part of our secret like the REAL REAL ME (SHIT).

So when Carmen goes to stay with The Psycho with my baby brother I have this place all to myself even though theres no food or $ and I wonder if Jake Junior is crying by himself scared shit less of his crazy father. But I like it when there gone and thats the truth cause its quiet and I go to my friends Jody and Hope to eat and some times stay the night cause some times its to quiet especially at night like thats the bad part. I hate it. In fact its night right now or almost so I'm going to Hopes house like maybe there haveing SPAGHETTI, I LOVE SPAGHETTI (I told you I spelled pretty good—a Champ thats me right?)

I want to ask you some thing, like is it against the law to pick CALIFORNIA POPPYS and will the cops really arrest you and put you in jail and all? You know me Virgen, some times I go to school and some times I don't cause I HATE IT THERE like why do they always teach the same crappy stuff and the windows are always closed and every one really wants to go to sleep but we don't cause thats really against the laws. Any way this White Lady Teacher told us that the little orange flowers that grow all over the place on the alley way home is a CALIFORNIA POPPY like our State Flower she said and if you pick it its big trouble. She even stopped and looked at us with her MEAN face but I notice she smiled at her Pets. The 2 blond girls with corny ribbons in there corny braids. Its like the suns in there hair some times (Jody has real short blond hair). But I think the ribbons are SISSY ASS SHIT HA HA! Well the other day I picked 4 on purpose and snuck them home in my pocket but they were deader than a door nail when I took them out, but still they were mine right? So I ate them and waited but I didn't die or any thing, so has God said any thing? Any way now I pick 2 or 3 California Poppys and I eat them and they taste kinda sour like orange peels but there pretty soft, and I throw away the green part. So far no cops and I just look at the White Lady Teacher and I feel like I'm laughing and danceing like El Diablo on the pham can, but I thought I'd check with you to make sure its really really OK. So let me know in a dream if I should stop picking CALIFORNIA POPPYS and I'll stop if you say I should OK?

I'm glad I wrote to you Virgen, but the street lights are on and I hope Hope (HA HA) is haveing SPAGHETTI. Pray for me

OK? And don't forget every thing I say here is true so I'm hiding this and don't forget—DON'T TELL GOD ANY THING!!! Maybe you can show me in a dream about this too, that what I write to you is our secret. Pray for me and tell Mamacita I remember how we laughed to much some times till we peed our calzones (Believe it or not). But that I've stopped looking for her cause I guess shes really really not here any more.

(SEPTEMBER INDIAN REAL SUMMER)

Dear La Virgen,

Well I guess you know by now I don't write every day kinda like a real diary, so I'm writing when I have a lot to tell you OK? Remember the weird stuff I was telling you about that happens all the time, well heres what happened—(Believe it or not.) When Mamacita died in that real mangy hospital PRISON for old people like after that they must've taken her old BEAUTIFUL body (She really really was beautiful cause she had soft soft skin, pretty eyes except for when she got mad at any one and thick thick gray hair to her waist so some times she looked like a kid when she put it down at night so I could comb it cause she loved me to.) They took her to this mortician (Thats a hard word.) This guys named (Believe it or not). MAURICE, like he gave us a card like he was PROUD of his JOB! I call him The Blood Sucker and he even looks like a VAMPIRE all white and DISGUSTING! Well guess what? Right before my eyes and my Tias eyes Carmen started making The Eyes with the Blood Sucker! You would think she was meeting some handsome irrisistible guy like CARY GRANT, like she said one time when she saw him on TV—He can put his slippers under my bed any time. DISGUSTING. Hard up I thought, but no she was just meeting a Blood Sucker who I'm not kidding looks and talks and walks like a VAMPIRE! Any way after this Weirdo takes all the blood out of Mamacita a few days later when we come back and who knows WHY like he asks me if I want to see where he WORKS like down stairs in his Vampire Headquarters. I look at Carmen and say The Blood Sucker is all yours, but I can't even look at her and just walk out the Vampires door FAST! And believe it or not I think shes doing it with a VAMPIRE!

It took us to dinner to Carmens favorite Italian place where she always remembers The Italian General who used to take her out there and when you hear that story 100 times you want to I mean PUKE and so there we are this time with the tall skinny white face VAMPIRE instead of the short fat red face GENERAL eating spaghetti (My FAVORITE food). With meat balls in a blood red sauce and all I'm really thinking is These are guts and eye balls and blood YUM YUM and I'm also sitting right next to The Blood Sucker YUM! Then he turns and smiles at me and I swear to you Virgen his teeth are yellow and he tryed to touch my hand with those long skinny VAMPIRE fingers of his and I mean I almost SCREAM but instead I jump up like I have ants in my pants and RUN right out the door leaving the SPAGHETTI in blood and Carmen drinking more red wine and I wonder for about one sec if shes going to be able to walk out the door, and then I wonder where Jake Junior is cause hes not home and thats where I'm going I guess cause my friends are probably in bed now cause they have rules. Not me. So instead I go to the play ground the one at Dolores Park. The one surrounded by bushes where all the Perverts hide and jump out at you with there weiners flopping around. When that happens I always laugh and run but usually I'm with a friend and tonight I'm by myself right? For some reason I just don't care so I swing as high as I can and leap in to the sand over and over, and then I go home to sleep on the couch and lock all the windows and door and wait for the Perverts to come till morning. At least I didn't let a VAMPIRE touch me and I really HATE Carmen. I really really do. There I've said it Virgen, and Mamacita never allowed me to say it but I knew she knew I was thinking it cause she'd say Don't hate your mother, niña, she can't help herself. Of course she spoke only Spanish and now I hardly ever speak Spanish cause Carmen speaks only English now. So I guess for the first time I'm writing it down and saying it—I HATE CARMENS GUTS! Don't tell God cause I know about the rule like Honor thy father and mother, like I've heard it in Church right? But I feel you understand cause if you don't who else can I talk to and tell the TRUTH. So please let me know in a dream if I can tell you every thing and that you won't tell GOD OK?

Any way this is what happened—Carmen tells me to come with her and Jake Junior to a house about 2 blocks from here on Guerrero Street and my job she says is to stand at the bottom of the steps when she goes up to talk to some one she says has been seeing The Blood Sucker, like some ones trying to TAKE The Blood Sucker away from her. (Believe it or not.) And I laugh but shes really serious so I go and stand at the door after we're buzzed in and she takes Jake Junior up the stairs with her. (She also drank some red wine.) And I hear her yelling and a softer deeper ladys voice talking back to Carmen. Then theres no sound like nothing and then I hear the ladys voice say Why don't you come up honey? But I don't move cause my job here is to run and call the cops right? So down comes this White Lady and asks me if I'm hungry and I am really REALLY hungry I just didn't think of it till she just asked me. She says Your mothers inside having a sandwich and coffee so do you want some thing to eat to? Of course I don't really believe her but I follow her up the stairs and I see that Carmen is having a sandwich and Jake Junior is sucking on his babow (Thats what he calls it.) So I walk in to this ladys house which I can see is pretty nice like she has curtains every where and LOTS of furniture and dishes and when she opens the frig its full of FOOD. After I eat every thing as fast as I can she says This kid needs a bath and she means me. I need one and thats the truth I know but I feel embarassed shes saying it right out loud, and plus theres this drunk guy named JERGENS like the lotion whos her friend and he keeps saying I'm so beautiful and hes so WEIRD I can't stop laughing and even Carmens laughing. This white ladys name is DARLING (Believe it or not!) DARLING. She takes me to the shower and says OK kid strip and I'll wash these for you. She gives me a shirt and some really baggy pants and so I lock the door and then throw my stuff out side the door (Except my under wear of course.) I lock it and shower with lots of HOT WATER and lots of NEW SOAP and theres LOTS of clean soft towels piled in a corner like on a shelf COOL. I really like this and so I wash my hair to. When I open the door the steam runs out and Jergens runs in cause he has to go to the bath room and he is really drunk and so instead he FALLS in to the soaking wet tub and hes (Believe it or not) Hes CRYING and saying YOUR SO BEAUTIFUL (To me.) For a split sec I kinda want to CRY but Darling comes running in and grabs Jergens by the arm and pulls him out of the tub. She says For Christs sake Jergens your so fucking drunk! And she really does say fucking Virgen, and she starts to laugh so loud and Jergens falls back in to the tub and I start to laugh with her and Jergens starts saying it again Your so beautiful! And she says Yeah yeah so what else is new ass hole? And I really REALLY like this DARLING lady Virgen, I REALLY REALLY do. Even if she is a White Lady—but she has green greener eyes just like a CAT like the way a CAT looks at you right?

So I spend the night and for the first time in a million years I wake up in sheets that are kinda stiff and kinda smell like the WIND out side and I had a Flying Dream like I used to when I was little with Mamacita, and I wish I could tell her this one cause every where I looked was LIGHT lots brighter than even the SUN, kinda like what she looked like when she came after the dumb ass funeral and sat on the couch by my feet and woke me up and scared the SHIT out of me like it was pretty creepy till I saw it was HER (Mamacita.) Maybe I'll tell Darling my dreams some times like maybe cause I don't want her to think I'm a Loca or any thing Virgen, but the Flying Dream still makes me feel pretty happy. Do you think I'm Loca—tell the truth OK?

So I'm staying with Darling now but I think about Jake Junior and wonder if his diapers are clean cause Carmen forgets all the time and then he crys cause hes dirty and his baby but hurts, like who can blame him but some times she yells SHUT UP! Believe it or not. When Jake Junior was just born Mamacita and I took care of him a lot like we fed him his babow all warm and changed his diapers all the time so his baby weiner always looked really pink and happy. Some times I sing him to sleep when he crys and crys and crys (I mean a lot.) And Carmen would yell SHUT UP! Pretty dumb to yell at a baby cause any one knows you have to sing in a soft soft voice so the baby will trust sleep to take them dreaming. Thats what Mamacita did with me and I know she did it with Carmen but I think Carmen forgot every thing like the time Mamacita and I were walking down the street and Carmen crossed the street cause one time Carmen yelled at Mamacita in a fight You look like an old Indian for Christs sake! (Believe it or not Virgen.) I think thats when I really really knew I hated her guts and you probably already know all this but Mamacita really really was BEAUTIFUL, like she had dark gray hair that was super thick and long cause she was a Yaqui Indian from Mexico from a place called Hermosillo (Like I visited some uncles and aunts and a COOL COUSIN named CHULA there one time and I'll tell you about that some time.) Thats where Mamacita met her husband who was a Baptist Minister and I think he'd kick Carmens big lardy but if he heard her say Mamacita looks like an old Indian like shes ashamed, but hes been dead a long time and all I know is storys I hear from Mamacita and Tia and even Carmen some times (Believe it or not.) Carmen always says in the storys that she was his FAVORITE and thats why he sent her to a special girls boarding school cause she was so SMART AND TALENTED and Tia stayed home to help Mamacita with the Cinderella stuff, like thats what she says and then she laughs just to prove it or some thing. I used to think her storys were so cool but now if I think of them they just make me want to like PUKE right? And then Tia told me like in a real mad way that when there father died Carmen sold all of the furniture for $ and that it was the BEST furniture and that it was Mamacitas furniture, and that she kept the $ for herself (Like these family storys aren't so happy right?) Like I know Mamacita used to go to Church cause she was still kinda like a Ministers Wife and I could tell some of the old bag ladys were jealous of her and that they really weren't her FRIENDS or any thing but I could tell she was pretty happy just to be there talking Spanish and kinda being the Ministers Wife right? Any way you know how really really BEAUTIFUL

Mamacita was and how sad her eyes were when she thought I wasn't really looking but then she'd turn on the radio and she'd sing and dance to some songs from Mexico, and she'd lift her long dress over her knees so I could see her dark brown rolled down stockings she used to wear to keep her legs warm even on hot days, so I'd start singing and dancing with her and we'd laugh till we peed our calzones and then she'd make us my FAVORITE thing to drink—cafe con leche with lots of cinamon and pan dulce all warmed up. Is pan dulce your FAVORITE thing to eat Virgen? I know it is or I bet it is any way cause Mamacita used to put a little piece on your altar some times with the flowers when she'd light the candles to you when she prayed. Some times we'd go to the Beach and find sea shells and we'd bring them home in our pockets and one time I put the prettyest one on your altar remember?

So any way I'm here with Darling or really shes out right now but theres always a TON OF FOOD in the frig and she calls me The Bottomless Pit cause I eat so damed much she says but she laughs at me a lot. She has a husband named Danny The Dane (Believe it or not). He works on a ship as an engineer she said or some thing like that so hes gone for months some times she said and then he comes home for a while, and then hes gone again so I guess she lives alone a lot so she probably likes company right? Some times she goes out at night but I don't mind cause theres a TV and FOOD in the frig any time I'm hungry and she gives me rules like I have to be here before dark and I don't really mind cause it feels like she really really likes me, like shes sewing me some thing to wear and I hope it doesn't look to WEIRD so I can't even wear it. I think she wants me to look more like a GIRL cause she says I have a pretty face but you wouldn't know I was a GIRL if you didn't check my DIAPER HA HA! She makes me stand on a chair and she puts pins on the HEM she calls it and I think of Jergens saying SHES SO BEAUTIFUL and I almost fall off the chair laughing cause this dress is weird, like I hate to say it but the only way I'll wear it out side is if I can wear a mask or every ones blind folded. But I like it when I stand on the chair and she walks back to take a good look at me and says Its just perfect Luna, its just perfect! And she smiles to herself and starts humming. So I'll have to figure out a plan like to hide some clothes out side in a bag so I can change if she makes me wear it cause the only way I'll wear it out side is at gun point like they say in Gunsmoke. But I really do like the way she says Its just perfect Luna! So I pretend I even LOVE the dumb ass BOW right on my neck cause no one but Mamacita has ever said stuff like that to me before but if the kids I hang around with like at the Salvation Army Club where I play basket ball with the toughest black girls in the neighborhood cause we're a TEAM, and if they saw me in this DRESS WITH A BOW they'd probably kill me. I can just hear them—Girl you so UGLY! And they'd laugh LOUD and probably fall on the floor and kick there feet cause I know I would right? I can just hear Jergens saying—Shes so beautiful (Believe it or snot.)

(October My Birthday TWELVE)

Dear La Virgen,

Well she did it. She made me wear the dress out to dinner to a really nice restaurant and there was no way I could hide my stuff out side and change cause Darling TOOK ME to the restaurant in her car and did I tell you she drives a car called a THUNDER BIRD and it has round little windows in the back so its pretty COOL and all. Or tan bonita as Mamacita would say about it and the only time Mamacita road in a car was when some one picked us up for Church or when Tias Cheap Skate Husband picked us up with a disgusted look on his fat tortilla face, like Tia has to keep his tortillas warm so she jumps up and down from her chair or he won't eat them (Believe it or snot.) He also eats all the food in the house and I'm not joking either and he hogs all the donuts even from his own kid whos pretty skinny and hungry all the time and I wonder why. So I call him The Cheap Skate and even Tia laughs in SECRET when I say it cause its the TRUTH right? Any way so as I walk to the Thunder Bird car I pretend I'm being kidnapped at gun point cause its the only way I can wear this weirdo dress with a BOW AT MY NECK and any way no one knows me at this restaurant cause its some where in San Francisco I've never been and its close to the

Ocean cause you can smell it, but you can't see it so its not that close. Usually I ride my bike to the Ocean (You know the one I stold cause it was laying right in the street and I didn't have one and no one was going to buy me one in a million years right?) It felt pretty WEIRD to walk in with my new SHINY shoes and feel like a GIRL and the man who took us to the table smiled at me like I'd done the best thing in the whole world, and Darling acts like a Rich Lady and every one runs around trying to make her happy or her Green Cat Eyes get narrow just like a Cat and MAD. I kinda liked pretending she was my Mom and she even told the guy I was her step daughter so I ordered a Coca Cola in a Rich Girls way (Kinda phoney.) But he smiled like I said the best thing in the whole world and then he brought it pretty fast and put it on a tiny piece of paper, like it might be fun with every thing on a tiny piece of paper so its clean and new and special right? Any way when she wanted me to wear the WEIRDO DRESS to school I wore it out the door and down stairs to the basement where the bag with my stuff is so I could change and not get killed by my friends or any of the guys I used to beat up (You know who I mean Virgen.) So at the restaurant Darling didn't drink to much, like just 2 glasses of white wine and she sent some thing back cause it wasn't cooked right she said and no one got mad at her or any thing or threw her out the door. Cool I thought. So I just watched her Green Cat Eyes and saw what they looked at and I thought COOL. And then for a sec I thought of Mamacita and what she'd say when White People treated her weird, like she'd say Que los Gringos, que mi chingan, los CHINGADOS!!! (You know this is the WORST swearing Virgen.) So I smiled as I looked at all the Rich White People eating and I even said it CHINGADOS like to myself and then I was <u>starving</u> and ate every thing on my plate as fast as I could and I was still pretty hungry so Darling ordered me seconds and I ate all of that to. Believe it or not—Me The Bottomless Pit right? Of course I know Mamacita would never come to this place cause going out for us was going to the Crystal Palace on Market street after a Mexican Movie and I'd order hot dogs with lots of mustard and hot relish and also some Coca Colas, and you know Virgen those hot dogs were DELISIOUS and some times I had 2. They tore down the

Crystal Palace cause they said it was a fire hazard cause it was to old or some thing but that place had every thing in the WORLD in it and I'm not kidding, like you could look at so much stuff even if you didn't have the $ like one time Mamacita loved some pearl ear rings but we didn't have the $ and now I wish I just stole them but I didn't cause I was to little and all right?

You know my birth day was a few days ago and I didn't even tell Darling I was 12 now but I did go by the house to see Jake Junior and Carmen, but they weren't even there. They were either with The Psycho (Jake Juniors father) Or with The Blood Sucker I guess. I was kinda sad cause the house looked so sad and dark and empty, and I looked in the frig NOTHING. So I was pretty glad I could go back to Darlings house with the nice curtains on every window and lots of nice furniture in every room, and most of all LOTS OF FOOD in the frig and she even brought a big bottle of milk just for me to drink cause she thinks I drink to much soda and its bad for my teeth which she says have cavitys so shes taking me to the dentist. The only time I went to the dentist was when Carmens boy friend who was a dentist took me to his office at night and it was all dark and creepy, and he was a MEAN ASS DENTIST so I kicked him and ran for it. So I told Darling about this guy but I made it in to a funny story and she just looked at me not even smileing, and said her dentist was a really nice guy who put your teeth to sleep first with a SHOT if he has to drill them and that I won't have to kick him or any thing. But I'm still not really THRILLED.

The other night a few days after my birth day I broke the rules and stayed out after dark cause I climbed a building they were building like the steel part and I counted each floor as I climbed to the top and there were 12 floors just like my birth day. I never climb buildings by myself especially at night cause I always climb and stuff with Jody whos a Tomboy like maybe even worse than me. My other friend Hope is more like a GIRL but I like her any way, but she would never climb a building cause she'd be scared she might die and all. Any way Jody is blond with blue eyes and she walks and talks just like a boy plus shes pretty strong with lots of mussles in her arms. Hope is Mexican like me and she also has green eyes like me, but there even greener than mine (More like

Darlings Cat Eyes). Hopes father calls her Esperanza some times and I think hes Mexican and her Moms some thing else kinda like me, like I'm Yaqui Indian, Spanish and GERMAN (like a GRINGA). My father was German and he was also blond and had blue eyes believe it or not, but I never knew him but I heard the storys about him. So I guess I'm part Mexican and part Gringa and part poor and part rich. I guess with Mamacita I was never confused cause with her I was just me Luna—you know Virgen? But with Carmen and now with Darling I AM CONFUSED you know?

So any way when I got way up to the top of the steel building it was petty cold and dark and scarey by myself up there, but some times when I DARE myself thats how I get (I think you know that right?) But the sky was so pretty like it was just the kinda sun set Mamacita used to love. That kind full of every color in the world and some times she'd say her Yaqui Poem To The Sun Going To Sleep, but I didn't understand Yaqui and I forget the poem now. Any way there were birds flying by me so I stopped feeling so lonely up there. I like the sound of there wings as they fly by my head and all so I sat down and just watched the sun set though I was starting to FREEZE and I could just hear Jody—Lets go get a hamburger and frys! And I was about to get up and go to Darlings house where I know theres some thing delisious to eat though I was probably in trouble for being out after dark and being so late so I kept sitting there freezing to death, and I'm not kidding Virgen. And then it happened—Can you guess what I felt like and did it ever happen to you? A warm weird feeling in my under wear DISGUSTING!!!! It was BLOOD when I felt myself so I thought I was really DIEING, LIKE BLOOD ON MY FINGERS! So I wiped them on my jeans and kept sitting on the frozen ass steel cause I was scared SHIT LESS to move (Excuse my swearing so much Virgen, but if this ever happened to you—You probably said SHIT LESS to right?) And then I'm not kidding I heard a voice in the wind and saw some faces in the clouds, and that scared me even more SHIT LESS than the BLOOD in my under wear so I almost flew down the steel to the bottom and ran all the way to Darlings house where it smelled like FOOD and I was pretty starved! But her Cat Eyes were pretty mad when I ran in but she looked at me funny and said What happened to you kid, seen a ghost or some thing? So I just told her every thing like I used to with Mamacita and she just put her arms around me and I could feel her giant boobs but I didn't mind, and she told me to get in the shower cause she was going to the store to get some NAPKINS FOR ME which sounded pretty DISGUSTING to me but I figured Darling knew what she was doing about this Girl Stuff cause she called it Girl Stuff and Getting My Period. She said Now you can have babys some day if you want, Jesus Christ thats great kid!

I myself don't think its so great. I think its pretty creepy, like WHERE would I even have a baby and WHY would I have a baby cause then I'd have a baby with a MAN right? Like I'd have to do it or some thing with a MAN (What a CHINGADO THRILL!!) And then I tryed just for a sec to think of The Blood Sucker as a baby and I almost did the OLD HEAVE HO like thats how much I wanted to know about all this Girl Stuff and Getting My Period which is really just BLEEDING all over your under wear right? And so believe it or snot I'm supposed to be a WOMAN (!!!!) Like now Darling says. I don't want to be a WOMAN ever and I HATE to wear these creepy napkins though I ended up laughing with Darling when I pinned them on the wrong way like back wards HA HA! SHIT Now I am wearing a dumb ass DIAPER and a dumb ass dress with a bow HOLY ASS SHIT!!!! I'm sorry for all the swearing Virgen—I really really am but I don't want to be a WOMAN or have BABYS or BLEED in my pants and wear a DIAPER like I don't even like to play with dolls, and the only doll I ever had I took the eyes out to see how the stupid things kept shutting by themselves, so I cracked her head open so I could take a look inside, and that was pretty cool.

When I really really think of all this Girl Stuff all I want to do is run and run and run and run until I come to the end of the World and then I want to fly and fly and fly FOREVER AND EVER like in a dream. Thats what I really want so don't go and tell God or any thing cause I'm just telling you about this Girl Stuff—OK Virgen? Like if he knew I'm saying I HATE this stuff he might smite me by giving me giant boobs or some thing so I'd have to wear GIANT BRAS like Darling, and I really like her but then I'd be doomed for sure (So don't tell God I got my Period OK?) Any way don't forget I'm 12 now and next year I'll be 13—Believe it or snot!!

NOVEMBER AND DECEMBER

(But I didn't write much in November though
I did write some storys and poems in Bolinas.)

Dear La Virgen,

(((About our secret—I dreamt a lady and I think she was you and she was putting her fingers to her mouth like she was saying to me this—I won't tell God. Thanks for the dream Virgen cause I know your real just like Mamacita knew your real—so thanks for the secret dream.)))

Well the crummy news is that Darling moved to the country to this place called BOLINAS which is pretty COOL and its even right by the Ocean, I mean Darlings house is right by the Ocean and you can hear it all night when your laying in bed, and you can even hear it when your dreaming right? Its an over and over and over sound that NEVER STOPS and I think its better than even music is (Believe it or not—and like they say in the Baptist Church that God CREATED every thing in the World—but I bet you created that over and over sound right Virgen?) Any way BOLINAS is across the GOLDEN GATE BRIDGE like over the Ocean (Where people jump and commit sewerside—I'm not kidding.) So Darling took me to her new house in the country for about a month and then Carmen said I had to come back to the city cause she and Jake Junior were moving to a new place and that I should go to school there, like what a joke right? All I can figure is that some times Carmen likes to PRETEND shes a regular mom and she goes out and buys cereal and milk and forgets about the rest of it like I eat dinner to and that I need CLEAN CLOTHES and then she just leaves, so I was not thrilled when Darling drove me back over the Golden Gate Bridge in the Thunder Bird and her forhead had lines which means shes worried and her Cat Eyes were pretty mad but I could tell she was trying to keep all this a secret, sort of right? She gave me her phone number and said Call me right away if you need me and I'll get here as soon as I can and don't take any SHIT, do you understand Luna? And I said Yeah I understand. But I didn't say BYE or any thing and I didn't watch her drive away in the Thunder Bird though I could hear her leave cause I started blubbering (Believe it or snot.) Thats how SAD I was. And when I went up stairs to the <u>new place</u> which looked pretty <u>old</u> to me—guess what? Carmen and Jake Junior weren't even there, like what a joke! And to top it off we have to SHARE the bath room, like go to the bath room and take a bath cause theres no shower or any thing. And then the guy we share the bath room with walks up the stairs and I'm trapped cause I can't run in to the house cause the doors LOCKED and hes staring at me like a PERVERT or some thing. And he says So are you locked out? And he says this I mean <u>real loud</u> like I'm deaf or some thing, what a Weirdo. And I say No I'm standing here for my health! I make a break and jump about 20 stairs and then I can hear the Weirdo laughing really LOUD. Then I remember I forgot my clean clothes that Darling put in a bag for me, oh well I'll come back tomorrow cause tommorows Saturday and maybe Carmen will be there.

I felt like calling Darling right then as I was trying to figure out where the hell to go and all but I knew she wasn't even home in BOLINAS and that she was probably visiting her old friend JERGENS (Remember him?). And I didn't have his phone number so if I was going to call her and ask her to come back I'd probably have to call in about 2 days. I wonder when her husband Danny The Dane gets back and I wonder what hes like? I saw his picture and his teeth looked huge cause he was really smiling and he had a pretty big nose with kinda nice eyes, like small and happy or some thing right?

Any way as you probably know Virgen I ended up at Hopes house which is pretty cool cause I always feel like 1 more kid cause there 8 kids there like mostly teen agers and the oldest is a brother who drives a motor cycle, and his names Freddy and he always bugs me (You still a boy, ain't it time your a girl?) But Hopes Dad is really nice and he always calls me Beautiful (Shit like Jergens right?) HA HA And I always laugh cause I know its a game cause I mean if any ones Beautiful its Hope. (She really is.) And then I ate dinner with every one like a TON of tacos Hope and her sisters kept making and they were good to. We made a bed from a sheet and blankets in the front room and told the SADDEST STORYS we could think of like starveing children and no one loved them and they were stuck on an island with no boat, and we CRYED and all (I made Hope cry the most.) Hope took me to the bath room and we turned on a RED light. She said her sisters put it in cause red lights make you look like beautiful so we looked in the mirror after we washed our faces, and we put on some of Hopes sisters lip stick, and we CURLED OUR EYE LASHES but the gizmo yanks about 1/2 of them out so its a pretty dumb thing to do right? Then Freddy walks in to the bath room and starts laughing at us and he says Is this the Red Light District? We start socking him and throw him out (And I figure the Red Light District is a place where a bunch of girls get together and try to be beautiful day and night or some thing—what do you think Virgen?) After he leaves I look in the mirror and for a sec I think I might be a little beautiful but my eye lashes look so PHONEY (Like I stold some hair off a horse and glued them on.) So I started laughing so hard I FARTED LOUD and Hope and I ran out cause it was a bomb. Any way Hope REALLY looked beautiful in the Red Light District thats for sure and I looked OK but I don't like to stare in to my own eyes like Hope does and say Do I look beautiful? (Its to embarassing.) I don't even do it by myself right?

After Hope stopped talking and we stopped telling sad storys and I knew she was sleeping I started thinking about BOLINAS and how quiet it was there with the over and over Ocean sound all night long (Cause I could hear cars barely making it up the steep ass hill Hope lives on and then I could hear a cop siren or an ambulance or some thing like that, and then some guy started yelling bloody murder, and then some drunk guy started singing some stupid song, kinda like The Psycho sings My Wild Irish Rose when hes a Drunk Psycho and he starts blubbering cause he feels so sorry for himself but of course not Carmen or Jake Junior who have to listen to a Drunk Psycho blubbering, and then I wonder if any one ever shuts up in the city right?) And I think about how Darling puts out some salt for the DEER to lick like you have to be <u>very quiet</u> and just wait AND THEN THEY COME and lick lick lick lick with there soft little tongues. (They have long long legs to.) Darling also brought her 2 old FAT AND FURRY CATS with her, in a box like one in each box, and then she put butter on there paws so they'd know they were home and I wished she put butter on my paws. I closed my eyes and saw the Ocean that was now her back yard she said and that she could walk around in her giant bra and no one would see her or give a shit (Thats what she said Virgen.) And then I remembered my clean clothes that I left at Carmens right?

The other night I dreamed this—I was at Darlings house walking down the stairs to the Ocean cause I was going for a SWIM! And I could really see the water like moving full of LIGHTS and I could really HEAR the over and over Ocean Sound LOUD and I was pretty happy cause she had a big fat ROAST in the oven (The kind I like with smashed potatoes and a TON of gravy). Then I woke up. If Mamacita was here I'd tell her the dream and ask her if she thought that maybe the dream might come true cause I can't believe I haven't called Darling to come and get me right? I guess I'm kinda waiting for an EMERGENCY or some thing. Other wise I'd feel like a BIG BABY. (But there is no FOOD in the frig like not even some rotten disgusting food right?)

Any way when I went back to get my clothes I tryed the door and it was open so I went in and my clothes were inside but no one was there. But there was $5 on the kitchen table with a note—See you tomorrow, mom. Excuse me if I don't believe you

Carmen, but at least she left me $5 right? And I look around at this New Place and its pretty UGLY like no curtains or any thing (Just some sad ass shades). In fact this place is kinda scarey and it smells bad like dead bodys right? So I change my clothes in to the clean ones Darling washed and just as I am about to leap down the stairs the Weirdo Guy next door comes out and says You hungry? Cooked moren I shoulda (He says should kinda like hes from the SOUTH or some thing.)

The next night I go back but YEAH theres no light in the window but I go up any way and the doors still open and no ones there in the Dead Body Place. Then I think I'll call Darling cause all of a sudden I feel like BLUBBERING cause I'm really like really all alone PLUS I'm hungry and the $5 is gone of course. In Carmens Flea Brain she thinks $5 will feed me for a MONTH. (So I feel for Darlings number and its there.) As I go out to call the Weirdo Guy opens his door and this time hes got a plate of chicken and stuff in his hand and he says You like fryed chicken and mashed tatos with gravy? (Yeah thats how he really talks.) It smells so GOOD I stop like I can't help it cause it smells SO GOOD. I say Yeah. Well come on in he says. And I say Just put it right here. And he does. He puts it right out side his door on a rug so I sit on the top stair and pick up the plate full of FRYED CHICKEN! Then he yells Do you want a sody? A SODY? HA HA I yell YEAH! And I try not to break out laughing till I pee my pants and plus who is this Weird Guy right? But the chicken and smashed tatos and mixed veges with a ton of butter is DELISIOUS! Then he calls me Pokahantas cause I won't tell him my name. (Of course Pokahantas is an Indian name and I kinda wonder how he knows about Mamacita, and then I realize this Weirdo knows I'm a girl like right away—usually people don't figure that out right?) So I'm keeping my eye on him and he laughs when I say in my boys voice that I'll take seconds if he has any and he says he has MOREN HE CAN SHAKE A STICK AT (Whatever that means.) And I watch him just in case I have to run for my life, like how do I know whats going on this Weirdos Pervert Brain right Virgen? (I even give him the Witch Power Eyes but this Weirdo Guy just laughs LOUDER.)

Later when I call Darling collect like she told me she tells me shes going to visit her mother in Washington (Where ever that is.) For Christmas. She asks me if I'm going to school and I say I'm going (Some times.) Then she tells me shes going to the school near her house in BOLINAS to see about me coming in JANUARY and she says if Carmen gives her any shit shes taking care of it this time, and I can tell Darlings Cat Eyes must be MAD. Which makes me feel pretty good. She wants to send me some $ so I give her Hopes address cause like Darling says Carmen might take it (She sure would.) Darling tells me to go to Tias house for Christmas and that she'll pick me up there and to call her from Tias so she can get directions in JANUARY and I say I will of course. I also say Merry Christmas and Darling says Don't take any wooden nickels kid. For a split sec I wonder if Danny The Dane is going with her to her moms in Washington for Christmas and then I wonder why I can't go, and then I'm not thrilled about going to Tias house mainly cause of The Cheap Skate but I really like my little skinny cousin Pablo and I always sneak him some thing cool to eat like SODYS and donuts and stuff. So I guess I'll take off to Tias after Darlings $ gets to Hopes house (Which I will hide from The Cheap Skate.) Are you still there Virgen? If you are send me a dream OK?

(A NEW YEAR JANUARY)

Dear La Virgen,

It turns out the Weirdo Guy next door to Carmens is named WHITEY and at first I thought it was a phoney name like he kept calling me Pokahantas till I finally told him my name is Luna and any way it turns out his name really is WHITEY! We're kinda friends cause every day I went back to Carmens she wasn't there yet and he had some DELISIOUS HOT FOOD in his hand like he was waiting for me, so now I sit on the top stair and he stands by his door and talks to me a little. One night I had THIRDS cause I was so STARVED and the next night Carmen came back with Jake Junior and they looked pretty bad, like Jake Junior had a stinky one and Carmen was all weird cause The Psycho had ripped up her clothes and of course she had to go to work tomorrow. This guy Whitey hears her story about The Psycho being drunk and all, and she had the bruises to prove it (If I was there It wouldn't hit her but of course we don't live together any more and I kinda wonder if Carmen ever had the Witch Power which he HATES and I'm glad he calls me The Witch cause I know hes scared I'll kill him or some thing—QUE LOCO FREGADO!!!! Thats what Mamacita would say Virgen and I know being a witch is supposed to be bad but if you see some one trying to kill some one like isn't it good to stop it Virgen?) So Whitey gives her some $ and then he gives me some $ and says Merry Christmas and be of good cheer! I think thats kinda corny but I guess he is trying to CHEER US UP right? I tell him I'm going to my Tias and then I'm probably going to BOLINAS and he says Right pretty country there. So I tell him Don't take any wooden nickels and he just laughs. See you when you get back Luna, like he says my name kinda like hes teasing me but when I look at his eyes I don't mind right? To tell the truth I wouldn't mind seeing him again but I don't ever want to see The Dead Body Place again in my entire whole VIDA.

With his $ and Darlings $ I felt pretty rich so I put all my stuff in to a duffel bag he gave me (Thats what he calls it, a duffel bag.) So I hopped the bus to Tias and Carmen was just glad to get her peace like she calls it, and I changed Jake Juniors stinky diaper before I left DISGUSTING! It was about 2 days before Christmas and Tia said to come any time so I bought some Pan Dulce and Coca Colas for Pablo and put them in the duffel bag. When I changed buses there was a Christmas Tree Lot so I started to look at the trees and I knew The Cheap Skate would make Tia put up the broken down tin one she keeps in the closet all year so when she puts it up I really want to laugh but I know it would really hurt her feelings and all (Plus its pretty SAD even when her and Pablo string this pop corn and it hangs there like DEAD pop corn right Virgen?) And then I saw this BIG WHITE TREE all sparkling like a ZILLION TRILLION STARS and this guy comes up and asks me if I want it cheap cause its almost Christmas. We settle on $3 and I pick it up and drag it to the bus stop and all these little sparkling stars start to fall from the Tree (Its sprayed of course.) So I'm waiting for the bus and its pretty late and I wonder if the bus to The Projects is still running cause here I am with a HUMUNGUS WHITE STAR TREE. (And I secretly name it WHITEY HA HA!) And I know if I dare to call The Cheap Skate he'll probably charge me $ for gas and thats the truth Virgen. Any way the Tree Lot lights go off and then the Tree Lot Guy is sitting in his truck saying Do you want a ride home? And I shake my head NO like I sure as shit know better than to get in a car with a MAN right? In one sec he jumped out and grabbed my Tree and put it in his truck and said Get in and I'll take you home, no problem (Some thing like that.) I just about DIED cause there was WHITEY in the guys truck and the Tree Lot Guys sitting there waiting for me to get in kinda like he was going to take my TREE. I held the door handle all the way and I was ready to leap out just like the movies but I told him like in my boys voice how to get to Tias through the longest darkest tunnel in the WORLD in to The Projects, and I was thinking if the bus had stopped running I'd be dragging WHITEY through this chingado tunnel by myself right? And as you know Virgen this man was very nice cause he drove me right up to Tias building where its all muddy when it rains and it started to rain to top it all off (Believe it or not.) To tell the truth I was a little embarassed cause of the mud (Like theres no regular streets here right?) And plus The Projects look worse at night and so I take a quick look at him to see if hes disgusted or any thing but hes just humming with the radio like he comes here all the time. And you know this Virgen but inside Tias house its SPICK AND SPAN like she calls it that and it is clean like no dead bodys there right? He picks up my Tree with one hand cause I guess hes pretty strong like the trees bigger than me, and all I can say (And my girls voice just popped out which was pretty embarassing.) Like all I can say is Thanks a lot. And he just says No problem and gets in his truck and then his head lights are entirely gone and I can't hear his truck any more and I wonder if he can find his way out of The Projects to the long ass tunnel where the real streets start on the other side where the regular people live.

So when I knock on Tias door its all dark inside so I have to keep knocking and when Tia opens the door her eyes pop out and she says Did you bring the whole forest Luna? She laughs and we drag it in to the house. The next morning Pablo went CRAZY and he LOVED the Tree (WHITEY). But I just kept the name to myself and hid my $ really good and brought out the TREATS after The Cheap Skate was gone and of course he didn't believe I paid $3 for it and that the Tree Lot Guy drove me here, and I could tell he wanted the phoney tin tree to stay up but Tia put it away after he went to work at the Steel Factory. When The

Cheap Skate comes home Tia always makes a BIG DEAL and says stuff like Daddys not hurt after all day in a dangerous job hijito (Pablo her kid.) I have to pretend I'm going to the bath room or I'll really puke. Like that night he had a STEAK and we had HOT DOG STEW like Tia calls it and she makes it taste pretty good with rice and her fresh tortillas and all. But Pablo kept looking at The Cheap Skates steak like he really wanted to eat a STEAK and The Cheap Skate just keeps stuffing his fat face while his skinny kid watches (I'm not kidding Virgen.) Tia says she has to go shopping but she has to wait for Her Husband (Like she calls him). Cause he drives her there like hes doing her a BIG FAVOR (PUKE!) She also tells me and Pablo that DADDY has to have his strength for the DANGEROUS JOB and thats why hes having the steak while we eat Hot Dog Stew (PUKO-LA!) Any way so I tell her to give me a list and I'll ride Pablos puny bike there (Yeah through the long ass tunnel.) So I go and get the stuff she has the $ for cause Her Husband still has to give her food $ she says but I buy a BIG ASS STEAK for us and I tell her to make it for us before you know who shows up. Shes kinda guilty like I can tell but she sure eats all of hers, and Pablo even has seconds it was such a giant ass ROUND STEAK. So any way we ate all of it and we had a whole bunch of donuts for desert and Pablo couldn't stop laughing. (Your my favoritist cousin he kept saying.) I hid the rest of the donuts in the duffel bag and then we had to string lots of new pop corn (And we ate some to of course.) This Tree is so tall and bushy and we wrapped the pop corn all around WHITEY and every thing looked alive and the sun coming in the window made all the stars really sparkle. When Pablos this happy he starts dancing like a funny Skinny Kids Dance which makes me laugh. I sure hope Pablo has some presents right? But I don't want to ask Tia so maybe I'll get him some thing on Mission Street with my $.

Virgen I've been thinking that since I got The Blood and all I've been kinda looking more and more like a GIRL like Whitey figured it out pretty fast and called me Pokahantas (A girls name right?) Cause usually people can't figure it out right away like only when I get to know them so this Girl Stuff is really really weird and I don't want to be a girl yet, like I know I'll be a girl e v e n t u a l l y right? But if I look like a girl now it means theres a TON of stuff I can't do cause girls don't do it like climb buildings and hop the trolly to the zoo through the tunnel going about 100 miles an hour and bike rideing to Play Land At The Beach and Golden Gate Park and the Secret Forest some times by myself and jumping roof to roof (And almost dieing). Its like flying and only Jody does it with me cause like I said shes a Tomboy maybe even worse than me. And I love to go fishing off the piers and some times Fisher Mans Wharf where I can sell the crabs I catch to these Chinese Guys who are pretty nice like some times they give me some of there tea and cookies, and one time even a bowl of noodles with chicken which was good. Any way these are my favorite places and you know all my FAVORITE stuff to do so if you'll help me not look like a girl till I'm maybe 16 that would be COOL OK? Also just to remind you—don't tell God any of this THANKS. Also is God your husband? Is he a Cheap Skate???? I kinda think he might be cause I used to pray for stuff and he never sent the stuff I asked for right? Any way don't take any wooden nickels Virgen or any shit either cause your LA VIRGEN and Mamacita used to say that without you she wouldn't have any under wear for her nalgas (She really did say that HA!) And then she'd laugh and I'd laugh with her. Some times I think I got the Witch Power from Mamacita cause when she was really MAD she'd say LAS ESTOY JUNTANDO FREGADO—which means she was going to remember EVERY THING and WATCH OUT and she wasn't kidding either. Like she might put the Pyramid Hex on some one (You know the kinda Hex you can't ever get rid of even if your sorry.) So if you can help me I don't want to LOOK like a girl till I'm at least 16 OK? And I don't care if I'm ever pretty cause I've never been pretty any way like Jergens is for sure a Loco Pendejo who not only needs glasses but a new pair of eyes. Also I sure don't need any BOOBS I think The Bloods enough. OK Virgen?

Tia took me to the Southern Spanish Speaking Baptist Church (Thats what they call it Virgen like DEL SUR so why don't they say stuff like—Moren I can shake a stick at?) Don't ask me cause every one at this Church speaks Spanish with me kinda back and forth and 1/2 and 1/2 but I can tell I'm starting to forget a little. Any way I refuse to go to Sunday School any more like the Sunday we went so I escaped to the Tower where they say an Evil Ghost lives, like where the bell is right? One time some kids were sneaking up and I waited till they opened the little door that comes in to where I was (You have to bend way over or you'll hit your noodle.) So when they opened it I SCREAMED and scared the HOLY ASS SHIT out of them HA HA! They ran so fast like screaming and crying till they fell 1/2 way down the stairs and after I went down to the Church basement where the Pan Dulce is waiting on a humungus table for after the sermon (Which I hate cause the Minister likes to act like he can read your mind or some thing which he can't cause why are his 4 daughters always getting in to big trouble right?) Any way I take 3 Pan Dulces and all of a sudden for no reason I miss Mamacita and I can hear the ladys talking and laughing in the kitchen cause there cooking, and some times one of them starts a poem and then they take turns finishing it. (She used to do that and she knew lots of poems to.) Mamacita didn't like the Minister either and I know she never told him about you or her dreams Virgen, right? Like one time his oldest daughter had a baby out of wed lock (She wasn't marryed yet.) And he made her stand up and TELL EVERY ONE SHE WAS SORRY and she was crying and he was smileing like what a CREEP!!!! Like I'm so GLAD I don't have a father cause I notice that most fathers (Except maybe Hopes) there really a bunch of idiots trying to PUNISH you like The Cheap Skate and my STEP father The Psycho, and kinda like God smiteing every one and Creation to right?

Any way at Christmas I don't even think of HIM so I think of your baby JESUS being born and I sing HAPPY BIRTH DAY TO YOU to your baby. Of course I sing this to myself or the people in the Church would call me La Loca like they do this old viejita lady who talks to herself out loud (I'd rather talk to myself than talk to some of them except for some really nice ladys who cook and laugh in the basement, and the Ministers daughter who had to say SORRY.) Like I can tell she really does like me cause she looks in to my eyes and smiles and asks me how I'm doing and all, and her little baby looks pretty happy and I can tell she really loves him even if shes not marryed. And I know the word for her baby BASTARD but he doesn't look like a BASTARD to me (In fact he looks perfect with nothing wrong like NOTHING.) And some times the ladys in the basement that cook ask me Do you want a taste hija? Some are from Mexico like Mamacita and some are from other countrys like from South America but they all speak Spanish, and they all cook together there different foods from there different countrys kinda like a contest, and every thing is super delisious with fresh tortillas waiting in covered baskets. Of course The Cheap Skate LOVES this cause its free and in secret he complains cause he gives $ to the Church and hes a Big Shot at Church (With the creepy Minister right?)

Any way we had a GIANT PINYATA Christmas Eve filled with candy and some really cheapo presents that fall a part when you even breathe on them but it was fun breaking it cause they blind fold you and twirl you around till your DIZZY and then I really WACKED IT THUNK!!! In fact I'm the one that broke it cause I could hear the pinyata whispering to me even though I was pretty dizzy WACK!!! And Pablo kept saying after I broke it—Shes my favoritist cousin, but he didn't dance his Happy Skinny Kids Dance probably cause he was in Church like in public, and now that I think about it Pablos Happy Skinny Kids Dance kinda reminds me of El Diablo on the pham can (I wish El Diablo would come up behind the Minister during one of his BORING ASS sermons when hes talking about God smiteing every one and how every ones really a SINNER and probably Lily isn't thrilled about that sinner stuff cause she knows hes talking about her and her baby right? I really really WISH El Diablo would stick him right in his MUY GRANDE NALGAS with his Red Hot Poker that he carrys around when hes haveing such a great time dancing HA!)

So I went out to Mission Street and took $10 and bought every one a Christmas Present (Even The Cheap Skate.) And the old guy at the store WRAPPED them for me with a ribbon so that was pretty COOL. I took Carmen and Jake Junior some presents over to The Dead Body Place (They weren't home of course.) And I knocked on Whiteys door with his present (A pen in a gold box.) When I handed him the present he looked like he wanted to CRY or some thing (Believe it or snot.) Then he laughed and called me Pokahantas which kinda made me mad like he forgot my real name but he didn't cause he said You hungry Luna? Thought you was stayin in Bolinas. So he fixed me some thing delisious of course and as I was eating some SWISS STEAK (Thats what he called it) all covered with fryed onions and I asked him why his name was WHITEY (And I thought of my Star Tree.) He said he used to be a toe head and I started laughing cause right away I saw a giant ass toe growing out of his head as a kid, and then of course I felt kinda bad. But he started laughing to and told me that a toe head is some one with white white blond hair, well thats news to me but his hair is still kinda blond so maybe its a true story (A TOE HEAD?) I noticed he was drinking some whiskey but it didn't make him a Psycho like you know who, like it makes him even nicer and he started telling me some storys about his father and growing up in Texas and that his mom died when he was almost just born, and then he looked like might CRY again but he didn't. He told me his father taught him how to hunt and that his favorite thing as a kid was rabbit and he asked me if I'd like to try some RABBIT STEW some time and I said Sure, but to tell the truth I can just see a rabbit floating around in a stew with its long ass ears right? YUM!!!! (Just kidding cause it makes me want to Heave Ho.) I think I'm going to kinda miss this guy when I go to BOLINAS like who will he cook dinner for and all right? Like when I left to go back to Tias he gave me a $20 for the New Year he said and then he said Now don't forget where I live Pokahantas! I'll make ya a cake to go with that rabbit stew next I see ya. What kind a cake do ya wanta order? And I told him a CHERRY CAKE and he was laughing as I closed the door, and I yelled HAPPY NEW YEAR WHITEY!!!! And this is really weird but I kinda wanted to give him like a kiss on his cheek (I have never KISSED A MAN never.) I stood out side his door for a while and I heard him talking to himself LOUD and I almost went back in like to tease him about talking to himself but I really felt like jumping him and giving him that kiss but I just couldn't (You know Virgen?)

I called Darling and told her how to get to Tias and Tia talked to her and then even The Cheap Skate told her directions

(Like a Big Shot Driver and all.) So I'm going TOMORROW TO BOLINAS where the deer live and I wonder if Darling put butter on there paws to. All I hope is that she doesn't sew me any more DRESSES cause the last one was really pathetic (The BOW.) Remember? I mean if I have to pretend some one is kidnapping me at gun point to wear the dress like I am NOT going to wear Little Bow Dresses to school in BOLINAS right? (If I do you can start calling me Little Bo Peep or some thing and then I'll commit sewerside, and I wonder what the kids wear in BOLINAS and if I'm going to be some kinda Freak Show right?) Any way at least in the city I just looked like another kid from the Mission like a boy I guess—HOLY ASS SHIT AND CHINGASOS TO!!!! Do you notice that I'm trying not to use the F Word cause to tell the truth I really in real life say it a lot like HOLY F SHIT right? But then you probably know that CHINGASOS is like the F Word in Spanish right? (I know I'm not fooling you but I just want to make sure that you know what I mean and that I DO NOT LIE TO YOU which is pretty good for me cause you know what a good liar I really am Virgen, right?) I guess what happens is that things get more interesting when you SPICE them up (Like Mamacita used to say—Los Gringos no tienen sabor, like the Gringos aren't SPICY HA!) So any way when I write to you I don't spice it up, so are you bored (Tell the truth OK?) I wonder if Darlings going to give me a new word every day like she used to and then I look it up in the dictionary and write a story with the new words at the end of the week (I used to really spice those storys up and make her really LAUGH.) But to tell the truth I don't want to go to school in BOLINAS (And be a Freak Show). Like maybe I could stay home with Darling and make her laugh with My Extra Spicy New Word Storys, and I could even write lots of poems and I'd read and read and do a lot more interesting stuff then I ever do at school (You know how BORING school is Virgen like the same old stuff over and over and over and the books have Gringo Storys I guess cause they have NO SABOR, NADA.) Like when I told that Stupid White Lady Teacher that I was reading The Diary Of Ann Frank cause she asked me if I was reading any thing kinda in that voice saying she really thought I WAS STUPID and probably never read any thing but maybe a cereal box, and then she looked all shocked and said Isn't that a little to much for you dear? So silently of course like in my BRAIN I just said Besa my nalgas, and I didn't go back to that class for about two weeks or so and when I did guess what?? Yeah BORING! Like I wonder if she reads RUN SPOT RUN and thinks thats spicy (In big giant letters of course cause shes almost blind with thick old glasses with her mean scarey eyes about 4 times there regular size.) So either shes stupid or she thinks we're stupid like the kids who aren't PURE WHITE, and just cause your a White Lady don't mean your smart, like Darling doesn't think that kinda stuff (And shes white and shes a Spicy Gringa I think cause she doesn't talk all in that phoney voice except for in public when I guess she probably has to like to tell the truth she calls people assholes and fuckfaces some times but they really have to make her MAD, and some times in the Thunder Bird she gives people The Bird and we both really break up laughing like yeah Darlings pretty SPICY and hardly ever BORING.) So when I told Darling I was reading The Diary Of Ann Frank she told me to write a Book Report on it so I did and I also wrote a poem about Ann Frank who was pretty brave (And I cryed at the end of the book cause she was killed just cause she was JEWISH, and you know I'mpart German cause my father was a German so in a weirdo way I felt like maybe my father who I don't know helped kill her but I didn't put this in the Book Report.) Ann Frank was pretty cool just being a kid and writing a whole book before she was killed by the Germans with bunches of other Jewish people like even her family, and it is kinda weird cause she died in the year I was BORN. When I was little like about 6 my best friend was Susan who was Jewish and she had redish curly hair and she had a regular family with a mother and father (And he was always nice and smileing about some thing). Susan played hop scotch really good I remember now and since I didn't know about Germans being so bad to the Jewish people, and I didn't even know I was GERMAN yet right? So Susan and I were just best friends (Some boys saw Mamacita pick me up from school and started calling me Dirty Indian (Believe it or not.) So thats how I found out I was a Yaqui Indian by asking Mamacita if we were Indians. She also told me that Yaquis are the Undefeated Indians like no one ever defeated them (Kicked there buts.) And so I went back to school and said in a loud ass voice I'M AN UNDEFEATED YAQUI INDIAN!!!! I yelled that when one of the boys started walking over to me and I just knew what he was going to say so I started yelling and I think thats kinda brave (Kinda like Ann Frank right?) And thats when I started fighting plus I think they thought I was kinda LOCA like maybe thats when I got The Witch Power right Virgen? HA! And I think thats when I stopped being best friends with Susan like she couldn't play out side any more, and thats when I became best friends with Peggy (Who was older and she had BREASTS cause she showed me them and said Some day you'll have some coco nuts.) And thats when the Bad Thing hapened which I'll tell you about some time OK?

Any way I really don't want to go to school in BOLINAS so maybe Darling will let me write storys and poems and read and do Book Reports, and maybe she can teach me decmals cause I'm lousy at arithmatic right? She says theres a guy with a horse named Cinamon cause the horse is dark brown she says and that he says I can ride it some times COOL!!!! But to tell the truth I've never ridden a horse and the only thing I know is to say GIDDY YAP and WHOOOOOAAAA like GO AND STOP but I didn't say any thing to Darling cause she might think I'm a chicken. I guess I'm not going to miss any one but Jake Junior and Pablo and Jody and Hope and probably Tia some times but I'm not going to miss Carmen or Tias house (Cause of The Cheap Skate.) Or the Mission or the Dead Body Place or even Hopes house, but maybe I'll miss Whitey some times and I wonder if hes drinking some whiskey or a sody like right now, and I wonder if he has any friends cause I could tell he liked being my friend and cooking all that food and saying . . . I got moren I can shake a stick at (Like I really hope hes not just talking to himself in that loud ass voice right now Virgen, you know?) Any way heres the truth . . . I HATE BEING POOR WORSE than being a girl and even worse than being called a Gringa, like a couple of really mean Old Viejas at Church say that to me all smileing cause of my freckles and green eyes probably. They say stuff like Que bonita es la Gringita and smileing at me like I'm supposed to be thrilled or some thing, and of course I can't beat up a little Old Viejita so I just give them the Witch Eyes and then they tell Mamacita I'm trying to give them El Ojo (I guess I am but I'm sure not trying to kill them or any thing cause I know El Ojo is to make some one really sick or kill them and I just want them to shut up and stop calling me La Gringita right?) Mamacita used to say Pay them no mind Luna and then she'd teach me a long ass poem to say by heart in Church in Spanish of course and that would make smoke come out of there ears. (She used to say that and we'd laugh LOUD.) And then I'd picture the Little Viejitas going home and putting raw eggs on there heads and leaveing it there for hours to get rid of El Ojo which they thought I was giving them and I'd start laughing even if I was all by myself just like La Loca. Like right now if I want to start laughing I just have to picture the Little Viejitas right? And you know they stopped calling me La Gringita HA! I also beat up a boy who called me a Wet Back (Which means Dirty Mexican). I guess I'm EVERY THING Virgen but the worst is being POOR cause it makes you feel ashamed cause if you don't keep it a SECRET every one will know even GOD HA! Like one time I asked him for a new dress for Easter Sunday like I PRAYED AND PRAYED and the next morning I opened my eyes picturing it on a hanger I put there NOTHING. I was pretty little and when I went to the Baptist Church Del Sur, the other girls had brand new dresses but mine was clean cause Mamacita washed and ironed it special but you know I wanted a NEW one of course. (And she put ribbons in my hair to and I didn't mind being a girl yet cause the Bad Thing still didn't happen so I thought I was pretty and all right?) Do you remember the time I prayed to you that I could have a bike and then I found that bike just laying in the street like every time I went by it was still there, and I knew you GAVE IT TO ME cause when I ride it every where I don't feel POOR at all cause then I can go any where I want and Jody rides her bike with me like thats how we found the Secret Forest in Golden Gate Park. Some times I took Hope on the handle bars but she screamed to much and now I wonder where my old bike is cause when Carmen moved to the Dead Body Place she didn't bring it and every time I ask her its like the hamster. (She doesn't know any thing right?) So I guess I need a new one Virgen, OK? And TOMORROW I'm going to BOLINAS where theres a horse named CINAMON that I can maybe RIDE (But I still want a bike OK?) And where the Oceans Darlings back yard and she can walk around in her BRA (Like she says.) And no one gives a SHIT and I will eat dinner every single night like I'm RICH and the sheets smell like SOAP (And the wind like Mamacita used to make them smell so clean to.)

Virgen does Darling think I'm a Gringa or a Wet Back???? (You can tell me in a dream OK?) The other night I dreamed Baby Jesus sang me songs but I can't remember the words or any thing, but I can still see his face singing. And you were holding Baby Jesus in my dream Virgen and you were really cracking up (Darling says that like cracking up.)

FEBRUARY IN BOLINAS

(And I can see the Ocean any time I want,
plus I can hear it even in my DREAMS.)

Dear La Virgen,

Guess what I did? The same day that Darling picked me up at Tias and I said Bye to Tia (And she started to cry and said Whos going to make me laugh Luna?) And even Pablo looked like he was going to start blubbering so I ran over like fast and gave him some $ to buy some treats and I whispered DON'T TELL THE CHEAP SKATE (And Pablo started kinda laughing and he even tryed to do the Skinny Kid Dance but it was kinda pathetic cause he still looked pretty sad right?) And then I whispered again Don't tell Tia I call Her Husband the Fat Tortilla Face like when she keeps jumping up and down trying to keep the chingaso ass things hot OK kid? And then Pablo said Your my favoritist cousin (And then I almost started blubbering, believe it or snot!) Any way I was glad The Cheap Skate wasn't there cause if he said any thing nice in front of Darling PUKOLA! So me and Darling hopped in her Thunder Bird and I waved to Tia and Pablo till they were 2 little dots in The Projects and then we turned and drove through the long ass tunnel. (That seemed short today.) When we drove over the GOLDEN GATE BRIDGE I was trying to spot some one trying to jump like you know sewerside but all I saw was cars and the grown ups staring straight a head like there going to there doom or some thing cause just the kids look out the windows. But Darling doesn't look like shes going to her doom like shes saying Look at that and look at that and did you see that JESUS F. CHRIST! (She says that a lot.) I looked up at the top of the G.G. Bridge and I saw BIRDS way up there and I wished I was a bird or maybe even climb to the top COOL!! Then we drove a road with TONS of curves that almost made me PUKE like all the way to BOLINAS. (And Darling drives fast.) Then we got to her Hidden House COOL!! And Darling gave some guy The Bird cause she said he was trying to take her lane and he was the only grown up I saw looking out the window, and his face was so red he looked like he was going to EXPLODE so I just ducked down cracking up but she didn't crack up till we got to her Hide Out (like she calls her house in BOLINAS.)

So what I did after I unloaded all the FOOD she bought and she was putting it away, cause she said I could get out of her hair cause dinner would be in an hour or so and I could tell she was tired after the long ass drive with the Death Defying Drops (Thats what Darling calls them). I said Why don't I go swimming and she gave me a towel and told me to stay close to shore and all, and I grabbed a snack and as I was walking to the Ocean like a 1/2 block from the back porch I thought I was in one of my dreams (HOLY ASS CHINGASOS for one sec I thought I could have a heart attack cause I was to HAPPY so I got kinda creepy and sat down on the sand.) Then I remembered the dream I had about swimming here and walking down this little dirt road just big enough for your 2 feet right? So I stripped down to my old sad ass swim team suit thats so stretchy it goes right up my but so I look around for any Stray Perverts. No one. Just me. And then I see a SEAL Then 2 SEALS. Then 3 SEALS. Then 4 SEALS. And there all staring at me (I think there wondering why I'm not in the Ocean right?) And then I wonder if SEALS bite and I sure the shit hope not and I wonder why I never saw so many SEALS the last time I came to BOLINAS. But I jumped in and swam a little kinda waiting to feel there big ass GIANT SEAL TEETH but they kept diving under the waves and up and just staring at me (Which is pretty creepy.) Then I layed down on the towel and the sun was so HOT and every thing was like super quiet (Except for some birds yelling at each other). So I fell asleep and dreamed—That I was a SEAL STARING AT ME on the sand sleeping WEIRD So I woke up laughing and I thought to myself (I'm a seal so they won't bite me right?)

Then Darling had my worst night mare dinner SHRIMP like I used to watch Carmen and the General Guy eat RAW OYSTERS and he tryed to make me eat shrimp one time (Count me out PUKOLA!) But Darling said I had to try one cause she was going to be cooking FISH once in a while and that its like healthy and all (And she gave me the Cat Eyes right?) So I tryed a couple and I ended up eating SECONDS cause she cooked the shrimp in a delisious sauce. So I guess I'll try fish like at least I promised I would right? So after Darling was watching TV and I was doing the dishes (Which is one of my jobs). So what I did was this—I put BUTTER on my paws and then I licked it off like the cats did. I even put some milk in a bowl and drank it like the cats LICK LICK LICK LICK (Do you think I'm getting MUY LOCA Virgen?) Are you surprised I still remember how to write Spanish? Remember how I used to read the Bible for Mamacita at night when her eyes were too tired? Remember how I read the poems for Church till I knew them by my heart? Remember how they put me in the Retarded Class cause I could only read and write in Spanish and do math in Spanish? Remember when I peed my pants when the Fuck Face Fat White Lady Teacher wouldn't let me go to the bath room till I asked in English like she kept saying Habla en Engles LORNA and I was so little I kinda thought maybe I was lost or something so I just peed my calzones, and thats how I went to Catholic school and finally learned English (But my name was NEVER LORNA.) Remember the Nun who taught me English? She used to wait for me in the Nuns House down some steps and when I walked in to the Nuns House there you were just like Mamacita said all in blue with your hands open and a Golden Crown on your head, and I think thats when I really started praying to you THEN. So the Mexican Nun always waited for me at the bottom of the dark steps with candles every where and she smelled kinda like ROSES and she sat by the black steel gate with GIANT ROSES on it and she smiled when she saw me. So I sat on a chair on my side and she sat on a chair on her side, and I learned English from the Mexican Nun who spoke Spanish and English through the Black Rose Gate and I could tell she was young and beautiful like when she smiled. One time Mamacita came to talk to her and later she lit some candles to you and she said to bless La Casita De Las Virgens, and some times I really wonder if you are the Mexican Nun who taught me English and laughed when we were all alone. I remember how brown and smooth your skin was and your teeth were so white and perfect and your hands were small and your voice sounded kinda like singing. Remember when I asked you if you were BALD and you showed me a tiny part of your black hair under your Nuns Hat that always hid it. Remember how you laughed so hard and I was laughing to right? So the old grouchy Nun came and put her finger over her mouth telling us to SHUT UP remember? And then I told all the kids—Nuns aren't BALD pendejos!

One of my other jobs is to feed the 2 cats and put water out for the deer. So far the deer are pretty scared of me and when ever I go out side they zoom away. I was thinking of having a Milk Licking Contest with the cats (Just call me La Loca for sure Virgen.) Any way Darling gave me a new word EXTRAORDINARY and like I've heard it before but of course I never even thought about it or used it like to talk or any thing. The other words are PARADOX CELLULAR MAMMAL. She decided to give me 4 words a week or so, but I have to really think about them and all and look them up and write a poem or a paragraph or a story with them in it. To tell the truth Virgen I really like the word EXTRAORDINARY cause have you ever thought of this—EXTRA ORDINARY. It's kinda cool when you really think about all this like some things are regular, but then some thing makes it EXTRA chingaso cool. Kinda like the other day I was going over to Harrys House to see his horse Cinamon to see about maybe riding it. (When Darling told me his name was Harry I cracked up cause I just pictured this guy that was born so HAIRY that his mom called him HARRY HA!) Darling gave me the Cat Eyes but she finally started laughing too (Now I know its <u>too</u>.) She said OK kid try not to scare the Old Cuss too much and now get out of here for a while and don't be scared of Cinamon cause shes about to keel over shes so old. Oh great I thought, like what a fregado thrill if she just dies while I'm yelling GIDDY YAP or WHOOOOOAAAA (Holy ass shit right?)

So I'm walking over to this Old Cuss Harrys House which is across the <u>mesa</u> (They call it a mesa here like a table cause its flat and the Ocean is right beside me the whole way.) So as I'm walking across the mesa listening to the Ocean cause the waves are pretty high today and its really windy like I see these little I mean TINY yellow and purple flowers and I guess I've been stepping on them all the time and I didn't even see them right? I look around really careful to make sure theres no Lurking Perverts or Weirdos and its pretty flat out here. (Like a <u>mesa</u> right?) Only out by the cliffs theres some really giant ass trees (I rode <u>my bike</u> out there cause Darling got it for me at the second hand store but I LOVE IT cause its a 10 SPEED!!!) Any way when I couldn't see any Pervs or Weirdos I flopped down on the grass and stuff and just stayed flat for a while, and every thing was still except for the tips of the grass that were waving around in the wind. And then I started looking at every thing like <u>close up</u> and the tiny (MINISCULE is a word Darling gave me a couple of months ago and it means tinyer than TINY.) So the miniscule yellow and purple flowers were like GIANT now and I could see really miniscule golden feelers (Like the Sea Anemones have and have you ever touched one and feel it taste your finger SO SOFT?) The golden feelers were just sticking straight up but you really have to <u>look</u> to see them, and then I saw a bee zoom in on the feelers and then I saw more bees and what Darling calls Dragon Flys which have rainbows on there wings EXTRA COOL see? Thats what I mean by EXTRA ORDINARY. So I just stayed there for a while spying on every thing like hardly breatheing or you scare every thing to death right? Darling makes me carry around a note pad and pen in case I feel like writing right? At first I thought it was kinda pendeja locita but I kinda like it now. (Did I tell you Darlings a Oil Painter and a Rock Polisher too?) When I left for Harrys House she was painting a picture of me standing in the Ocean with some seals staring at me (I told her about the seals and some times she comes down to watch me with her sketch pad she calls it). Darling says shes going to teach me how to draw cause she says I just forgot like she says every kid knows how to draw, but to tell the truth Virgen I'll believe it when I see it (Like me drawing some thing that looks like some thing? HA! and HA!) So I slowly got my pad and pen out and kept laying down on my stomach QUIETLY and I wrote this poem (Believe it or not.)—EXTRA ORDINARY

> Because I'm a MAMMAL that walks
> on 2 feet CLUMP CLUMP CLUMP
> I squished I don't know how many
> regular MINISCULE flowers cause
> I'm going over to Harrys House to see
> a 1/2 dead horse named Cinamon.
> Now thats a PARADOX, but laying here
> on a windy sunny day I can see
> the yellow and purple flowers
> with golden feelers and
> tiny zooming bees that stop
> to taste the gold and
> I'm so HAPPY for one sec
> I forget if I'm a bee
> or a Dragon Fly
> or a flower
> or even the wind thats singing
> like a CELLULAR song for every
> thing like even me.

Do you like the poem Virgen? Tell the TRUTH (Tell me in a dream OK?) When I showed Darling the poem she really laughed and she probably read it 100 times and she really hugged me with her GIANT BOOBS (I'm not kidding Virgen cause there the biggest boobs I've ever seen so please DO NOT give me boobs that big PLEASE!!!!) And she kept saying that she loved the poem cause I'm extraordinary (Kinda embarassing right?) But I guess I'm just a MAMMAL cause to tell the truth Virgen I kinda like it (That she LOVES my poems and stuff.)

So any way after I wrote the poem and I ate a couple of the miniscule flowers (To see what they taste like SOUR but OK). I'm thinking maybe the golden part is sweet where the bees zoom in and eat right? So I finally got to Harrys House where Darling said his mail box is RED with his last name WALSH. I was kinda expecting Cinamon to be tied up on his fence waiting for me (Like in the movies). But I have to BANG on the door and then I see a sign that says—RING THE BELL. Theres a huge ass BELL with a ringer right next to it so I start making this RACKET. (If I were in S.F. I'd probably get arrested or some thing.) I was really SMACKING it and kinda haveing fun cause certain parts of the bell really sounded COOL. Then Harry comes yelling WHO THE HELLS THERE GOD DAM IT!!!! And he just keeps swearing even when he sees me right? So I say You said to ring the bell (in my boys voice). Well Jesus F. Christ and his disiples (HA!) I didn't mean you to wake the damed dead did I? Thats what he said. How do I know? Thats what I said. Then he looked me up and down (And I looked him up and down like he was DECREPIT with some bushy ass eye brows and hairs coming out of his NOSE and do you know who he looked like Virgen? YOSEMITE SAM like in the cartoons and I'm not kidding either but lots older right?) Fuck this (I said to myself). And I jumped down the rickety ass stairs and I was almost out the creeky ass gate when he yells COME ON OUT AND HELP ME FEED THE DAM HORSE CAUSE SHES BEEN WAITIN ON YOU ALL THE DAM MORNING AN I DON'T HAVE ALL DAM DAY YOU KNOW!!!! (He sounds kinda like the Whitey guy in S.F. right?) So I followed him really really careful like at a distance right? And then I saw Cinamon (Shes a GIRL HORSE!) She didn't look 1/2 dead at all in fact she was HUGE and when she saw me she looked a little MAD cause she snorted and clumped around with her horsey ass feet (I didn't know horses were so CHINGASO ASS BIG!) Did you Virgen? So Decrepit Harry hands me a bucket and tells me to go get the feed (And he shows me where it is like in a scarey old barn but he walks back to the house and I figure I could kick his but if I had to right?) Then he puts some of this FEED in his hand and feeds Cinamon and tells me to do it too so I figure like there gos my fingers, like what a fregado THRILL!!! So I put some on my palm cause Decrepit Harry is kinda laughing at me (I can tell he thinks I'm scared SHIT). So I put my hand out really flat so my fingers aren't in the way and Cinamon looks like shes thinking about it too (Like whos this mammal right?) And then she breathes and slobbers all over my hand with her GIANT LIPS and guess what Virgen? Her lips are so soft just like the Sea Anemones so I just start laughing like a pendeja. Then he says Do you know how to ride? I look at him (Cause I don't want him to think I'm a chicken) And I say NO.

So I fed Cinamon some grain and filled up her bath tub (Thats where she drinks water, probably cause horses drink a TON of water I guess plus she kinda ducks her head in to the water and comes up all wet and slobbery which kinda cracks me up cause it looks like shes kinda haveing some fun too.) Then Decrepit Harry showed me how to brush her fur but it was pretty creepy cause I kept waiting for her to step on my feet and smash me so I kept jumping around when she moved which made Decrepit Harry LAUGH (And he has a weird ass laugh kinda like hes learning how to laugh or some thing.) So he tells me Cinamons getting used to how I smell and how I touch her and that next time he'll get me in the SADDLE and he tells me which days I can come back if I want to. Whats your name? He says and I tell him. And he calls me LORNA (My night mare name right Virgen?) So I say my name right LUNA. Then he says Means MOON doesn't it? You a Spanish Girl? And I say You a Hermit? And kinda like that Whitey guy in S.F. he looks really mad for a sec and then its the Weirdo Learning Laugh (Kinda like Pablos Skinny Kids Dance right?) So he says See ya next time LUNA And I say Probably on Monday Harry The Hermit. So thats what I call him now—Harry The Hermit cause hes all alone way out on the mesa exept for Cinamon of course.

I really wish Pablito were here Virgen cause I think he'd LOVE Cinamon (After he got over being terrifyed and all.) He could feed her from his hand and feel the most giant and softest lips in the whole chingaso world EXTRA ORDINARY!!! And he could have some of Darlings Beef Stew and not Hot Dog Stew and he could have seconds or thirds and maybe he could even get

FAT right? And then he could do the Fat Kids Dance or some thing and I think of him far far away over the Death Defying Road and the Sewerside Bridge and in to the long ass dark Killer Tunnel to his Projects House where he lives with Tia (And the Cheap Skate.) And Tia keeps the house Spick and Span (Thats what she says—Spick and Span like after shes done cleaning and every thing smells kinda like a brand new house with no dead bodys any where in Tias house.) But if the lights burn out at night when every ones sleeping—believe it or not its Cock Roach City, and you don't want that to happen Virgen like believe me it is NOT EXTRA ORDINARY. Its cellular its so creepy and thats no paradox (The end—Luna The Mammal.)

MARCH RIDEING CINAMON IN MARCH

Dear La Virgen,

Thanks for the dream (It was a little creepy but I really liked it too.) I dreamt Mamacita reading one of my poems in Spanish and she looked SO HAPPY like she used to look like in Church when she'd stand up on the stage and say a poem by heart especially at Christmas Time at Midnight Services when she'd be Death (I'm not kidding either.) And she had a spear in her hand cause in the poem she'd say by heart Death had a STING and thats the only time I saw her in public with her hair down like to her waist remember? (So in the dream she was happy like that and if you saw her from the back she kinda looked like a kid I remember.) When I woke up I was pretty SAD and then when I got up to see if the deer were here yet it felt like I could still hear her reading my poem. Then the weirdest thing happened like it felt like she was right here with me watching the deer and the cats just lazeing around the house (Some times they bring a beat up lizard or dead snakes in to the house DISGUSTING and Darling praises them. cause she says the cats need to be praised cause there good hunters DISGUSTAMENTO!!!) So she takes there Gifts she calls them and one time she said if the snake were bigger she'd COOK it cause she says SNAKE tastes just like chicken YUMMY!!! And I said Thats the one thing I'm not ever never going to try even ONCE. (And Darling just smiled but I AM NOT KIDDING like no snake for this mammal cause I know the difference between a SNAKE and a CHICKEN right?) Any way I told Darling the dream and I even told her about how Mamacita and I always said our dreams in the morning (But I didn't tell her about my Flying Dreams yet.) I watched her Cat Eyes really careful to see if she thought I'm La Loca, but she looked regular and asked me some stuff about Mamacita and then she gave me these words—REINCARNATION DILEMMA OXYGEN FETUS. These are some <u>cool</u> words and she explained REINCARNATION. (It turns out that Darling is a BUDDIST and thats why she lights incence and candles kinda like the Nuns House right Virgen?) And she puts flowers and special sea shells in front of this little fat guy she calls Budda who I guess is kinda like your husband GOD right? But he doesn't look <u>mad</u> like hes smiteing any one and in fact he looks like he eats 5ths or 6ths, and in fact he looks like hes <u>smileing</u> cause of his flowers and all the food he gets to eat right? So any way Virgen what do you think about this guy BUDDA like do you know him and why is he so <u>fat</u>? To tell the truth I kinda like him and I even put some flowers I picked right in front of him but its no big deal cause I'm just checking him out right?

Darling told me REINCARNATION is when some one like any one dies and doesn't breathe OXYGEN any more they become a FETUS and get <u>born</u> again. At first I was pretty confused to tell the truth but then the dream about Mamacita reading my poem in Spanish felt <u>so</u> <u>real</u> so I decided like maybe Mamacita is BORN again some where which would <u>make me older than her</u> WEIRD!!! So I picked the flowers and put them in a glass of water like Darling does and gave them to Fat Boy BUDDA and I said (I'm not kidding) If Mamacitas born again don't give her so many <u>dilemmas</u> this time OK?

You know Virgen I think I'm getting kinda used to this place especially in the day time like I don't have to look around any more for Lurking Perverts (Darling says if any man tryed to get in her house he'd wish he was <u>dead</u> when she gets through with him and I say You mean REINCARNATED and we crack up.)

You probably know that Harry The Hermit finally taught me how to ride Cinamon and like all I really have to do is not be afraid of her cause even when I went way out by the giant ass trees on the other side of the mesa and it got dark all of a sudden (I was really kinda lost right?) Cinamon finally figured it out (That I was a lost pendeja). And she took us back to Harrys House NO SWEAT!!! But I'll tell you the truth cause being in the DARK out by those scarey ass trees and LOST was pretty chingaso ass creepy (I thought—This is a Perverts Dream Come True, so I figured if they were waiting to get me nows the perfect time right?) And then I started thinking about REINCARNATION (Believe it or not.) Like maybe there were some really POed (Which means Pissed Off which Darling says a lot) OK some Pissed Off GHOSTS that might like a girl body like mine with blood and all (Cause I was wearing The Diaper FREGADO!!!) So while I'm thinking all this freako stuff Cinamon just keeps walking back to Harrys House and you know I think I'd be embarassed if Cinamon could read my mind like what a CHICKEN I secretly am like a GIRL CHICKEN, but then I think maybe she likes me cause I'm a girl and shes a girl, OK shes a GIRL HORSE (You ever think of this—em-bare-assed—SORRY VIRGEN but I really do think of this stuff SORRY!)

Any way so when I tryed saying GIDDY YAP the first time I finally got in to the SADDLE (Which is pretty COOL!) I thought Harry The Hermit was going to have a heart attack he was laughing so hard like hes getting better at it maybe cause hes laughing more like a mammal these days right? And he finally says—This ain't the movies Annie Oakly. (And I think SHIT now I'm ANNIE OAKLY like in S.F. I'm POKAHANTAS right Virgen?) So he tells me what to do and its so easy I feel like a real dumb ass PENDEJA and I'd give him the Witch Eyes but I'm not really mad or any thing, and then I remember who Annie Oakly is (That White Lady in the movies whos a COW GIRL and she shoots and rides better than even guys COOL!) So I don't give him The Witch Eyes and I say Maybe I should get a DAM COW BOY HAT (And I kinda can't believe I even said it right?) So Harry The Hermit REALLY cracks up and tells me to Keep movin the old girl around and he hobbles away and then he finally comes back with A COW BOY HAT and tells me—Its for you Annie so go on a head and put the dam thing on. (And of course hes laughing.) But I do. I put the dam hat on my pendeja head and I don't even want to think about what I probably look like, and for one sec I think—Maybe this is what happens when you put butter on your paws and have a Milk Licking Contest with 2 cats right? HOLY ASS CHINGASOS!!! So what am I Virgen? Am I POKAHANTAS or ANNIE OAKLY????

So I haven't gone way out to the Giant Ass Trees since the last time I got lost when it got dark on me and I thought ghosts were after me (OK I know I'm pretty pathetic Virgen.) But I've been rideing Cinamon about 1/2 way there where I found a COOL Hide Away Beach and so I wear my beat up swim suit under my regular clothes (And of course it gos right up my nalgas so maybe I'll see if Darling could get a <u>new</u> one cause this ones about 100 years old right?) So I bring a sandwich and some apples and I tie Cinamon to a branch and I feed her a cut up apple (Danny The Dane sent me a SWISS ARMY KNIFE with a bunch of cool knives and sissors even and its the <u>best present</u> in my life so far!!) Then I jump in the Ocean and scream cause its FREGADO FREEZING and I swim and ride the waves with the Seals cause they always come to kinda keep me company and stare at me (Some times like right now I miss Jody my Tomboy Friend cause I know she'd <u>love</u> it here and of course she might not even recognize me with the COW BOY HAT and rideing a HORSE right?) Also I'm reading a book about a boy around my age whos stranded on an island after a ship wreck and he finds a Secret Tunnel in to the island, and inside the island is a whole SECRET WORLD and also a BLACK STALLION and a bunch of other wild horses. You know Virgen I feel kinda like that boy in his own Secret World and even if it would be fun to see Jody and even Hope and my friends at the Salvation Army Club, and play basket ball and goof around, the TRUTH is I'm not sorry I'm here but some times I wonder if Jake Juniors OK, and if Carmens still alive (Like has The Psycho murdered her yet?) And I wouldn't mind droping in on that Whitey guy like he promised me a CHERRY CAKE (And maybe I'm his only friend?) OK so even if I think of those guys some times this Secret World is even better than the Secret Forest in Golden Gate Park in S.F. cause it feels like its all mine probably cause I don't have to worry about Lurking Perverts all the time like in G.G. Park.

The other day when I was rideing Cinamon back to Harrys House I suddenly felt like laying down on her stinky ass neck and so I did and then I put my face close to her mane which is her hair and I sniffed and she was pretty stinky like a HORSE but the more I stayed there and she just clump clump clumped back to Harrys like for some weirdo reason I felt just like a horse with the sun on our back and bunches of birds yelling at each other flying over our heads and I watched the grass and the flowers under our horsey ass feet and I just about fell a sleep like wouldn't that be WEIRD if I just fell off and she just kept clump clump clumping over to Harrys House HA! HA! But I didn't of course (I'm not that Loca Pendeja yet.) But do you know what it felt like Virgen? It felt like a DREAM like maybe I was really dreaming this Secret World and it was kinda creepo to think that, but to tell the TRUTH I like feeling like a HORSE IN A DREAM (Do you know what I mean Virgen—tell me in a dream OK?)

And I was thinking it kinda reminds me of how Mamacita and I had Secret Worlds like China Town in S.F. when I used to go with her after Catholic School and the Mean Ass Sister Superior WACKED my hands for being late cause I was watching a GIGANTIC line of ants marching in to this hole in the side walk and I thought it was pretty cool like where were they going right? And the tops of my hands got these big RED marks on them and of course I grabbed the humungus ruler and WACKED her back on her thick ass Nuns Dress so it didn't hurt her or any thing of course (Darling says HUMUNGUS but she says its not a real word but I like it OK, in fact its better than GIGANTIC I think.) Also the pathetic part was that when the Mean Ass Sister asked to see my hands like a PENDEJA I thought she wanted to see my hands cause they were BEAUTIFUL (Believe it or not.) Cause back in those days I used to squint my eyes in the sun light when we were sitting at our desks in these straight rows and I felt like looking at some thing cool so I'd see all these beautiful lights SPRAYING off my hands, and thats why I thought my hands were so beautiful right? Plus every one was pretty bored and the Nun who was the Teacher was pretty boreing herself and plus in those days I couldn't understand every thing cause I spoke mainly Spanish still and I could tell the Nun thought I was a real pendeja right? So when the Mean Ass Sister wacked my hands they were BURNING and I ran out of there and Mamacita said I never had to go back to Catholic School again (But I did miss the Beautiful Mexican Nun who taught me English and some times I wonder if shes still sitting there by the Cold Black Rose Gate?) So Mamacita and I took Cable Cars to China Town and the Mexican Movies and the Ocean some times, and it felt like our Secret World (And you know how some times she did GRITOS like thats a Chingaso Mexican Yell when you're REALLY HAPPY and she did GRITOS to the Mexican Rancheras on the radio, and she even DANCED.) But you know what happened Virgen cause she got really old and sick and they put her in the Old Peoples Prison, and you know that I saw her die there REINCARNATION. So I had to steal my first bike (You know the one you left for me on Guerrero Street.) And I had to find all the Secret Places by myself till I met Jody and I guess if any ones Annie Oakly its Jody cause she has blond hair and blue eyes like a real Gringa but I never thought of her like a Gringa or any thing cause shes my best bestest friend in S.F.

The other day I asked Harry if he liked being a Hermit and then I thought wouldn't it be cool if Old Whitey could visit Old Harry cause I bet they'd really like each other and maybe even get drunk cause Harry drinks HOOCH, any way thats what he calls it WEIRD. For one sec I thought he was POed but then he said—I lived here all my life and built this palace (Thats what he said PALACE and we kinda cracked up cause his house looks more like a shack but a nice shack I think)—For myself and my wife and I had one kid and hes gone and shes dead now, she was an Indian Woman, marryed over 40 years me and her. (You know thats how he talks kinda twangey like Whitey, The South and Tia said thats how my real father talked WEIRD.) And then he said some other stuff about how he wouldn't live in no city if they paid him a million bucks cause theres no freedom there even to think your own dam thoughts and stuff like that (And I kinda know what he means right Virgen?) So I asked him what kinda Indian his wife was and he got <u>really sad</u> and I was really sorry I asked so I said—My grandmother was a Yaqui Indian from Mexico and shes dead too or like Darling says REINCARNATED and I really for real miss her cause she was always like my real mom and all. Then he said some thing like—Well Miss Moon I thought you might be my old wifes daughter WEIRD. Then he just went in to his house and he yelled—Cinamons waitin on you for her ride so get your but in gear Miss Moon!

Miss Moon HA! I kinda like that. No ones <u>ever</u> called me Miss Moon. When I was a baby I had my fathers Gringo name but after Carmen divorced him and brought me to S.F. from some weirdo place in LOUISIANA (A farm she said where his whole family lived in The South where they probably said stuff like sody and down yonder you all) Carmen said his family tryed to make her work in the fields cause she was a Mexican (And Carmen always tells this part too, that being a Mexican there was the same as being a Nigger like a slave but of course if you were to say NIGGER to any of the kids at the Salvation Army Club you'd be instantly KILLED and I don't blame them cause I've been called a Wet Back and a Dirty Indian and I almost KILLED those ass holes SORRY VIRGEN but its the TRUTH.) But some times the black girls call each other Nigger goofing around, but of course thats different you know? Any way I guess they couldn't believe he marryed a Mexican (Tia says he had the bluest eyes and blond blond hair and she says he was a really nice guy cause she met him on the Army Base where Tia and Carmen worked like Tia was a nurse and Carmen was a medical secretary and Mamacita lived with them and took care of me the baby.) Tia said this was after there father died and Carmen sold all Mamacitas good furniture Tia said and first they moved to a place called Santa Barbara where I was BORN. So when Carmen brought me back to S.F. from The South she changed my name back to her familys name VILLALOBOS cause she didn't want him to find me I guess. Which I like cause Mamacita used to call me her Lobita some times and that means Baby Wolf which is cool, and some times I really did feel like a Baby Wolf, kinda like being a horse with Cinamon right? And Mamacita said that a wolf is pretty smart and strong plus she said there also good dreamers, and so I always really liked being called Lobita and she was the only person in the world who ever did of course. So maybe Harry The Hermit figured out my secret name for this Secret World and you know Virgen the mesa really does feel like an island cause you can hear the Ocean every where you go, and maybe Cinamons not a BLACK STALLION cause of course a stallion is a boy horse with a PENIS (Darling makes me say penis like the proper name she calls it but saying PENIS to me sounds worse, and then she tells me the other proper word VAGINA but I can tell shes trying to be like a mom and teach me some thing right?) But I can not really say PENIS or VAGINA without laughing my ass off, but I guess I can write it (Cause I am writing it.)

So maybe Cinamons not a stallion with a PENIS but shes a mare with a VAGINA (I know this is pretty weird Virgen SORRY). So maybe in my Secret World here on my Secret Island like my name is Miss Moon and my friends from S.F. even if they saw me (Rideing Cinamon way out on the mesa right?) They'd probably say—Look at that creepy Hermit Kid HA! Now I'm wondering what Harry The Hermits Wife looked like and maybe he has some pictures he could show me so maybe next time I'll ask him. He probably thinks I'm a Royal Pain In The Ass (Darling calls me that some times). But I guess I'm the kinda mammal that wants to know EVERY THING especialy if I like some one (I guess I like Harry The Hermit and now I'm wondering if I'm getting pretty hard up to be friends cause he is pretty old and all.) And like Darling calls him a Cranky Old Cuss but maybe thats why I like him, and to tell the truth he doesn't even look like Yosemite Sam any more WEIRD. Well some times he does like when he starts yelling HA! HA!

One night Darling brought out a HUGE BOOK that had thousands of pictures glued inside and there she was as a BABY WITH HER BABOW and then she was a kid, and she had her own PONY in Washington like she grew up on a ranch she said and she was a tomboy, and so thats whats so COOL about Darling right Virgen? And then she told me storys about being a kid and growing up and climbing trees and fishing, and she said her father even taught her how to HUNT and she said she even killed DEER for the table like they ate a DEER. I guess she saw my face like how DISGUSTED I was and she said she wouldn't kill the deer that come here unless she were pretty hungry cause she buys all her meat now (And I wonder if shes still planning to kill a SNAKE FOR THE TABLE PUKOLA!!!) And then I asked her what she was and she said German, Scotch and Irish, and I said I was German too but also Yaqui Indian from Mexico like mi Mamacita and she said she already knew that I was some kinda Indian but she didn't know I was a Yaqui Indian. And then I had to SAY IT. (Believe it or snot.) Do you think I'm a Gringa or a Wet Back? And she didn't even laugh but her Cat Eyes looked kinda sad (Darling never looks sad.) So she said—Your a Human Being Luna period. And then she said Come on kid lets make some pop corn with a ton of butter, and then we ate our asses off like 2 HUMAN BEING MAMMALS (Tell the truth—What do you think Virgen?)

When I left this morning to go to Harrys House Darling was watering her flowers dressed in her jeans and HUMUNGUS BRA and she promised to cook Honey Chicken for dinner (Which I really love!) Some times I wonder if I maybe drive her muy loca cause shes not used to haveing any kids like just herself and then Danny The Dane shows up once in a while I guess. So any way during the day I take off kinda like in S.F. (I told Darling maybe I'll go to school in September but I don't want to be a Freak Show yet and she said OK.) But here in BOLINAS its my Secret World and I'm Miss Moon HA! HA! And I don't feel like a Freak Show even with Harrys Cow Boy Hat and rideing Cinamon all by myself all day long WEIRD.

When I got to Harrys House there was a note—WENT TO TOWN. TAKE HORSE. SEE YOU NEXT TIME. Your Friend, The Hermit. I guess he went to Town with his rusty old truck that he says runs on fumes and a prayer probably to buy some more HOOCH and what ever it is he eats like Hermit Food. So I just fed Cinamon her apple (She paws the ground now till I do cause she knows I have it.) And before I put my up the nalgas bathing suit on heres a poem with the 4 new words (Which I'll show Darling tonight after the Honey Chicken YUM!!!). Already theres 2 Seals out there just stareing at me (They sure are NOSEY!) But I like them any way and so far they haven't taken a bite out of my nalgas or any thing (There kinda like dogs cause they follow me around when I'm swimming and of course I've never had a dog so maybe your giveing me these guys for FREE right Virgen? SUPER COOL!!) So heres the poem with my new words—1. MAGMA 2. DORMANT 3. GALAXY 4. VOYAGE

ZEN KONE POEM

If the MAGMA is in the middle of the earth
and if the winter is when every thing is DORMANT
and if the GALAXY is where every one
lives like a miniscule speck on Buddas
eye ball, and if he ate us and we took
a VOYAGE down his throat to his stomach
and we got even smaller—
What would we be?

Darlings been telling me these Zen Kones which are pretty goofy so I thought I'd write her a ZEN KONE POEM (Can you guess what it is Virgen?) Do you ever have to go to the bath room? Do you get a Period every dam month and have to wear a dam diaper? (Tell the TRUTH Virgen OK?)

So now Miss Moon will leave the Brave Brown Mare (With a VAGINA) and go swim with her Pet Seals and see if she can swim way out to where those giant ass rocks are (I think she wants to TOUCH them.) Me Miss Moon (Or is it me La Muy Loca?)

APRIL THE MONTH I ALMOST DROWNED

Dear La Virgen,

The last thing I said in March was that I was going to swim way out to the Giant Ass Rocks where the Seals take a break from swimming so I thought COOL maybe I can take a break too when I get there, but it was way the chingasos out there right? And then an UNDER TOW just grabbed me (I'm not kidding Virgen!) And it took me even further out than the Giant Ass Rocks and I was pretty stupid too cause I fought the Under Tow (My swimming coach always said to never fight it and it'll just let you go but I fought it any way cause I forgot all the rules.) And the only reason I stopped fighting it was I was too TIRED to fight any more, but then I could barely swim and then it let me go THANKS A LOT UNDER TOW and it felt like the Ocean had some GIANT ASS HANDS and my Miss Moon Body was like PUNY out there like a speck like a tiny dot of sun light or like some spit compared to the whole OCEAN. So when I started to swim back to shore I knew I was DOOMED and I knew I was going to DROWN and I couldn't even see any of the Seals so I knew I was really all by my pathetic self right? And then its really WEIRD but all of a sudden the sun light on the water all around me was like jumping around and danceing every where and for some reason it just made me HAPPY (So I must be La Muy Loca for sure now!) Was it you Virgen? Cause then this miracle (My new word for the week from Darling of course.) This really happened NO SHIT!!!! All of a sudden this really PERFECT WAVE came (Was it you Virgen?) And it picked me right up like a GIANT SUPER GENTLE HAND and just like a ride at Play Land At The Beach in S.F. it took me back to where the Seals were waiting for me and I just kinda floated back to shore and flopped on the sand for a long time, and the sun felt SO GOOD and I was SO HAPPY to be a MAMMAL and breathing AIR with WARM SAND all around me (Also lots of rocks that Darling brings home to her Rock Polisher and then all these Regular Rocks turn in to Super Cool Shiny Rocks.) So I survived even though I nearly drowned from EXHAUSTION (2nd new word.) Darling said I didn't drown cause of my STAMINA (3rd new word.) But I know it really wasn't me cause I knew I was a goner (So was it you Virgen?) On the beach when I passed out for a while I felt like this—A baby mammal kinda dreaming in your warm WOMB (4th new word.) And when I woke up the sun had moved way over by the cliffs (And heres the TRUTH.) I felt like a NEW Hermit Girl Miss Moon La Muy Loca Pokahantas Annie Oklay MAMMAL (Like Jody says some times—Have you lost your fucking noodle? And she really does say that A LOT Virgen.) But it felt like maybe I'm not scared of ANY THING any more, and then I was STARVED!!! Maybe the most hungry I've been in my whole entire VIDA and so I threw my clothes over my up the nalgas swim suit and untied Cinamon (And I felt bad cause she had to just stand there all day so tomorrow I'll just ride her and I told her like a promise.) Harry still wasn't home so I fed and watered Cinamon and put every thing away like he showed me, and I brushed her and watched her skin shake and jump cause she likes it and some times she nuzzles me (Horses do that only if they really like you and if they don't they just show you there HUGE scarey teeth.)

I was so STARVED when I got home to Darlings I almost fainted when I smelled what she was cooking A ROAST!!!! Smashed potatoes and lots of peas with tons of butter and a giant ass salad full of tomatoes and onions (And artichoke hearts which

Darling made me like and now I do pretty much with mayo.) When I told Darling about the Under Tow and how the Giant Wave saved me and how I fell a sleep in the sun, and I even told her about my up the nalgas swim suit and that I know a new one won't stop the SEALS from biting my ASS (But I don't really think they will cause there good DOGGYS!) So Darling laughs with her Cat Eyes and says—Time for a new swim suit for the SURVIVOR. And then later she gave me the four new words. She also said she was going to S.F. for about 3 days and 2 nights but that shes calling me in the morning and then at night, and that shes leaving lots of food in the frig. I've never stayed here by myself but I told her its cool (Like maybe I'm really not scared of ANY THING any more—So what do you think Virgen am I?)

Darling gives me a 1/2 glass of vino with dinner and she tells me what kind it is but so far it all tastes the <u>same</u> to me and I don't even drink all of it, but its fun to sip some with Darling. She took me down in the basement to her Rock Cutting Room and it was really <u>dark</u> down there till she turned on a light. Then she showed me all the Polished Rocks and she told me to take 10 just for me and so I chose some COOL ones, and then she turned on her Rock Cutting Machine and she picked up a regular old rock like if you saw it laying on the ground you'd think "No big deal" cause its just a rock like the size of a baseball right? Then she slides it in to the Rock Cutter (Which makes a chingaso NOISE!!) And it splits in 1/2 and the MOST BEAUTIFUL ROCK I've <u>ever seen</u> is INSIDE. Darling calls them <u>crystals</u> and its like a whole Secret World is inside an ugly regular old rock and its like the regular old rock caught the sun inside cause when you open it up theres a ton of crystals. (Darling says rocks are born from the <u>womb</u> of the earth and then there spit up to the top, kinda like I was spit out of the Ocean she said cracking up, and then there born she said after centuries of time and then I wonder how the sun was born like do you know Virgen????) So thats how the Secret Crystal World is made and then Darling gave me the split open Crystal Rock and she told me she'd polish it later so every thing will be super smooth. Any way I put the Secret Crystal World Rock next to my bed and its the first thing I see in the morning when I wake up (I think some times theres a smell when your happy or feeling pretty good like Darlings House and Bolinas smells that way right Virgen?) So heres the 4 new word poem.

SECRET CRYSTAL WORLD

Because its a MIRACLE I didn't drown
I brought a PERFECT sea shell
to Buddas Altar (The one Darling
has with candles and flowers.)
An Under Tow caught me in the Ocean
and took me so far out my STAMINA
disappeared and all I had was
EXHAUSTION. Then La Virgens

hand scooped me up or other
wise I'd be reincarnated right now
and she brought me to the sand where I
fell a sleep (in her WARM WOMB.)

And I dreamed this—
A Secret Crystal World
you don't always see,
but its there any way.

Also Darling said that what splits the rock in 1/2 is made of DIAMONDS cause she said DIAMONDS are the hardest things in the world like I guess there pretty strong (I know this is all kinda hard to believe but its true Virgen DIAMONDS). And the other thing Darling wants me to find out is if theres any thing in the WORLD that doesn't have water in it (Cause she said even our BODY is mostly WATER!!) So far I can't think of any thing like the first thing I said was ROCKS and she said "Rocks have water" and then I said an ATOM and she said "Atoms have water" (So I give up I think.)

Before Darling left to S.F. for 3 days she brought back all the mail and I got to pick out sodys HA! chips, cookies, stuff like that at the store which has saw dust on the floor like the Old West or some thing but it smells kinda cool, and they even sell clothes there like very WEIRD clothes (And some other freako stuff like chawing tobacky like Harry calls it and lots of Hooch and a giant ass barrel with giant ass PICKLES floating around in it kinda like The Hermits gather here and make a fire in the morning in The Pot Belleyed Stove and they SPIT chawing tobacky juice in to the SPITOON—DIS GUS TING!!!!) Any way I didn't actually see any one do it (Darling told me about it.) And then I had to stop myself from doing it cause all of a sudden I wanted to spit in the SPITOON so instead I got a HUMUNGUSLY UGLY PICKLE for 5¢ and darling bet me that I couldn't eat the whole thing but I did and in fact I got 6 more to bring back to the Hide Out like there sour and creepy looking but I just can't stop eating them DELI-SIOUS!!! So part of the bet was that I could buy any thing in the freako store and luckily they had some regular tennis shoes so Darling bought me some RED ones which I chose. So now I'm Miss Moon with Red Feet HOLY ASS CHINGASOS and when I look at myself in the big mirror on the back of the bath room door I start to laugh cause maybe I'm starting to look like some one from BOLINAS (Who has a friend named Harry The Hermit and her Private Pets The Seals with a swim suit that goes right up her NALGAS who writes Zen Kones and talks to a horse with a VAGINA named Cinamon.) And I even lit a candle after I gave Budda the perfect shell and then I said—"I know it was La Virgen who saved me but maybe you helped her out a little cause you live here in Bolinas with Darling." (So now I'm wondering if I'm also becoming a kinda BUDDIST who lives in BOLINAS and writes Zen Kones and thinks shes a MAMMAL like maybe I'm doomed HA!) OK Virgen so what I want to know is this, OK Budda is kinda fat but he looks pretty happy like hes not smiteing any one and all of Creation right? So if your SICK OF GOD why don't you MARRY Fat Boy Budda? Do you want to know the TRUTH? Poor old grown up Jesus nailed to the CROSS with blood on his head from the THORNS and his chest all bleeding cause some soldier stabbed him, and God doesn't even give a shit cause his Only Son died for OUR SINS (Like the creepo Minister used to say a lot). So when I'd see grown up Jesus on the CROSS I hated it cause it was so CREEPY like maybe thats why Gods always smiteing every thing right? You know cause hes secretly POed (Like Darling says PISSED OFF). Any way I'm starting to kinda like this Budda guy and I'm thinking maybe hes not a Cheap Skate either (Let me know what you think about maybe marrying El Budda like with all the candles and all the flowers in front of him and my Perfect sea shell and you know I think hes kinda cute, right Virgen?)

So before Darling took off to S.F. we shared our dreams (Like I told her Mamacita and I used to do in the morning.) Darling told me she had a dream about painting Danny The Dane (Her husband of course.) So she thinks thats because hes going to be here next month and so I get to meet this guy with the giant ass smile in the picture (But I think Darlings right about her dream that hes coming next month, plus shes all happy that hes coming too.) And I tell her mine like I'm planting a tree in the back facing the Ocean and in the dream I really want it to grow HUGE and I almost feel sad cause I don't ever want it to DIE but then I see the trees growing these YELLOW LEMONS but there still pretty small, but it makes me pretty happy any way. So Darling says we'll do that like we'll plant a LEMON TREE in the back COOL!! I really think Darlings catching on to this dreaming stuff like some times dreams tell you what to do and whats going to happen (Thats what Mamacita told me all the time which is why you say your dreams in the morning so you don't forget them.)

So in the mail was a letter from Pablo and Tia so I'll just stick it in to the diary OK?

Deer Favoritist Cusin,

We miss you. When are you coming to visit again? Send us a picure of you in the cuntry. Here is a picure of me.

LOVE PABLO XXOOXXOO

(And the picture of Pablo makes me kinda miss him cause hes still so SKINNY and hes standing next to his sad ass puny bike and I wish he could meet Cinamon and I'd let him ride her and wear my Cow Boy Hat even though its probably too big for him and would cover his eyes entirely, right? Then we'd come back to Darlings and have some roast or some thing, and Pablo would think he'd died and gone to Heaven like Darling says some times and maybe he'd do the Happy Skinny Kids Dance right?)

So heres Tias Letter.

Dear Luna,

I know you're probably very happy in Bolinas so I'm happy for you. But if you can please send us a photo. I promise not to show the cheapskate! Your mother and brother moved to a new place and its much nicer and as far as I know she doesn't see the "nut" anymore. Your step-father Jake. In fact shes being friends with a new neighbor named "Whitey". I met him and hes a very nice man. He lives in the place over hers and he even asked about you. He said he met you at the old place. So maybe you could visit us for a few days in the summer. Give us a call any time soon.

Con Mucho Amor, Tu Tia

BELIEVE IT OR NOT right? Carmen is friends with WHITEY! Well maybe thats pretty good cause he'll cook her and Jake Junior some dinner and maybe if The Psycho does show up Whitey can kick his ass good (If I were there I'd help for sure!) But to tell the truth Virgen I don't even want to visit cause I know it'll be DEPRESSING like I know Carmens place will be The Dead Body Place with all her crap laying every where and of course Jake Junior will be CRYING for some thing, and of course Carmen won't know what to do as usual PUKE. So count me out but maybe Whiteys feeding Jake Junior fryed chicken and sodys (I hope he is and thats the TRUTH Virgen.) But its pretty weird to think of Carmen and him being friends like I wonder what happened to The Blood Sucker (Probably went in search of fresh blood PUKOLA).

So after Darling takes off to S.F. I go over to Harrys House to ride Cinamon like I promised her and I find Harry drinking his Hooch but hes OK just kinda sad or some thing. So for the first time he says to "come on in to mi casa Miss Moon." And he shows me a picture of his wife when she was really young and I think she was beautiful like she has the best eyes, kinda happy and sad at the same time, and shes not trying to look really happy so she just looks like her self (And I think she looks maybe a little like mi Tia but Tia doesn't think shes beautiful cause shes so SHY.) And then he shows me a picture of his boy when he was little (And I'm not kidding Virgen he looks like PABLO weird!) And then he shows me a grown up picture in a Army out fit and he looked pretty handsome and strong like a man, and Harry kept saying stuff like "Missin in action" and he kept drinking his Hooch so I told him to "Take it easy" (Cause he wasn't making too much sense any more.) And I went down to Cinamon and got her ready and then Harry yelled "Bring her in for the storm comes in! Storms comin in! Battin down the hatches Miss Moon!" He was really YELLING all this kinda like Yosemite Sam, so I started cracking up to my self of course (And I then I wonder what the chingasos Battin Down The Hatches is like do you hit some thing with a bat till it hatches?) OK don't ask me but I heard the storm part and I looked up to the sky and it was getting kinda cloudy but I sure didn't see any storms. Also Darling didn't say any thing about hatches or storms so maybe its too much Hooch for Harry, but I decide to keep an eye on the CLOUDS.

Any way Darling gave me some really weird ass words for the week—1. ECSTASY 2. SORROW 3. FERTILITY 4. WORSHIP. So I brought my diary out to the cliffs and I'm sitting here trying to think of a poem for these weird ass words but I can't—what kinda poem would I write about FERTILITY (Darling says "Women have the gift of FERTILITY" like she says haveing kids and stuff like that, but then she said thats why she paints and she even said thats why I like to write WELL MAYBE but if women have FERTILITY maybe I don't want it right Virgen?) I just looked up and the clouds are getting chingaso DARK and like Mamacita used to say—I smell the rain. Any way Virgen maybe I like the way Darling has fertility but I don't like the way Carmen has fertility. OK I'm getting my but out of here cause its going to rain any sec (I also like the way Cinamon has fertility.) Con Amor, La Loca

Well I got back and made dinner and just in time too cause a STORM is here with lots of WIND and a ton of RAIN so the TVs not even working like one time in a storm the lights went out and Darling lit a bunch of candles and it was kinda fun (We watched the Ocean in her back yard and we roasted marsh mellows in the fire place COOL). But tonight to tell the truth I guess I'm kinda lonely, in fact I might even go over to Harrys House but hes probably all weird cause of the Hooch (I put Cinamon in her stall and gave her some extra grain like you know Virgen some times I think I LOVE HER better than a human and maybe better than any one I know, and like maybe I'm losing my noodle for sure but thats the way I really feel right?) Darling reminded me that Cinamon was a mammal just like me and so are seals, whales, dogs, cats and deer she says. And in a weird loca way it makes me feel like I have a TON of friends (I can just hear Jody "You lost your fuckin noodle Hermit Girl") OK. I have to know some thing Virgen—Do you see every thing? Like some times the Nut Case Minister used to say "God sees every thing". I sure hope not cause I think some stuff is none of his bees wax and also I figure if I don't pray to him maybe he can't see me all the time (But if you really do SEE EVERY THING I guess I'm kinda embarassed OK?) Heres the deal—I found my Tickle Button (You know in my private place) When I was kinda little by accident when I was slideing off a couch and so probably this is none of your bees wax right? TELL THE TRUTH—Do you have a Tickle Button? Jody and I talked about it one time and we were really cracking up and all, and she said she has one too, so do you have one TELL THE TRUTH OKAY?

Guess what? The lights just went off so I lit a bunch of candles and I tryed the phone but its not working either so I guess Darling can't call right? And the Oceans making a LOUD NOISE like FREGADO THUNDER and its for real in Darlings back yard CHINGASOS AND HOLY ASS SHIT!!!! So heres the deal—If the Ocean gets to the back stairs I'm going to run for it over to Harrys House (Maybe I could sleep with Cinamon YEAH!) So I'm going to sit right here by the slideing glass window thats really a giant ass door that opens with a WOOOSH sound and my TWO EYES on the Ocean, and you know Virgen if it wasn't for the candles the in side would be just as DARK as the out side, so its pretty weird like all I can barely see is the Ocean and it looks really PISSED OFF like its trying to get me so thats pretty CREEPY (But you know Mamacita used to love to take the street car in S.F. to the Ocean when it was storming and now I wonder why she loved the Ocean when its MAD right?) Any way so far the Ocean hasn't touched the back stairs but I can tell it wants to SHIT! ! ! !

OK so if you do see every thing Virgen then you probably already know about The Bad Thing that happened to me when I was 7 like I was in a park with Peggy and it was getting dark but she said it was OK (And she was about 12 so I trusted her.) And this Weirdo came and said it was against the Law to be there after 5 oclock or some thing so one of us had to go with him and Peggy said "She'll go" and pendeja me cause I thought she wanted me to go cause I was the smartest even if I was only 7 and pendeja me cause I thought I was the PRETTYEST GIRL IN THE WORLD cause I was wearing a brand new twirly dress, and I thought he thought I was the prettyest girl in the world too so pendeja me and thats the truth of course (And he showed us a Cop Badge too.) So I thought he was takeing me to a Cop Place and then the Weirdo kidnapped me to some bushes like he picked me up and wouldn't put me down even though I kept telling him I had to go home cause Mamacita was probably looking for me (And I also said some thing DUMB about Carmen being rich cause I had a new twirly dress and she'd give him $ right?) But the Pervert didn't even listen to me and instead It put Its PENIS in my mouth (First he said "Do you want to eat some thing"? And I thought it was going to be some thing that tastes BAD cause he wouldn't let me go so I knew it had to be really bad.) Then he said he'd kill me if I ever told any one and he even showed me his GUN (But I did tell and I found his PICTURE in a giant ass book full of other Perverts like a zillion and they put him in JAIL! ! ! !) But you know how SCARED I was and then I wasn't cause I got away and just walked home in the dark by my self and it was funny cause I didn't even feel like running so I just walked all the way back home, and I didn't even cry or any thing even when Tia saw me and said "Luna what happened to you"? (Cause Peggy told her about The Pervert and Tia called the cops.) And then you know how I never ever let any one kidnap me again or even touch me (Like a man.) And you know how I started to look and talk like a boy so maybe I wouldn't be DOOMED (But then The Blood came any way right?) FERTILITY And do you remember Virgen what Carmen said to me later when I still trusted her (Cause I was so little of course.) She said "Its your fault hes going to jail" (And I NEVER trusted her again cause I may be a pendeja but I'm not a Loca Pendeja.) And I never told Mamacita what she said when I was 7 or any one (So I guess this is another secret Virgen, and now that I'm 12 and looking at the pissed off Ocean I'm wondering WHY Carmen hates me so much cause why else would she say that right?)

OK so right now I'm pretty SCARED waiting for the Ocean to wash Darlings House to maybe CHINA so I'm going to stop writing, but if you do SEE EVERY THING VIRGEN please keep both of your eyes on me and Darlings House just in case I pass out cause I'm pretty tired too probably cause its 3 oclock at night. Con Amor, Luna

ITS MORNING!!!! I WOKE UP ALIVE AND DARLINGS HOUSE IS STILL HERE IN BOLINAS AND THE OCEAN IS STILL OUT THERE!!!!!!

And all the lights are on and its still raining but not too hard and I made my self scrambled eggs and bacon YUM ! ! ! ! With CAKE for desert YUMMMYYYYY! ! ! ! ! ! I had 2 pieces of CHOCOLATE CAKE WITH CHOCOLATE FROSTING!!!! All the candles were burned away even the ones I lit to Fat Boy Budda and I told him to keep both of his eyes on me too (Mamacita too if shes not born again yet right?) And I lit the tall blue candle that was just for you Virgen, I told you to watch me just in case the Ocean snuck up on me when I passed out remember? So the tall blue candle is gone now and the rain out side is soft soft soft and heres the poem I wrote with the weirdo words while I was haveing desert like maybe I'll write another one later, but here it is.

THE STORM

Darlings House is still here on the mesa
so I'm in ECSTASY and if it weren't
I'd sure be in SORROW. Last night
the storm made me WORSHIP candles
and Fat Boy Budda
and La Virgen too.

This morning I'm still ALIVE
and the rain is so soft.
Heres the deal—I guess I'm a girl
and I've got FERTILITY
and I'm strong and pretty smart
and I'm not afraid to give any
one The Bird like Darling.
And I'm not afraid of the dark
like Cinamon the mammal.

Hey Darling just called me on the phone ITS WORKING and I told her about the Ocean almost washing her house away (With me in it.) So shes comeing back tonight with a new swim suit she said so I don't scare the Seals HA HA! Did I tell you theres a zillion California Poppys every where out by the meadow so I picked a bunch (Remember how the White Lady Teacher in S.F. said it was against the Law to even pick them and all?) So I put a bunch in Cinamons mane and I even put some in my mane. HA! And I even put some on El Buddas altar (Which is secretly your altar now too—what I did was this—I cut a picture of a lady in a magazine that I think kinda looks like you, and I wrote at the bottom LA VIRGEN and I put the picture behind El Budda under some gold paper Darling put there.) The gold paper sparkles when the candles are burning and I remember how your there on the altar, but I know your every where I go and if you showed up right now this minute do you know what I'd do? I'd take all the California Poppys on the altar and put them in your mane (But of course you'd have to show up in a regular mammal body like just for a sec.) CON AMOR, Miss Moon

All The Mammals in May And
The Secret World Of Miss Moon
GIRL HERMIT WHO LUNGERED IN A
SPITOON DIS GUS TING
CHING GAAAA SOOOS
(And I'm not kidding!)

Dear La Virgen,

You know I did it when no one was looking cause in a creepy way I figured this is how you join the Hermits Club here in Bolinas, so I dropped a lunger that I saved up while Darling was getting some weird ass lace for my new dress shes making for the fall when I start school cause she says girls can't wear pants to school and of course I know that right (So of course I'm really THRILLED like lace and a bow—I'm DOOMED) I'm thinking how some times they have air raid drills in case they drop The Bomb and every body runs under the fregado desks like thats going to save you from The Bomb (I think that every time we do it and one time I asked Darling if she thought going under the desk will save your but, and she said "And while your at it just kiss your ASS good bye") And she really cracked up and thats what I always kinda thought right? And I started cracking up just picturing every one like especially the MEAN White Lady Teachers kissing there asses good bye HA.

Cause there was like 2 really OK White Lady Teachers who I liked, like one time in the fifth grade one of them read some thing I wrote and she said "This person is the best writer in the class" and I scrunched down in the desk cause I was just waiting for her to say my name but she didn't. And so the truth is I'd rather let The Bomb drop right on my head and put me out of my misery right? (Than wear this weirdo dress and all the other LACEY dresses shes buying stuff for.) OK its really TORTURE so I finally told her I can not wear BOWS but that I think she sews like a PRO (To not hurt her feelings or PO her too much.) So her Cat Eyes got kinda narrow for a sec and then she said "OK kid no bows and you can help me pick the colors and how long you want them too." And then she said if she had it her way I'd go to school any way I felt like it cause she likes jeans the best too, but I could tell I kinda hurt her feelings about the BOWS and I didn't even say any thing about the LACE right? (But you know Virgen—I can't wear that freaky stuff to school even at gun point and I'm not kidding.)

So I wrote her a Mammal Story where all the Mammals have to wear BOWS and they start to lose there fregado noodles cause the BOWS either make them want to laugh all the time or else puke all the time (And every Mammal in Bolinas is in the story and I even give Cinamon a few horsey friends cause I know in real life she'd like some right?) Any way all the Mammals In May figure out how to rip off the bows, like with there teeth and paws and they do it for each other cause they can't eat or any thing being that there laughing or puking all the time. So after all the bows are off they have a PARTY a big CELEBRATION where they have a bar-b-que and drink a ton of sodys and then some nosey idiot shows up with a truck load of HATS and starts putting these freako HATS on the poor Mammals, and of course they start laughing and puking again (But they figure it out pretty fast and ditch the HATS and so they have another PARTY right?) Any way Virgen when I showed Darling the Mammals In May Story she super cracked up (Which was a fregado relief!) And then she said "why don't you have some one put diapers on them next and how about jewelery?" I said "Do you mean ear rings and a necklace?" And I was kinda laughing like a hyena, like

Harry The Hermit says that, "laughing like a hyena." And the first time I heard it I almost fell on the ground cause I couldn't stop laughing just picturing a HYENA cracking up (And don't start me thinking about HYENAS as Mammals MUY FREAKO) Any way Harry was looking at me like I'd "Gone round the bend." (Another weirdo thing he says.)

Any way I really like the idea of diapers and the jewelery but don't ask me why. So I'm going to make the story a little longer but I'm wondering if the Mammals will be able to take off the jewelery WEIRD (You know cause some times it looks pretty hard for PEOPLE type Mammals.) So Virgen when ever I think of the SPITOON in town I kinda laugh like a hyena cause now I'm a Bona Fide Hermit Girl and heres the deal—All of a sudden I can just see myself (Luna The Mammal) In a lacey dress with a diaper for The Blood wearing ear rings and a necklace NECK LACE. So I am doomed to be a Freak Show, and I have to hand it to Darling like I think she gave me a Wooden Nickel. Yeah I think she really did like shes pretty sneaky when she wants to be FREGADO! (Like I'm the Mammal with the diaper and the jewlery only I will never wear jewelery cause then I'd be Little Bo Peep for sure and COUNT ME OUT!)

Danny The Dane came for about 2 weeks and I made myself scarce so they could have some PRIVACY and get sexy right? Well there marryed and all and I don't really want to be a Royal Pain in there ASS. Hes kinda funny looking and a little fat but he has nice really BLUE eyes and he laughs sort of like Santa Claus right? Actually Virgen he really looks like El Budda and especially when hes sitting down and smileing (He really SMILES A LOT). So I think its cool that he looks like El Budda and maybe thats why Darling marryed him right? Also he brought me back some gifts from JAPAN—A Japanese KIMONO (Thats a bath robe but really nice and its made from SILK) A Japanese FAN with flowers and birds on it and Japanese SILK SLIPPERS with flowers on the toes (Cause he says every one in Japan takes there shoes off at the door and Darling does that too so now I wear the SILK SLIPPERS) And a Jewelery Box with rainbow shells glued in to the top of a shiney black wooden box which is pretty especially in the sun—And DANGER DANGER 2 pair of Mother Of Pearl Ear

Rings (Darling calls them that). And OK Virgen there pretty (There made like flowers and sea shells and I kinda like just looking at them in side the Jewelery Box.) But if I started wearing them then every one in the entire world would know I'm a GIRL and there goes all The Secret Places and haveing FUN (So count me out!) And best of all BINOCULARS from Japan. Danny The Dane said "You can keep a look out for Pirate Ships and take care of Darling when I'm gone. I hear your quite a tough young lady and good for you!" Then he laughed like Santa Claus but I LOVE these BINOCULARS and now I really wonder what Darling told him about me being tough (I mean I don't give him The Witch Eyes right?) I like him so far and also hes really from DENMARK like thats where his family is right now (Darling and him visit there once in a while and he says I can go too, so Luna The Mammal in DENMARK sounds OK to me—What do you think Virgen? Do you like DENMARK?) I looked it up on a map and its way the chingaso over the ATLANTIC OCEAN and Danny The Dane says we'd fly and that most every one there kinda looks like him, so I guess DENMARK is full of White People that look like El Budda (And the ladys probably look like El Budda with a VAGINA right Virgen? Sorry. Luna La Loca.) Now I'm trying to picture Luna The Mexican Mammal in DENMARK (Are you laughing like a hyena Virgen? Should I go to DENMARK and tell the truth OK?) Like the ATLANTIC OCEAN looks pretty humungus and I wonder if the White People over there ever even heard about Yaqui Indians or if they know about stuff like Wet Backs and Gringos right? I also found GERMANY over there and you know my real father who lives down South in a place called Louisiana (Thats what Carmen and Tia always say, so if Tia says it too it must be the truth.) But his family really came from GERMANY and he had BLOND hair and BLUE eyes (But you know I'm not blond with blue eyes and I look more like Mamacita like a Yaqui Indian from Mexico.) And now I wonder if the Danes know about Dirty Indian stuff cause I don't think I can beat up a WHOLE COUNTRY right? So tell the truth Virgen, should I go to DENMARK some time????

Any way the other day when I was making myself scarce as usual I ended up at Harrys House after I rode Cinamon for the whole day and I swam with the Seals a little, but it was pretty windy so I froze my ass off (But its cool haveing a swim suit that doesn't go right up my but plus she picked a orange one and not any thing pink or freako or any thing with BOWS—TORTURE— And I figure the Seals can see me a lot better cause its really ORANGE. And I have to admit when I first went out to swim with the Seals I hoped they didn't think I was some thing orange and really juicey to eat, and you know I still can't figure out if Seals really have teeth but I figure if they do there probably pretty HUGE (What a chicken I am.) So I got out of the freezeing ass Ocean and I tryed to write a poem with my new words but every thing I tryed to write was really STUPID. Heres the new words— 1. DIAMOND 2. OPAL 3. CRYSTAL 4. RUBY. So I'm thinking maybe its the jewelery thing like maybe Darlings trying to give me another Wooden Nickel, but any way I gave up. So when I got to Harrys House he came out after I made Cinamon all comfortable and he said "You been spyin on me with those BI noc U lars?" (Thats how he says BINOCULARS.) And I said "You a Pirate or some thing cause I've been looking for pirates but I'm starting to think there extinct." I could tell he was trying not to crack up and keep his Poker Face (Like Darling says Harry has a Poker Face cause when you play a card game called Poker you try to not let any one know what your really thinking so you end up haveing a Poker Face.) So I guess Harrys pretty good at Poker and Darlings teaching me Poker and I'm practiceing my Poker Face in the mirror (Which is really pathetic to tell the truth Virgen, so I always crack up and then I practice again and I end up thinking how I look like I just farted and don't want any one to know PA THE TIC.)

So Harry says "Wish I was a Pirate but how bout some chow Miss Moon, got some beans and I'm thinkin of makin some burritos, so you in the mood for chow?" (I'm trying to write down the way Harry really talks OK?) So I said "Do Hermits always say chow instead of FOOD?" And then he laughed like a hyena and he sure is better at laughing now cause he doesn't sound like hes learning any more. "Got me pegged Miss Moon, yeah thats right, thats Hermit Talk all right." Then I said "OK and I'll help you fix the burritos if you want cause I used to make them with Mamacita and they were delicious too. I helped my Cousin

Chula make burritos a couple of times too when I visited her in Mexico like Mamacitas whole family lives there, and I really like my girl cousin named Chula, but every one else was pretty strange like too many rules for me, and Chula said there were so many rules cause I was a girl and she used to hate it too cause every time you left the house some old lady called a DUENA followed you every where like a SPY." (I watched Harry open the cans of beans for the burritos and he just nodded cause he doesn't like to talk too much, but he kinda likes to listen to me tell him stuff so I'll try to remember every thing I said to Harry The Hermit OK Virgen?) "Like one time I just wanted to go to the Mercado, its like a Market Place out side where they sell a *ton* of stuff and some really delicious Pan Dulce and candys plus it was pretty interesting cause they had *live* chickens, pigs, parrots, canarys and some times puppys and kittens and even some smelly goats. One time Chula came with me and she told the DUENA she'd take care of me, but the other time when I wanted to go by myself I looked behind me and there was the creepy DUENA *spying* on me, so guess what I did? I ditched her and of course she got in trouble from my elephant sized Uncle, and even though I can tell he'd like to really *whip* me cause I heard him *say* it. Well he sure didn't plus I was really giveing him The Witch Eyes so it must've worked." But for one sec I was sorry I told Harry about The Witch Eyes cause I've *never* told any one about my real Secret Weapon right?

Harry put some water in the beans and I chopped up lettice and tomatos (I thought you'd like to know every thing OK?) Then he said "Don't CHULA kinda mean DARLING? Like that Darling lady you live with I mean." And then I laughed just like a hyena cause I hadn't even thought of that and it felt like some one just wacked me on the head like a *surprise* plus I think its mucho COOL cause I really truly like CHULA and DARLING of course. When I finally came back round the bend I said "So did your wife speak Spanish?" And Harry said "Yup she was Mexican too and she taught me some and the boy as well. Do you see Chula any more?" And I decided to not ask him any more questions about his wife cause his eyes got really SAD and he might start with the Hooch right? "I haven't seen her in a year since that time in

Mexico, but maybe some time I'll see her again. She was pretty cool like she was a teacher and she taught 6th grade I think plus she used to sketch a lot and take her sketch book every where and she also did water colors, and thats kinda like Darling cause Darling paints pictures. You ever see any?" Harry nodded NO and I could tell he was really listening to every thing (I like Harry a LOT Virgen.) "So guess what else Chula is?" I waited for a sec and said "Shes a BULL FIGHTER, I'm not kidding and I even saw her do it one time cause she took me with her and all. She had her own car and we put all the windows down and then she put the radio on like FULL BLAST and she sang with the radio LOUD and then once in a while she'd do a grito. Thats a loud yell Mexican people do when there really happy and theres good music on the radio (I can tell Harrys trying not to smile.) So any way me and Chula were doing gritos all the time in her car. We were pretty quiet at the house cause of her father like he never did a grito when I was there. He was a judge Chula said and I believe it cause I could just picture him sending a ton of people to jail of course. Chula had a humungus room kinda seperate from every one and every ones room faced a really nice garden with flowers and fruit trees and lemon trees with GIANT yellow lemons and a fountain full of water where a ton of birds were always takeing a bath and makeing a racket. We used to pick lemons every day kinda like Mamacita used to put a lemon in her purse in case I got sick so I could suck on it and feel better fast like there sour but they really work some times like a miracle or a milagro, thats what Mamacita used to say, a milagro." (I looked at Harry to make sure he was really listening and he was, I could tell.) "So one day Chula takes me to see her Bull Fight and it was pretty cool like she wore pedal pushers which are pants and a really pretty white shirt with RED ROSES on it, and she had a Bull Fighting Cape so the bull would chase her around, and she said stuff like HEY HEY TORRITO!!!! Chula said these were the young bulls but that some day she wants to fight the grown up bulls cause I guess thats harder for sure. So as Chula was doing the cape thing with the bull and she'd stand really still when the bull went by her and some people I was sitting next to started to yell OH LAY!!!! So I started to yell OH LAY!!!! too and Chula smiled at least twice like at me, so I wonder if Chulas fighting the grown up bulls yet, like they have GIANT ASS HORNS and I guess there kinda mean but I still feel sorry for them cause they get stabbed to death. But Chula said people get to eat them like the poor people she said so maybe thats not too bad then, but it can't be to much fun for the bull I think."

Then Harry said some thing. "Thats fer damed sure." Then Harry was warming up some flour tortillas for the burritos. "After the Bull Fight we went to a really noisey restaurant and there was a bunch of guys in Mexican out fits and humungus SOMBREROS playing some loud ass music and singing too" ("You sure swear a lot Miss Moon" Harry said but he kept on cooking.) I started to give him The Witch Eyes and decided not to. "Any way lots of people were doing GRITOS and so were me and Chula and Chula even danced and had some BEER but she told me to not say any thing to you know who (The Sour Puss Judge) Which of course I never would. And I had about 10 Coca Colas but I sure didn't dance. One time The Judge told me he wished Mamacita would come home so every one could take care of her the right way he said like cook and clean for her, and then he said she was too proud for her own good." Harry was flipping the tortillas and then covering them with a towel to keep them warm like Mamacita used to do, so for a sec I close my eyes and pretend hes Mamacita but if I open them its Harry The Hermit right Virgen?

"Do you want to hear a story Tia told me about Mamacita crossing The Border from Mexico to here cause its kinda funny I think." Harry nodded YES and he let me have a warmed up tortilla so I put some butter on it and sprinkled a little salt like I always do SABROSO! Now I kinda wonder what a BULL tastes like—a Bull Burrito or Bull Tacos or Bull Stew (Or STABBED Bull Stew!) I think I'll put a bull in my Mammals In May Story and maybe I'll have the bull chase the guy with the diapers and the jewelery away (Cause the guy would be petrifyed of the bulls giant ass horns and the bull would charge him HEY HEY TORRITO!!!!) Then the BULL can be the hero of the whole story THE END (Maybe I'll make it the bull that even knows Chula but he runs away from Mexico cause he doesn't want to be in a Bull Fight and get stabbed to death.) THE END.

So any way Virgen heres the story Tia told me pretty much the way I told Harry, and its probably why The Sour Puss Judge says Mamacitas too stubborn for her own good right? "Mamacitas husband (You know my grandfather) He was a Baptist Minister and he had a news paper and he wrote poetry too Tia said, so one day he wrote some thing that pissed off Pancho Villa so they tryed to kill him but Mamacita begged for his life and she was really pregnant with my mother Carmen OK? So the deal was he had to leave Mexico if he wanted to LIVE and so Mamacita packed every thing and my grandfather Pablo was going to have a Baptist Church in Los Angeles California instead of staying in Mexico for the rest of his life right? So as they were crossing The Border to over here the Border Cops went through all her stuff which made her MAD. So when they asked about what she had in a sack where she was carrying some food Tia said she threw the stuff out of the sack and she blew it up kinda like a baloon right? Then she POPPED it really CHINGASO LOUD!" (Harry looked at me with his eye brow up probably cause I said chingaso but if he can drink Hooch I can say CHINGASO right Virgen?) "So when she popped the sack with her hand and it made a CHINGASO POP Tia said she yelled probably like a grito AIRE MEXICANA!!!! And that means Mexican air!!!!" I yelled it really grito loud and Harry covered his ears and laughed "Miss Moon ya got a pair a lungs on ya Christ All Mighty!" Then I did another loud ass GRITO even louder than before AIRE MEXICANA! ! ! ! Then I started cracking up like a regular hyena and poor Old Harry kept his ears covered cause he was scared I'd do it again I guess. Finally he said "Well thats a story to be proud of and your grandma she never went back to Mexico?" Harry gave me the first burrito and I was starveicating (And I'm not kidding.) He even had some Coca Colas for me in his ice box and theres really ice in it which he brings from town (From the Hermit Store, you know, where the spitoon is.) And those sodys were pretty COLD too and the burrito was hot with a ton of chilie sauce and onions (Just the way I LOVE them.) So I chewed and drank sodys and kept telling Harry stuff.

"Tia said she wouldn't go back cause they threw her whole family out of Mexico, so I guess she was pretty STUBBORN like maybe the only way she would've gone back is if I went with her to live with The Sour Puss—you know her brother The Judge but I really hated it there cause I couldn't do any thing without a DUENA chaseing me around and I bet if I lived there he would've tryed to whip me like Chula said he whipped her some times when she was little. Any way the only reason I liked visiting Mexico was Chula and escapeing in her car and the last time I saw her she said she was going to move to her own house pretty soon so I could just see me liveing there by myself with The Sour Puss, so count me the chingaso out!" Old Harry sucked in his breath but didn't say any thing for a minute—Then he said "I never did whip my boy, guess I just loved him too chingaso much Miss Moon." I was really tempted to remind him he was SWEARING but of course I know better than that cause its like Harry The Hermit is really being my friend (right Virgen?) And I bet he never did whip his kid, but I wonder if he ever yelled at him like Yosemite Sam (but of course I'd take Yosemite Sam over a Psycho any day, thats for chingaso ass sure.)

I had 4 HU MUN GUS burritos and I pretended they were Bull Burritos and that Chula stabbed the bull to death in the Bull Fight, and that Harry and I got the bull cause we were poor and that also Chula was going to teach me how to Bull Fight so that every one would yell OH LAY! every time the bull just missed me while I stand there so chingaso COOL! ! ! ! So then I thought of the ear rings (Mamacitas Ruby Ear Rings she always wore.) Maybe it was the Mammals In May Story about tortureing Mammals with jewelery or maybe it was thinking about why Mamacita didn't go back to Mexico and her dieing in that prison right? But then I remembered what else Tia told me Virgen—That Carmen took Mamacitas Ruby Ear Rings right off her (Dead ears Tia said.) And she paid her Gringa baby sitter that took care of Jake Junior for her and Tia was POed cause she said those Ruby Ear Rings were mine and that I should have them and not some Gringa baby sitter who we don't even know right? So when you think about Mamacitas good furniture in Los Angeles being sold and you think of The Blood Sucker (Who took all her blood right?) And those times when we lived in The Projects on Army Street in S.F. when Jake Junior was just born and Carmen would just leave us with no $ so I had to steal the El Diablo Pham and take a ton of sody bottles to the store for some bread, plus the RUBY EAR RINGS—I WANT TO REALLY PUKE (Of course I didn't tell Harry all this muy freako stuff.) Any way you know Rubys are RED right Virgen? So guess what I did on Mamacitas Funeral Day? I wore a RED really RED shirt (And the Church people were POed but I really didn't give a fregado and thats the truth.) Tia kept saying "Luna maybe you'd better wear some thing else today." And I kept saying "I don't want to." So finally Tia gave up. And you know I was glad that no one tryed to hug me (Cause of the red shirt like they were so SHOCKED). All those phoney Church people plus the Nut Case Minister when he tryed to make me cry in front of all those phoneys and I didn't cry even once (A couple of the Church people were OK but the truth is most of them were Dos Caras which means Two Faced, cause Mamacita used to say Dos Caras had a face for God and then a face just for regular people like us, but she used to say Los Dos Caras must think Gods really a PENDEJO if he can't figure that one out.) So the Nut Case Minister (You know the one who made his daughter say she was sorry and CRY in front of every one in Church cause her babys a bastard right?) He asked me to say some thing about Mamacita and I could see his weird ass SMILE hideing on his pendejo poker face just waiting for me to cry (So I said to myself "Kiss my farty nalgas." Out loud I said "I don't want to.") Lilly the daughter he tortured was the only person that gave me a hug and I let her, and her baby kinda patted me on the head or he was smacking me, one or the other right? So she and I got some red roses and we threw them on Mamacita as they lowered her with these creepo ropes in to the creepo grave, and one of my roses landed on the bottom first cause I aimed for it SQUISH. And every time I thought of Mamacita (Even right now) I think of the squished RED ROSE thats always keeping all of her bones company, right Virgen? Cause like Darling says shes probably reincarnated and I wonder if she remembers me (Like maybe in her dreams, maybe.)

That night Old Harry The Hermit drove me home in his rusty old Jalopy (Thats what he calls it cause its got DENTS every where.) It was pretty dark by then and he stopped for a couple of secs and said "Will ya look at that." (And of course I was looking but thats how he talks Virgen.) "That Milky Way (A zillion stars that look like shiney milk) looks good nough ta drink tanight Miss Moon." And I had to say it, "Better than Hootch Harry?" He pretended like he didn't hear me so I told him how Darling taught me about Night Eyes like how we walk at night some times and we get our Night Eyes so we can really see in the dark and then we watch for Shooting Stars later when we lay out on her patio, and how some times we even sleep out there in sleeping bags (Which I love better than even a bed any day, plus you don't have to make a sleeping bag cause you just roll it up COOL). But I didn't tell Harry about how Darling always sleeps out side with her GUN (And I'm not kidding of course.) And how she said shes a "Damed good shot and that if any one ever trys to even bother us I'll BLOW THERE ASSES AWAY! ! ! !" And she showed me the GUN and said its like our Cow Girl Secret, she said "Out here kid, we're Cow Girls and we aim to kill." Then she'd crack up, and of course I'd crack up too just thinking of Darling blowing some Pervs ass away (And there weirdo weiners too.) And then I kinda secretly wonder if Annie Oakly would live with a bunch of Pervs like in S.F. cause I think thats why Darling moved to her Hide Out in Bolinas right? Of course I know that EVERY GUY isn't a Perv in S.F. but theres moren you can shake a stick at, especially if you happen to be a girl. Any way when me and Darling and her GUN sleep out side in sleeping bags I wake up all night so I can see Shooting Stars, so I told him the part about the STARS and how I keep counting them till I finally pass out (Then in the morning I'm kinda POed cause I know I missed a ton of Shooting Stars—Do you sleep Virgen and do you ever stay up all night counting stuff like stars and comets—Do you close your eyes when you sleep and do you dream—Let me know OK cause I'm curious about all this kinda stuff.)

Then Harry said "Well do you make a WISH?" And I said "Damed straight!" I could see him smileing in the dark with my Night Eyes and he said "Now ya gotta make dam sure they come true, see what I mean Miss Moon?" (Do you want to know my wishes Virgen cause I'll tell you later OK? And of course there secret wishes like in dreams.) So I tell Old Harry "Yeah kinda like dreams cause you have to believe there real or they won't come true, yeah I know thats true." And then since Harrys old Jalopy doesn't have a radio like Chulas we ended up singing this super corny song I learned at school one time (And Harry knew it too probably cause its a song from the Good Old Days, thats what Harry says like a lot.) Its this one—She'll be comin round the mountain when she comes eeeeehhhaaaaaa!!!! And then I started singing She'll be comin round the bend when she comes eeeeeehhhhaaaa!!!!! So Harry and me and me especially really yelled this song out the windows and I also did a bunch of gritos and Harry laughed like a REAL HYENA and we saw a COYOTE run right in front of us, and of course coyotes are mammals (So I'll put a coyote in my Mammals In May Story right?) Then Old Harry made some real loud ass coyote yells and I started doing them too really loud like gritos, and I bet that coyote is wondering why a coyote looks like a Jalopy with 2 weird ass head light eyes (Like one head light points kinda UP and one points kinda DOWN.)

Darling and Danny The Dane were in S.F. so when I fell asleep by myself I could hear the coyotes doing there gritos way out on the Mesa in the dark like a whole family of coyotes and I didn't feel lonely at all maybe cause now I know what a coyote looks like (And for one sec I pictured them all with RUBY EARRINGS just shineing in the dark like RED STARS way out on the Mesa and I could see them with my Night Eyes right Virgen?) Do you have Night Eyes? Do you have Ruby Ear Rings? And don't forget to tell me if you DREAM OK? And now I wonder if I had Mamacitas Ruby Ear Rings (They were pierced and she wore them all the time I remember) I really wonder if I'd WEAR THEM. Do you think I'd wear them if they were mine Virgen? Also I really want to know if you have Ruby Ear Rings OK?

GRACIAS FOR THE DREAM VIRGEN but you still didn't tell me if you close your eyes when you sleep (If you sleep.) Or if you dream and I still want to know some time OK? So heres the poem I wrote with the new jewel words Darling gave me, and I hope you like it (Thats why I read it out loud so you can hear it.)

JEWELS 2 RED STARS

Last night I dreamed Cinamon
and she had a DIAMOND necklace
and OPALS glued to her pretty mane
that I just brushed and brushed
and her tail had a ton of CRYSTALS.
So I was rideing her way out on the Mesa
where the Giant Trees are at the edge
of the cliff (In fact a pretty good place

for sewerside for sure.)
In my dream it was dark and scarey
but then all the jewels on Cinamon
lit up like STARS, so with my Night Eyes
I saw bunches of coyotes and they had jewels
and I saw some Seals and they had jewels,
and I even saw La Virgen for one sec
and she had a ton of jewels but

she didn't have the RUBY ear rings and
she was laughing at me (Which made me
MAD.) Then she was gone.
And guess what?
La Virgen gave me the Ruby Ear Rings
and they were mine—2 RED STARS
Cause I was wearing them and
in the dream they were mine.

To tell the truth when I woke up I was pretty sad I guess cause the dream was better than wakeing up (Cause Cinamon looked so BEAUTIFUL with all her jewels and the other Mammals too.) Also when I woke up it was kinda weird but I checked my ears for the 2 Red Stars—NADA. And I almost started blubbering which kinda surprised me cause I never ever wanted GIRL STUFF right? But I guess its the truth like if I had Mamacitas Ruby Ear Rings I'd probably wear them maybe even at night and even if I looked like a Girl Mammal with Ruby Ear Rings (And a DIAPER—PUKOLA!!) Is that why you were laughing at me Virgen (Cause I'm becomeing a Girl Mammal In May with b r e a s t s cause when I run now I can feel them kinda like jello and if I tell Darling she'll make me wear a BRA for sure and then I'll be really and truly DOOMED so don't even tell you know who—God.) But if I had the Ruby Ear Rings I'd never ever take them off NEVER especially at night (Cause like in the dream Mamacitas 2 Red Stars are magic and maybe if God doesn't know about my jellos and maybe in the dream La Virgen really did give me the Ruby Ear Rings, so maybe there really on my ears but no one can see them when there awake, so maybe the magic will keep the jellos small like really small and not humungus like Darlings). So when I look in the mirror I squint my eyes and I can kinda see a Red Star on both my ears, so its another one of our secrets Virgen and GRACIAS for Mamacitas Ruby Ear Rings cause I didn't even know I wanted them (As you probably know of course.)

Tonight I'm going to sleep out on the patio by myself even if the Vampires get me cause I've never slept out side by myself like only with Darling (And the gun.) Any way Darling and Danny The Dane are coming home tonight probably late so I can SCREAM chingaso loud for help (What a BOCK! BOCK! CHICKEN I secretly am, right Virgen?) So I'm taking some garlic out side with me cause Vampires hate how it smells NIFTY (Thats a weird word Darling says but I kinda like it.) Any way Virgen as far as the Girl Stuff—Just as long as I don't turn in to Bo Peep or any thing like thats the limit OK? I just had an idea—Darling has a phoney diamond necklace so I'm going to put it on Cinamon tomorrow maybe on her mane (Like in my dream.) But first I'll brush it super smooth and super shiney.

When YOSEMITE SAM saw Cinamon with the phoney diamond necklace that I put between her ears at the top of her mane (I pinned it with Darlings bobby pins and it worked too). He just stood there in dis-belief right? And then he finally said "Why doncha put some high heel shoes on the poor dam animal HOLY SHIT MISS MOON!" Then I got POed and I said "I've got news for you cause Cinamon is a MAMMAL and so are you BELIEVE IT OR NOT Harry The Hermit, so if people can wear jewelery so can horses and she looks better than people any way and she sure looks a zillion tons better than you!!!!" So his ears got all PINK and I really saw his nose hairs like I did the first time I ever saw him and he yelled at me like Yosemite Sam and I figured he was an ass hole right? And then Virgen all of a sudden I felt like blubbering so I jumped up on Cinamon FAST (And I whispered to her "You look PERFECT Cinamon!!") Then Old Harry yelled "Miss Moon LUNA how bout some hot the dogs later on!" (That's what Y.S. calls hot dogs.)

So I just yelled OKAY but I didn't stop or any thing or even look at him cause thats how POed I was—and then I started to CRY and its so weird cause I couldn't stop CRYING (I didn't make any noise or any thing but it was like some one forgot to turn off my eye ball water and I felt so SAD like some where in my fregado stomach, and I was so glad no one could see me and Cinamon kept walking and walking and walking.) I layed my head down on her mane and then when I looked between her ears to see where we were like all the phoney diamonds had a ZILLION RAINBOWS so I just looked through the ZILLION RAINBOWS and the smell on Cinamons mane made me happy (Even though I still felt kinda pathetic.) I thought of Pablo and Tia cause I sent them a photo of me in my New Red Tennis Shoes and I wrote on the back DO NOT SHOW THE CHEAP SKATE!!!! I told Tia I might not be able to visit in the summer cause I might be going to DENMARK with Danny The Dane and Darling right? I wanted to ask Tia if Whitey is cooking food for Jake Junior but I didn't and of course I didn't ask any thing about Carmen (Cause you know Carmen hasn't even sent me a smoke signal like Darling says, which started me thinking it might be fun to send some one a smoke signal and I wonder how the Indians really do it right?) Any way maybe I'll call Tia up and talk to Pablo for a while cause I don't think they could see a smoke signal from S.F. and maybe Pablo can tell me some of his super corny Knock Knock Jokes that I always pretend there funny and crack up, but boy there not (But when I laugh it makes Pablo so fregado happy and then I can just picture him doing his Happy Skinny Kids Dance over the phone right?) So any way looking at every thing through the DIAMONDS between Cinamons ears is the best thing in the whole wide mundo and I'm thinking if every one had a horse with phoney diamonds between there ears and they just layed there head on the horses mane (And saw ONE ZILLION RAINBOWS)

Maybe people wouldn't be so fregado SAD. Any way thats what Luna The Mammal thinks (What do you think Virgen?)

After I finished the Mammals In May Story I read it to Danny The Dane and Darling and I'm not kidding they were laughing like a couple of Muy Loco Hyenas and they said they loved it about a million times which made me kinda happy, and then I started laughing some times cause they were laughing so hard some times Darling had to kick her feet to not pee her pants she said, so I had to stop the story (But I didn't tell Darling about Cinamon borrowing the phoney diamond necklace and the zillion rainbows cause I figure thats my bees wax.) And any way its like they have a BIG SECRET I don't know about like some times they look at each other and there eyes are saying "Shes just a pendeja freak show kid." (Do you know what I mean Virgen?) Like maybe they can't help it cause they don't live together all the time so when he shows up its Gooooochy Goooo Time so I take off and do my own bees wax like secret stuff (Which I only tell you Virgen—OK maybe I keep 1 or 2 secrets even from you but thats all—OK?) Also I think Danny The Dane is leaving for his ship again in about a week or so for a short trip he said, so it'll be just me and Darling (And all the other Mammals).

Any way me and Danny The Dane went for a long ass hike across the Mesa to a place I never went to but he said he liked cause of some fields and stuff. So we packed up a HUMUNGUS lunch and I was hikeing around looking through my BI noc U lars when all of a sudden I saw some thing so UGLY I did a GRITO (I mean I really yelled.) And guess what it was Virgen? It was pretty embarassing cause (Believe it or not!) It was a C O W and Danny The Dane started laughing so hard I thought his lips were going to fall off cause they got stretched all over his face right? I just kinda said to myself "I didn't know COWS were so fregado ass ugly." (And then I decided then and there to NEVER EVER DRINK MILK again in my entire fregado ass vida and I'm not kidding!) So I just walked over by the cliffs and sat down cause I didn't appreciate being laughed at by a Danish Hyena (D.T.D. has a BIG NOSE). And then I noticed a TON OF COWS all over the place munching grass and M O O O I N G. I ran down the trail to the beach cause I didn't feel like looking at a ton of ugly COWS or D.T.D. I guess I like him OK but its just that he acts kinda phoney some times kinda like he loves me so much but I know he really doesn't cause we hardly even talk to each other right Virgen? Its kinda like he wants to like me but then he just thinks I'm a boreing pendeja kid who Darling feels sorry for cause shes poor and has a weirdo muy loca mother (Carmen). And how she had to give me a shower and wash my clothes and feed me cause I was starved when she first met me right? But I bet he doesn't know about Old Jergens (But I won't tell of course—"Shes so beautiful" HA). So any way I take off my Red Tennis Shoes and stick my feet in the cold ass water and I'm thinking maybe D.T.D. just thinks I'm a Charity Case Kid right? So when he finally does come down and I see he still has his lips on and all but I don't even try to smile (Cause all of a sudden I feel like a Freak Show and I don't even know this guy right Virgen?) Then D.T.D. puts out a blanket and spreads the lunch out and theres even some giant ass PICKLES which I love of course. So he sits on the blanket and eats and I sit on a rock and eat some DELICIOUS sandwiches with a ton of mayo and hot mustard (Which I made Darling buy.) And raw onions and all thats missing is the hot chilies but Darling promised to get some. Then I hear this loud ass M O O O O O and I look up and a COW is stareing at us CREEPY But I finally crack up and tell D.T.D. "If thats where milk comes from you can count me out." And he says "Cows are rather funny looking but I can assure you (He says assure you a lot) They are harmless Luna. Cows certainly aren't dangerous. No not at all." And then he started telling me The History Of Cows (Believe it or snot). So I asked him if he grew up on a farm or what cause I was trying to change the pathetic subject cause I was trying to eat and I sure didn't want to hear Cow Storys M O O O O O O O O. So then he said "A small farm and then I went to the city for my education." So I asked him if the citys in Denmark were like S.F. maybe and he said the citys there were safer and cleaner too, but then he said real fast that he thought S.F. was a beautiful city any way and that he met Darling there which I figured. "I like it better here in Bolinas" I said. He tryed to smile at me and said "I hear your a tough little cookie (All of a sudden his nose looked like a BIG

RED tough little cookie that just about covered his whole PINKY face so I cracked up.) And what they call a tomboy. Am I right?"

I gave him The Witch Eyes and he sure didn't like it but he didn't get mad. He just turned away and looked pretty sad like I hurt his feelings or some thing. So we just sat there for a long ass time without even talking and D.T.D. just stared at the Ocean like maybe he was wishing he was back on his ship instead of with some creepo kid whos giveing him The Witch Eyes right? So I started fooling around with the Swiss Army Knife he gave me (Which I really love like my best present EVER.) And I start to tell D.T.D. this story but he never turns to look at me cause he just keeps stareing out at the Ocean, but he doesn't seem sad any more (Probably cause I'm talking to him instead of giveing him The Witch Eyes.) "You know I think I became a tomboy when I was around four (I kept watching D.T.D. cause if he started laughing I was going to get the chingasos out of there for sure.) Like I have 2 uncles who were visiting from Mexico where my grandmother came from cause she was born there. Ones a teacher and ones a judge, and the judge is an Old Sour Puss and the other one seems nicer cause he laughs a lot but I think The Laugher is really pretty mean like he used to kinda torture me right? (D.T.D. looked at me surprised and then he looked back at the Ocean but he didn't laugh or any thing.) The Laugher uncle was really a fatso like a tub of lard and he'd say he had some thing for me and put me on his fatso lap, and then he'd hold a piece of candy in his hand way up high over his head and start saying in a super creepo voice kinda like a song LUNA LUNA COME LA TUNA—ECHA LA CASCARA Y COME LA TUNA!! And that means MOON MOON EAT THE FIG—PEEL THE SKIN AND EAT THE FIG!! My grandmother told me what it meant cause I couldn't figure out what a TUNA was when I was four (I said all this in the super creepo voice Virgen.) So TUNA isn't like a fish in Spanish, its a FIG which I wouldn't eat if some one paid me a zillion bucks, and of course it was extra creepy cause Lunas my name right? So when he got to the COME LA TUNA part at the end he'd tickle me like almost to death till I started blubbering, so my grandmother told him to cut it out but he'd see me and do it again The Weirdo. One time I saw The Laugher coming and saying he had some thing for me so I hid under a humungus table with a table cloth on it almost to the floor, so I thought I was safe there like I used to do secret stuff like draw and cut stuff up with these baby sissors under there so when all of a sudden his fatso hand tryed to grab me I STABBED HIM and I made him BLEED too!!!!" Then D.T.D. looked at me and said "Thats heroic" (And I looked this word up in the dictionary later to spell it right and of course it means some one super BRAVE but the dictionary also said this—Hero is the priestess of Aphrodite, so Hero is really a GIRL—COOL). Any way when I read this I did a loud ass GRITO (I was by myself of course.) And I kinda like that he said that I'm a HERO and that he didn't start laughing like I'm a freak show joke or some thing, plus I told him the whole story like a test (You know how I am Virgen—sneaky.) Then he said "Did you get punished?"

Then I kinda closed my eyes (And I heard the cows MOOOOOOOING but I was starting to kinda get used to it.) And I remembered the blood on his fatso hand (Like I could really see it for a sec Virgen.) And I remembered how I wondered if I did the right thing cause I remember thinking I was REALLY BAD when I saw the blood. (I didn't tell D.T.D. this cause the truth is I was also glad when I saw the blood just for 1-1/2 secs.) Then I remembered how he grabbed on to me and Mamacita grabbed me back and how I stood behind her dress. "No my grandmother saved me but I could tell he wanted to kill me and both my uncles wanted me to live with them in Mexico so I could learn to be a regular girl instead of a weirdo tomboy, but I really hated it there cause you can't have any fun cause some ones always spying on you. Like some times I think Bolinas is kinda like a Secret Island cause no one spys on you and I don't have to keep a look out for Perverts all the time like I used to in S.F., like I'll take a Vampire over a Pervert any day." (And then I was instantly sorry I said that cause I thought D.T.D. wanted to crack up.) But then he saved me from feeling totally STUPID cause he said "I know exactly what you mean Luna, I can assure you that I truly do." And I pretty much believed him and I started to notice how his eyes were so blue they kinda looked phoney and I even stopped thinking about his big ass nose, and I stopped giveing him The Witch Eyes of course. Then he told me a story about being a kid in Denmark on the farm and how him and his grandpa milked the cows before dawn and how fresh milk he says has CREAM at the top, and that maybe we could get some fresh milk from the guy that owns these UGLY COWS but I said "Thanks any way". Then he said when his grandpa died and that he loved him the best in the whole world, and he said he was POed for a long time but he was lucky he said cause he really loved his mom and dad too, but not as much as his grandpa (Thats what he said.) Then he asked me if I wanted to FLY way the chingaso over to DENMARK and meet his 3 brothers and 1 sister cause he said he knew they'd really like me for sure. And for one sec I tryed to imagine his 3 brothers and 1 sister standing together in DENMARK and I saw all 4 of them with these BIG ass noses (But they also had nice BLUE eyes.) So I had to pinch my arm super hard till I got pretty dented so I wouldn't start laughing like a hyena (You know I can be a real pendeja some times SORRY Virgen.) So I said "Can you swim in DENMARK and do people spy on you 100% of the time, and do they know about Yaqui Indians and Mexicans over there?" (Now I really felt like a REAL PENDEJA but the truth is I'm not going to go ANY WHERE where people just stare at you like your from Outer Space or some thing like whos this Weirdo Wet Back and whats she doing in DENMARK). Then D.T.D. looked at me kinda like the way I think a <u>father</u> might look at you if he really likes you a lot right Virgen? Then he said "Yes you can swim in DENMARK, in fact I'll make it a point to take you swimming if you want (He talks this way and I'm not sure I'm getting it all right but I'm trying.) And I can assure you that no one will spy on you even 1% of the time and of course we know about Yaqui Indians and Mexicans in DENMARK and I can assure you that you'll be welcome in DENMARK. I promise Luna."

(And you know Virgen he really did say I PROMISE and I don't remember any one ever telling me I PROMISE but I realy liked it and the way his eyes looked exactly like the color of the Ocean when he said to me I PROMISE—COOL.)

Darling gave me some new words I'll probably NEVER say in my todo vida—1. POSSESSION 2. DESIRE 3. ILLUSION 4.

INFINITY. She said these are kinda Buddist Words so I guess El Budda says these words a lot like ILLUSION. I looked it up and it pretty much means some thing thats not all that real (But the dictionary said "Like in a dream" but I know better than that cause Mamacita always said dreams are real so thats kinda confusing right?) So I'm thinking that in the Gringo Dictionary ILLUSION means to pretend or you think some things are real, but guess what? Its not (At least in the Gringo Dictionary right Virgen?) So I went over and sat down by El Budda and I lit a candle (Darling and D.T.D. were still eating and drinking wine by the fire place and I could tell they wanted to be by them selves and not have some nosey kid spying on them ME). So I lit the candle right in front of him and I said just loud enough for him to hear right? And I wonder if my friends in S.F. saw me talking to El Budda like would they think I finally turned in to a Psycho HA! So I said "Look the other night I dreamed Mamacitas Ruby Ear Rings and I was wearing them in the dream on my ears like 2 Red Stars and it was night time and I mean DARK and the coyotes were wearing jewels too. Any way wearing the Ruby Ear Rings in my dream still makes me HAPPY and the only people I've told this to is you and La Virgen, so even though I know you love this word ILLUSION the Ruby Ear Rings are real. I promise."

OK heres the deal Virgen—I'm going to PROMISE you some thing (Cause I never promised any one any thing right?) And I think its COOL if you can promise some thing and really keep that promise, so here I go—I promise that I'll NEVER STEAL AGAIN (And you know how hard that is Virgen.) Like the other day in the store I amost put some candy in my pocket like stealing here is super easy BUT guess what? I paid for it BELIEVE IT OR NOT.

Last night I probably shouldn't have done it but I spyed on Darling and D.T.D. while they were drinking there wine by the fire place and I heard Darling say this—"I'm used to liveing by myself and shes a wonderful kid but you know I'm used to just being on my own except for you Sweety" (She called him Sweety.) And D.T.D. looked pretty pathetic and SAD and he said "We can't just send her back to S.F. Darling. Don't you think she deserves better?" And he started saying some other stuff but I didn't feel like spying any more. I wonder if I could live with

Harry The Old Hermit and I could just sleep with Cinamon and then Darling could be by her self all the fregado time, and then I tryed to remember if Darling ever promised to keep me (But I can't remember her promiseing me that.) Or really promiseing me any thing and thats the truth. So I guess D.T.D. is the first person to promise me any thing (You know to take me swimming in DENMARK and make sure no one spys on me, and he even said later that some time we could even visit Mexico, and then I thought D.T.D. and Darling could meet Chula COOL.)

Its pretty dark out side but I'm going to pack some stuff and go see Cinamon and I'll see if I can have dinner over at Harrys House and I'll ask him if I can sleep with Cinamon tonight so Darling doesn't have to see me for 2 days right? And its weird cause for some stupid reason I feel like visiting the COWS and hearing them MOOOOOOO to each other in that dumb ass field, and I know this is really chingaso WEIRD but I wonder if in Cow Language MOOOOOOO means I PROMISE cause it sounds like it kinda like one cow gos MOOOOO and the other cows go MOOOOO all day long to each other right? And the stupid cows never seem to get tired of it MOOOOO MOOOOOO MOOOOOOOOOOOO (Do they MOOOOOO at night too Virgen—I wonder.) So heres the poem with the El Buddas favorite words

PROMISE (MOOOOOOO)

I promise not to steal POSSESSIONS.
I promise not to DESIRE too much candy.
I promise to remember dreams are not
ILLUSIONS and that there real
like the Ruby Ear Rings.
I promise I will always be Miss Moon
even in DENMARK, even in S.F.
(If I visit Tia and Pablo.)
I promise I will be a Mammal in to INFINITY.
But what I secretly wish is that some one
would promise me some thing
and that they'd keep there promise.
MOOOOO MOOOOO MOOOOOOOOOOOOOO

THE WISHING MONTH—JUNE

(With a TON of crickets makeing a racket)

Dear La Virgen,

I had 2 Loba Dreams (Or as Mamacita used to always say Lobita Dreams, so I'll call them that from now on.) In the first Lobita Dream I was chaseing COWS and haveing a ton of fun, but I was by myself and I was kinda lonely cause theres only so many cows you can chase right? In the second Lobita Dream I was running around with a friend and then I was wondering how I was going to talk to this new friend in Lobita Language (Which cracked me up when I finally woke up.) Mamacita used to tell me to pay super attention when I dream Lobita, so of course I'm telling you about it (Like maybe I might get a friend here and I am kinda starting to feel like Hermit Girl Who Lungers In Spitoon In Bolinas right?) Any way do you remember how I promised to tell you some of my Secret Wishes? In the Fairy Tales you only get 3 wishes (Which I think is a GIP So I'll make it 3-1/2 HA! #1—I never want to be hungry in my whole entire todo VIDA like ever cause it just makes you so desperate and then you have to STEAL some thing to eat. #2—I NEVER want to be bothered by some Pervert ever ever again like not even some Perv trying to show me his weirdo weiner and thats what I LOVE about Bolinas—NO PERVERTS LURKING that I can see. #3—(I really thought about this one especially after the Lobita Dream.) I want a friend to goof around with cause I'm tired of being Hermit Girl every dam day like you know some one my age OK? And I'm saveing the 1/2 for later just in case I really need it.

Any way Darling hung up this weirdo sign after Danny The Dane took off for his ship till next month cause its a short trip she said. It says I LOVE MANKIND, ITS PEOPLE I HATE. She put it in the kitchen and I guess I feel like that about a lot of people (You know all the Lurking Pervs.) But then when I think about Old Harry The Hermit, D.T.D., Whitey in S.F. and the Tree Lot Guy who took my Christmas Tree to Tias (There all MEN) I guess I do kinda love MANKIND in a way, right Virgen? "And how about WOMAN KIND?" Thats what I said to Darling and she cracked up and said "Your a PHILOSOPHER Luna, no shit." So you guessed it like PHILOSOPHER is one of my new words and Darling said its some one who <u>loves</u> to think about every thing in the world and figure every thing out for them selves like a Royal Pain In The Ass she said (Like me right Virgen?) And Darling has NEVER seen my Diary to you cause all this stuff I write to you is PRIVATE NO ONES BEES WAX STUFF. So I guess its true that I love to think about stuff (Then write to you.) And I also love SECRETS (Which is why I don't tell you 2 or 3 things probably cause it makes me kinda feel like I swallowed some RUBYS and there glowing in the dark way down in my STOMACH, and no one knows there there but me, and I know thats kinda creepy but I still like it, the Secret Rubys.) And now you know there glowing in my stomach but you don't know WHY—Sorry.

So guess what Darling calls me now? PLATO!! Cause he was a famous PHILOSOPHER in Ancient Greece (Greece is kinda close to Denmark but its different now Darling says than when PLATO was figureing every thing out). So any way now when Darling yells that dinners ready she yells "HEY PLATO COME AND GET IT!" And you know me cause I'd run in for dinner if she called me SNOW BALL, one of the cats names with the most beautiful thickest whitest fur I've ever seen, plus shes pretty fat and spoiled but I like her cause she sleeps on my stomach (Where the Rubys are.) And she purrs like a lepard or some kinda motor you can't turn off, but I think its pretty cool (Like in Cat Language that probably means they love you.) Or some times I wake up and shes curled around my neck and her furs all in my mouth DISGUSTAMENTO. Like one time I woke up and she was licking me with her Cat Tongue (I looked up TONGUE in the Gringo Dictionary and I remembered how much I hate silent Gs.) Any way Snow Balls Cat Tongue kinda gives me the chingaso creeps, but then I kinda also like it and she was purring LOUD so I pretended I was sleeping till she started licking my nose (Did you ever smell Cat Breath—MUY PUKEY).

Also me and Darling planted the lemon tree in back and the tiny white blossoms fell off where these tiny like really tiny hard green things which Darling says will be LEMONS and then she said some thing pretty embarassing cause I wouldn't even laugh right? She said "There kinda like your nipples becoming your breasts," and of course she started cracking up. So now I'm doomed to see my pathetic (nipples) on the lemon tree getting bigger day by day WHAT A CHINGASO ASS THRILL. It's kinda like Darling doesn't want me to forget I'm a girl, but at least she calls me Plato which kinda takes my mind off all the Girl Stuff (Like nipples, The Blood, fertility, The Goochy Goo.) Like one time she showed me how she puts lotion on her arms and legs and she says she puts it every where on her BODY right? And she actually and for real said "You want your skin to be smooth for your HUSBAND." Like thats not what I ever think about and I bet Plato never put lotion all over his body to make it smooth for any one cause he was too busy figureing stuff out right Virgen? Do you put lotion all over your self like for GOD—tell the truth OK? (Or how about El Budda cause I think you'd be a lot happyer with El Budda cause I bet he even laughs some times and I NEVER heard about God laughing.) And now I want to know of course—have you ever heard God laugh? What about El Budda? Let me know in a dream OK? GRACIAS cause I'm really super curious about this one being that God just smites people when hes POed (Like the Nut Case Minister always used to say in a loud ass voice that was supposed to be SCAREY).

And I don't think the Bible ever says that God laughs or even smiles (Like El Budda does.) So now you know why Darling calls me PLATO but this stuff just jumps in to my brain, plus I kinda like it to tell the truth, you know THINKING about every thing and then writing to you in the Diary (Which is starting to get pretty fat even though I'm writing really tiny to save pages, so I'm going to have to get another one pretty soon.) Any way Darling even said I could shave my legs and wear NYLONS with my new Bo Peep Dress she sewed me but then she saw my face (Which was in disbelief.) She laughed for a sec and said "Some day you will!" "Maybe when I'm paralyzed or some thing" I say to her (And then I think—Or when The Blood Sucker gets me and thats really chingaso ass creepy like to think of The Blood Sucker shaveing my legs after I'm DEAD.) So I ran for it over to ride Cinamon and I jumped on my bike. "See you back here for dinner Plato!" she yelled and when I turned around to wave I saw her putting lotion on her BOOBS but she looked kinda nice in the sun all smileing (Just keep that stuff off me right?)

Virgen, remember when I spyed on Darling and Danny The Dane and I heard Darling say she was used to liveing by herself (And not with some kid.) When I didn't come back that night she went over to Harrys Palace and told me to come HOME (So I think she changed her mind, but she still didn't promise me any thing.) I was kinda thinking of making a Contract where I say—Darling here by promises to keep Luna The Mammal till she grows up here in BOLINAS, CALIFORNIA. And then giveing it to her to sign COOL. And then maybe my part of the contract would say—LUNA THE MAMMAL VILLALOBOS promises to stay out of Darlings hair and follow all the rules (Which I do any way.) And then I'll sign it too MUY COOL. So maybe I'll do that (What do you think Virgen?) So my 1/2 wish is—I want Darling to promise to keep me HERE till my lemons come in HA! (Cause I do not want to go back to S.F. and leave Cinamon.)

So these are my new words I've been thinking about—1. PHILOSOPHER (Plato) 2. COURAGE 3. NOBLE 4. CREATIVE. I always think the new words Darling gives me are pretty weird till I start really thinking about them and then I start to think there pretty NIFTY. Also just in case you haven't noticed or maybe even recognized me (I've switched from the Cow Boy Hat to a Base Ball Hat when I ride Cinamon and its got a deer on it MUY COOL DADDYO) Darling says DADDYO when she dances to some really junkey music she calls Jazz, and then I start doing the Charleston and mixing my knees up like La Loca which of course cracks her up till she starts crying and peeing her calzones right? Any way I bought the Deer Base Ball Hat at the Hermit Store and I did it <u>again</u> (I lungered in the SPITOON but I don't really look when I do it cause I could really heave ho so I do it FAST.) Also Harry The Hermit took me to his Secret Fishing Spot and I caught more fish than him which I think kinda POed him, but he said that some time we'll go out in a boat where the smart ones are (And of course there bigger he said.) One thing about fishing he said is you can't talk too much or the fish will SKEDDADDLE (Thats Harry Talk.) And then Plato (me) had to ask him what he was (Like I'm part Mexican and part Gringa.) And Harry said he was English and Irish so thats why he was always fighting with himself (He explained to me that England won't get out of Ireland and that Irelands POed about it.) Then I said "Your son was part Gringo and part Wet Back kinda like me." But Old Harry didn't even look at me cause he kept looking at the Ocean (Trying to think like a fish he said.) Then he said "That Darling ladys calling you Plato these days you said right Miss Moon?" "Yeah" I said. "Ain't that the dam truth" he said.

Then I started thinking about Chula (My girl cousin in Mexico who fights bulls.) And I wish (Wish #4) I could visit her in Mexico this summer and stay in her new house (Not with The Sour Puss Judge, her father.) And we could ride in her car with the radio FULL BLAST and do GRITOS and I could yell OH LAY!! like when she stands <u>so still</u> when the bull zooms by OH LAY!!!! Then Harry said "Miss Moon I wouldn be worryin bout all that horse shit if I was you cause in the end all most people will remember is what you did and who you were and not the color of your bare but cause all our blood and all our bones is the same dam color and the rest of its just plain old steamin horse shit Miss Moon." And thats the most I EVER heard Harry say at one time and for once Virgen I couldn't say any thing back so I just looked out at the Ocean with Old Harry (Pretending to think like a fish and maybe it really worked cause I caught one pretty fast.) Then Harry took the 6 fish we caught so far and he said he was going to make a BARBQUE for lunch for us so he took off and I wrote this poem—

NOBLE HORSE SHIT FOR HARRY

I asked Harry The Hermit about
Gringos and Wet Backs while
we were supposed to be thinking
like a fish. (Fishing)

And he said "Thats horse shit Miss Moon
cause our blood and bones the same dam color."
So I'm thinking—Harrys really the
PHILOSOPHER!!

But he'd probably say
thats horse shit too right?
And so I start thinking how no one
will ever know about Harry The Hermit

(Or even me right?) Cause when
he said that stuff to me it sounded
NOBLE and I think it takes COURAGE
to say that kinda stuff out loud

to some one else. (I think)
So this poems my CREATIVITY
and my way of saying "I know what
you mean Harry The Hermit!!!"

So when I got to Old Harrys Palace (it cracks him up when I call it that, but I actually got it from him so maybe he forgets) He was keeping every thing hot and he made french frys too (Which I really love) With a ton of ketchup and like he says hes stocking up on it cause I'm a Ketchup Fiend HA! While we're eating I tell him about D.T.D. wanting to take me to DENMARK and how I was kinda worryed about haveing to beat up the whole country if I went cause I don't have blond hair or blue eyes of course, and I told him Darling made me some Bo Peep dresses and that she wanted me to wear one when she takes me for my I.Q. Test and I told Old Harry thats how they figure out how smart you really are, right Virgen? I think its kinda weird like I wonder if there going to measure my brain but Darling says its just some writing tests that tell you what your POTENTIAL is (She says POTENTIAL is what your kinda born with and how much of its still in your brain I guess.) So Harry just says "Thats a big pile a horse shit CHRIST ALMIGHTY even I know your smart Miss Moon!" And his face got all red like you know who (Yosemite Sam right?) And its funny the way his nose hairs stick out when hes POed and it kinda made me feel better cause in a way it secretly did feel kinda like I'm getting the I.Q. Test to see if I'm really worth keeping or not (But thats my secret which I didn't even tell Old Harry of course.) What I did was copy the Horse Shit Poem real fast and I gave it to him just before I took Cinamon for her ride to the Giant Trees (Which is now my favorite place to watch the sun set PLOP at the end of the world in Bolinas and I'm even pretty used to the dark like rideing back with Cinamon.) And June is definitely Cricket Month here in Bolinas especially rideing back in the dark, and Darling says they make all that cool racket by rubbing there wings together (I wish #5 I had wings REAL WINGS when I'm awake to fly with to the end of the world where the sun sets if I felt like it, right Virgen?) (DO YOU HAVE WINGS????) But then I guess I wouldn't be a Mammal if I had wings when I'm awake (I wonder if Plato thought of all this stuff in Ancient Greece?)

So when I gave Harry the Horse Shit Poem he musta read it pretty fast cause he yelled "YOUR A GOD DAM GENIUS MISS MOON!!!!" So I did a grito to let him know I heard him and then I cracked up like a psycho hyena all by myself like even out by the Giant Trees I'd start cracking up just cause Old Harry called me a GENIUS (Boy am I a Mammal, and I wonder if Plato liked being a Mammal, and I wonder if Plato was a genius?) What do you think, Virgen? Do you think I need an I.Q. Test to find out how much POTENTIAL I still have left in my brain? (Which is almost 13 YEARS OLD.)

So I'm sitting there with Cinamon tied to a tree and I do a loud ass GRITO just for some fregado fun I guess and then I almost fell off the cliff cause some one said "You really sound like a mountain lion." And it was a BOY—NO SHIT and for real!!!! For one sec I was so POed I felt like kicking his but and then (Believe it or not) He was smileing at me like he knew me or some thing and then my face felt all RED so I thought—Oh shit I probably look like Yosemite Sam right? So I pretended to fix my Deer Base Ball Hat like it was probably crooked, and of course I probably looked pretty pathetic (Like all I needed was some long ass nose hairs right?) But I finally looked at him again and he was looking at the sun trying to get to the end of the world, and then he SMILED at me again CHIN GA SOS!!!! So I said in my boys voice "How do you know what a mountain lion sounds like?" "I've heard them thats how right here in Bolinas, but theres not as many as there used to be cause people shoot them like my dad shot a couple cause we have some cows." "Well I've never heard a mountain lion here I guess cause I didn't even know mountain lions lived here, like can they kill you or what?" Then he said "My dad says only if there sick or starved cause they usually like to eat stuff that tastes good to them like deer, so I guess humans don't taste so hot like they might go for your horse if you left him out all night maybe." So I had to set him straight, "Its not a him—its a her like a girl horse and her names Cinamon." Then he said "My names Jeff." And he was waiting for me to say my name (Pokahantus, Annie Oakly, Miss Moon, La Loca, Plato, Luna).

I liked his eyes cause they were just nice and I think hes probably around my age, and for one sec I even think of telling him my names CHULA (But thats a girls name and its also Spanish.) And then I think of telling him its JODY (Cause its like a boys name too and a Gringo name also.) So hes looking out at the sun set kinda waiting of course for the PENDEJA to say her fregado NAME, so just as the sun poked the end of the world I just say "I'm Luna". "Luna means moon doesn't it? And theres the cresent moon and my mom always said the cresent moons good luck. Thats what she always said." And boy did his eyes get sad and you know me cause I said "Is she dead or some thing?" It was getting dark but the sky was turning all of Mamacitas favorite colors and I could still see his face, and now I felt pretty lousy BAD for even saying it but he said "Yeah she died last year from cancer." And I said (Believe it or not!) "My grandmother died last year cause she was pretty old and she was like my real mom and all, and now I live here with a lady named Darling. Do you really think the cresent moons good luck?" And Jeff said "Yeah for sure."

It turns out that Jeff has a horse too (A boy horse named Midnight which I think is a cool name and Jeff said his mom named him and all.) He said his mom helped Midnight to get born and that Midnight was really pathetic and skinny when he was a COLT (Jeff said kid horses are called COLTS.) He also said his mom taught him how to ride a horse when he was about 5 years old. I told Jeff that my mom (Carmen) forgot me in a store in S.F. when I was 5 (We were rideing Cinamon and Midnight real slow and I think they like each other like FRIENDS!!) I told Jeff how I was 5 and sitting under a table watching all these ladys legs go by and how the sound of there nylons sounded like Carmens so it felt like she was there some where, but then finally when I tryed to find her I couldn't and I was yelling CARMEN but she wasn't any where. The store lady called the cops and the cop was pretty nice and gave me an ice cream, and luckily I knew my phone number (Pretty smart for 5 I think.) And Tia answered and came and got me in down town S.F. on Market Street. It turned out that Carmen FORGOT I was with her and then I started laughing like a pendeja right? But Jeff said "You musta been pretty scared being just a 5 year old kid cause I'd a been terrifyed thats for sure." And these BIG ASS TEARS jumped to my eyes with no warning. OK but I didn't let them pop out or any thing so I asked him if he wanted to use my binoculars and he said "Sure."

We got to my favorite swimming place where all the Seals hang out and then suddenly I realized if I'm going swimming I'll have to wear the Swim Suit (Well at least it doesn't go up my nalgas cause I wouldn't FOR SURE then.) But then I realize my Lemon Tree Nipples will be sticking out kinda so I decide to keep my shirt on like even in the water. After we tied up Cinamon and Midnight kinda close together so they can talk I had to ask "Did you know I was a girl right away when you first saw me?"

"Yeah" Jeff said. And I told him how thats kinda bad cause in S.F. I always had to look like a boy so the Pervs wouldn't spot me a mile away and then of course I was sorry I said that stuff, but Jeff said real fast "Hey I don't blame you, it must be pretty weird being a girl and worrying about that kinda crap especially in the city where its got to be 40 Pervs per square inch probably." And for the first time in MY LIFE I SMILED AT A BOY!!!! "My mom always used to say she was glad she lived in Bolinas where its safe for her to be a woman and she really used to say stuff like that my mom, like she'd read stuff in the paper and get pretty infuriated. You'd a liked my mom I think." Then he smiled at me and it was a <u>small</u> smile (Not a show off smile.) But the kinda smile that means—I think we're friends, right Virgen? Then I asked him "How old are you?" "13" "I'll be 13 in October" I said but now I was DREADING taking my jeans and stuff off. "You know I HATE wearing dresses." Then Jeff said "It must be a pain in the but to wear dresses all the time, but I think they look nice some times, you know?" Jeff had his clothes off and he was wearing some super pathetic baggy looking shorts that made his legs look like pathetic little WHITE PENCILS so I started laughing like a pendeja hyena, and I tryed to stop but then I'd look at his little white PENCILS and the hyena was at it again till I was on my back kicking my legs right? Then all of a sudden I felt like a PSYCHO and that probably I was hurting his feelings (Some friend, right Virgen?) But he was in the Ocean with the Seals already so I took off my stuff <u>real fast</u> (Even my shirt.) And for one sec I wished #6 that <u>my legs</u> didn't look like pathetic browner pencils and I jumped in to the water before he could see me. We raced and I'm a faster swimmer than him but he didn't get all weird about it, and he had names for the 3 seals that followed us around (Sam, Fred, Egor—believe it or not.) And I asked Jeff how he knew those were there names and he said "Cause they TOLD me is how." Then I told him how some times I put my head down on Cinamons mane when we're rideing around and how I feel EXACTLY like we're a horse together, and Jeff said "Thats the magic." Then he ducked under the water and I couldn't see him for a long ass time like so long I was starting to get SCARED SHIT LESS and then he popped up behind me laughing just like a Psycho, and then one of the Seals popped up and I SCREAMED which was kinda embarassing, but he said "Its OK thats Egor." So I went under the Ocean and for the first time I opened my eyes for a sec cause they burned too much, but I thought I saw his white pencil legs and I was glad he was there with me in the Pacific Ocean with Sam, Fred and Egor (Do you know what I mean, Virgen?)

And when we got out and layed on our towels he didn't stare or laugh or any thing (I guess hes NICER than me to tell the truth.) My eyes were still kinda burning so I just kept them closed and I could see reds and purples kinda like the sun set and if I squeezed them tight all the colors EXPLODED and then I started thinking how its different to lay in the sun with some one else instead of by your hermit self, and then I thought—Jeff is my first real friend whos a BOY. And then I thought—Jeff is a MAMMAL. And then I heard Cinamon and Midnight snorting so I figured they were figureing stuff out too (I wonder if hes Cinamons first horse friend—what do you think Virgen? And I wonder if Cinamon remembers her Horse Mom cause it must be pretty weird to NEVER see your mom again, right?) Any way I was laying there thinking about all this Mammal Stuff when Jeff says "I was just thinking that I've never really had a friend whos a girl, you know?" For one sec I got scared to THINK any thing cause it felt like he could READ MY BRAIN!! WEIRD!!!! So I opened my eyes and I saw his Pencil Legs and I remembered how he named the 3 Seals Sam, Fred and Egor, so I said "This is pretty weird but I was thinking kinda the same stuff like I've never really had a friend FRIEND whos a boy cause my best friend in S.F. is a Tomboy named Jody and we used to do a TON of daring stuff together like jumping roofs and rideing the street cars through I mean a long dark ass tunnel about 100 miles an hour, and we used to jump on the back of the street car when the driver wasn't looking and hang on for our lives." (I didn't tell Jeff how Jody and me laughed if a Perv tryed to show us there weiner especially in Golden Gate Park some times—I wonder if those guys LIVE in the bushes?) "Do you miss Jody?" he said and for one sec I got kinda MAD like he was asking me some thing personal, but then I thought how nice his voice was kinda like his pathetic white Pencil Legs (And then I looked at my pathetic Pencil Legs only mine are browner than his cause hes 100% Gringo, of course.) And then I thought—Well some ones asking YOU questions for a change, right Virgen? So I said "The lady I live with calls me Plato cause he was a philosopher in Ancient Greece and I'm always thinking about stuff and I was just thinking how you and me are MAMMALS like even if your a boy your still a Mammal, so why can't I be your friend is what I kinda figured out, so what do you think?"

Then Jeff laughed but it wasn't mean (But I kinda sat up to see his face and he just looked kinda happy.) "My dad calls me The Old Man cause I'm kinda serious some times I guess, and I write stuff in a journal like my mom got me started when I was about 9 so I've been writing in it for about 4 years. Any way my best friend whos Ray is gone for the whole summer and we always go fishing in my dads double KAYAK, so do you want to go?" "Sure" I said trying not to sound too excited (But I've NEVER been in a KAYAK kinda like the Eskimos, so MUCHO COOLO!!!!) I was laying down again with my eyes closed watching the sun set colors EXPLODE and I thought—I didn't know <u>boys</u> wrote in journals kinda like me and my diary to you Virgen, and then I wondered if he wrote it to any one like maybe God (or El Budda—and then I wondered if he knew about El Budda cause I didn't till I met Darling.) And then I wondered <u>what he wrote</u> (And I pictured myself in a burgler mask climbing in his window and STEALING his journal so I could read all his SECRETS). Wish #7—I wish I had X-RAY Vision like Super Mammal and then right from here I could just read his journal, but then if I had X-RAY Vision I'd probably have to see through a bunch of MOOO cows on the way to his house, and then maybe I'd accidentaly see his dad sitting on the toilet before I could even find his journal (But I still would <u>love</u> to have X-RAY Vision any way!)

Then I kinda just BLURTED out (Cause Darling says I blurt a lot but she always laughs when I blurt) "I write in a diary which is kinda like a journal I guess, but I just started mine last year after my grandma died so thats where I keep most of my secrets and stuff like that." Then I stopped blurting cause I was scared I was going to tell him about you, so instead I blurted this—"To tell the truth I was wishing I had X-RAY Vision so I could read your journal right from here." (But I didn't blurt about pictureing myself in a burglers mask or accidentaly seeing his dad sitting on the toilet right?) Then he blurted "Every one wishes they had X-RAY Vision I bet, like you could probably find buryed treasure and see to the bottom of the Ocean and even way out to space to see whats really there, like wouldn't that be the Cats Pajamas?" Then I started cracking up just pictureing Snow Ball in pajamas, and then I had to ask him "Do you write your journal to any one?" Then Jeff covered his eyes with his arm and he said "Yeah to my mom probably cause I started writing it to her to read at first and if I didn't want her to read it I'd write PRIVATE on it and cover it up, but I guess now that shes got real X-RAY Vision shes probably read all that stuff too, but thats OK cause I don't mind any more you know?" (He said some more stuff but I can't remember every thing, but this is pretty much what he said.) So when he said "you know" it sounded like maybe he was CRYING and I have <u>never</u> heard a BOY CRY. Well one time when this boy got his but kicked by a mean ass bully and his nose was bleeding and he was blubbering, and I really felt pretty sorry for him so when that bully kid tryed picking on me later I punched him right in the face and made his nose BLEED (Was he SURPRISED cause I just punched him right away cause I saw what he did to that other kid.) So I kinda kicked his but for the other kid too, but to tell the truth Virgen, I was kinda surprised to see all that BLOOD on his face and he was hideing his nose saying "My nose, my nose you broke my god dam nose!" I felt pretty crummy for one sec but then I knew he'd a punched out my eye balls too cause I NEVER picked him for base ball and I could tell he hated my GUTS. So any way I peeked at Jeff and I thought about how Hope and me made each other cry with our phoney storys (And Jeff still had his arm over his eyes and then I saw how boney his chest was with his ribs sticking out.) And you know what Virgen? I couldn't SAY ANY THING!!! And thats the TRUTH!!! So what happened was my <u>hand</u> blurted cause it kinda just flew over to his arm like a Blurty Bird (Call me La Loca cause its the TRUTH). And it kinda landed on his pointy elbow and just stayed there for about 4 secs and I wondered if he was watching the sun set explode on his eyes, but then I realized he couldn't cause his eyes were covered by his boney arm. So I said "If you take your arm off your eyes and you close them super tight for a sec you can see some cool colors." He lowered his boney arm and I took a FAST peek (His face was kinda wet but he looked OK.) "Yeah I do that too. You know I think my mom was my first friend who was a girl, so I guess your the second friend whos a girl, so maybe some time I can show you my journal." "OK" was all I could say even though I kinda knew he was probably waiting for me to say I'll show him my diary, but I just couldn't Virgen. Wish #8—I wish I could've said "OK I'll show you my diary some time like 1 or 2 pages."

So when he took off to the Moooo Farm on the other side of the Mesa and I took off to Harrys Palace we waved a couple of times, and then he yelled SEE YA LATER MAMMAL GATOR!!!! And I yelled AFTER WHILE CROCK O MILE!!!! (Which sure isn't as good as MAMMAL GATOR but I couldn't think of any thing good fast enough so I yelled MILE like a pendeja, but I guess thats OK cause Jeff laughed like I yelled some thing pretty zingy.) When it was really pretty pathetic (MILE?) Which really proves Jeff is a lot NICER than me cause I don't know if I'd laugh at some thing I didn't think was really funny (But then I remember how I laugh at Pablos BORING Knock Knock Jokes just so I can hear him crack up on him self and do the Skinny Kids Dance right? So maybe I am kinda NICE????) Any way tomorrow we're going fishing in the KAYAK and we're going to wear Life Jackets (I told Jeff about almost drowning to death right?)

When me and Darling were eating dinner tonight (Meat Balls and Spaghetti YUUUMMM with Super Buttery Garlic Bread cause she puts more butter on my bread cause she says I'm all skin and some bones) She said "Do you have a buddy now?" But then she changes the subject real FAST cause she can tell I'm POed (And now I'm wondering if Darling has X-RAY Vision Super Cat Eyes to spy on me FREGADO!!) Then Darling tells me my I.Q. Test came out real HIGH and I'm One Smart Cookie (Like D.T.D. calls me a Tough Cookie FREGADO again.) But I have to admit Darling didn't make me wear the Lacey Ass Dress cause she said I could think better if I was really my old comfortable weirdo self, and thats the TRUTH. But theres no way I'm telling her about Jeff being my friend cause I can just hear her—"Your first boy friend." And hes not. Hes a BOY whos a FRIEND. So I thought about what he yelled and smiled to myself super sneaky SEE YA LATER MAMMAL GATOR!!!! I wonder what my I.Q. looks like—Is it a map of my BRAIN? Darling said the guy who told her about my I.Q. said its better not to tell me a NUMBER but just to say its "Well above average." Thats what Darling says it is. So I'm putting my brain on a map with an average line on it and my I.Q. NUMBER up by my eye brows right? Then as I'm washing the dishes I think—If I had X-Ray Vision I could see every ones I.Q. number on their BRAIN (And then I remember Harry The Hermit saying "Thats horse shit Miss Moon." Steaming horse shit HA!) So wish #9 is I wish I could SEE Jeff like what hes doing right NOW but then I think what if hes on the toilet or takeing a shower FORGET IT!!!!

Any way tomorrow I'll teach him to think like a fish. Good night Virgen and do you like Jeff? Send me a dream if you want to OK? And SEE YOU LATER MAMMAL GATOR!!!! (Are you part Mammal Virgen, like 1/2 Mammal and 1/2 Super Mammal?) And don't forget—Do you like Jeff and his boney self, and do you think hes boneyer than even me?

So you sent me this dream—I'm out side and it feels SUPER REAL and its night time and I'm just looking at the cresent moon (Like with Jeff right?) And then your on the cresent moon with a shawl over your face (Like the ladys at Church always wear.) Then you say "Thats the magic." And for one sec I wonder if your Jeffs Mom or even Mamacita, but then I know its really you Virgen, telling me you LIKE JEFF COOL and GRACIAS for the dream!!!!

First of all I LOVE the double kayak and we paddled together real good like we didn't go in circles or any thing, and Jeff knows where the Baby Seals hang out so we went there, and the Baby Seals followed us every where COOL. We named them but there were too many to remember who was who so we gave up and just called them Baby Seals. I brought some lunch and Jeff brought some lunch so we had a TON of food, then we fished and I told him how Old Harry The Hermit taught me how to think like a fish so the fish will get tricked and come to check you out. Jeff said his dad kinda does that too and then he said his dad got drunk last night (And I thought right away about The Psycho in S.F. right, you know my step step step father Jake Juniors dad.) So I said "Is he a Psycho when he gets drunk or is he just kinda goofy, like my step step father Jake in S.F. acts like a real Psycho and hits my mom Carmen" (Jeff was in front of me in the kayak so I couldn't see his face but I could tell he was really listening you know?) "And like Harry The Hermit just gets goofy and sad when he drinks too much Hooch, so I'm not scared of Old Harry or any thing but with The Psycho I have to be prepared to fight for my life and I'm not kidding either." And then I told him how I knocked Its tooth out that time and Jeff turned his head and looked at me in disbelief (Like maybe he thinks I'm lieing, right Virgen? But you know I'm not!) Then he said so quiet that for one sec I thought maybe the Baby Seals said it "I wish I could knock his tooth out." "Why?" is what I said to Jeff. "Since my mom died hes meaner and meaner I guess cause she used to stop him from drinking too much." So I'm waiting for Jeff to say some more stuff but he doesn't and the sound of the Ocean is LOUD all of a sudden, so I'm stareing at our fishing poles and I can just see the fish sticking their tongues out at our bait (And we caught about 4 each, but we just kept 3 cause the rest were too small to eat.) Finally I had to blurt "What does he do when hes being a psycho?" Then a bunch of Baby Seals are just kinda STAREING at us and I wanted to say "Quick Jeff name these guys!" But I was waiting for him to say some thing so I just shut up. "The bastard hits me." When Jeff says that I want to yell at the Baby Seals some thing stupid like "You heard him THE BASTARD HITS HIM" But I don't of course and instead the Blurty Bird (You know my hand) flys over to Jeffs shoulder and sits there on his boney ass shoulder and then I'm so MAD I wish #10—I could give his Psycho Dad one of my Witch Power Knuckle Sandwiches right? Or if I really had X-Ray Vision Witch Eyes I'd burn his hands right off and I could just see him blubbering cause he has <u>no hands</u> to hit any one with or even to pick up his Hooch with (Or eat or shoot mountain lions NADA). But the Blurty Bird just kinda stays on his boney shoulder cause now I know why Jeff has a cut eye today.

After we land the kayak without even flipping over and we carry it up to the road and hide it in some bushes even though Jeff said no one would steal it, like maybe they'd borrow it but thats about it he said. We ride Cinamon and Midnight over to the Sun Set Cliff but I can't wait for the cresent moon cause I promised Darling I'd be back by 6 o clock and she even bought me a watch so I know what time it is (its a super corny Elvis Presley watch which she thought I'd love so of course I pretend I love it, but I know I'd NEVER scream for Elvis The Pelvis—thats what Darling calls him and don't ask me why.) I don't tell Jeff all this so I just check the time cause Darling says now I don't have any excuses to be so late cause I'm always late and tonight we're going out some where for dinner and I'm doomed—The Lacey Ass Dress FRE GA DO!!! Any way when Jeff first saw my watch he kept saying (Like Elvis The Pelvis does) "Thank you very much." So I had to clobber him to make him stop but he was pretty funny.

So I said "Do you ever sleep out side and count shooting stars?" I probably sound like a pendeja but I don't know what else to say cause I'm going out to dinner with Darling and Jeff has to go see a Psycho right? And Jeff says "Yeah some times Ray and me sleep out in my tree house down by the creek." "You have a tree house?" "Yeah." "Is it far away from your regular house?" "Yeah." "Maybe some time I can meet you there and we can stay up all night till like dawn" I say. Then Jeff smiled for the first time today I think and he said "When?" "How about tomorrow night?" "OK meet me here at 2 o clock and I'll show you where its at and don't worry about sleeping bags cause I've got some in the tree house, and I've even got a lantern and cards and Scrabble, do you play Scrabble?" he says. And I say "I'm a CHAMP like no one has ever in my life beat me." And Jeff laughs but I can tell his cut eye kinda HURTS. "Look I'm not kidding if your father trys hitting you again tonight come to my house, you know the place I showed you like I'm not kidding! Do you promise?" And for one sec I wanted to tell Jeff about MOOOO maybe meaning PROMISE but I figure he might think I've gone round the bend (Like Old Harry says.) So I don't and then Jeff just looks at me kinda like the Baby Seals and he says "How would I know which windows yours?" And I say "Mines on the side where the kitchen door is but what I'll do is put my binoculars right in the window cause I sleep with it open all night and if I'm sleeping out side I'll be on the back patio, but if I'm inside just knock on the window OK?" Then all of a sudden Jeffs Blurty Bird Hand comes flying over to my Blurty Bird Hand like maybe a 1/2 sec and we say Bye and See you tomorrow for sure at 2 o clock, and I turn and yell "Don't forget the binoculars in the window OK?" And Jeff yells SEE YA LATER MAMMAL GATOR And I don't yell any thing back cause Jeffs is the best thing to yell.

Virgen, please do me a FAVOR—Take care of Jeff with your Super Mammal X-Ray Vision Eyes and make sure Jeffs father goes BLIND or some thing if he trys hitting him again OK? And you know I just realized that Jeff never asked me what I am like he just said "Luna means moon doesn't it and cresent moons are good luck." So I wonder how he knows Spanish and I wonder if he knows about all the Wet Back and Gringo stuff like in S.F.

So heres my poem with the new weird words—1. ALIEN 2. SACRED 3. SOLITUDE 4. TRUST (I wonder how Darling THINKS of these words cause when you think of each word they start to mean a lot of stuff, and you know me I start thinking about every thing.) Like ALIEN—An alien from S.F., an alien in Mexico, an alien in Denmark, an alien to the Baby Seals, an alien with 2 friends, a boy named Jeff and a hermit named Harry, an alien named Plato with an I.Q. up by her eye brows (See what I mean, Virgen?)

2 BUDDYS

I guess haveing a friend
(And whos a BOY)
Makes me feel like I'm not
an ALIEN on the planet

BOLINAS and tomorrow night
I'm going to his SACRED
Tree House and we're going
to stay up till dawn

counting shooting stars,
playing cards, playing Scrabble
(I know I'll win too!!)
And we'll stay up till

dawn not in <u>SOLITUDE</u>
like 2 Hermit Kids, but maybe
like 2 buddys with Blurty Bird
Hands that <u>TRUST</u> (Each other—right?)

Good night Virgen cause I'm so TIRED I can hardly see the paper and I put the binoculars in the window and so far no knock. And you know I almost couldn't even WRITE DOWN the word <u>TRUST</u> but I did (Cause I remembered his boney pathetic shoulder, his white pencil legs, his cut eye that hurt when he laughed.) So MAYBE I TRUST HIM like you said in the dream "Thats the magic"—Is that the magic, Virgen? Still no knock on the window so good night and keep one X-Ray Eye on Jeff OK? Also gracias for answering my pathetic prayer about the Lacey Ass Dress cause Darling let me choose what ever I wanted to wear to the Gringo Restaurant (But it had GOOD FOOD). Good night Virgen and don't forget you still haven't told me if YOU HAVE WINGS OR NOT (You know me, I'm a curious Mammal even when I'm 1/2 dead.) Keep <u>both</u> of your X-Ray Eyes on Jeff OK? Wish #11—I wish I could really really TRUST Jeff MOOOOOOOOOOOOO

2 Heros in JULY
More Wishes and More MOOOOOOS and
LA LOCA RIDES AGAIN!!!!
And—
La Virgens RED WINGS

Dear La Virgen,

I had another Lobita Dream where I was a Lobita (But I really want to fly again cause I haven't in a long time and I miss flying in my dreams and thats the real TRUTH). Anyway it was still pretty GROOVEY (You guessed it like Darling says GROOVEY and DADDYO when shes in a super good mood, so its all right with me of course.) So it was groovey cause I was chaseing this butterfly when suddenly it landed on the Most Beautiful Flower I've ever seen like ever, kinda like a humungus ROSE but it kept turning different colors (Like pink, purple, red, green, blue, yellow, orange, even white.) When I stopped to look at every thing I saw YOU Virgen with GIANT RED BUTTERFLY WINGS and you kept opening and closeing your WINGS. And then I heard Jeffs voice saying "Thats the magic" but in one sec I knew that cause I looked like Lobita he wouldn't know it was me, and then I got a real WEIRD feeling like maybe his dad might try to shoot me kinda like he kills Mountain Lions and even Coyotes Jeff said cause they might get his MOOOOO Cows (What a fregado creep!) So the last thing I saw before I woke up was your GIANT RED BUTTERFLY WINGS opening and closeing and when I woke up I didn't open my eyes for a long ass time cause when you do the Dream kinda goes away, and I didn't want the humungus ROSE to go away or your GIANT RED WINGS. I was surprised you have RED WINGS and they were the red-dest color I ever saw in my whole entire vida (Do you change wings or do you always have RED ones, I wonder.) Also I kinda wanted to keep Jeffs goofy voice in my ears like "Thats the magic" cause for some goofy reason it just made me pretty chingaso happy.

Heres the deal cause I know its only been a couple a days in July but if I don't write all this stuff to you I might forget a lot of the creepo de-tails (When I write DETAILS I like that theres TAILS in it kinda like Lobita with her bushy ass tail, so de-tails.) But some OK details too cause I had a lot a fun too of course. So you remember I was going to Jeffs Secret Tree House and I did when he showed me how to find it at 2 o'clock and then he told me to sneak over at 9 o'clock (Cause he knows Psycho Dad would be weirded out if he knows I'm a girl, and I sure don't want Darling to know either thats for sure.) So he told me to HOOT like an Owl 3 times and he'd drop his ROPE LADDER MUY GROOVEY!! So Darling went to S.F. for 2 days so of course it was perfect cause if I sneak off and Darling figures it out that I'm gone, and if I have to tell Darling about Jeff being my FRIEND you know she'd think all this weirdo boy friend stuff and thats all I need, right Virgen? So I pack A TON OF FOOD (Ham sandwiches with cheese, onions and sliced humungus pickles from the Hermit Store, plus 4 peanut butter and jam with sliced banana sandwiches, apples, a WHOLE BAG A COOKYS, chocolate bars and a bunch a bubble gum so we can have a Bubble Gum Contest like who can blow the biggest BUBBLE in el MUNDO, plus 4 icey coca colas which I wrapped in dish towels so they won't bust when I went over some killer pot holes which you can't help doing especially in the PITCH DARK.) Darling has a Army Back Pack cause its a real pukey green color but every thing fits in it so I use it a lot and I can even pack some clothes plus my Swiss Army Knife and Binoculars too, no problem right?

So I put this chingaso Army Back Pack on my chingaso back and I really started to feel like a chingaso Soldier kinda like I was on Patrol or some thing (Especially about Jeffs Psycho Dad cause I don't want him to spot me of course.) Any way it was so HEAVY my shoulders kinda started burning (And I'm not kidding either.) But I couldn't wait to see Old Jeffs face when he sees my Supplys, right Virgen? So I jumped on the bike and tryed to keep the flash light on the trail but I almost fell on my fregado head twice (The FREGADO pot holes!!!)

I turned off the flash light when I saw the lights in Jeffs House and I hid my bike real good, so when I got to Jeffs Tree House I hooted 3 times like a OWL (We even practiced hooting right?) "Move back!" He kinda yelled and its a good thing he did cause if I didn't leap out of the way his Rope Ladder probably woulda KILLED me and I'm not kidding cause this giant ass Rope Ladder Thing comes flying out and lands about 1 inch from my toes, so I climb up but its kinda hard probably cause of the chingaso Army Back Pack being full of all the SUPPLYS and every thing else I brought, but I finally make it like 1/2 dead. Then Jeff pulls the Rope Ladder UP so no one can get in NIFTY (Even Super Nifty). Theres a lantern on and theres a bunch of games like Checkers, Chinese Checkers, Cards, Scrabble, Monopoly—right between 2 sleeping bags COOL!! Then for about 2 secs I realize I'm in a Tree House by myself <u>at night</u> with a B O Y. But then I see Jeffs cut eye where Psycho Dad hit him and I picture his skinny white pencil legs and his boney ass shoulders, and I say to myself "Jeff is just a Human Being Mammal and a skinny one too" (Plus I know IF I HAD TO I could kick his but, right?) When I unpack my Supplys Jeff starts drooling (He has some stuff too but I brought us a FEAST). So we eat the ham sandwiches and drink a icey coca cola and I ask him if his dad hit him or any thing since I last saw him. "Hes drinking but hes not plastered so hes OK I guess, in fact I could tell he was sorry like hes always sorry later, you know?" So I say "What a psycho, so hows your eye, still hurt and all?" And Jeff says "If my Mom were still alive and she saw my eye she'd probably cold cock him with a frying pan cause some times she used to yell that at him like 'I'll cold cock you with a frying pan if you don't watch your step Donald!' " "Your dads name is Donald?" I say starting to crack up just thinking of you know who (Donald Duck—Quack Quack). Then I'm laughing like such a hyena I'm laying there kicking my legs in the fregado air and holding my fregado stomach—finally I do a couple a QUACKS and Jeff gets it and we both almost PUKE our ham sandwiches so we have to stop and just rest for a couple a secs, and its a good thing I peed in some bushes before I got here and then I wonder where I'll pee later on but I don't say any thing of course.

So we ended up playing every game and of course I won in Scrabble EVERY TIME (Cause I guess I know a lot of new words now that Darling keeps saying "Look it up in the Dictionary PLATO!") And I don't tell her I call it the Gringo Dictionary cause of what they say about DREAMS, you know like Dreams are illusion (in fact I even crossed that part out HA!) OK but Jeff won in some games like Checkers and Chinese Checkers and <u>once</u> in Monopoly (Cause you know I started CHEATING and I know its crummy but I HATE TO LOSE so I stold some $500 bills and hid them under the board—I guess what it is is that I HATE BEING POOR Virgen.) And I know Jeffs dads a ass hole but hes not <u>poor</u> like I guess all those COWS make $ with there milk cause they have a ton of them moooooing around every where. Still I PROMISE I won't cheat Jeff in Monopoly next time (But its hard to resist those $500 bills especially when he isn't even looking and you know me Virgen—I like to do the Winner Kids Dance!!)

Finally I had to PEE so bad I thought I'd EXPLODE so I told Jeff I had to go check my bike right? He started to say my bike was safe unless I was worryed about a Coyote rideing it (HA HA) But then he just shut up and threw the Rope Ladder down and climbing down was like flying without a ton of stuff on my back of course. Then Jeffs dad yelled "When you going to turn the damed lantern off boy? What are you doing up there any way?" "Holy shit" I said to myself but I ran way out to where my bike was for real and it was still there (No coyotes had borrowed it HA). And of course I forgot my flash light like a fregado pendeja so I said to myself "Holy fucking shit" (Sorry Virgen but thats the <u>truth</u> right?) For one sec I felt like going over to Old Harrys Palace cause its closer than Darlings Hide Out, but then I kinda knew Jeff was waiting for me to get back so I started singing a Baptist Church song that always reminds me of Mamacita so I could PEE in the bushes like a Perv ("Yo tengo gozo gozo en mi corazon, en mi corazon, en mi corazon" like over and over, which means "I have a joy joy in my heart" cause of Baby Jesus your kid who I really like a lot, Virgen.) Any way usually in Sunday School we used to really yell this song with lots of GOZO but being that I was trying to hide in the Pervy Bushes to PEE I was singing it just so you could hear it, and finally I PEED like what a fregado GOZO that was (I think I peed a CREEK.)

By this time I had my Night Eyes so I could pretty much see where I was going and I could see Jeffs Rope Ladder still hanging there waiting for me, but his lantern was out cause of Psycho Dad and then I had a loca idea like what if Psycho Dad was waiting for me to come back (Just like Psycho Jake—my step step step ex father would probably do.) So I switched my Night Eyes to my Witch Power Eyes and I found a branch the size of a base ball BAT and I didn't go right to the Rope Ladder, and I hoped Jeff wouldn't yell "Hey Luna, you there?" But every thing was super quiet and all I could hear was the crickets makeing a racket and once in a while some moooos then a coyote or maybe a dog, so any way I turned in to LA LOCA and scrunched down kinda invisible. I figured if Psycho Dad was waiting for me to climb the Rope Ladder I'd fool him, so I snuck all the way up to where Jeffs House is (Like an Indian does cause I didn't make <u>one noise</u>.) I scouted around so sneakey I was smileing to myself (I couldn't help it Virgen cause thats how I get when I turn in to La Loca.) So I scouted to the window with the light on like a TV light and there was Jeffs dad sitting in his UNDER WEAR drinking some Hooch from a bottle, but I didn't see his face real good just his sad ass skinny ass legs (Well at least I didn't see him on the chingaso toilet right?) Darling showed me where the FUSES are so when shes gone I can put a new one in just in case the lights go out, so La Loca scouts around till she finds the old fuse box and then I loosen some till all the lights go OFF and the TV too of course, and then I hear a really loud "GOD DAM IT TO

HELL" and some thing smashing in the house. So I can just picture Psycho Dad comeing out in his UNDER WEAR so La Loca runs for the Rope Ladder the circle way so he can't see me, and I FLY UP the Rope Ladder and when Jeff sees me he looks kinda POed. "So did you go back to your house or some thing?" And then I told him what I did to the fuse box (Not about peeing like a Perv.) But I didn't tell him about La Loca of course cause thats my bees wax (And one of my Secret Weapons like the Witch Power Eyes which only you really know about, Virgen.) Some times I wonder if I'll ever be able to tell any one about La Loca cause when I'm her I'm not scared of NOTHING (And thats the TRUTH). In fact scarey stuff (Even really scarey stuff) It kinda cracks me up and makes weird PLANS pop in to my brain (Like the fuse box.) Any way Jeff was in <u>disbelief</u> but I told him I (LUNA) really and truely had done it, so we were kinda laying there with our heads pokeing out the door listening and we heard his dad swearing and stuff, and I said "I hope he steps in Coyote Ca Ca." Then Jeff said "I hope he steps in Mountain Lion Doody." And I have <u>never</u> in my whole vida heard that word DOODY so I almost fell out of the Tree House. And we started to say all the DOODY Psycho Dad could step in like Racoon Doody, Deer Doody and even Mouse Doody but we had to crack up REAL QUIET and I was glad I peed of course. And then I wondered why Jeff didn't pee (Like maybe he just puts his p e n i s in to one of the holes in the wall and like Darling says some times PRESTO). And of course I really want to know how hes peeing but even La Loca says FORGET IT PENDEJA!)

Any way Jeffs dad really bumped in to some thing and started really swearing cause I think he probably crippled himself cause we could see him limping around (Boy did that make me ECSTATIC). But he finally fixed the fuses and he even limped close to the Tree House for a sec but me and Jeff were QUIET like invisible so he just limped back to the house (And I thought to myself—I hope he cut himself and hes bleeding too like Tough Shitskey, Darling says that too and she cracks up and says "Thats Russian for Tough Shit.") So Jeff says "Do you think hes really hurt?" and he sounds kinda worryed. And I just say "Tough Shitskey like didn't he cut your eye, Jeff?" Jeff started cracking up "Where'd you hear that?" "Its Russian for Tough Shit." Then he started imitating Elvis The Pelvis cause he knows I HATE HIM and all those pendeja girls who go around screaming "ELVIS THE PELVIS, I LOVE YOU! ! ! !" So Jeff started singing "You ain't nothin but a hound dog" and "Love me tender love me true" but he really LOVES to sing the Hound Dog Song (Till I threatened to throw him out of the Tree House even though I was cracking up.) We finally got in the sleeping bags which were WARM and he said "Thank you very much" a couple a times like E.T.P. till I punched him but not that hard (On purpose.) "Do you have to get up at dawn to milk the moooo cows cause like this guy told me thats what they did in Denmark." "We used to all the time but my dad has a couple a guys that do it now, but he checks up on them regular, any way thats what he says, so my dad sleeps in till 8 or so or if hes getting up early its dawn to check stuff."

So we promised to stay up till DAWN and then we ate most of the cookys and stuff but we decided to save the Bubble Gum Contest for later like when we can see every thing. I asked him "Whats the best thing you can remember about your mom?" And he said "She used to read me a story every night ever since I was really little and she used to tell me storys about her being a kid like she grew up in New Jersey and her parents were divorced so her mom raised her and her sister by herself. She used to always say Bolinas is Paradise and that its MAGIC here and all. She used to rub my back at night too till I went to sleep so when she died I could barely sleep any more, in fact I thought maybe I was turning in to a Zombie or some thing cause I could barely even sleep." (This is pretty much what he said like I might a forgotten a sentence or 2 right?) So I was laying there in my sleeping bag thinking how Mamacita and me used to rub each others backs some times like I used to rub hers with alkohol cause she liked that but not me cause it kinda STINKS. So I told Jeff about all that and how I used to read her the Bible in Spanish some times like her favorite parts, and how she told me storys about Mexico and I told him this one—"Mamacitas mom was a preacher and a healer kinda like a doctor is here down in Mexico, and she was teaching Mamacita all about how to heal people with plants and stuff while her brothers went to school" (You know The Sour Puss Judge and The Laugher Teacher.) "But her brothers taught her how to read and do math when they came back home at night she said. But any way one time her mom sent her to the river to get some special plants at sun set cause she said you had to pick them at sun set so they'd work really good." (I didn't tell Jeff how she used to talk to plants when she'd pick them kinda like they were old friends cause of course he might think shes a weirdo, right?) But I kinda peeked at Jeffs face to see if he was feeling like cracking up but he was just laying there listening. So I said "Did you ever hear about La Yorona?" "La who?" Jeff said. "OK La Yorona is a Magical Lady but shes pretty scarey too cause she either kidnaps kids and you never ever see them again cause she just keeps them or if your really really LUCKY she might give you a GIFT" I said. "So what happened?" Jeff said and I could tell he really wanted to know. "Mamacita said she'd heard about La Yorona like about how she might be super ugly or super beautiful, so when she was picking the plants for her mom at sun set this SUPER BEAUTIFUL lady in the most beautiful black lacey shawl she ever saw asked her if she was La Claras daughter (Thats what they called Mamacitas mom cause she could tell what was wrong with some one just by looking at them—Can you do that, Virgen—I bet you can.) She wasn't through picking the plants for her mom La Clara but she knew she might have to run for her life any way cause of course she didn't want to be kidnapped, but she also didn't run cause La Yorona knew her moms name and then suddenly as La Yorona was getting closer she just disappeared in a super bright light Mamacita said, and right on the ground was the beautiful black lacey shawl that Mamacita wore only in the house and I was the only one she ever told her secret to so I guess your the 2nd person to know all this stuff." "Thats a pretty cool story but I think I'd a run for it." "Yeah me too" I said but I didn't tell him about the Bad Thing like when the guy kidnapped me when I was 7 temporaryly and how I heard La Yorona CRYING (And I'm NOT kidding.) And how maybe that was her GIFT to me like how I got away and SURVIVED right Virgen? Also my new words are—SURVIVOR, COMPASSION, REVENGE, KARMA (Like Darling calls me The Survivor some times when shes not calling me Plato or The Bottomless Pit cause I eat so much, and of course she cracks up cause I'm skinny like a bone she says.) Any way I've been thinking about KARMA cause Darling says KARMA is any thing you do (And thats the good stuff or the bad stuff you do.) It comes back to you sooner or later or like she says in this life or the next WAMMMO! !

I could tell Jeff was trying really hard to stay awake but he said "Whats the best thing you can remember about your real mom named Carmen?" Which really SURPRISED me and I didn't even know what to say till kinda like a movie I saw her playing the piano all dressed up before she went to her secretary job and I was probably 6 or 7 and she had a piano (Before they took it back cause she couldn't pay for it—thats what she told me later.) She used to play super early in the morning like I mean really early in the morning, and she used to play some classical music that kinda sounded like bells (Which I found out later her favorite piano song was Moonlight Sonata which was my favorite one too kinda like my name, right?) Luna Luz Sonata—so I always thought she was playing it kinda for me and I wish some times I could play the piano like maybe Carmen coulda taught me, right Virgen? Any way I thought she was probably the most beautiful mom in the whole wide MUNDO cause she was all dressed up wearing lip stick and LOTS of perfume right? So I told Jeff that part and he said a weirdo thing—Yeah I can just see your mom all dressed up playing the piano with the Magic Shawl from La Yorona on her and all." And thats the last thing I can remember thinking of (Carmen wearing Mamacitas favorite black lacey shawl from La Yorona.) And it was WEIRD cause it really made me happy and the next thing I opened my eyes and the Tree House was sunny and I also saw that Jeff was sleeping with his mouth WIDE OPEN and for a 1/2 sec I really wanted to put some thing weird in it, but I passed out again.

So Jeff made sure his dad was gone before I climbed down the Rope Ladder and I told him how I almost put some thing weird in his mouth cause he sleeps with it wide open like a GUPPY and for one sec he looked kinda POed till I said "Just kidding", but I guess I'm not cause I really do want to do it HA! ! Then I turned around and yelled "You ain't nothin but a Hound

Dog, Jeff!!!" And he yelled back "Thank you very much" like Elvis The Pelvis and then he started singing the Hound Dog Song and I was GONE. So after I made some breakfast at me and Darlings Hide Out I took off for The Secret Beach but first I visited Old Harry and he was drinking the Hooch, so I just took Cinamon (Cause he could barely stand up like thats how Hooched Up he was.) But Old Harry The Hermit cracked me up cause he kept saying stuff like "Miss Moon yer a god dam GENIUS and don ya ferget it, ya could be the next Shakespere and don ya ferget it! ! !" Now I'm SHAKESPERE (He was a writer with a TON of thees and thous so don't ask me, like Darling kinda made me watch HAMLET with her and I got so bored I fell asleep cause every one seemed real excited but I couldn't tell what they were saying—Do you know Shakespere, Virgen?)

Any way I wrote this poem with the new words and I ended up reading it to Jeff later on when I spent the 2nd night in the Tree House (After Darling calls at 6 pm I take off.) Of course I'll tell you about the exciteing 2nd night in a minute but first heres the poem (Also when I took Cinamon back to Harrys Palace I covered Old Harrys boney ass hoochy self up cause I found him SNOREING chingaso loud on the kitchen floor, and I hate to say it but he really STUNK but I put some blankets on him while holding my breath cause the floor was an ice cube.

YOU AINT NOTHIN BUT A HOUND DOG, JEFF!!!!

This friend of mine
whos a boy is like
me, cause he lost
his mom (She died.)

And I lost my real
mom (She died.)
And now no one loves
us in the old way

like the Best In The Whole Wide Mundo
way, so I think were <u>SURVIVORS</u>
me and Jeff. And I like the way
we can tell each other secrets and

storys and stuff we really think about,
and so no one else knows,
and we know what it feels like to be
each other COMPASSION (Darling says.)

So last night we had some REVENGE
when I twisted off the fuses and his dad
got kinda crippled and we cracked up on
Doody Jokes while his dad limped around.

(I kinda like REVENGE so is that bad
or what?) I think what I really did was
I gave Psycho Dad some KARMA—HA!
And I think Jeff sings better than

Elvis The Pelvis (Just kidding! ! !)
What I really like is when Jeff says
"Thats the magic."
And I'm not kidding either.

So after I packed the pukey green Army Back Pack with EVERY THING I snuck up to the Tree House and climbed up the Rope Ladder, and then we had the Bubble Gum Contest (Which I almost won every time but I got gum in my fregado hair when they popped some times cause I was chewing about 20 PIECES of gum, believe it or snot! ! !) So my jaw got sore from chewing and so did his too, so then we had a long ass game of Monopoly (And I only cheated 2 times and you know thats real good for me, Virgen.) And then of course I had to PEE cause I ate a ton of food plus 2 sodys, so down I go super sneaky like La Loca but tonight I don't feel like revenge (Since I got Jeffs dad last night, right?) So after I make myself pee in the pervy bushes (But tonight I don't have to sing The Gozo En Mi Corazon Song) Any way I still sneak up to Jeffs House to make sure Psycho Dads not lurking out here but I don't see him in the rooms with the lights on, so I figure maybe hes in the bath room and I sure don't want to see that of course.

Then I hear a loud ass voice in the Tree House and then some yelling, and when I run over the Rope Ladders down. Then I hear "YOU'LL DO AS I SAY YOU LITTLE SHIT!" And its a really weird mans voice kinda like hes lost his fucking noodle and he keeps saying it, and then I hear Jeff kinda yell "LEAVE ME ALONE JUST LEAVE ME ALONE!" So I grab a giant ass stick thats laying by the ladder and then La Loca Rides Again cause I fly up the ladder and for 1/2 a sec I feel like yelling (Like I used to some times in S.F. with Jody) "NEVER FEAR LUNAS HERE!" But of course I don't and before his Psycho Hoochy Dad can turn around I CLOBBER HIM—KA THUNK! ! ! ! "Is he dead?" Jeff says over and over. I bend down to check but not too close cause I could really heave ho hes so PUKEY but any way hes breatheing through his hairy nostrils so I didn't kill him, Virgen. So I told Jeff "Hes still alive and hes sure breatheing so don't worry, so did he hit you, Jeff?" "He was pushing me around so he was sure going to, he was going to hit me for sure." I just looked at Jeff cause nothing was popping in to my brain plus his dad kept laying there 1/2 dead. Then Jeff said "The old bastard" and Jeff started to CRY so I said to grab his stuff and I grabbed my stuff and we RAN FOR OUR LIVES to Darlings Hide Out. So we slept inside in the front room with the curtains closed and I checked all the doors and windows about 1 ZILLION times in case Psycho Dad figures out where we are, but I really didn't think he could cause he doesn't know me but just in case of course. Finally we got in our sleeping bags around 3 am and I could tell Jeff was kinda embarassed about crying, so any way I asked him if he was POed at me for clobbering his dad and I told him about my ex ex step step father (Jake) And how I had to clobber him twice but I didn't tell him how I clobbered him the 2nd time (With a giant ass MARBLE ASH TRAY which knocked him out, in fact I even thought I'd KILLED him for sure and when I saw he was still alive I was really SORRY and thats the truth, Virgen and I did it cause IT was trying to kill Carmen by strangleing her to death.) So I didn't tell Jeff about that time like maybe he'll think I'm a La Loca in a creepy way (Not the hero way.) So I just told Jeff about knocking out ITS tooth and Jeff said "You ever cry about it?" "In secret I guess" and then I thought about the time I couldn't stop crying with Cinamon and all those rainbows I saw on her horsey fake diamond necklace, remember? "I wish I could clobber him" Jeff said. "Its pretty hard to do it if you can't sneak up, thats for sure plus hes all over you like a giant ass gorilla" I said (And I still felt pretty MAD). Then I said "Plus if you go back after I clobbered him hes probably going to really kick your but, right?" And Jeff said "Yeah thats the truth."

So we decided that Jeff would wait for Darling to show up and that maybe she could help or think of some thing to do to save Jeffs VIDA. Then I read him the poem I wrote kinda for him and then at the end when I said "Thats the magic" the way Jeff does (I couldn't help it and thats the TRUTH) I started to CRY I felt so fregado lousy for him like whats he going to do now, right? Then he started singing "You ain't nothin but a Hound Dog" which made me kinda laugh like La Loca. Then some MUY LOCA ideas popped in to my brain—"Could you live with your moms sister? Where does she live? Do you like her? Do you think she'd come and get you? Do you have her phone number?" Jeff started really smileing and finally he said "That's the magic, Luna."

Then he told me about his moms sister whos named Laurie and how she lives in OREGON (I looked it up on a map and its pretty far away.) And she teaches 8th grade and she has 2 kids and that he really likes her and her husband whos his Uncle Louie (I don't tell Jeff about my Tio The Cheap Skate, plus I'm really glad he likes these guys.) In fact he wanted to live with his Tia when his mom died but his dad wouldn't let him, and his Tia Laurie even asked and when she calls he never ever tells her about Psycho Dad being an ass hole. Finally when its dawn we pass out and Jeff asked me if he could touch my hair so I said OK. Then he kinda petted my mane over and over real soft and nice, and I thought about Cinamon like when I brush her mane and she kinda shakes her horsey fur cause she really likes it (What a Mammal!) So Jeff was petting my mane and it was so QUIET it felt like me and him were the ONLY MAMMALS in the whole mundo (You know what I mean, Virgen.) So I told Jeff about what Darling told Danny The Dane about not being used to hanging around some weirdo Tough Cooky Pokahantus Annie Oakly Plato Shakespere Miss Moon La Loca 12 year old KID—ME every single day of her fregado vida, and I told him how I don't blame her or any thing cause she never had kids and it was really pretty nice of her to bring me here to live (And of course I didn't tell Jeff about The Blood Sucker cause its too DISGUSTING like Carmen and Darling FIGHTING over IT and now I wonder what Danny The Dane would think, right?) So I told Jeff how I'm going to make a Contract for Darling and me to sign cause I DO NOT want to go back to Pervy S.F. and live in Dead Body Places with zero food or see The Cheap Skate if I can really help it (But you know I kinda miss Tia and Old Pablito like when I close my eyes I can see him doing The Skinny Kids Dance with his legs and arms flying around in these goofy circles and of course hes cracking up, and I wonder if Jake Junior is talking yet, right?)

So I told Jeff if me and Darling signed the Contract and she PROMISED moooo moooo me to keep me till I'm at least maybe 17 and I PROMISE mooooo moooooo her to stay out of her hair most of the time and do all my chores and get good grades when I go to the creepo school here in BOLINAS and wear the Bo Peep dresses when we go out to dinner and keep writeing storys and poems that crack her up—Then we'd have a DEAL and we could both sign it. Jeff was petting my mane when I was telling him all these moooo plans and he said "Why don't we write the Contract tomorrow so I can help you do it, OK?" And I could really tell he was kinda sad for me like I don't have a real family, right Virgen? And he kept petting my mane over and over and then I could tell he wanted to do some thing for me to HELP so if I said "No thats OK" I'd really hurt his feelings cause he was trying to help me out with stuff. So I said "OK." And then I realized that if Jeff goes to live with his Tia in Oregon he won't be HERE any more and I'll be a hermit again and have to go to the creepo Bolinas School with a bunch of other hermit kids. But mostly I was so fregado happy that my mane was being petted and that Jeff really was my friend and that tomorrow we'd write the Contract together, and so I just passed out and the last thing I thought was this—Con Amor, La Loca The Mammal (And I guess I was talking to you and probably to Jeff too cause he was petting my mane so nice and soft like Mamacita used to some times when I was little.)

And this is what I dreamed—Did I tell you Jeff has kinda blond hair and dark blue eyes kinda like my best friend Jody in

S.F. whos a Tomboy only her eyes are more like sunny sky blue. So I dreamed I'm my usual dark fured Lobita self, but then theres a blond fured Lobit<u>o</u> and we're raceing and kinda barking like Coyotes till we get to the Sun Set Place where I met Jeff, remember? (When he scared the shit out of me and I almost fell off the cliff and I was pretty POed at first, remember?) So me and the blond Lobito are raceing as fast as we can and we're kinda barking and talking Wolf Talk and its pretty nifty haveing a Lobito Buddy, and its night time and every thing really smells super good. So we get to the Sun Set Place and kinda jump all over each other and I can feel his blond fur and I'm just HAPPY. Finally we calm down and then we see a GOLDEN FULL MOON (I've seen those with Cinamon and Darling too.) Then both of us start to sing like real loud and long HOWLS but I really think its the most beautiful singing en todo el mundo cause we're howling <u>together</u>, and we just keep on singing cause now we can't stop its so much fun, right? Then I see you Virgen right on the GOLDEN FULL MOON with your GIANT RED BUTTERFLY WINGS and I can tell your pretty happy cause we're singing, and then your GIANT RED BUTTERFLY WINGS turn in to 2 GIANT WHITE STARS and I wonder if Jeff can see you but before I can ask him I wake up (Fregado!) And Jeffs still sleeping with his mouth WIDE OPEN like a guppy but I really and truely don't feel like putting any thing weird in it (! ! ! !) So I pass out again and I wonder if I ever sleep with my mouth wide open cause I sure hope not like when I think of all the times I stayed at Tias House in the Projects and how the cock roaches come swarming out when the lights go out PUUUUUUKE.

Later when I made us some scrambled eggs and stuff I told Jeff about the Lobita Dream and I could tell he thought it was pretty neat (Jeff says that some times NEAT so thats what he said—"Thats a neat dream".) But I didn't tell him about you, but I really wish I asked him in the dream if he could see you too, right? Then Jeff told me he dreamed being at his Tia Lauries House and that he was so <u>ecstatic</u> (Jeff likes that word.) So he was so ecstatic in the dream he said he started singing (You guessed it) "You ain't nothin but a you know what". And then I told him it was pretty cool that we both had kinda singing

HOWLING dreams and I also told him about how dreams come true especially if you remember them (Like Mamacita taught me.) So I said "It probably means your going to live with your Aunt Laurie, so are you happy about it?" And he said "I was pretty ecstatic in the dream thats for sure and I sure can't stay with Doody Dad any more." Then we cracked up. "But it means I'll move away from Bolinas and I guess we won't be able to be friends you know like this." And Jeffs eyes got REAL PATHETIC so I said "Yeah but if you go back to Doody Dad he'll probably try to kill you and you won't be my friend that way either." Jeff kinda laughed and said "Yep".

So we wrote up my Contract for me and Darling to sign and we did it about 20 times till we finally got it to look right—So here it is—

I LUNA LUZ VILLALOBOS, also known by Darling Van Der Veer as PLATO here by PROMISE—

To not lie, cheat or steal
and to do all my chores and responsibilitys
(Like doing the dishes, mopping and waxing the floors and vacuming, washing the windows, feeding 2 Cats and putting the salt lick out for the Deers and feeding the Birds seeds, plus any thing else Darling needs for me to do.)
And to go to school and get PERFECT GRADES
And to not be a PEST (And if I am just
let me know, OK?)
And to wear dresses once in a while
and to write better and better storys
(And poems too.)
And to pick wild flowers when ever you
tell me, and to be home right on time
(Especially now that I have the Elvis
The Pelvis Watch.)
So I'm leaving some space for any thing
you can think of, OK?

So you have to PROMISE me to keep me
kinda like your real kid till I'm at least

17 or maybe even 18 years old.
Then you can throw me out if you
really want to, OK?
So I Darling Van Der Veer
PROMISE to keep this Mammal
named LUNA LUZ VILLALOBOS
(PLATO) In my Hide Out
in BOLINAS till shes at least
17 or maybe even 18.

Then I made a space for her to sign and for me to sign, plus a space for the date when we do it. Jeff is a really good drawer so he drew some stuff on the Contract like flowers, suns, moons, stars and even some Lobos, and he even drew a Fairy (Thats what he called it like a girl with Star Wings.) And I made him draw a lemon tree with a couple a lemons on it but of course I don't tell him about Darlings Lemon Nipple Joke, so I just told him me and Darling planted it together and he said "Neat." So by the time we finished the Contract it was about 2 o clock and Darling still wasn't back but that was OK cause some times she gets back kinda late, but theres still a ton of food in the frig so of course I won't starve or any thing, plus Jeffs here and I'm starting to kinda feel like hes my brother even better than a friend, but I don't tell him of course. When I explained to him about the Mammal Stuff he cracked up so maybe I'll show him The Mammals In May Story later. Any way Jeff was still kinda worrying about Psycho Dad (if he was really still alive after I clobbered his but.) So Jeff called and we put a towel around the mouth part and when he answered the phone Jeff hung up. "How does he sound?" I asked. "Really really POed in fact he said—Jeff is that you? Creeepeee!" Then Jeff called his Tia around 5 o clock when I was makeing some hamburgers and Jeff peeled a bunch of potatoes for French Frys so they were cooking and I could hear Jeff telling her EVERY THING and it took a long ass time (So its a good thing he called COLLECT.) But I pretended like I wasn't really noticeing cause he cryed a little but not much, so when he finally hung up he said "Aunt Laurie was so POed you wouldn't believe it Luna, like she was calling dad names and she never does stuff like that. So I gave her this phone number and how to get here and she told me to stay here till she can get down which will probably be this week end, so shes going to call Darling later and talk to her about me staying till she gets here, and she said if dad trys to bring me back shes takeing him to Court and all, boy was she POed." So I said "Cool—Do you want Cheese Burgers?" And he said "Yeah I'm starveicated." And we cracked up. So Jeff turned the French Frys and I finished cooking the Cheese Burgers and it really felt like we were better than friends kinda like a brother and a sister or like the Dream (The dark fured Lobita and the blond fured Lobito makeing a racket singing and HOWLING at the Sun Set Place.) And the golden full moon and you Virgen with the GIANT RED BUTTERFLY WINGS that turned in to 2 WHITE STARS (And now I wonder—if Jeff really did see you in the Dream.) You know cause of the drawings on the Contract and the Star Wing Fairy, right Virgen? Also to tell the TRUTH some times I wonder what it would be like (To kiss a boy) like Jeff maybe ON THE LIPS and I wonder if its like one Lobita giveing the other Lobito a LICK. I guess the truth is I feel like giveing Jeff a lick some times kinda like pounceing on him and licking his face. Cause when I think of KISSING Jeff ON THE LIPS I start to think about my eye balls and then I think about his eye balls (Kinda like if you kiss some one on the LIPS you probably have to look at there chingaso eye balls, right Virgen?) Any way I guess I'd rather lick him. Con Amor, La Loca.

The Contract With Flowers, Moons, Suns And
A Fairy With Star Wings—Also an Elvis The Pelvis Movie
And Jeff My BEST FRIEND and Lobito Amigo Is Gone
In August To O R E G O N (And I even miss his skinny
white pencil legs, and I even miss him singing like
E.T.P. and I really miss his horse named
MIDNIGHT) Remember when Jeff used to say
"That's the magic!" And no else ever says that.
And Amazons and 1/2 Amazons F R E G A D O!!!!

Dear La Virgen,

I guess you know I couldn't write you till after Jeffs Tia came for him and so after her and Darling talked for about 10 hours they decided she'd come down the next week end so that gave me and Jeff about 9 days to go, but Darling said we couldn't go to my favorite swimming place or ride our bikes cause of Psycho Dad. Even though Jeffs Tia called him up and he says its OK for her to take Jeff for a while he said, but Darling doesn't trust him probably especially since I KATHUN-KED him (Like Darling says "I bet he'd like to wrap his fingers around your scrawny neck, kid.") Then she kinda squints (Thats a Q not a K kinda like psycho, like you don't say "P syko" cause the P is silent and it just sneaks in there, but they don't say WHY in the Gringo Dictionary of course and you just have to remember all this stuff, Virgen.) Also, I'm SORRY about saying FREGADO about the Amazon Dream you gave me, but I still feel pretty creepy about the 1/2 part (Like almost creepyer than the Bo Peep Dresses, believe it or not, so any way we'll talk about the Dream later, OK?) So Darling squints her Cat Eyes at me and says "Where'd you learn to do that any way?" And I say "2 guesses." And she says "Saveing Carmens ass I bet." Then she tells me a story about the only time in her whole vida she ever really clobbered some one. She said she was in a bar with her friends when some drunk guy punched one of her friends and I said "Was it Old Jergens?" Cause I had to know of course but it wasn't Jergens, so any way this friend fell like a sack of potatoes (Thats what Darling said.) And this drunk guy starts kicking him so Darling clobbered him over the head with a BEER BOTTLE and then the bar tender grabbed the drunk guy so Darling could drag her beat up amigo and run for it. It sounds like a Cow Boy Movie doesn't it, Virgen? I guess Darling kinda liked ka thunking that guy cause she even got a sody bottle to show me exactly how she did it and then I told her about Psycho Jake my ex ex ex ex step father and how I just about murdered him with the chingaso marble ash tray (His favorite one HA!) Then she said this— "There used to be a whole TRIBE of women who lived in a really beeeuuutiiiful (Darling says beautiful like this some times so you know) beeeeuuuutiiiiful place some where in AFRICA. They were called AMAZONS and they were as brave and as good a fighter as any man any where, and they didn't take any shit or shineola (Darling says that too) From any one any where. So I think your an AMAZON kid." And then she told me how the Amazons cut off their right BREAST (if they were right handed and their left BREAST if they were left handed, right?) So they could shoot their arrows better cause the bow had to be where the boob was, and then I started thinking about how that would be to CUT OFF YOUR BOOB (What do you think, Virgen, would you do it?) You know cause here I am DREADING my (Lemon Nipple) BREASTS or getting big boobs and then Darling tells me about these Amazons plus I guess these Amazons are African ladys like my friends in S.F. from the Salvation Army Club who were on my Basketball Team who were the <u>toughest</u>

black girls in the Club or at school, and they could even kick the boys buts. So when we had the Camp Outs at the Club and we played pool and watched super corney movies like Laurel and Hardy and The Three Stooges, and also played some basketball of course, any way the boys NEVER messed with these girls and now I really realize thats because there Amazons (But they didn't cut off their breast, but I bet thats where their family comes from COOL!!!!) They used to say stuff to any guy who was even thinking of messing with them "What you lookin at, boy, you got a problem wich yer eye balls or what and I can take care a that for ya with my FIST!" And now that I'm writing this I really realize how much I kinda miss those Amazon girls (And I wonder what Jeff would think if he met them, and what he'd think about the Salvation Army Club in the Mission, right Virgen?) Any way you know me cause I'll have to really REALLY think about all this Amazon stuff and cutting off your boob to be better at fighting weirdos.

So I gave Darling the Contract Jeff and me figured out together and she really liked Jeffs pictures, and she read it a couple of times kinda SLOW AND SERIOUS. Then she said she was going to put it away till Danny The Dane gets back in a couple of weeks (Cause she said they'd have to sign it together of course and I didn't think of that.) So shes saveing it for D.T.D. but she told me its a really good Contract and it made a lot of sense (Thats what she said.) And she told me this "Don't worry about it Plato cause it'll all work out." And then she gave me a Big Boob Hug which was kinda embarassing cause Jeff was there but it didn't bother him probably cause his Mom hugged him a lot he said (He also told me his Mom died of BREAST CANCER and that one of her breasts had to be CUT OFF!!!!) So I didn't tell him about the Amazons cause it might just make him creepo sad (You know how they just chop them off with their SWORDS!!!!) But maybe Jeffs Mom WAS AN AMAZON and I wonder if I should tell him some time (Should I tell him, Virgen?) Any way I liked how Darling told me not to worry about stuff and how shes saveing the Contract to show D.T.D. and maybe you could give Darling and D.T.D. a Dream telling them what a really GOOD IDEA it is to KEEP ME, OK Virgen?

So me and Jeff probably played Scrabble, Monopoly, Checkers, Fish, and War, even Poker about 1 Trillion times cause we couldn't leave Darlings Hide Out like the only place we could go is the rocky ass beach down the path, but theres too many killer rocks in the Ocean to swim so we just skimmed a ton of flat rocks and had contests doing that (And of course I WON the most skips on record cause we kept a record in my note book.) Any way guess what happened while me and Jeff were playing our 1 millionth game of Scrabble—we were wrestling (I HATE silent letters like wrestling.) Like almost a real fight and I pinned Jeff down and I could tell he was kinda POed cause his face was RED HA!!!! And I LICKED HIM right on his eye ball cause I was really aiming for his cheek but the pendejo moved. "Your turn!" He started yelling that and he tried his hardest to lick me but the truth is hes just not strong enough to pin me down so finally (Believe it or snot, Virgen!!) I let him lick me and it was SUPER WEIRD. He ended up licking me on the fore head and I ended up being kinda POed so I punched him and told him to keep his tongue (Silent sneaky G) to himself. Then just as Darling yells "Chows on now!" Jeff starts to sing "Love me tender love me true" like in the Elvis The Pelvis Movie Darling took us to see in S.F. and we also went to the Zoo (I used to go to the Zoo with Jody some times on our bikes and some times by jumping on the trolley and flying through the long ass I mean DARK DEATH DEFYING TUNNEL and I mean flying through there like Amazons!!) So it was fun and kinda weird going to S.F. with Jeff over the Sewerside Bridge and we made a bunch of Sewerside Jokes then Darling said "I don't know how women have 2 or 3 kids cause I'd kill myself for sure." She sounded like she kinda meant it so we tryed to talk more quiet and Jeff told me his whole family went to the Zoo in S.F. one time only so I didn't tell him this was probably my 20th time cause I don't want to be a creepo Show Off, and to tell the truth, Virgen I was counting Pervs the whole time (Cause I can tell just by looking at a guy if hes a Perv like I'm a PRO). So on the ride to S.F. and at the Zoo where I counted the most Pervs for the whole day and then the movie and then the fancy Gringo Restaurant where Darling took me before—The Grand Total For Pervs in S.F. for one day came to 128 PERVS.

Any way Darling told me and Jeff to meet her back at this hot dog stand in one hour so we took off running all over the place like 2 Psychos kinda yelling and stuff (And for 1/2 a sec I thought about my Lobita Dream where me and Jeff HOWL and goof around, right?) Then suddenly as we were standing there stareing at all these Monkeys in a place the Zoo Guys call Monkey Island (Super sneaky silent S) I really realize how all these Monkeys are Mammals of course and if you stand there stareing at them long enough you can start figureing out whos in what family like whos the kids and the moms and stuff like tias, primos, abuelitas, abuelitos, and then I see this skinny little Monkey start to make a RACKET and I swear Virgen, he started doing the Happy Skinny Kids Dance and of course I thought of my Primo Pablito, and that if he were here I'd buy him 4 hot dogs, 2 pop corns, 2 sodys and a candy apple and I know he'd eat the whole fregado thing and do the Happy Skinny Kids Dance too. I guess I miss him but not enough to LIVE in Pervy S.F.

So any way I told Jeff about the Mammal stuff and how its kinda weird how the Monkeys are all locked up like in a PRISON and we get to come and just stare at them like a bunch of chingaso creeps and Jeff said "You know I was kinda thinking the same stuff and when you really think about it every one here is a Mammal and I sure wouldn't be too ecstatic to be a Lion Mammal and have a bunch of Human Mammals watching me eat and do my doodys." So we tryed to crack up but the truth is we were both kinda DEPRESSED. So when this rich looking White Lady with her 2 Perfect Kids next to us said "These Lions really smell. Lets go children," I said "I bet the Lions think you stink but they can't go any where." Jeff looked SHOCKED or some thing and then the White Lady said "Didn't any one teach you manners Young Lady?" And then I said "Besa my nalgas!!" HA!! HA!!! And I took off running with Jeff right behind me saying "What did you say, what did you say, Luna?" Finally I stopped and we were in front of a beautiful pathetic TIGER who kept marching back and forth in her cage kinda like to her DOOM and I really think it was a Girl Tiger and then I wondered what it would be like to be in a CAGE and have all the Pervs in the whole mundo come up any time they felt like it and just GAWK (That means stare while your probably even drooling.) And also have all these Rich People stand there and say you STINK cause your in a CAGE where you have to eat, sleep and doody, so instead of Zoo they should have this sign up MAMMAL PRISON—I Luna The Human Mammal promise to never ever come here again MOOOOOO. So I tell Jeff "I said Kiss my but!" Then I teach him how to say it (And some other stuff.) "Thats not bad for a Gringo" I say. "Thank you very much" he says like E.T.P. and I punch him. Then we end up in a really STINKY place where they keep all these birds prisoner and there pretty and all but you can tell there MISERABLE hopping around instead of FLYING. So we get the fregado out a there and find Darling whos drinking coffee and talking to some guy who looks a little pervy to me, and I hope the White Lady I said "Besa my nalgas" to doesn't suddenly come by with her 2 Perfect Kids like I wonder what Darling would do. I really do like maybe I'd have to put it in the Contract that I wouldn't embarass her in Public, right Virgen? So any way Darling writes some thing down and her and the Pervy Guy (#86) really smile and she says "I'll get in touch." (And I wonder what Danny The Dane would say like does he know she likes all these Pervs and I sure don't even want to think about The Blood Sucker, right?)

Any way I was just glad to get out of Mammal Prison and then we went to see Elvis The Pelvis in the movie where he sings "Love me tender love me true" and all these girls are SCREAMING when E.T.P. is just a dot way out in some fields like I really couldn't tell it was him but they sure could, and for 2 secs I thought I was going DEAF cause they were screaming so chingaso LOUD and Darling says to me "If you want to scream go on a head" and I just rolled my eyes kinda like I had to heave ho (And hoped I wouldn't go deaf, right?) It was a dumb (Silent sneaky B) dumb story but I was glad Jeff was sitting next to me, and then he did a Blurty Bird so sneaky I didn't notice at first cause he was holding my baby finger (And I let him so DO NOT TELL God, OK?) Darling was kinda sad that E.T.P. died at the end but I didn't make any jokes about how he was still singing even after he was DEAD—REINCARNATED (Cause of course its really nice of Darling to bring me and Jeff to Pervy S.F. kinda like a Going Away Party she said.)

MUCHOS CHINGASOS AND FREGADOS cause thats the TRUTH cause that Saturday his Tia Laurie came to get him and she kinda looked like the rich White Lady I said "Besa my nalgas" to but she was a lot nicer of course like she thanked Darling for keeping Jeff about 1 Zillion times and she even tryed to give Darling some $ but Darling said "Jeff was a pleasure so its not necessary" in her White Ladys Voice, and of course Darling didn't say to Jeffs Tia that she kept her GUN LOADED all the time just in case Psycho Dad tryed to attack us. Plus I could tell that Jeffs Tia was kinda worryed about P.D. showing up and I know I shouldn't wish this, but I kinda wished (Like a 1/4 wish) that P.D. would show up so Darling could scare the "The Bee Jesus outta him" like thats what Darling says HA!!! So Darling and Jeffs Tia ended up haveing coffee and talking in there White Ladys Voices and I heard his Tia say "He will not get his hands on Jeff again over my dead body!" And I triple liked her cause she loves him so much with no Contract either, but then there a family (Like I guess my Tia would take me to live there but you know me Virgen, I can't just sit there and eat Hot Dog Stew while El Cheap Skate chomps on his STEAK). Maybe I am an AMAZON—Tell me in a Dream if you think I am, OK? Kinda like I think Jodys an Amazon too and probably thats why we were the only White Girls on the Salvation Army Club Basketball Team, but the Black Girls used to call me a 1/2 White Girl some times (Cause I told them one time when we were camping out at the Club that I was only 1/2 Gringa and 1/2 Wet Back.) Jody was 100% Gringa but shes still an Amazon I think, so let me know if you really think I'm an Amazon, OK Virgen?

So me and Jeff walked down to the rocky ass beach right in front of Darlings Hide Out and its got all the rocks Darling likes to bring to her Work Shop and polish and cut with her Diamond Saw (Which I love to watch a regular ugly rock sliced in 1/2 to the Secret Crystal World and for 1/2 sec it SMELLS like it too.) Like I never knew rocks have a smell but now I kinda pick them up and sniff them, but they smell the best when Darling saws them open especially the big rocks of course plus there really beeeuuutiiiiiful. And I'm not kidding cause its like they have all these super secret lights inside of them, but you'd never know if you just saw them laying around pretending to be ugly (Do you know what I mean?) So me and Jeff end up haveing one more Rock Skimming Contest like who can make a flat rock skim the longest or skip the most skips, and you have to wait till the tide comes in and its pretty flat for a sec. So I was winning as usual and Jeff said "You have an arm like a boy cause girls usually throw like this" and he acted like a girl throwing a rock (Like really STUPID). And I said "Do you think girls are stupid?" Then he looked pretty stupid cause his face got all PINK so he picked up a flat rock and skimmed it at the wrong time when the wave was still curling so it just PLOP disappeared (HA!) "Well OK your my first REAL FRIEND whos a girl and I think its neat that you can skim rocks better than me." "I can run and swim faster too" I said. "Yeah I know and you cheat in Monopoly too." Jeff just looked at me and now my face was probably REDDER than your wings, Virgen CHINGASO!!! Then Jeff started cracking up "I saw you take those $500 bills" and then he started singing "You ain't nothin but a Hound Puppy" (You know instead of DOG). And I guess he thought he was pretty nifty cause he started danceing too kinda like E.T.P. does on TV which is why they call him The Pelvis of course, but Jeff is so scrawny I start cracking up and singing "You ain't nothin but a hot dog" (And don't ask me WHY). So me and Jeff are singing at the top of our LUNGS kinda like Darling says to me some times "Do you have to talk at the top of your damed LUNGS?" And hes singing HOUND PUPPY and I'm singing HOT DOG and we're kinda danceing together (Believe it or not!) Then we hear Jeffs Tia call him over and over and we stop singing and danceing cause we know hes going to go to OREGON now, right? Then he yells "I'll be right there!" And his Tia yells "I'm waiting Jeff and its going to be dark in a few hours so we have to go now!" Then I see his eye balls have these BIG ASS TEARS right in them and then one leaks right down his face (And for 1/2 a sec I try to hear if La Yoronas crying but I don't hear her or any thing cause thats how crummy I feel.) And then all of a sudden I feel like BLUBBERING cause I bet I'll never in mi vida see Jefferino again. And then (Heres the TRUTH) Jeff said "Can I kiss you?" and like a pendeja I said "Where?" and he said "On your cheek" and I said "OK," and when he got so close I could see the Ocean in his eye balls and like maybe he saw some clouds in mine, right? He kissed me on my cheek so s o f t it felt like some thing I never felt before kinda like a Butterfly thought by accident you were a flower or some thing pretty special like a flower (Do you know what I mean, Virgen?) Then Jeff said "I think your the smartest person I ever met, Luna." And then I did it. I just LEAPED over and kissed him but I think mine wasn't as soft as his cause I kinda pounced on him (And I wanted to tell him he was the smartest and the nicest person I have ever met but I couldn't cause it might make me blubber right there in front of him CHINGASO). Then his Tia yelled for him again and we kinda ran up to her car and she told Jeff his dad was sending all his stuff by mail. So while me and Jeff are just standing there this giant YELLOW Butterfly flys by us and its really flaping its wings to get by us cause its pretty windy and I say "Bye Einstein like thats you Jeff cause hes the smartest and the nicest guy in the world maybe." And Jeff started smileing "Write me back, OK?" "Write me first then." "OK" he said and "OK" I said and then I noticed the Butterfly was on the ground opening and closeing its yellow wings over and over, and I hoped no one squished it with there fat foot.

Jeffs Tia said "Maybe you can visit Jeff in OREGON some time" and I said "OK." And as the car started moveing away Jeff just kept waveing both of his arms at me and then I heard him really yell "SEE YA LATER MAMMAL GATOR!!!!" And I didn't yell any thing back cause Jeffs was the best thing to yell but I did wave my arms over and over till the car turned on to the regular road that'll take him past Harrys Palace, Psycho Dads MOOOOO Cows, Town, The Hermit Store (Jeff said he never lungered in the spitoon but I could tell he was kinda jealous that I did it TWICE) And then the car will go on some road I don't even know about that'll go all the way to OREGON and for 1 sec I kinda wonder if Jeff thought I looked like a giant weird ass Butterfly cause I was waveing my arms up and down like I wanted to FLY or some thing, right Virgen? I guess I shoulda yelled some thing back but it was like my brain was frozen and the truth is what I really wanted to yell was ("I love you, Jefferino!") But then I'd have to jump off a cliff like commit sewerside cause then every one would know, right Virgen? So please don't tell God or even El Buddha that I wanted to yell what I just said or that Jeff kissed me kinda like a Butterfly (And then I kissed him like La Loca.) Cause I don't want them getting any Girl Ideas about me cause I DON'T EVER WANT TO GET MARRYED but I would like a friend. A boy whos a friend like Jefferino. Thats all.

Then I went down to the rocky ass beach again and skimmed about 1 million flat rocks but I didn't count how many times they skipped or even wait till the waves were really flat probably cause Jeff wasn't there for me to beat of course. Then it was super weird cause (I'm NOT kidding) I heard Jeff say like he was standing right behind me "Thats the magic, Luna." And I turned around so fast I fell on my nalgas and my elbows got scraped and one was kinda bleeding but for 1/2 a sec I thought Jeff had come back to play a trick on me, right Virgen? You know cause no one ever says "Thats the magic" but Jeff. And then I realize thats what I shoulda screamed "THATS THE MAGIC, JEFFERI-NO!!!!" But of course my brain was FROZEN and all I could do was wave my pendeja arms like a fregado Butterfly that can't even fly, right? So I kept sitting on the rocky ass beach kinda watching my elbow drip and then I started thinking that my blood was kinda neat so I tasted it (Like a chingaso Vampire, sorry Virgen.) And then I took some drops and painted a HEART on a perfect flat skipping rock and I said it. "Thats the magic, Jefferino." (DO NOT TELL GOD OR EL BUDDHA PLEASE.) So I stood up and waited till the wave was perfect and I skipped the rock about 20 times. Then I saw the giant yellow Butterfly and I was really glad no one had squished it and it was flapping its yellow wings kinda fast cause of the wind and it looked kinda tired to me, but it also looked kinda happy all super yellow in the sun and I wished I could touch it like maybe capture it, but Darling told me if you touch the dust on there wings (Which is what makes them yellow) They can't FLY any more and I think thats worse than being squished, right Virgen?

I finally talked Darling in to letting me go to Harry The Hermits and ride Cinamon but first she called The Sheriff and told him about Jeffs Psycho Dad and The Sheriff said he'd go over and talk to him about not attacking me or else he'll have to go to JAIL (Kinda like the weirdo that bothered me in the Pervy Park in S.F.

when I was 7 years old cause he went to JAIL.) Any way when Old Harry saw me he said "I was startin to think you'd gone round the bend, Miss Moon" and then of course he laughed kinda like his old hermit laugh probably cause I haven't been around these days. He said he heard from The Sheriff about me clobbering Jeffs Dad and that I'm pretty famous down at the Hermits Store, and then I told Harry WHY I did it and he said "Sure can't blame you none, Miss Moon and thats down right courageous!" And then he said "I sure hope you don't do that to your HUSBAND some day" and he cracked himself up of course so I left him standing by some weird ass flowers I see all over the place now. But I was so happy to see and smell Cinamon I forgot about clobbering any one and I could tell Cinamon was pretty happy to see me too cause her ears started really twitching, and she was kinda doing a Happy Horse Dance, and I'm not kidding either, Virgen.

When I came back out with Cinamon Old Harry was sitting on one of his rickety ass porch chairs kinda stareing at stuff and I then I wondered what he was stareing at, so then I asked him what kinda weirdo flowers these were like there all pink and smell so SWEET they almost make me puke and the stem is really long and dark with no green leaves, but they are kinda pretty if you really look at them as long as you don't sniff them. "Thems Naked Ladys Flowers, Miss Moon, you ever smell one?" "Yeah they make me puke cause there too chingaso sweet." (And of course I don't really believe Old Harry like that there called NAKED LADYS.) "Some day you'll love how they smell I bet." "When I'm dead and there growing all over me maybe, but I'm never going to get marryed, Harry The Hermit!!!!" Then I leaped on Cinamon and squeezed my knees and clicked my tongue (Which is GIDDY YAP in Horse Talk.) OK Old Harry taught me, but some times I want to STRANGLE HIM! "Thats what they all say, Miss Moon!!" I didn't even yell any thing back cause I mighta said "Besa my nalgas" or even "Fuck you and the horse you rode in on" (Darling says that too.) So thats how POed I was, so sorry Virgen, but thats the truth. Plus I bet if I said that about the horse Cinamon might get POed, so any way I just layed my head down on Cinamons mane which is my favorite place in el mundo and even before I got to my favorite swimming place I knew it wasn't going to be the same without Jeffs skinny white pencil legs, right? And I sure don't want to go to the Sun Set Place cause thats where he found me, remember? So before I jumped in to the Ocean I wrote this poem with my new words—FUTURE, LOYAL, EMPATHY, CRUELTY. Also Danny The Danes coming back in a couple of weeks so I guess thats when shes going to show him the Contract me and Jeff made together. Also I like the way Darling doesn't say any corn ball stuff about Jeff kinda like she understands hes my BEST FRIEND, right? OK Virgen, since I wrote about my Top Secret in this poem I'll have to write another one to show Darling. And its really weird cause if I close my eyes and shut up I can still feel how SOFT it was, and of course Jeffs the first boy who ever kissed me and maybe the last boy ever, right Virgen???

BEST FRIEND

I guess todays the FUTURE after
Jeff went to OREGON with his Tia Laurie
and I guess I'm still his LOYAL friend
and I wonder if hes still my LOYAL friend.

Cause me and Jeff had a ton of EMPATHY
with each other which is why I let him
(Kiss me—TOP SECRET!!!!)
And we never did CRUELTY to each other

like when I saw him sleeping with his mouth
open I didn't put any thing weird in it,
and Jeff let me cheat in Monopoly
and no one ever let me cheat in any

thing and win (And I'm thinking if I saw him
cheating I'd a screamed and stuff, but not
Jeff.) Cause now I really and truely know
hes my BEST FRIEND.

P.S. And thats the magic, Jefferino.

Por Vida, Luna The Mammal, your first best friend
whos a girl.

I wrote Jeff a letter and put this poem inside the letter kinda folded up like a surprise, and I told him about me being famous at the Hermits Store for clobbering his dad, and I promised MOOOOO him to lunger one for me and then one for him when I go there next time, and now I wonder what he thinks about his new name—JEFFERINO. In the first letter he wrote me he told me some names of people I might like when I go to the Bolinas School and he told me these guys weren't weirdos or creeps (4 boys and 2 girls). After being Jeffs friend I guess its kinda creepy to me to be The Hermit Girl again so if these guys are 1/2 as nifty as Jeff maybe I'll have a couple of friends even though I DREAD wearing the Bo Peep Dresses to SCHOOL and I've been thinking about asking Darling to make me some skirts like maybe 2 or 3 so I'm not doomed for sure cause skirts and blouses can be groovey, daddyo (As Darling always still says while shes danceing to some corn ball music.) And I hate to say it but some times I start danceing with her and cracking up of course cause we're so GROOVEY, DADDYO!! Like maybe we can put that in the Contract—Luna The Mammal promises to dance with Darling when ever she feels like being muy groovey.

So when I got back to Harrys Palace he wasn't there but he left me a note that he went to Town and would I come for dinner tomorrow. "Mark your X" he said if I was, so I put a humungus X on it and I also wrote MAKE TACOS!!!

Here's the <u>truth</u>—I feel like I NEVER missed any one like Jefferino almost like if he can't be my best friend I don't want any friends, right Virgen? But then I really and truely do not want to be Hermit Girl cause its muy creepy.

So that night you sent me this Dream—I was with Jody my Tomboy friend in S.F. and we climbed way to the top of a building at night and theres no fog and we can see the Sewerside Bridge kinda like all the lights are a necklace far away and it makes me feel SAD like I lost some thing for ever. Then Jody says "If you want to be an Amazon for real do it" and she CUTS OFF HER BREAST but theres no blood or any thing, and her breast isn't big like it looks kinda like a tennis ball laying there by itself. So it looks pretty easy and she hands me the SWORD to do it and I really and truely want to and I almost do it, but then a

Butterfly that's kinda glowing in the dark like a Star with wings lands right on the sword (I'm not kidding!) And I drop the sword cause all of a sudden its super hot and its burning off my chingaso hand which makes me even sadder in the Dream but I'm also kinda glad I have TWO BREASTS (Muy weird!)

So does that make me a 1/2 Amazon, Virgen?

P.S. Con Amor Por Vida, Hermit Girl

P.S.S. Please don't forget to send Darling and Danny The Dane some Dreams about keeping me till I'm at least 17-1/2 cause that should do it, OK Virgen?

FOGGY AND HOT IN AUGUST
Hermit Girl Lungers In The Hermit Store
(1 for me and 1 for Jefferino) And I spot
my first Perv in BOLINAS in the Hermit Store
SHOOTING STARS—SHOOTING DREAMS

Dear La Virgen,

I got a humungus Banana Box (And I'm not kidding either!) It had pictures of yellow bananas on it, but my name (And Darlings name) Was on it to BOLINAS. So when I ripped it open with my bare hands like I didn't get a knife or any thing and then I was FLABBERGASTED cause there was a TON OF GIFTS inside for me LUNA!!! Tia sent me 5 skirts and 3 sweaters and there pretty nifty!! Probably she had El Cheap Skate drive her to The Mission and for him thats like going to The Moon cause it costs gas $. But I bet he did and Tia went to her favorite 2nd Hand Store where she buys all the clothes for her and Pablito (And you guessed it, El Cheap Skate buys his stuff brand new.) And then of course she bought my stuff too, and of course she washed and starched and ironed every thing so there "Just like new" like thats what Tia always says all happy cause some times stuff is 10¢. Like one time I found some sneakers for 20¢ and they looked NEW and they were black High Tops too so I bought them even though they were a little too big cause I figured I'd grow my feet, right? And I also found a basket ball and some marbles that same day (I paid for the basket ball but you know me—The marbles snuck in to my jeans pocket and some of them were even Lucky Cat Eyes!!) So any way Tia kinda saved me cause I don't have to wear the Bo Peep Dresses. Plus Darlings also sewing me MORE skirts and blouses and now I feel kinda like The Princess And The Pea, but I don't care (Cause The Princess And The Pea is so spoiled she feels a PEA at the bottom of 100 mattresses HA!!) I like being spoiled but I don't brag about it of course, just to you cause I know you understand my noodle (You know my BRAIN). Then Pablito sent me a bunch a comic books of every weirdo kind and some a them had stains and some were like brand new, and he tied them all up with a long ass RED RIBBON And he wrote on piece a paper "To my favorite Cousin Luna and I miss your jokes. Love, Pablo." I think Tia helped him with the spelling cause usually he says Favoritist Cusin, right? But his comic book gifts is muy GROOVEY!! And then (BELIEVE IT OR SNOT!) Carmen sent me a brand new book like you can tell its brand new cause when you open it up its like it wants to stay shut and not tell you its Top Secrets, and its a thick ass book called Hans Christian Andersons Fairy Tales and there are drawings inside that are kinda spooky but if you keep looking at them they make sense. But I've never seen drawings like this (Kinda like a dream, right?) Kinda like I dreamed it and then its in a BOOK or some thing.

So Carmen wrote on the first page when you open the book—From her mother. Miss you. Love, Carmen. And I was SUPER FLABBERGASTED cause Carmen under lined LOVE. And then I remembered some thing from when I was probably 6 or 7 years old when Carmen used to say about me like "Her breakfast, her shoes, hers so pretty" meaning me. And then I super remembered how I always tryed super hard when Carmen was around to be PRETTY (So she'd like me of course, Virgen.) So now when I sniff the brand new book of Fairy Tales and I open it up to read the Top Secrets I kinda wonder when I stopped being PRETTY cause in fact I didn't even want to be pretty cause I really wanted to look like a BOY and boys sure aren't PRETTY. Anyway Darling said Hans Christian Anderson was a famous Story Teller from DENMARK and that Danny The Dane probably knows these Fairy Tales back wards of course. D.T.D. is comeing back in about 5 days so then Darling can show him The Contract. And then just as I was about to take the giant ass Banana Box to the trash heap where a guy with a truck comes to get it—I see an ENVELOPE and some really weirdo scratchy writeing on it that barely says "To Luna Villalobos" and then a pathetic drawing of a dog sitting there stareing at my name (Muy chingaso WEIRD). So I opened it real SLOW just in case some thing creepy popped out, right? And guess what I found??? $20 Buckerooos!!! And a piece of paper like some one tore it off like they were desperate or some thing and it said "To Pocahantas, Ever things the same old thing here. How you doing there in the country. I hear you ride a horse, don't fall off. I wonder what you look like these days. Your friend, El Blanco." For about 2 secs my noodle froze and I could not figure it out till I said "El Blanco" out loud about 10 times and then I cracked up of course WHITEY! You know the guy who gave me the delicious dinners and a ton of sodys (Who I thought at first was a Perv cause we had to share the same bath room in S.F.) But I ended up likeing this guy just like Harry The Hermit. In fact when you really think about it Old Whitey and Old Harry could be Twin Brothers especially when they start with the Hooch, right? But they even kinda talk the same and a bunch a other stuff, but Old Harry is probably older cause hes more rickety then Old Whitey (El Blanco). So $20 Buckerooos and all the other Loot (Thats what Darling calls it LOOT.) If this is how The Princess And The Pea always feels then I want to be The Princess And The Pea forever Por Vida, OK Virgen?

And then after I took the Banana Box out to the trash heap I started thinking about the one other time when I was maybe 6 and I felt like The Princess And The Pea. I remember it was my birthday and Carmen bought me a Hop Along Cowboy Bike with Saddle Bags (Cause I had begged for it in the store.) And then I remember I wouldn't let her die my hair BLOND unless she promised MOOO to buy it, and so I let the Hair Lady put this pukey stuff on my head that smelled beyond belief (I can still remember I almost couldn't even BREATHE). But it made me turn blond and I remember Mamacita looking at me and kinda shakeing her head and saying "Pobrecita la niña" me. But after the Hair Lady washed that junk out of my hair and she told me to keep my eyes shut or I'd GO BLIND and its super spooky to remember all this stuff from my child hood like I told Darling and she said "Thats a child hood memory." And she also squinted her Cat Eyes at me and said "For the life a me I can't picture you as a blondie. I hate to say it kid, but your moms off her ass." And thats the truth but I'm still pretty flabbergasted about Carmen sending me a brand new BOOK (And that she under lined LOVE.) So anyway I super remember how chingaso HAPPY I was when I saw the Hop Along Cowboy Bike with these long ass red white and blue ribbons hanging from the handle bars, and now I realize that my hair was BLOND and CURLY cause she made Mamacita curl my hair like Shirley Temple!! Its pretty funny cause when you remember one little thing you end up remembering the whole fregado thing like a dumbo movie where Elvis The Pelvis dies but hes still singing at the end, right Virgen? So there I was in Pervy S.F. rideing my brand new Hop Along Cowboy Bike with the brand new Saddle Bags and I look like some creepy ass Shirley Temple when I was 6 years old. And the bike had training wheels. And then I remember this—I was kinda POed cause I also really wanted a GUN AND A HOLSTER but Carmen said "Girls don't have guns" so I used my finger, but of course I knew it wasn't a real gun, Virgen. And I remember it was kinda foggy so when I rode to the end of the block I'd hear Mamacita yelling her lungs out "LUUUUNNAAAAA!!" And I remember how I rode to a Secret World Place where she couldn't see me, but then it scared the shit out of me so I raced right back to where her face was in the window, and then of course I'd go back down to the Secret World Place again, and I bet that later she told me how the Sepetio Guys (Gringos probably call them The Boogey Man, right?) How they take kids when no ones looking. Los Sepetios. I haven't even thought of them in 1 million years or the Hop Along Cowboy Bike. Or the blond hair. Or Shirley Temple. But I will not tell Darling that I was supposed to look like Shirley Temple cause if she calls me that I will for sure PUKE (Hers so pretty—Hers so fregado FREAKO.) But its kinda funny cause I think I knew I was blond for about 10 secs and then I just forgot about what I looked like (Cause I think really little kids are like that, right?)

And now that I'm thinking about all these muy freako child hood memories I'm remembering my EX step father The Psycho Jake and his daughter who was exactly my age and her name was Mary Jane, and I remember how he made her cry a ton when me and her lived together for about 1 month (The time I almost murdered him with the marble ash tray.) He used to tell me to go out and come back later when Carmen got there and every time I came back Mary Jane would be in her twin bed crying her eye balls out cause she was sick (Thats what The Psycho always said.) And I remember when he said she was the PRETTYEST I was always glad she was and I barely got to know her cause I was always out side, and then of course I just about murdered him so I had to high tail it out a there (Like Old Harry says.) I wonder how people ever think of saying stuff like high tail it out a here or there, I really do. So when ever I think about Mary Jane now I can just see her red looking eyes, and they were blue and they kinda made her look like a baby I thought like a super sad baby cause I don't remember her ever cracking up or even smileing, and now I wonder why she was so fregado SAD I really do.

The other day I was over to Harrys Palace and we were watching his NEW TV which gets one station but he says "All ya needs one in my book and besides I tend ta watch with one eye and do my chores with the other one." So we were watching a movie about SLAVERY and they were takeing these whole bunches of African People on a ship to be slaves when all of a sudden this woman whos holding her baby runs real FAST and she JUMPS in to the Ocean with her baby. So the mean ass White Guys on the ship say some thing like "She went insane." And I said to Harry "Shes an Amazon and shes not crazy cause she'd rather be DEAD than be there pathetic SLAVE" (Like at the Mammal Zoo, remember?) And Harry said "You sure do figure things out, Miss Moon cause I think your ab so lut ly right." And then Harry asked me how I knew about Amazons and I told him what Darling told me and I told him about the Amazon Girls I know in S.F. and I could tell he was pretty FLABBERGASTED that he kinda knew a real Amazon. Me (Luna La Loca) Cause he said "I think I met 2 or 3 Amazons in my day when I really do stop and think about it, and your one for the books, Miss Moon!" And he cracked himself up of course, but I didn't say "Fuck you and the horse you rode in on" (And even if I did Cinamon was too far away to hear it.) I figured Old Harry was trying to give me a COMPLIMENT so I asked him "Do you think she was crazy?" He was quiet for so long I suddenly got the spookey feeling maybe he'd DIED and read my brain about The Fuck You Part, so I was just about to check him when he said "Nope, she was an Amazon." Thats why I really for real like Old Harry cause he never says stuff he doesn't mean, right Virgen?

I slept out side with Darling to watch a Meteor Shower (Darling calls it that.) But it looked like it was kinda raining SHOOTING STARS for a while. And I kept thinking about the Amazon Lady and her baby, and how she all of a sudden just RAN FOR IT AND JUMPED INTO THE OCEAN where its so deep and the beach is a zillion miles away (So you can't swim for it of course, you know, to the beach.) And I kept thinking about how dark her skin looked and how she was probably the most beautiful lady I ever saw (And I didn't even see her face, right Virgen?) So I kept kinda wondering if I'd rather be DEAD than be a SLAVE and I was going to tell Darling about it but before I could (You guess it) I passed out I think with my eyes still open stareing at Shooting Stars raining every where (And for 1/2 sec I wondered if Jefferino was stareing at them too, so was he?)

So this is what I dreamed when I passed out—I dreamed I was swimming in the Ocean full of Shooting Stars and then I saw the Amazon Lady and her baby, and guess what? She was swimming with one hand and holding her baby with the other hand, and then she looked at me and smiled at me kinda like she knows me. And in the Dream I was even HAPPYER than being The Princess And The Pea (And don't ask me why either.) And her face was really BEAUTIFUL and I think I'll always remember her face for ever, and her baby too. Por Vida, Amazon Girl (Luna).

JEFF CALLED!!!! JEFF CALLED!!!! JEFFERINO CALLED!!!! And we talked for 10 whole minutes and then I called him back and we talked for 10 whole more minutes like this—"So hows OREGON?" "Not too bad, so hows BOLINAS?" "I spotted my first Perv in Bolinas at The Hermit Store." And Jeff cracked up "What did he look like?" And I said "Like a Perv. And I lungered in the Spitoon for you, Jefferino." "Is that my new name?" "Do you like it?" Then he was really quiet and finally he said "Better than Jeff probably." And then he started singing "Love me tender love me true" but I couldn't punch him over the phone of course. So when I called him back he said "I really liked your BEST FRIEND POEM so I sent you a present in the mail." And then I told him about the Banana Box Gifts and how I felt kinda like The Princess And The Pea who could feel a measley pea under 100 mattresses SPOILED. And then I asked him what was he was sending me and he said "A surprise, top secret!" So I said "OK I'm sending you a SURPRISE TOP SECRET!!" Then Darling said "Times up." So we said "See ya later mammal gator!" At the same time. Then as I was putting the phone down I could hear Jeff yelling THATS THE MAGIC!! But when I tryed to yell back he was gone and then I wondered if he was standing there like me stareing at the phone like a pendeja. And then I thought about the Bolinas School next month and all of a sudden I felt like comitting sewerside (And I wonder if Jeffs old friends will even like me and I wonder if they have forts and a horse—I hope so.) I really do, Virgen. Have you sent Darling and Danny The Dane the Dream yet like about keeping me and signing The Contract? Don't forget cause its pretty important, right?

GRACIAS, Luna La Loca

I told Darling about another freako child hood memory about the one ONLY TIME I ever in mi vida tryed to write my real father whos name is LEO (I sent it to the address on the Army checks for $10 that came every month and which I had to find before Carmen, right?) I think I told him some real DUMB STUFF about me being a Spelling Bee Champ and how I was the Captain Of The Baseball Team (Which I was then.) But I didn't tell him about Psycho Jake or stuff like that, but I did ask him for a picture of him cause I don't really know what he even looks like (Except for what Tia tells me—He's tall, skinny, blond and has sky blue eyes the last time she ever saw him before Carmen went to Louisiana with him to the Weirdo Farm where his whole family lived.) Anyway thats what Tia tells me and of course Carmen told me stuff too like she says she came home from her office job in town one day (Cause she told me she would not work in the fields and that one of his sisters said "Mexicans are no better than a nigger" like to her face, right?) So she found her bags on the front porch and she had to walk 2 or 3 miles to a bus stop carrying me she said on a hot ass day. So all these months go by and I forgot about even sending him the dumb ass letter (But I keep trying to get the $10 before Carmen and usually I did too.) And then one day this humungus Banana Box (with no bananas on it) shows up from LOUISIANA so was I in <u>disbelief</u>. But when I opened it up the most disgustamento smell like MOTH BALLS was all over every thing (like what a chingaso THRILL, right?) So like I told Darling "Guess what was inside?" She just looked at me with her Cat Eyes so I said "Carmen called them Southern Bell Gowns, believe it or not cause they were like 2 PINK and 1 PEACH looking ones and they were all kinda silky and long and they were so CREEPY I started to crack up till I peed mi calzones, and even Carmen peed hers too and I'm not lieing cause these GOWNS WERE UGLY <u>beyond belief</u>." And all Darling could say was "No shit." And her Cat Eyes looked kinda SAD (And Darling <u>never</u> looks sad.) And then she said "I'm makeing us some hot chocolate with plenty a marsh mellows, you with me kid?" And of course I said "Sure." Plus it was all foggy again and then I told her some one wrote some super phoney letter which was inside an envelope (Some lady Carmen didn't even know but she figured it was his new wife, right Virgen?) And there was $5 but no picture so I still don't know what this Leo Guy looks like. But Tia says "Go look in the mirror. You have your mothers eyes, but the rest is your father." And I wonder if thats why Carmen used to die my hair BLOND—

So I could tell Darling was starting to feel pretty SAD so I told her the story about what I did with the Southern Bell Gowns that STUNK like moth balls—I kept the worst one (Believe it or snot!) like the <u>uglyist</u> one and stold some Blue Waltz Perfume from the 5 and 10 and just poured it on so the moth ball skunk smell would go away, and then I hung it up on the clothes line for

2 whole days—and then I wore the fregado Southern Bell Gown for HOLLOWEEN. And I ran around saying saying stuff like "Trick or treat you all!!" And "I'm going down yonder" to my weirdo friends and we went down yonder to some a my favorite bars where some a the guys kinda know me, and I had close to $100 BUCKEROOS by 12 midnight cause they really cracked up when I said "Trick or treat you all" of course, plus I ran some errands too which is cool cause thats how I get $ in pervy S.F. and its kinda weird but <u>most</u> a the guys in the bars aren't Pervs, but I don't let any one even breathe on me (Breath and breath<u>e</u> SNEAKEY.) So any way Darling cracked up about the Holloween part and she told me to write it like a story so I think I will cause she said its a GREAT STORY. But she also said this "I think your fathers a real TURD" which cracked me up, so me and Darling drank our hot choco and I ate about 40 marsh mellows for real.

Also Darling gave me these new words—ADOPTION, LEGAL, COMMITMENT, CHOICE. And she also talked about ADOPTION like she asked me how I'd feel about maybe her and Danny The Dane <u>adopting me legaly</u> cause she said that would make me her REAL LIFE DAUGHTER!!!! So I said "Would I live here then?" And she said "We were thinking of sending you to The Best School In The World in DENMARK" and like D.T.D. kinda said (That time with the MOOO Cows, remember when they scared the shit out of me?) He said they'd go with me so I could get used to DENMARK and Darling said I'd come back here to BOLINAS for the Summer Time and also Christmas Time too, and Darling said his sisters who live there would also keep an eye on me there in DENMARK. So I told Darling I'd really and truely rather live here in BOLINAS and watch Shooting Stars and ride Cinamon and see 1 Perv per year (And even go to the corn ball Bolinas School which is probably not The Best School In The World, right?) Its kinda like Darling wants me to be a GENIUS cause of my IQ but I just want to be a Regular Mammal with 2 friends (Not counting Old Harry The Hermit.) Like just 2 friends with some forts and a horse so we can goof around some times. Or even a BIKE thats OK too. Plus would you be able to go to DENMARK with me Virgen, cause I was thinking its pretty FAR AWAY FROM MEXICO like you don't have to go very far to get here. So heres the TRUTH—I don't think I could go to DENMARK without you (Even if I am a 1/2 Gringa.) I really and truely don't. So now I'm really wondering what to do about all this ADOPTION STUFF cause Darlings going to write Carmen about it and it turns out D.T.D. says all this stuff is OK with him cause Darling already asked him. And I guess I really and truely do want to be ADOPTED by Darling and D.T.D. And then I was also wondering if that would make me a real life Princess And The Pea HA! ! ! ! And I guess it would be OK if I went to The Best School In The World in DENMARK (MAYBE!!!!) But I guess you'd have to go with me, Virgen so let me know in a Dream (Right away PLEASE!!!!) So I guess you gave Darling and D.T.D. the Dreams I asked you to so GRACIAS POR TODO! ! ! ! But I can't go to DENMARK if you can't go, so send me the Dream telling me all this stuff, OK? Also if you want to talk about all of this with El Buddha thats OK (But not God cause I think he might want to smite me or some thing and thats all I need, right?) Like maybe El Buddha can come with me to DENMARK (And I pretty much like him OK cause I put flowers and stuff on his altar and of course your there too where I HID you, muy sneakey.) But I know I can't go without you Virgen, even if I am The Princess And The Pea and a LEGALY ADOPTED GENIUS in The Best School In The World in DENMARK. Any way I have to write this—BESA MY NALGAS and don't ask me why, Virgen. Just send me the Dream, OK?

BESA MY NALGAS

Hermit Girl in Bolinas is bad enough, right?
But Hermit Girl in DENMARK makes me want
to say "BESA MY NALGAS!!"
ADOPTION means I would be Darling

and Danny The Danes real life LEGAL
daughter, but I wonder if I weren't smart
would they still do the COMMITMENT
which makes me say "BESA MY NALGAS! !"

Like I wonder if I couldn't write poems
and storys that crack Darling up

would she still make the CHOICE
to make me her real life daughter?

And then I'd have to go to The Best School
In The World in DENMARK where all the
Gringos probably have a big nose like D.T.D.
So BESA MY NALGAS!

Hop Along Shirley Temple, La Gringita
(Like the old Church Ladys used to call me)

Virgen, I tryed to write this poem a bunch of different ways but this is how it finally came out (SORRY!!) I went to the Sun Set Place for the first time since Jefferino left and I wrote it, but I sure can't show Darling this poem so maybe I'll still have to write another nicer poem about how lucky I am to go to Gringo Denmark of course. I got Jeffs present in the mail and I could barely believe my eye balls cause he sent me a RING with a PEARL in it. It fits my fattest finger and when I wore it to the Sun Set Place I kinda talked to Jeff and told him that I thought the ring was the best present in mi vida so far, and that it means THATS THE MAGIC every time I look at it. So I sent him one of Darlings ugly regular rocks sliced in 1/2 (The Secret Crystal World) And I wrote this poem—

Dear Jefferino,

If you miss me some times
just look inside this
Secret Crystal World.
I'm standing in the middle
where the lights really sparkle.
Thats me waveing my arms like a nut case
cause I miss you.

Hermit Girl Luna

And then I told him under the poem that I will never EVER take off the RING and I really wanted to say some other stuff but I felt too much like a weirdo cause I wanted to say—Maybe we're engaged now (See what I mean, Virgen?)

Dear La Virgen,

You sent me this Dream—First I saw all the lights on the Golden Gate Sewerside Bridge cause it was night time and I'm flying FAST so fast the wind kinda hurts my eyes but I have to keep them open so I can see where I'm going. And then I fly over S.F. and its DARK AND QUIET. And then I'm supposed to land on a roof I see, but I don't want to. I really don't want to Virgen, so instead I wake up.

Amor Por Vida, Luna La Mammal

May 1973
The Farm in Sebastopol
La Loca rides again,
and I'm not kidding either!

DEAR LA VIRGEN!!!

I'm crying and laughing at the same time!!! ITS ME, LUNA!!! And I SURVIVED just about everything! ! ! !

First of all, let me tell you how I found the diaries. My twelve-year-old daughter Tania, who'll be 13 in one month, found them in her "baby box" at the bottom, all wrapped up in a bag with a string. I remember wrapping it. In fact, I was just about Tania's age—12 going on 13—when I piled all the diaries together, wrapped them in one of my favorite T-shirts, put it all in a bag and folded it all together, and made my 12-year-old self resist the temptation to write TOP SECRET STAY OUT ALL SNOOPS!! on it (because obviously someone was bound to notice that, I told myself, Pendeja—I can just hear myself, remember me, Virgen????). Then I tied string all around it a dozen or so times until it resembled a kind of desperate time bomb; but now, I realize a time capsule.

And so, Tania found it first when she found her "baby box" full of her old baby clothes—some of which I stole from the old "5 and dime" store in the Mission. I kept all her baby clothes till age one or so, and her first blankets too—one with pink roses all over the border because you sent me a Dream telling me she was going to be a GIRL, remember? (I can't believe I'm talking to you, Virgen, just like "the old days" when I was Luna La Loca.) And so, Tania was so tiny, barely 5 1/2 lbs. and she was full-term too; but she was perfect, absolutely perfect. And born right on Mamacita's birthday, June 28th, to her 15-year-old mom. Me. Luna La Mammal.

So, Tania read the diaries first—even though she said she was a little worried because of The Hex. She even kept it a secret from me for about a month till one morning when she was up early to bake because sometimes she has insomnia and baking's one of the things she does at 5 am. And so, I woke up to the marvelous smells of my daughter's cinnamon (The horse, remember?) roll bread and freshly brewed coffee, which she brought on a tray with her signature rose in a vase—she always has a flower for me. I love that girl. And a note surrounded by circling red buds and green leaves which she drew herself with crayons—another Tania Treat, she's been decorating little notes to me since she was about 7—and, boy, did I need them, I realize now—I needed to be loved. On this morning her note said: "Dear Mom, I found your La Virgen Diarys in my baby stuff. I hope you don't mind but I read them, so don't hex me, okay? I just want to say that I love you when you were a kid like me. And you had a LOT really a lot harder life than me. THANKS FOR BEING MY MOM. I LOVE YOU MOM! Tania The Mammal."

And then she brought the diaries. She'd wrapped them up in what she calls "fairy paper"—white tissue with gold sprinkles all over it, with gold ribbon, from the old Xmas wrapping, all around it. And she gave it to me like a gift. Which it is, of course. I'd forgotten all about these diaries, this diary to you, LA VIRGEN, till now.

It makes me remember the last 16 years so clearly. So, what I'm trying to do is tell you what's happened, more or less, and also tell you what I'm doing NOW.

I'm so happy Tania found you, these diaries, and me, La Loca. Can you imagine, Virgen? But of course you can, and I'm talking to you again (Believe it or snot!).

And I don't know where to begin, but I'll try, step by step like some crazy dance you do just because you're TOO HAPPY, with no real steps you have to learn. Remember Pablito's Happy Skinny Kid's Dance? . . . Okay, like that. And now I know you can only dance that way if you've really suffered and known real sadness, like Pablito watching his father (El Cheap Skate) eat steak while Pablito ate Hot Dog Stew, remember? As you can see, Virgen, I'm going to try to write to you like I always did. I think I was always writing to you all these years in my head and in my heart, and so finally I can catch up with you. Finally. Here.

First of all, I have 3 children—Tania who's almost 13, who's sweet half the time (and she's truly sweet in her nature), but the other half she's a real pain in the ass and fights with me, holds her own ground, so STUBBORN, and I can just hear you Virgen: "Just like Luna La Mammal." And of course, you're right. Then there's Theo who's going on 11 in September, and another half and half (the agony, the ecstasy). He's the one that looks most like his father, my now ex-husband, but I can see Theo's going to be even handsomer than Theo (Sr.). And finally, Jason who will be 8 this November—this one was born with the gift to make me blindly love him, and then, just as swiftly, to make me want to murder him (a real half and half at the extreme reaches of the spectrum). A real PAIN IN THE ASS, but I love him of course. This one's blond and blue-eyed like my biological father (Leo) was/is, and in a family of dark-haired Latin-looking types (my ex is French) I had to contend with the usual Milk Man Jokes. I even gave up saying, "My father's blond. . . ." And I'd say things like, "My milk man is Chinese, Black, Indian, etc." You know me, Virgen, a Royal Pain In The Old Ass. What can I say after all these years . . . because in my secret heart (and in my dreams) I always talked to you . . . "I survived this, I survived that"—I used to say that a lot when I went back to S.F. at 13. And I suppose I still do, just a little more quietly so my kids can't hear since I'm "the mother" now. But in my secret heart I'm still the same. La Loca.

Who else can I tell this to but you, Virgen? I know you've been hearing me all these years, but now I'll write it all down, or at least most of it. But you also know this—there were times I didn't want to survive. There were times I was at the bottom, the very bottom, of the darkest well, and the walls were slick and mossy. No Hope. None. Nada. Then suddenly, a kind voice. A kind hand. A kind heart. Kindness. You've sent me so many kind people. Like Whitey. He died and left me some money, enough to buy this farm in Sebastopol. I'll be teaching the 8th grade in the fall. I was with him when he died. I gave him morphine so he'd feel no pain from the cancer. I gave him a kind voice, a kind hand, a kind heart, as he once gave me at 13 when I returned to S.F. that October when my family wouldn't let Darling and her husband adopt me.

I stopped eating when Carmen told me the food she worked for was only for her and Jake Jr., and I remember she even put a lock on her closet door and put the cereal, bread and other food in there, locked. From me. So, I stopped eating, and I slept most of the time on the couch in the front room. When I came back to S.F. I didn't have a bike and it was getting harder to look like a BOY because my breasts, though small, were starting to show, so I hated even walking down the street sometimes, I remember. And I didn't go to school for about 6 months or so—and my gums started to bleed (and my mouth really stunk, even to me). Whitey came by one afternoon after work, looked at me and said, "Holy shit, what happened to you, Pocahontas?" The next thing I saw was a Chinese doctor who looked like El Buddha—in fact, I was sure it was El Buddha. He touched me very gently as though my chest and back were made of extremely thin glass—and then he looked at my bleeding gums (and I remember I was so TIRED I wasn't even embarrassed). El Buddha said, "If you don't start eating you're going to DIE, young lady. Do you understand me?" I remember his kind and firm Buddha eyes just looking at me. He wasn't mad or sad or anything—he just wanted me to know the TRUTH. And then Whitey's voice, "She'll eat all right, doc, if I gotta spoon feed her like a baby." "You make sure she does, Whitey," El Buddha said.

And so, first thing in the morning before Whitey went to work, probably about 6 am or so, he came by with hot cereal, toast and tea. When he threatened to feed me like a baby it POed me, but he'd wait and watch me eat some of it. He'd leave me a bag lunch in the frig, and I heard him tell Carmen, "It's for your daughter, so don't go eatin it." And then I'd hear him mutter, "What's goin on here's criminal, goddammit, wolves be better mothers, fer Christ's sake." Then in the afternoon after work, he'd bring me soups at first until I graduated to my favorite: batter-fried chicken with buttery mashed potatoes, with rich, smooth pan drippings all over everything and mixed veges floating blissfully in butter. But he wouldn't bring me sodys—instead, he brought me giant glasses of icy cold milk which I strangely craved, even though I gave him dirty looks, The Witch Power Eyes. He just laughed. Loudly. Like I was the most novel thing since a light bulb. While I drank my third glass of icy cold milk.

And then, the grayness, the darkness that was overtaking me at the bottom of the slippery, mossy well—the awful coldness that had begun to seep and settle into my extremely skinny 13-year-old body, to the very center of my bones, and, most crucially, to the very center of my Amazon La Loca Heart—the darkness began to recede. And I saw the tiny squares of neon-orange carrots, the grass-green peas in melted sun-yellow butter, the deep, tempting brown of thick gravy spilling over pure white mashed potatoes flecked with black, black pepper. And the steaming chicken, stews, piles of red tomatoes and green pepper sauce flung over mounds of spaghetti. I ate color. I saw color. And my teeth stopped hurting. My gums stopped bleeding. And of course, Whitey kept teasing me all the while, "You wanna blow away in the goddammed wind, Pocahontas?"

The slippery moss dried and tiny rainbow flowers appeared. Then, small carved ledges. And when I climbed to the top of the well, I saw that the sun was gold and hot, and though I craved its heat, it also blinded me. When I climbed out of the darkness, I knew I was a 13-year-old woman. I knew I'd never be the girl in Bolinas again. Something in me was forever broken. Yet something in me was forever yearning to be healed, to be made whole, to be fed. To be, simply, loved. And at 13 this longing was blind, like my craving for the gold sun's heat. So, picture me, Virgen—a shaky 13-year-old girl-woman standing in the healing, golden sun that blinded her (keeping her Witch Power Eyes in reserve)—you know that was me. And you know how scared shitless I was. But there was color, tiny flowers, in my dreams, Whitey's voice, Jake Jr.'s temper tantrums, even Carmen's angry eyes.

I've heard that people who have shock therapy lose their memory for awhile—that's how I felt. Empty. Blank. Waiting for what must happen next to happen. So that I could remember. Me. Of course, I didn't know all of this then. It's how I felt. It's how it really was, Virgen.

(2 days later . . .)

And I want to tell you this part, about the ride over the Golden Gate Bridge in Darling's Thunderbird, with the port-hole windows in back, as I watched the clustered lights of the city grow closer and closer, as I felt the dark, silent safety of my Secret Crystal World (where Cinnamon and Harry The Hermit lived) grow farther and farther away like a dream I just couldn't remember no matter how hard I tried or wanted to remember. And then I heard the noise. I'd forgotten about the noise. I remember I wanted to cry, but I had too much pride to let Darling see me blubbering. I remember thinking about the African Amazon woman, with her baby in her arms, jumping into the ocean, and I imagined leaping out of the car at the toll booth and jumping—imagining how everyone would feel about Pocahontas, Plato, Shakespeare, The Genius, her, jumping to her death rather than doing what everyone wanted her to do. But I didn't. I wasn't that much of a real Amazon, and I remember how ashamed I was because I was such a coward, secretly.

As Darling paid the toll the amnesia began to cover Cinnamon's face, eyes, her whole body, her horsey smell that I loved—and now I know that to remember was to die of grief, over and over. It was the same with Mamacita. I forgot her too. I forgot for a long while that I was ever loved. Until I gave birth to my daughter Tania at 15, on Mamacita's birthday. It was then I began to remember. Love. Me. Who I was. Who I am. Luna La Mammal. And maybe even Luna La Loca.

(3 days later . . .)

Dear, Dear La Virgen,

This farm is the most beautiful place in the world—it's like a separate country on these 2 acres of walnut trees, an immense and old magnolia tree blooming in front (by Tania's bedroom), pear trees, an old grape arbor in the driveway (where wild turkeys perch in the morning), three ancient, graceful weeping willows that dominate the small creek that runs through the middle of the property separating the house from the fields and two huge barns that smell like old hay and old dreams, so wonderful. And then the thickest tangle of blackberries, where even a bird would get lost, on the field side of the creek by the largest willow, where my sons found a tree house. Theo has announced he's going to make it stronger this summer and sleep outside every night. He waits for me to forbid him to, but I don't (to his surprise). And when I silently dare him to, his eyes shine with the joy of proving me wrong (one of my dirty mother tricks).

In the fields, in the early morning, there are wild turkeys—and the other morning I saw one perched on the grape arbor, its long and lovely tail feathers making it so beautiful I was frozen to the spot. Also, in the early morning, and in the twilight, there are small, brown quails with little commas on their heads, scurrying everywhere as though they're late for work. Next door, to the left, our neighbor has some steers and a cow (MOOOO). To the far front of the fields, sheep bleat softly. And to the right, our neighbor has a beautiful, black horse with a white comet between his eyes. In front of the house, our neighbor is a very old woman, in her eighties, who keeps chickens and plants an enormous garden. We see her working in her large garden, the size of a tennis court, as she hoes and mulches. Already she offered to teach me the mysteries of mulching when I asked her what she was doing with all that newspaper and hay. She places this stuff all around her seedlings to keep them warm and cut down on the weeds—that's what she tells me, and now I'm curious of course.

We moved in the first week of April with the help of my friend Steve from school—we took a lot of classes together, and he's teaching now. His four children also helped (they're aged 10 to 16)—and Steve's my first real black man friend. We helped each other with homework and took our kids to Golden Gate Park on the weekend sometimes, and having a man friend to talk to, when I left my ex, helped keep me sane. I have two other men friends, but they're married to women friends of mine; so, Steve is my friend just by himself. I like that. (He's divorced too, and sees his kids regularly—in fact, they live with him part-time—he's a great dad.) Anyway, Steve has a beautiful Afro and he doesn't understand WHY I want to live here, "out in the sticks," he calls it. Also, my cousin Pablo helped with the move-in; and you wouldn't recognize Pablo now. He's tall, built like a man, with a beautiful, bushy Afro hairstyle that suits him. He also has a mustache, so I call him Zapata sometimes—which makes him laugh, crinkling his eyes at me. And some other friends, who look Mexican and Indian, showed up with their children with pots and pots of delicious food. They brought tents, sleeping bags and guitars.

It was chilly at night in April, but it was pretty warm in the day, so that weekend we made fires outside, and after we ate, Pablo and Roberto played guitar and sang. Sometimes we joined in, especially when they played "The Yellow Submarine." The kids love that song, so they'd end up screeching it at the top of their healthy lungs, "We all live in a yellow submarine, a yellow submarine . . ." And I thought how wonderful it was that they could screech once in a while in the darkness of this farm, and that we were really and truly in a Yellow Submarine. As in a safe and magical place, right Virgen?

So, after my friends and Pablo (who's not so skinny anymore, and he's learned to play the guitar and sing songs that make him close his eyes in pleasure)—after they all left, about three or four days later, someone BURNED A CROSS ON OUR LAWN. Just like in some bad movie or like you hear they did years ago "in the south." But here we are about 70 miles north of S.F. with a black burn mark on our thick, green grass, on our just-bought farm, in our Yellow Submarine. SHIT AND PURO CHINGASOS!! Okay, I'll say it—we're totally surrounded by Gringos or should I say Red Necks. My children's father (my ex-husband Theo) is a Gringo: French and Russian. So, my children, let's face it, are half-gringo (as I am), yet these cross burners see us as Dirty Mexicans, Dirty Indians, Wet Backs, Niggers, Outsiders, and as they say in the old cowboy movies, Vermin. (Well, we are Dirty Indians and Wet Backs also—so what!) Virgen, this is the last thing I expected—a cross burning. . . . I guess I was expecting the safety I remember in Bolinas (Harry The Hermit, Jefferino, Cinnamon The Horse).

Anyway, Tania saw the cross on fire first because her bedroom window faces the front, so when she screamed I came running. Then a truck sped away, raising dirt as its wheels found traction. Then the sound of bottles exploding and ugly laughter shattering the peaceful night, my children's dreams.

I turned on all the outside lights and called the police. They were polite but not very sympathetic. All they could say was, "Did you see the license plates?" And I hadn't. All that night, after the police left, I lay on my bed (with the kitchen and bathroom lights on, and the sharpest knife I could find next to me), listening for their return. For their ugly laughter. I lay there thinking about why we moved here, why I'd actually bought this two-acre farm 70 miles north of S.F. on the outskirts of a small town (with one movie theatre and one ice cream parlor) called Sebastopol.

The reasons were—and they were especially painful to face that night alone in bed with the image of a fiery cross etched on my brain, my daughter's screams lodged in my ears, and the sheer terror in Theo's and Jason's eyes, as well as my own terror I was trying to conceal with no-nonsense anger—Whitey died and left me the most money I'd ever had in my entire life. (And which I may never have again, right?). In one of our last talks he said, "Ya oughta buy a place way the hell out in the country where there's some trees left for these kids a yours." That was the seed, or maybe Bolinas was the seed, but he watered it with his wise words and the money he left me. Only now I thought, his insane words, as I waited for the fucking Ku Klux Klan to return to do whatever the fuck they do to ethnic City Slickers.

So, as I waited I kept thinking about why I ended up here on a farm 70 miles north of S.F. . . . I'd left and divorced my husband after 10 years of very sporadic happiness, bouts of joy, with larger portions of misery and even larger bouts of drinking and gambling his paycheck. Then, he finally hit me. Once. In the face. Both my eyes were black and blue, swollen shut. And just before his fist connected to my face—in that split second of eternity I saw his fist raised—he said, "Here's for your pretty face." I'd modeled for about three years, making more money in one or two hours than he did all day long as a construction worker. I did this when he was in the Marines stationed in Vietnam for two years, and when he returned he was an often violent stranger with only glimpses of the sensitive 16-year-old boy I first loved.

During this time my first son, Theo, was born—we lived in the cheap, low-income, but drug and violence-ridden Sunnydale Projects on the outer edge of S.F. I still can't believe we survived that place, and that I had the 18-year-old GALL to contact a modeling agency, go in for an interview and get hired for work that saved our asses and also gave me the adventure and optimism I needed to not be <u>crushed</u> by what I saw and heard—daily—in the projects: violence, great poverty, theft, rape, general hopelessness and DESPAIR. Tía would watch the kids during the week, and Whitey would come over on the weekend if I got a weekend job.

By the time Theo hit me we no longer lived in the projects but in a large Victorian flat, the lower one, under friends who were like my family. This place was nicer with warmer weather, but there were still kids on the street who didn't have what my children had (regular meals, clean clothes, someone who really loved them)—so, I gave out free food to the children who were amazed to see LIVE APPLES AND ORANGES on our kitchen table. But my kids still had to deal with the realities of the street without my help, of course. And so, Virgen, after my ex hit me in the face he left for a week and returned, and when he did I told him, "If you ever hit me again, I want you to know that I will stab you to death when you're sleeping." He believed me when I said things in that calm, deliberate way; and I did mean it. I'd do it.

Once in the projects—while he was still in Vietnam—I was settling in to sleep when I heard my neighbors arguing (they were teenagers like me—he was the biggest drug dealer in the area I'd been told, and she'd just had a baby). She called him a long list of vile names and slammed the door behind her. For the next two hours I listened as his friends showed up, the music growing so loud I could feel it in my body (yet my children continued to sleep). The walls in the projects were THIN—and then I heard the high shrill cry of a newborn. After about an hour of this, that calmness came over me and I knew what I had to do: I threw on a coat, marched next door, marched right in without knocking (looked at the group of men gathered in their front room: some of the largest black men I'd ever seen; they just stared at me, silently), stomped up the stairs toward the shrill cries, wrapped up the urine-drenched baby, stomped back downstairs and yelled: "I'm taking this baby home with me, you should all be ashamed of yourselves, and turn down that fucking music, NOW!" Anyway, that's where I go when I get "calm and deliberate" (like La Loca). The next day, Sonny (his name) came for the baby, made me promise not to tell his wife—"She'll kick my ass"—and from that day forward NO ONE ever bothered me again in those projects, and Sonny always took my garbage can out to the streets with his on Mondays. As I was laying there (in my Yellow Submarine), I kept waiting for that calmness, La Loca, to appear and tell me what the fuck to do, right?

And so Virgen, back to the time my ex hit me. . . . I lived in a kind of Neutral Zone for a few months till he came home drunk one night and tried bullying me. He wanted my purse. I wouldn't give it to him. He pushed me down on the bed. I leaped back to my feet. He pushed me down again and I sprung right back in stubborn RAGE, screaming something like, "I'm not giving you my fucking purse and I'm not going to fucking stay down!" (This from a woman who'd picked her way carefully around this violent and wounded man who'd killed but wouldn't speak of it or cry, ever; who cleaned up his tantrums, found a way to stretch the money to the next paycheck when the money was mostly gone; this from a woman who tried to believe that if only she were good and the house was clean, the floors shiny, the children she loved cared for, the dinner on the table when he walked through the door—he'd love her, he'd change; this from a woman who'd forgotten about the Amazons of her childhood; this from a woman who was trying to remember you, Virgen).

Of course, my children were listening, and I think for my daughter Tania hearing me hold my ground gave her courage—she called the police, and they took him away. I packed his clothes, put them in a box, went on welfare, went back to school to become a teacher. I divorced him. He disappeared and welfare couldn't find him—secretly, I was glad. It felt strangely like he never really existed (except for our children). Then I finally started to teach the 8th grade and earn my own money, and see how troubled so many children are in the city at that age. Their homes (many of them) are violent (wasn't ours once?), the streets are violent, and I guess somewhere in my mind, in The Secret Crystal World of my memory, the long fearless rides I used to take with Cinnamon, all that returned and returned until I could almost smell the open meadows and the ocean all around us as I put my face in her silky, dusty, brown mane—the best smell in the world, I remembered. But I think when Whitey said those words, the tiny dark seed broke open, sending its delicate and pale green hands toward the sun.

Then, it became unbearable. A homesickness for the unknown, what I never really had, but what I knew I wanted, now. Some thing. Some where. Maybe the place I'd find you again, right? Here (this farm). And I kept dreaming the four-poster bed I bought Tania for her 7th birthday—she pins notes to herself on the canopy, her daily schedule, starting at 6 am—who is this kid, I sometimes wonder, Virgen? So, I kept dreaming Tania's four-poster bed floating up from the floor, through the walls, moving somewhere, and the homesickness for what I never really had began, and it terrified me. Period. Every time I dreamt her four-poster bed floating away it made me sick to my stomach for days. With terror and longing.

For over a year my oldest son, Theo, had been running home from school trying to avoid a gang of Mexican guys who wanted him to join or they'd beat him to a pulp (he told me all this later, when we decided to move, because he didn't want to seem "like a chicken"). They sniffed glue, did petty robberies, and got drunk when they could get it. I saw them in the neighborhood—6 or 7 kids ranging from 10 to maybe 13 years of age, but their eyes looked about 100. They hung out on the corner, some steps, some run-down grocery store and glared at every passing car. So, Theo ran home that year, double locking the door behind him until I arrived with Jason around 4 pm.

But what finally got me in contact with a realtor, who had listings "in the country" in my price range, was Tania. On the last day of school, just before Xmas vacation, Tania was surrounded by a group of girls she'd gone to school with since kindergarten—now they were 7th graders—they were all black girls, five of them, and one of them, Ruby, had been her best friend in the 4th and 5th grades. Ruby had stayed at our house, Tania at hers. Ruby lived in the projects on the other side of the hill (Potrero Hill it's called), but I trusted her mother once I met her, that she'd take care of Tania, and she always did. But on that last day of school before Xmas vacation, Ruby and the other girls had hand hatchets and knives. They ripped Tania's "coming-of-age dress" (which I'd made for her—it was so beautiful—and in fact I told her I didn't think she should wear it to school, but she insisted) and they pushed her around, but then Tania got ANGRY—and she's 5 foot 8 and pretty strong, right Virgen? She pushed one of the girls to the cement and ran for a door that opened just as she started to bang on it for help. So, that did it. . . . And here I was awake all night waiting for the KU KLUX KLAN to finish their fregado job and I didn't even have a hand hatchet, just some sad assed semi-sharpened kitchen knife that barely chops up stew meat.

La Loca rides again.

Every once in a while I'd make myself get up and check all the doors and windows, looking out to the pitch black country darkness. There's no street lights here, and the far away stars that night just made me LONELY. So Virgen, as I looked at the bright, pulsing, far-away stars I thought . . . If they're just icy cold little dots in that black COSMOS, what am I here on Earth with no light of my own . . . a woman hiding (with her children), that's what I really felt, so alone with all my bad, stupid, dumb, pendeja decisions, with no husband to protect her (but who would protect me from him, I asked myself, so as they say in chess, "Stalemate"—but it didn't make me feel any better, believe me) . . . a woman with no light of her own in the fucking dark, and here I'm telling you THE TRUTH, what I don't tell anyone. Too much pride, that's me. And what would my children do if they knew I didn't know what the fuck I'm doing, so I tell myself . . . shut up and check the doors and windows, be prepared to use your pathetic knife that barely cuts stew meat because, girl, that's all you have, so deal with it—a typical Pep Talk from La Loca to La Pendeja, right Virgen? Anyway, just looking at it made me want to laugh, so I figured that's a good sign: laughter. And I kind of laughed, but I probably sounded like Harry The Hermit, remember?

As I lay back down on the bed, my eyes on the curtainless windows that look over the creek, barns, walnut and willow trees, blackberry bushes, the fields beyond, the neighbor's black horse with the white comet on his forehead who puts his beautiful head over the fence to eat our still high, wild hay—I waited for the sun. Morning. With my ears cocked for the sound of a motor. Four cars passed that night, and each time I ran to the wide front-room window. Twice it was the police patrolling as they'd promised, so that was a relief. The other two cars were probably neighbors further up the road, as they say here—not "the street." Then back to the darkest bed on Earth, eyes on the curtainless window, jealous of the bright, pulsing stars with a light of their own—and I'm not kidding, I was really and truly JEALOUS. And petrified. Waiting. For the fregado sun.

And I started to think (though I really tried to stop myself, but of course I couldn't—good old Plato, right Virgen?) So, I started to think about that song Billie Holiday sings, "Strange Fruit," and what it really means, the "strange fruit" dangling from southern trees (and northern trees as well, no doubt)—lynched black men dangling from trees. The KKK dragging people from their houses, lynching fathers in front of their children, or sons in front of their parents, or raping mothers and daughters in plain view, burning their houses to the ground, then burning the fucking CROSS while wearing their "pure white" cowardly hoods and robes—in short Virgen, my imagination went chingaso wild while I waited for the KKK to roar up and throw a burning torch on our cedar-shingled roof.

I saw it all. Germany, the year I was born, and what the KKK's soul brothers, the Nazis, did to over 6 million human beings, and I'm part German (from my birth father, Leo). And then I started thinking about the Indians in our own country, the genocide of MILLIONS of human beings here—and of course I'm also Yaqui Indian, and you know Mamacita was a full-blood Yaqui Indian from Sonora. So, I just lay there on my bed thinking . . . I'm Mexican but I'm also German and my father was from the South so maybe his family was part of the fregado KKK, them and their Big Plantation, as my mother Carmen always said . . . and I'm also a Dirty Indian, a Gringa, a Wet Back, granddaughter of the Ku Klux Klan, waiting for the KKK to burn my fregado house down and run me and my half-breed vermin kids out of the farm I just bought. . . .

Then I just passed out cold because when my eyes flew open, ready to see just about anything, what I saw was the curtainless window filled with MORNING, and the almost deafening singing of birds brought me to my feet in a flash. All the kids were still sleeping as I checked each one. Tania had her head under a pillow, with her arm flung out over the side of her bed, trustingly it seemed. Theo had crawled into a sleeping bag, his slingshot on the floor beside his bed. And Jason was drooling into his pillow, mouth open—and his shock of blond hair surprised me for the zillionth time, his clear, blue eyes even more—I guess I've never gotten used to a real life Gringo in the family. Someone who'd actually arrived from my own body with that blond hair—and now I wonder what the KKK would make of him, but I let it go because I'm back at the beginning: I am a human being mammal. What a genius. I knew this when I was 12. 1 guess the hard part is remembering it, over and over, etc. . . .

I very quietly opened the back door and as I stepped out onto the damp earth, the early morning sun seemed to create mirrors of light on every wet leaf, hundreds of them, everywhere. Surrounding me. And the silence, the perfect beauty as far as I could see, the SMELL of the damp earth made me weep with a weird kind of happiness. I really don't know why I felt so happy, Virgen—I just felt, suddenly, perfectly happy. Right then. Right there. That's when I saw the wild turkey perched on the grape arbor—at the time I didn't know it was a wild turkey, we looked it up in Tania's bird book, and there it was. Now, Theo wants to hunt one for Thanksgiving, we'll see.

Then I slowly walked to the front lawn where the burned spot was, and as I was staring at it someone said, "It'll grow back so green you'll never know that crap was there, dear." I jerked to attention, not knowing for a few seconds whether to run for the house or find the person this voice belonged to. I made myself hold still and look up. It was my 84-year-old neighbor.

"My name's Sally," she said. "I've lived here for over 40 years and never seen folks act like such fools in my own back yard." She gazed at me patiently, waiting for me to speak.

Finally, I relented to the kindness I saw in her eyes. "My name's Luna and I've been wondering if I should just pack up my kids and run for it. You're saying no one's ever burned a cross here before?"

"Not to my knowledge, but these kind of fools do what they want, don't they? And if you leave that's what they want, isn't it, dear?"

I just stood there still staring at the burned grass and earth, remembering what I had come to just before I passed out—that I'm the whole chingaso shebang and I'm NOT going anywhere. This is where I want to be. Here and now, as the LSD guys say.

"Now, I've got some jams put up in the cellar and some fresh eggs from my hens I want you to have. Have you had your coffee yet, dear?" Sally began to walk, slowly with care, toward her house. 'What you do is to take a rake and just scratch that burn away, and give it some water every day for a while. It'll be green again before you know it."

I glanced toward the house and saw Tania staring out of her bedroom window. I waved and put one finger up, meaning . . . See you in a minute. She waved back and closed her curtain.

As I watched Sally pour me coffee, I saw she had pain in her body and that everything she did was done with focused economy. She handed me fresh muffins and as I ate them, sipping the strong, hot coffee, I told her I was going to be teaching 8th grade in the fall in Santa Rosa, but in the meanwhile I was doing substitute teaching wherever they needed me. And then I told her I was from S.F., my children's names and ages, and then she said, if I didn't mind, she'd hire them for yard work and chores from time to time. By the time I left, Sally had loaded a box full of jams and pickles, and 6 beautiful brown speckled eggs in a bowl.

"Just tell one of your children to bring back the bowl, dear," she said as I walked back to the house. "Oh Luna, I just want you to know something."

I turned around to see Sally holding a rifle in the crook of her 84-year-old arm—she'd told me her age proudly, like she'd won the lottery that morning, and that she'd outlived three husbands.

"I keep this right over my back door, and my daddy taught his daughter to be a damned good shot. Can you shoot, dear?"

"No, I don't think so, not any good anyway," I croaked.

"I'll set up a target practice for you, and then you go out and buy a good rifle for yourself and your children, if you want to learn that is, dear."

My mouth was probably open and my expression not too bright. I was stunned. Sally looked kind of like that nice, genteel white lady, Betty Crocker. But I realized, with a burst of clarity that made me want to laugh out loud—this was Annie Oakley at 84!

"Where do I buy one?" I asked stupidly.

"Oh, I'll show you, just take me in that car of yours to town and we'll pick a good one out. Just let me know in advance, dear,

I have to plan my day at this stage of the game so I don't wear my old self out." She laughed, and I swear for a few seconds she could've been a girl of, how's TWELVE, Virgen, no lie.

The kids were up, so I made them scrambled eggs and toast with jam from one of the jars Sally gave me. I told them about Sally, but not about the rifle, yet. (I guess I'm trying to tell you all this like a story, plus it's more fun this way for me, and somehow everything makes more sense even to me, okay Virgen?)

"Are we going back to S.F., Mom?" Jason dared to ask. His clear blue eyes were so large and trusting. And afraid.

I looked at Theo and Tania, and their hazel and brown eyes were just as large and trusting. Trusting me. Their mother. The one in charge, holy shit.

"Last night I stayed up and the cops patrolled like they said they would, and Sally said she's lived here for over 40 years and never saw anyone do that, here anyway, that's what she said." I paused to remind myself: I'm the one in charge. "So, anyway, like Sally said, which I agree with, they're trying to scare us out like a pack of cowards, and the way I see it, we bought this farm and we belong here as much as anyone else. We bought this farm with our own money, right guys?" (I said this as much to myself as to my wide-eyed children, Virgen.)

Then we talked about the Ku Klux Klan and why they probably wear the white hoods and robes—because they're really afraid to be SEEN. And that we hadn't actually seen the men who burned the cross on our lawns, or if they were wearing the KKK outfit. So we talked about that for a while. And finally I told them about Sally offering to teach me how to shoot a rifle, and how she hangs hers over her back door like ANNIE OAKLEY.

"Who's Annie Oakley?" Jason wanted to know.

"A cowgirl, stupid," Tania answered him. "Are you going to do it, Mom, like learn to shoot?" She stared me down.

I thought of Darling and her gun in Bolinas, then suddenly of 84-year-old Sally standing in her doorway cradling her rifle, and I said (trying to sound firm), "Damned straight, I'm going to do it just in case."

"Can we hang it over our door too cause that's so cool!?" Theo wanted to know.

"Oh, shut up, Theo, besides it'll probably fall right on your head," Tania started giggling.

"Can I learn to shoot, Mom?" Theo ignored her.

"Maybe when you're older. . . ."

"Me too, Mom!" Jason joined in.

I tried to picture a rifle over my door, a rifle in the crook of my arm, a 29-year-old Annie Oakley. "Jesus F. Christ," I sighed.

After breakfast I went out to the shed, where I'd seen a rake, left by the former owners. I took it to the burned spot and raked it smooth. Then I watered it by hand with the hose as I pictured the rifle over the front door, then over the back door, then front door, and out of nowhere this image came to me: I was cutting down the bodies, the "strange fruit" Billie Holiday sang and broke your heart about—and as I cut the ropes, each one, they floated to the ground like ripened leaves and disappeared into the earth I was standing there watering. Then I, good old Plato, wanted to think about the whole genocidal chingadero century, but I knew it was too much to bear at that moment, so I kept watering the dead grass.

And then I started to picture myself holding a rifle, learning how to shoot. Just in case.

Well Virgen, La Loca rides again in SEBASTOPOL.

Early June, smells like SUMMER

Dear La Virgen,

Sally helped me pick the rifle and I'm doing target practice in her field. First I watched her do it, and she is a good shot! So, when it was my turn, the first time I had to pull the trigger, hear the loud KABOOM, feel the kick of the rifle shoot up my entire fregado arm to the top of my head, I tried to act like it was as natural as frying an egg (that's what Sally Oakley says). Plus, watching this 84-year-old woman handle a rifle with SUPREME CONFIDENCE made me feel like a 29-year-old wimp for even wanting to whine, "Maybe I shouldn't do this. . . ." So, now I'm getting a little better at it, steadier. But I still haven't hung it over my back door—it's in the closet on the top shelf, unloaded. I keep the ammunition box hidden away in my underwear drawer, figuring the boys won't go through that drawer, ha! They're at the "Girls are gross" stage and I say hooray for that, for now, right Virgen?

As far as I know the KKK (or whoever it was) never returned. I search the faces I see when I go to the small downtown for clues, a sneer, a sign of hatred, a desire to kill me. Obviously, that's futile so I've made myself stop looking for IT.

In the meanwhile, Tania has made best friends with a black girl her age named Minnie. She lives with her grandmother and cousin Sam, who's just a year older. They're the only black family in town it appears, and of course they live right down the street, or road as they say here—Tania says there's a couple of other black guys at school, but that they've been adopted into white families. Anyway, I wonder if anyone's ever burned a CROSS on their front lawn, but I can't bring myself to ask Minnie, and I guess Tania feels the same way because when I ask her she says, "God, Mom, how do I know?" It's Kid Shorthand for "Shut up," so I do because I don't want to mar their friendship or hurt Minnie's feelings either (but of course I still want to know).

And last week the principal of the junior high called and in a spy-like voice he said he wanted to know if I knew who my daughter was "keepin company with"—and I said, "Do you mean Minnie?" And I swear to you, Virgen, he actually said, "I was jus wonderin if you knew your daughter's spendin time with a nigger-o." "I'll be right there," I said between clenched teeth and hung up. At first I was irritated with the drive to Santa Rosa to teach as there were no openings here. Now, at that moment, I was GRATEFUL—but then to be honest, I was relieved to see the school in Santa Rosa had a good population of brown and black kids mixed in with the white ones (unlike this place)—and I also reminded myself that my kids were going to school where they lived, here. And as I was taken on a tour of the junior high in Santa Rosa, it was the weirdest thing, but I remembered that 6th grade teacher telling us it was against the law to pick California Poppies, and how I even ate them—my big secret. And so, here I am going to be a regular 8th grade teacher, and all I could think of was "Why do white people think they OWN all the beautiful places, and that we're just visitors?" And I really wanted to find a California Poppy and eat a few, but I haven't seen one here yet, Virgen.

And so, in short, I went directly into the principal's office, past his startled secretary, and had a FIT (though the sight of him stopped me for one sec right in my tracks—he was entirely dressed in <u>white</u>, even his shoes, believe it or snot!). So I shrieked, "The color of a person's skin means nothing to me or my children, and I will not have you calling me to report such things, do you understand!!!!" He didn't even answer me, he just kept standing there in his white shoes, white socks, white pants, white, very white, shirt, and, unbelievably, a white TIE, and most likely pure white boxer shorts on his immense, white belly (which I really did NOT want to imagine), so anyway he was staring at me like I was something he couldn't recognize or understand my language—so I marched back out past his still startled secretary. Then two days later a teacher from the school called me to say he'd heard about my confrontation with Mr. Stewart, and that he and a group of like-minded teachers and parents wanted to get him out of there. Would I go to a school board meeting and lodge a formal complaint with about 20 or so other parents? "Count me in," I said, overwhelmed with joy that I wasn't alone in my own private rage here in Sebastopol.

So that's encouraging, Virgen, especially when Tania came home crying the other day—some girls started calling her "nigger lover" as she waited for Minnie to come out of the bathroom. And then Tania said, "They call Minnie 'Little Black Sambo' and she's even kind of used to it cause she doesn't even get mad, Mom." But that did it for Tania—she went into a RAGE and started yelling, "You shut up, you little white patty bitches!" (She was pretty proud of the "bitches" part—her face lit up as the word turned into a smile that covered her face with glee—she is such a trip!) Tania the trip, as in Luna la loca, of course. So Tania said, "And Minnie couldn't believe those little white patty bitches did shut up, and when they walked away Minnie started to crack up." "Don't get too fond of the bitch word there, Tania," I said, trying not to smile, but she caught my eye and continued to be proud of herself, though she'd run in the door red-faced and crying till she told me the whole story.

Anyway, I told her to go take a nice hot bath (her favorite thing—she surrounds herself with candies, and bubbles up to her eyes)—and I told her she did the right thing, and I'm so glad she didn't let the last horrific incident with her four ex-friends in S.F. (with the hand hatchets) tilt her toward white pattydom. Whenever I look at Tania I see someone with a wide open heart, ready to love, and when I look at myself—the truth—I see a heart covered with loads of scar tissue, and that it opens a little crack, then slams itself shut, the Tough Cookie Syndrome. So as I started cooking dinner I could hear Tania humming to herself and running a trickle of hot water into the tub. This month, June 28th, she'll be 13, the age I was when I went back to S.F. from Bolinas, and the same age I was when I lost you, La Virgen. I didn't even realize she was born on Mamacita's birthday until Tía told me with tears in her eyes, and it felt like all the scar tissue trembled and heaved, and I remember my heart actually hurt in my chest—and I realize now I had NO IDEA what I was getting into with this new daughter of mine (at 15)—gracias a La Virgen for the scar tissue or I'd be a drug addict prostitute, dead, my children in some shitty foster care place. But the thing is, Virgen, what I'm starting to understand is that I'll probably never be able to really love someone (like a man)—my heart's too tough. It softens only for my children, and other children, my students. The truth is it gives me such pleasure to just be in their presence—because even with the wise-ass stuff most of them are so willing to love (even me).

I've been thinking about The Cheap Skate, you know, my uncle—when I had Tania I stayed with him and mi Tía for awhile before I found a place to live with a friend over a bar in the Mission, but it was ours, both of us 16. She worked as a waitress and I was on welfare for that year, and I also did babysitting on the side for cash. I'd pack up Tania and the diaper bag, taking 2 buses five days a week to babysit a baby about Tania's age. So while I was staying with mi Tía she told me his story: He's the oldest of 22 children, started working in the fields at about 7, never finished grammar school, had his first pair of new shoes in the Army—I guess that explains it, but I still don't think it's an excuse to eat steaks while your kid eats hot dogs, that's my opinion. But then if I picture him, a skinny, hungry 7-year-old kid up at dawn to work in the fields, and the oldest of 22 children, year after year, I see his heart overgrown with stinging nettles. I've stepped on that stuff and nothing, like nothing, takes away the PAIN.

And then Whitey's story: He and his brothers and sisters were beaten pretty badly, he ran away at 12, hopping the rails (he told me all this in pieces while very drunk, when I'd take his paycheck $ and hide it from him till Monday morning). Got to L.A. and found jobs selling papers on the street, ran errands, slept in a burlesque house where some of the women looked out for him, cooking for him on a hot plate sometimes, and he said they were so beautiful, the most beautiful women he ever saw—and when he said this I could see the wide open boy in his bleary eyes. I loved it when he told me his stories, so I'd hang out when he was drinking just to get him going. And yet from his hard-ass childhood he chose to give, to inflict the pain on himself mainly—when I see Whitey's heart I see clusters of wild roses in a riot of full bloom.

The hallmark of his personhood was that he couldn't stand to see a child suffer and do nothing about it—when he saw me hungry and scared shitless (while trying hard to look BRAVE), he fed me in spite of my Witch Power Eyes, remember Virgen? He named me Pocahontas, daughter, though he never called me "daughter" or told me, in words, that he loved me—but I know he did. Love me. The way he showed up at my first apartment (over the noisy bar) with an arm load of food 2 or 3 times a week, always giving me some cash "For whatever you might be needin." When I lived in the Sunnyvale Projects later, he came at least twice a week with the arm load of groceries, and always something special for the kids. And the truth is I always knew he was coming, and it always made me feel safe (but of course I'd never tell him this).

And now, that's how I'm here on this 2-acre farm, this slightly dented Yellow Submarine—his final gift to me and my children. The last time I saw him, and he could still speak, I told him, sitting on the bed with him (he was so skinny and small, as though he was shrinking back to how he came into this world)—"I love you, Whitey, and I couldn't have done it without you." Of course I was crying, and he looked mortified, as I've never said it, that I loved him. "Now don't start that fer Christs sake, I ain't dead yet!" But I could see the wide open boy in his eyes.

Virgen, I forgot to tell you—the grass is growing back a young fluorescent GREEN. Tania and I made you a small altar in the front room by the window, no Buddha this time, just you. There are wild roses out by the creek, so will pick some tomorrow for the altar. Here's a question, send me a dream: Is it possible for wild roses to grow from layers of scar tissue?

con amor, La Loca With A Rifle

Mid-June . . . California Poppies all over the fields!!!!

Dear La Virgen,

Last night a neighbor across the road, and up from Sally—the houses are separated by FIELDS here—this guy woke me up. He was obviously plastered and yelling something at the top of his lungs. Sally had warned me, "He's the most arrested man in Sonoma County as he's a drunk and sometimes he beats his wife, a good woman too and a damned shame, her with six children to feed. Well, the county helps her out I'm told, someone's got to." For a second I wanted to tell her about my ex-husband, how I had to be on welfare for awhile to survive and go to school, but I decided not to considering how gossip can spread in a small town—exactly the way she's telling me about them, right?

So, I woke up to The Most Arrested Man in Sonoma County yelling something, and I mean he was YELLING at about 2 am. I picked my way through the dark, checking my kids as they slept through it. I opened the back door to hear him better, what the hell he was shouting about, and the soft summer air was so sweet and tangled with unnameable things somewhere out there in the dark, tears sprang to my eyes. I had actually been ready to scream, "SHUT UP!" But the night took me by surprise, it was so soft, and I sat down on the top step and just listened for awhile. And finally I heard it. He was quoting a poem, Dylan Thomas. (I studied his poetry in school and his book's in my book shelf in the front room.) I recognized the first stanza and just followed his voice, which was thick with hooch and a thick Irish brogue (he must be Irish). I was amazed and enthralled—The Most Arrested Man In Sonoma County seemed to know whole poems by heart, by memory, unless he was reading it, but I couldn't see any lights on his porch, where he obviously was standing in absolute darkness at 2 am yelling wonderful poetry. So I just listened, Virgen, sitting on the top step of my dark porch, breathing in the soft, sweet unnameable things of summer. June. Almost my daughter's 13th birthday. I was tempted to wake her up to hear him, but then I knew she'd wonder if living on the farm for almost 3 months had made me go koo-koo (if she only knew, right Virgen?)—so I didn't.

And his voice kept breaking my heart, it was so full of defeated longing. At the end of each line it sounded like he was going to give it up, but then he'd come back with a ROAR. Here's the first stanza of my favorite one, and the last poem he shouted:

"I see the boys of summer in their ruin
Lay the gold tithings barren,
Setting no store by harvest, freeze the soils;
There in their heat the winter floods
Of frozen loves they fetch their girls,
And drown the cargoed apples in their tides."

It's a long poem, nine stanzas, and he'd been out there shouting poetry for at least 20 minutes, so when the cops arrived, no siren with just the slowly flashing lights, he was almost to the final stanza; he continued as they approached, and then he was just silent as they led him to the car. I imagined his wife and kids were probably sadly relieved he was gone (he was so hooched), and I hope the only damage he'd committed that night was poetry. After the cop car floated away into the night toward jail, I went inside, found my flashlight and Dylan Thomas, and brought him out to the back porch. By flashlight I read the last stanza out loud—here it is:

"I see you boys of summer in your ruin.
Man in his maggot's barren.
And boys are full and foreign in the pouch.
I am the man your father was.
We are the sons of flint and pitch.
O see the poles are kissing as they cross."

Then I read the last stanza out loud, again and again, and each time it meant more to me, and tears just poured down my face. There's such grief in this poem, such sorrow, regret, and redemption. "O see the poles are kissing as they cross." Forgiveness. The cross. The fiery cross. Where it's thick and green now.

Virgen, you probably know it's been a long time since I've even talked to my mother Carmen, and it's been an even longer time that I've hated her. But sitting on the porch reading this stanza over and over, I remembered an old story Carmen told me when I was little, how she carried me as a baby of about 2 years, on a most likely unbearably hot summer day, down a dusty Louisiana road—she said it was summer and you could fry an egg by the sun—she carried me and her suitcase to a bus stop because neither my father nor his racist family—Carmen told me one time that she heard one of them say she was no better than a nigger—would drive her. And her choice was to leave me behind. But she didn't. She carried me all the way. To the bus stop. And home to Mamacita. So, I change the words to: "I am the woman your mother was. We are the daughters of flint and pitch. O see the poles are kissing as they cross." The cross. The fiery cross. Where it's green now.

And I think of the last time I saw her, when Whitey died (left his body)—how I couldn't stand her, and at the same time how I noticed her stubborn spirit was still entirely intact, and I realize clearly now at this moment that both things are true for me. I can't stand her, but I must know she's intact. (That I must love her . . . I am the woman your mother was.) That I'm grateful she carried me to the bus stop and brought me home to mi familia, Mamacita y Tía. (That she must've loved me . . . I am the woman your mother was.)

Finally, I read the whole poem through out loud from beginning to end—kind of wanting to yell it, but I'm not that brave, and that's the truth. My tears had stopped and it was as though I could see in the dark. Night Eyes like in Bolinas (remember?). And I knew I'd call Carmen. It will be very weird and awkward, but I know I have to do it, call her. (I haven't done it yet, but I will, I promise, Virgen.)

Then I carried the flashlight (but didn't use it) as I walked toward the creek and across the wooden bridge to the back fields where the hay is starting to get high. Sally advised me to put a steer or two back there for the meat, she said, and that they also eat the hay like automatic lawn mowers, plus they get nice and fat, she said, and healthy on all that good hay out back that's just growing for free. So maybe I will. But then of course we'd have to KILL the steers to eat them (whine whine). . . .

I bent down to see the California Poppies, but they were all closed up against the night and I imagined them dreaming about the SUN—how they open their fiery sunlike petals first thing in the morning. And then I suddenly heard the white lady teacher's voice, "It's against the LAW to pick California Poppies because they're the State Flower." How she glared her words into the eyes set into the brown and black faces—how she glared the words into my eyes. And I realized, 18 years later, what she really said—that it was against the law to love the sun, the moon and stars in the sky, the flowers and trees that grow on the earth for FREE, especially if you're poor and brown/black-skinned. It was against the law to trust your Secret Crystal World Dreams (if you had any)—to trust them (and never ever speak of them in that class, of course) but most of all, <u>most of all</u> it was against the law to love your OWN SELF. So, I picked a bunch of dreaming California Poppies and I ate one just like I did as a kid, La Loca.

There I was at probably going on 4 am in the morning in the middle of June, sitting in the back fields, and I wasn't afraid of the KKK, perverts, muggers or vampires for that matter. I ate another California Poppy and thought about the principal we just impeached at the junior high—I went to pick Tania up for the dentist, so while I waited for her I saw him drive off (his last day there) in his white Cadillac with a white interior, with his wife sitting next to him, and she had (no joke) white hair that looked so stiff it could've been cement the way the waves of her white hair obeyed her. I could only stare (and stare). And he was dressed ENTIRELY in white, though of course I couldn't see his shoes, but every time I saw him they were. . . . I guess that was his final statement to us all, or maybe that's just the way he normally lived his life (free from all darkness and nigger-o lovers).

I ate another California poppy and I thought about how we—the like-minded teachers and parents—also abolished "Slave Day" (believe it or not)—a practice of auctioning a student slave for a day to the highest bidder in the name of school funds and "good clean fun." They would actually stand a kid on a crate and auction him or her off—and the kid looked pretty embarrassed as the other ones really got into it in a nasty way, probably because it wasn't them being a slave, right? Tania came home and told me about it so I was there the next day with a group of other parents, then the teachers who heaved every year also spoke up. Anyway, I know this isn't ending racism here, but it feels like it might help, bit by BIT. Of course, I know the boys don't want anyone to know I'm their mother (The Trouble Maker), especially their new friends, but then I also know they count on me to do this stuff, secretly, like all's well in the world if Mom is being a pain in the ass to whoever currently needs it—but they actually duck down in the car to not be seen with me, and I pretend I don't notice for now.

I ate another California Poppy and remembered the very last time I talked to Whitey and he still understood me. I told him for the second and last time in my life that I loved him, right to his face, his mortified eyes, "Now don't go gettin mushy on me fer Christ's sake." But I could see how (secretly) pleased he was. And then I kissed him on the cheek, as he pretended to get away, but of course he was in the bed he'd die in (leave the body) within the week. My lips remember the feel of his cheek: fragile, temporary. Ripe wild rose petals.

I ate one more California Poppy and I heard myself speaking to Mamacita, welcoming her to this farm in Sebastopol, my home, my children's home, because I know she'd love it here. And then I started thinking about planting chilis, onions, scallions, tomatoes, squash, corn, and then I <u>knew</u> Mamacita was really here—and I swear to you, Virgen, I felt her SWELL up inside me and I thought of Dylan Thomas' words: "I am the woman your mother was." And then I felt Whitey swell up inside me too, so I welcomed him: "I am the man your father was." And I thought of his love of steaks and fried chicken with mashed potatoes, smothered in butter and gravy, on the side—so I decided to get 2 STEERS, some laying chickens and some FRYERS—those are male chickens you eat (kill). Sally said she'd help me figure all this out, the best places to buy them, even what you call these animals (pullets are fryers) when you actually grow them to be your food—whine, whine—I'm beginning to love this woman who picks out the layers who don't lay as much anymore for The Stew Pot, she says, because if you don't do it quick enough they get too tough to eat with any pleasure, and you just eat them to not waste food. So, for Sally: "We are the dark deniers, let us summon / Death from a summer woman." (The same poem.)

How can I ever thank The Most Arrested Man In Sonoma County for this night, Virgen? I just wish he didn't beat his wife and terrorize his children—a California Poppy for each of them. But I am grateful for his muy crazy (brave) self that woke me up and kept me up till DAWN reading Dylan Thomas' poems (poems I haven't read in years), and writing one of my OWN. . . .

I REMEMBER

When I went to search for you at
twenty-one (the year my third child
was born)—to find your brittle bones
ten years later, under a number 13—

there is no headstone they tell me,
so they give me a map of the cemetery
and a #13 circled in red. Finally,
I found your bones, your empty eye

sockets (you were no longer there)—
but I wept anyway, and since
I didn't weep as a child, I wept
long and hard the 10 years past.

And the ripe, red rose I threw into your grave
gave me its magical seeds, blooming
from my eyes, running down my face,
I devoured them, unknowingly.

Until now. As a child I roamed
the city as a boy (my only freedom,
defended and disguised)—on star-nights
climbing buildings being built where men worked,

sweated all sun-foggy-day—fishing on piers, watching ships
full of men and treasures, and all around me were the
fisher men—bike riding through Golden Gate Park,
the Secret Forest Place where I heard fairies

whisper "hello" (it was so beautiful,
a small lake, giant ferns, flowers everywhere)—
where I was watchful but somehow safe.
And Playland At The Beach where the men who

worked the rides let me ride for free
after paying only once, and I wonder now if
they saw through my disguise, my defense—
that I was a girl dressed up like a boy.

That I was a spic, a wet back, dirty Indian,
gringa. That I was a kid brave enough
and crazy enough to keep seeking
some real joy. Her, La Loca.

And I see now, Mamacita, that when
you taught me to Dream—each star-night
to sun-foggy-day—you were teaching me to
love my self. My true self.

And I see now, Mamacita, that the Dreamer
isn't a woman or a man, isn't Mexican,
English, German, Yaqui, African, Chinese,
Japanese, French, Spanish or Irish.

The Dreamer is the lover loving
the Dream, and La Vida is

the child of their union. The mystery
of loving. And dreaming.

Tonight a drunk, Irish-brogued man,
shouting poetry to the June star-night,
wasn't crazy or just drunk—he was
trying, in the only way he knew how,

to love his very own self.
He was just a Dreamer trying to remember
the child that loves to dream and fly.
He was just a Dreamer—disguised

and defended—trying to be free for awhile
on his porch, poetry on his tongue,
California Poppies shut and hidden, waiting
for the great-light-sun. But it was

still against the law, and they took him
away (The Most Arrested Man In Sonoma
County). And so, 18 years later, Mamacita,
I just want you to know—your spirit, what

I feel inside me, so full, expanding—
I am the Dreamer loving the Dream, and
I am the child who loves to dream
and fly. I remember. La Vida.

Your great-granddaughter, born on June 28th,
your birthday, remembers—your great-grandsons
also remember (because I remember)
what you taught me.

Now, my California Poppies are waking up.
They tell me: "It's not against the laws
of the sun and moon, the stars,
to love your fairy-thumbed self,

remember."
We wait for the sun
as I try to remember what
I remember. LA VIDA!

One last thing, Virgen—it was a little past dawn when I fell into bed, and for the first time since I left my children's father I didn't miss his presence, or any man's presence, in my bed, and the bed didn't feel like a huge ocean with me on a tiny life raft. It felt more like I was floating in the wide open ocean with my old pals The Seals in Bolinas (I even thought of Jefferino, and I actually remembered his FACE, what he looked like), remember? And for the first time since I moved here to this farm (where Tania's 4-poster bed landed), I didn't feel foolish, vulnerable, terrified or lonely ALONE. I thought of the rifle on the top shelf of the closet and the box of bullets hidden carefully at the bottom of my underwear drawer. And I was glad they were there just in case I really needed them (if the KKK returns with torches or worse)—and I was glad Sally taught me how to shoot straight, pretty much on target, no more whining (with the rifle).

But before I finally got to my bed . . . I was really and truly glad—sitting in the cool, wet field—in that moment, that The Most Arrested Man In Sonoma County got me to remember Dylan Thomas' poetry. So just as the sun began to touch the tops of the trees, just as the California Poppies began to <u>sing</u> very loudly to the sun—and I swear I could hear them singing high and whispery, but loud, Virgen—I re-read this stanza about the fairy thumbs:

"I see the summer children in their mothers
Split up the brawned womb's weathers.
Divide the night and day with fairy thumbs;
There in the deep with quartered shades
Of sun and moon they paint their dams
As sunlight paints the shelling of their heads."

It makes me happy to type it out for you—it feels like doing it makes it more like mine. Was I smiling when I passed out, Virgen? Or was I just drooling with exhaustion? I slept till noon and the kids were so quiet and good. It turns out they thought I was sick because I <u>never</u> do this—but I've been eating California Poppies all night, and that sun(dawn)light painted the shelling on my head, and the California Poppies were singing: "It's not against the laws, no, no, it's not against the laws of the sun, moon, stars, earth. . . ." And I, for one, believe them.

Also, I picked one last California Poppy just as the sun lit up the fields entirely, and I suddenly (for no good reason) thought of Carmen's WOMB (the poem of course), imagining her heart beat as the sun began to pulse and hum (I could actually hear it hum in the silence like I used to in Bolinas)—and the air was so soft with dawning breezes—and Virgen, I was so glad to be ALIVE (La Vida). "Thank you for my life, Carmen," I whispered with the poppies. And then I ate the one I picked, and I wondered what I'll say to Carmen when I talk to her—it's been almost 2 years. I know I can't say, "Thank you for my life"—but maybe something will come to me. And then I hope she doesn't say something mean and stupid, because that's what she tends to do, right Virgen? "I am the woman your mother was. We are the daughters of flint and pitch." I wish I had a mother who could say something like this to me—Mamacita did, but she's not HERE in the flesh and blood—so I'll say it to myself. And Tania. My fairy-thumbed sons. "I am the woman your mother was. We are the daughters and sons of flint and pitch."

(A secret dream . . .

When I finally woke up at NOON I remembered this dream: a heart kind of suspended in the middle of nothing, but it's not heart shaped, yet I know it's a heart. I can see it beating, and then I hear it, and I love the sound of <u>my heart</u>. Suddenly I know it's my heart. I see layers and layers of really ugly scar tissue, and I feel sad for my heart, that it's so beat up and ugly—but as I watch, a miniscule seed pops open, and very slowly, a skinny green shoot begins to grow, then two tiny leaves, a ridge of thorns, the tiniest rose bud. And as I watch, the tiny rose bud decides to open—and I can feel it like joy and sorrow all mixed up with so much joy it hurts—and slowly, slowly it blooms. A tiny, bloody, so beautiful RED ROSE. Now I have a secret in my ugly scar tissue heart, and for whatever it's worth it's mine—gracias, mi Virgen.)

Con todo mi amor,
Luna La Fairy-Thumbed 29-year-old Mammal,
With her own FIELDS of California Poppies
SINGING!!!!

Early July, firecrackers at the football field, Tania's 13th birthday, her party with a piñata even Sally took a swing at—and waiting for the chingado KKK . . .

Dear La Virgen,

Well, I did it—I hung the RIFLE over my back door, but I still keep the bullets hidden away in the taboo underwear drawer. The kids and I started singing "Home home on the range" and other cornball songs after we got it up there, but strangely enough I can tell it makes them feel safer, like we ain't takin no BS on this here farm, so put that in your pipe and smoke it EEEEHHHAAA!!!! (Stop me before I kill again, that's a joke, Virgen.)

When Sally saw it perched over the back door she said, "Now that's the place to put it so you don't have to be searching for it like a damn fool." Then she laughed, handing me the morning's eggs, and she sat down to wait for the tea kettle to boil so I could drip our freshly ground coffee. Jason asked her, "Are you a cowgirl, Mrs. Jensen?" She looked at him dead serious and replied, "The genuine article, son." Jason was speechless for once as he stared back at her in a rare moment of respectful awe. Then he laughed his Bugs Bunny laugh (I feel slightly sorry for them as we have no TV and I'm not planning to buy another one, but they plead, "Saturday morning cartoons, Mom!" I just want to see if we can actually live without it for a while, so I'm the monster who ate the TV, fregado!). So Jason blesses Sally with his Bugs Bunny laugh, runs out the back door with the rifle perched over it, hops on his bike to go meet his new friend Rocky who we call Rocky Raccoon because he has dark circles under his eyes, but he's full of life like Jason (but I worry he has a vitamin deficiency so I give him a vitamin when he's here). And I can just see them watching cartoons at Rocky's house, right Virgen? Maybe that's why Rocky has dark circles, too much TV . . . but Jason comes home absolutely muddy and filthy, so much so he takes his outer clothes off outside to be hosed off first. Then he does a comet streak to the shower—so I know they're out there having their quotas of adventures also. I guess TV is like heroin, you have to withdraw a little at a time. I keep piles of books, as does Tania. Also, everyone's writing in a diary now—I read only what they let me, but I glance at the date and entry to make sure they write something every day. And I make everyone do the trek to the library once a week to bring home at least 2 new books, so at night it's quiet, some music, everyone reading something or a game of Monopoly, Scrabble, cards (and no new crosses on the front lawn). Peace. Is this peace, Virgen? It's beginning to feel like it, just a little.

And so, when I see Jason and Rocky together roaring around on their bikes, I wonder, I truly wonder what these over-charged, glittery-eyed 8-year-old boys do with all the apparent freedom they have to just roam on their bikes this summer, finding places in the nearby Swains Woods where a year-round creek still draws fox, coyote, deer, Sally tells me—she also says that's where the wild turkeys hide out, and that wild turkeys are shy but smart, unlike the ones we buy to roast. All the wildness has been bred out of them and they've become so stupid that young chicks must be forced to drink or they'll die of thirst—then colored marbles must be placed in their water to remind them to keep drinking, talk about pendejos, and we EAT them too. Anyway, I guess I'd love to join Jason and Rocky for a whole day, but that's ridiculous of course. I can just see them trying to put up with my 29-year-old self, and having to be <u>good</u> all day long, as in no putting their lives in danger—and I think of myself as a kid on her bike in S.F., how DANGER was the best part, remember Virgen?

So instead I yell, "Be home by 1 o'clock for lunch!" And Jason yells back, "Okay Mom!" But I know he'll be at least 30 minutes late, and he'll be so muddy he'll just eat outside, him and Rocky. I watch them zip down the road, the early summer morning so ripe with yellow light, and I think of Dylan Thomas, his poem "I See the Boys of Summer"—then I hear Jason's Bugs Bunny laugh and Rocky yells something I can't hear, and they're gone. And I go to the "little garden," a fenced-in spot, where I'm putting in lettuce, tomatoes, cucumbers, squash. Sally asked a neighbor with a tractor to hoe my HUMONGOUS side field by the house—we'll plant corn, staggered, so it comes in at different times (more Sally Advice). After I finish in the garden, I'll take a walk in Swain's Woods—tomorrow we go to the beach for a barbecue, each kid taking one friend to fit into the VW bus. Is this peace, Virgen?

And Theo has a new friend his age up the road, way up the road where we followed the sign that said they were giving away puppies. We brought home a fat, fluffy, perpetually licking puppy that's a German shepherd/husky mix (and his friend claims also WOLF). The puppy picked us, leaping on Theo, who would not let him go. The puppy does have a wolf-like mask and ruff, and he's powerfully built at 6 months old. We named him Wiley as in the Coyote on the Road Runner cartoon (which is secretly my favorite—I love that Road Runner, beep beep). So, Wiley it is. . . . Wiley The Wolf we call him. Theo's training Wiley and sleeping with him out in the fort he quickly built for himself in the redwoods—he says he plans to make it better later, and I believe him, as Theo does pretty much what he says, just as he hasn't come into the house as he said he wouldn't for the whole summer. Once in a while Theo lets me hug him, but no kisses—he holds still for maybe 3 secs before he disappears. To the back fields, his fort or his new friend Bill's.

I met Bill formally when we got Wiley, getting a good look at his face, his shy "Glad ta meet ya." Since then I catch glimpses of him slinking around with Theo in the back fields and barns with their dogs running behind them. They look like they're hunting or something just as furtive (and again I have that impulse to join them, my undying curiosity, right Virgen?) . . . Anyway, Bill could be the legendary Big Foot since I just glimpse him now from time to time. I've even forgotten what his face really looks like, but to tell the truth I crack up as I watch them on Their Mission, knowing they believe no one can really see them. And of course I remember The Secret World, the boy (me) on the island with The Black Stallion where no one could see me it was so magical like my dreams—and I'm just a little jealous, and I can't help it. Is this peace, Virgen?

And of course, Tania's best (or bestest, as Tania says) friends with Minnie down the way (the only black family in Sebastopol, remember?), and now Marta, a Mexican girl whose family lives in the so-called "Farmworkers Town" about 15 miles from here—they bus the farmworkers' children into the town's high school as they only have a small grade school where they live. I can see how happy Marta is to have a friend IN TOWN, someone to visit here, and that we're Mexican too. Tania said Marta didn't believe her at first, that she's Mexican too—and when she saw Jason with the Golden Fleece (hair), "liar" flashed across her face. But when I told her some stories about mi Mamacita, that we come from S.F. and that my name's VILLALOBOS, she laughed, "That means village of the wolves!" So now she makes herself right at home, even going to the frig to get a drink on her own (after our constant, "Just help yourself, Marta"). She even asked me, in a voice I could barely hear, "Why is Jason blond?" "My father was blond." "Why aren't you blond?" "I don't know." (And I don't.) She laughed and I glimpsed her beautiful smile I'd never seen as she disappeared into Tania's room. Then there's Sharon, a Jewish girl who lives tucked away in a beautiful 3 story house on an apple orchard—her mother drops her by on the way to work at the hospital where she's a nurse. Marta I go pick up usually, but one of her older brothers comes to get her when it's time to go home.

When one of her friends is over Tania closes her bedroom door (or Jason would spy and torture them for sure)—and their voices sound like the steady hum of bees with fits of high laughter.

Sometimes they take a blanket and something to eat out by the giant willows by the now small trickling creek, and I admit it . . . I spy on them. I can barely breathe they're so beautiful. Innocent. Was this peace, Virgen?

I say was because I didn't know it yet when I was spying—Tania just told me everything, and she didn't even cry as she spoke. She was so enraged. And confused. I could tell she wants me to somehow "fix it" or do something like the principal or Slave Day—at the same time she told me to keep everything secret as her friends made her promise to not tell anyone. Marta told her she's been raped by her two older brothers and their friends, but she's learned how to stay away from them and fight back. She was only 11 when it started to happen, the year their father died in a tractor accident. Tania said she's too ashamed to tell her mother, plus Marta says her brothers act like they're in charge now that her father's gone. And then I realized she must be terrified to get in the car with her older brother when he takes her home—and I of course understand why her face is so frozen and stern as she leans against the car door, as far away from her brother as possible, as they drive away. I thought it was just the normal brother, sister war zone thing.

And to top it all off, Tania told me that her friend Sharon has been sexually molested by her stepfather, that Sharon has tried to tell her mother repeatedly, but that her mother refuses to believe her or protect her. Tania says Sharon sleeps with a knife and one night when he tried to molest her she stabbed his hand, and she was punished—but she still sleeps with a knife. Unbelievable. I may have had a weird childhood, but no one did these things to me—repeated molestation and rape. Ongoing terror. The one time in the park when I was 7, but thanks to you, Virgen, he didn't rape me or kill me. And Tania is still innocent, but she still has to know her friends' truth and horror. But again, she made me promise NOT to do anything because of course she knows I always tend to do something, and I don't know how long I can NOT do something and just watch these young girls . . . we'll see.

Now I fully understand Marta's nervousness when she's waiting for one of her older brothers—and Tania also says both of her older brothers threatened to kill her if she tells anyone what they did to her. But I really do not understand how Sharon's mother smiles and smiles so charmingly when she picks her up—I feel like punching her right in her smiling mouth—thus far, I've restrained myself, Virgen. But I know I'm going to have to talk to this PENDEJA soon. And Marta's mother, a sweet person from what I've seen, and she looks so tired—what about her, telling her?

That cornball song "Home home on the range" just won't leave me today. It keeps playing like a squeaky record in my head. I look at the rifle over the door and imagine myself loading it up to pay a visit to Sharon's pervy stepfather . . . remember my stepfather Jake and his daughter, what I'm pretty sure he was doing to that poor kid? Me and my Witch Power Eyes that saved my ass—my bony fist in his face, marble ashtray on his booze-crazed head, remember? And so, I imagine loading the rifle, driving over to the house, him answering the door, and I blow his pervy genitals away. There, much better. But I will have to talk to Sharon's pendeja mother, and what about Marta . . . she's afraid they're going to get her alone again, Tania tells me.

Tell me in a dream what the fregado to do and I will do it—please, Virgen, I need some advice here real fast. Tania said they can stay in her room, and I think, "Sure, why not?" But that would probably mean police, child protection, all that—it's not that easy. Not unless their mothers let them come here for awhile—I'm willing. Just let one of those assholes show up here, Luna La Loca will ride again—okay, I won't blow their pervy genitals away (or I'll try not to), but they will not want to visit here again. And then I start to imagine the girls walking home from school, being kidnapped by the brothers, which means I'd have to drive them every day. . . . SEND THE DREAM, VIRGEN!

(After a 2-day break—I've been in the fields planting the first corn and 4 rows of potatoes.)

Here's the dream. . . . I saw Sharon living with us, sleeping in Tania's room—and then I saw Marta riding away on her horse (she has a horse, Tania tells me). But I think I have to talk to both mothers soon, so will do it.

Okay, all that horrible stuff said, let me describe Tania's birthday bash—it was unbelievable, even better than I thought it'd be.

Tania was heaped with presents, she was in hoggy heaven, and most everyone brought some kind of farm-warming gift—from a yoghurt maker to an apple peeler. COOL, I say! We had tents pitched all over the fields as people spent at least one night, some two. And so, the guests . . . My brother Jake Jr. came with his beautiful girlfriend, Laura, with long red hair and green cat's eyes like Darling in Bolinas. Every time I'd look at her beautiful eyes, it made me want to find Darling, and I bet she's still in Bolinas (so maybe I'll try). Jake Jr. also brought an enormous plastic bag of "Acapulco Gold" Mary Juana—and they'd already taken some "acid"—but they were just a little confused by all the activity. They were gentle, smiling, laughing and kind of holding each other up, their arms around each other. Both of them still teenagers, 19 and 17, so beautiful together, their newness with each other made me wonder if I've ever felt like that with anyone (I must be getting OLD). After they pitched their tent, which kept caving in until they got some help putting it up—every time it would cave, they'd fall on the ground howling, holding onto each other—so finally, after the tent was up I didn't worry about them so much—they could pass out in there if necessary. They were so happy with their tent, like two kids playing in their fort, in their very own world.

My cousin Pablo (remember the Happy Skinny Kids Dance?), he came alone, bringing a shopping bag full of good wine and 4 dozen delicious tamales from Tía, with a note telling me to enjoy them, and that somehow she was going to visit me on the farm after I got settled in. Pablo said he'll bring her up later (mi Tía is still a Baptist who doesn't drink or dance, much less smoke Acapulco Gold—ha). Just the sight of his bushy Afro head and Zapata mustache made me do the Happy Skinny Kids Dance, and he cracked up of course, remembering the olden days in S.F. in the sad-assed projects he and Tía (and The Cheap Skate) lived in. He was also carrying his guitar in its case, and I could see he was ready to play and sing. I decided not to tell anyone about the cross burning (and made the kids promise not to either)—I'll tell people later like after the party in a few months or so. Why ruin the get-together, I figured.

Everyone from S.F. brought a shopping bag of wine, beer, tequila and more. My kitchen began to look like a liquor store, but a very free and friendly one. My black friend (and fellow teacher) Steve and his 4 kids, who all helped with the moving, also brought hooch and some home made potato salad—"A secret family recipe passed down from slavery days," Steve said in a solemn tone. I guess I looked pretty sad all of a sudden because Steve started laughing, but I wonder what he'd say if I told him about The Cross and Slave Day. He used to call me "a worrying little spic" whenever I'd fly off the handle, get POed, about any racism we'd encounter. He used to laugh at me and tell me "to go with the flow." To which I'd answer, "I will not go with the fucking flow." Hence, "worrying little spic"—but I bit my tongue about the KKK and showed him where to put up their tent, which was so enormous it looked like The Big Top out in the field as it vibrated with neon orange and green. I started laughing finally, it was truly bizarre but strangely wonderful . . . like a circus, us the amazing, exotic and ethnic Circus People in Sebastopol, right Virgen?

And then I flashed to the (very real) possibility of the KKK in some tree tops with binoculars—who knows, maybe even rifles, another flash—trained on our multi-racial festivities. Finally, I made myself stop peering into the distant trees for movement, shape, anything at all. I made myself look at all these (beautiful) people gathered together in plain old joy, to celebrate, and the hooch was flowing from the Free Liquor Store, my kitchen—but at the same time I told myself to be prepared (kind of like turning on The Witch Power Eyes in my stomach, that one) . . . for another cross burning visit or worse. I kept seeing myself (as I poured hooch and served food) shooting out their tires as they tried to make their chingado getaway, and then I wondered if I could do it in the pitch country-road dark, right Virgen? And then I had to consider: Do I want to <u>kill</u> them for burning a cross on my lawn? And then, would I want to kill them if they shot at us? And then I knew I'd want to kill them if they hurt my children, simple as that. . . . So, Virgen, if they're coming back please let me know in a DREAM. (I keep you busy, don't I?)

Anyway, after I tried to stop worrying with my brain about the KKK I started to worry about how ALL these people were going to go to the bathroom, and then I noticed the men were going out to the way-back field behind a stand of redwoods, so I surmised they were bonding via their prolonged beer pisses. The women lined up at the 2 small bathrooms in the house—it was working out so I let that problem go. And of course Steve kept laughing and calling me a worrying little spic while he handed me another glass of champagne, my favorite.

My old neighbors for years in S.F., Jorge and Anita, came. They picked up 2 of Tania's best friends from S.F.—Kathy who's black and Lupe who's Mexican. We lived next door to each other for 8 years during my chaotic marriage to Theo Sr. Actually, I lived in a lower flat and they lived right over my head with their 5 children who were in the same age range as my 3, so we were all best friends. They're from Guatemala and are the most loving people I've ever known. We shared almost everything those 8 years like an enormous slapstick family (butter via their kid flying upstairs, tampons via my kid flying downstairs). They used my car when theirs broke down, and I used theirs when mine did (I marvel now at such trust). And noise traveled easily through our 2 old Victorian flats, so there were nights when my husband would come home drunk and stupid—then Jorge's knock would be at the front door and he'd come in to make some good, strong coffee (or join Theo with a glass of wine). He'd stay up talking with my drunken husband till he finally passed out—this was the kind of friends they were to me. Rare. When Anita had to do something on her own (or just needed some precious time to herself), I'd watch her 5 kids. She did the same for me. And we often took everyone out to Golden Gate Park as one huge familia, and that's how I survived the general chaos of those years—their love for me. (The years I lost you, mi Virgen—I love writing everything down for you and knowing you're here, you're here. . . .) "O see the poles are kissing as they cross." The last line of the Dylan Thomas poem, which I repeat to myself when I start worrying about the KKK spying on us, and it helps. (And you're here, Virgen—send me a DREAM if they're coming back, gracias.)

And so, Anita and Jorge decided to return to the city that night since Anita <u>hates</u> camping of any sort, but they'll come back again during the summer for a visit (maybe I can talk them into staying in the front room). Kathy and Lupe stayed the night and went back with Pablo the next afternoon—anyway, when I watched them all burst from their Chevy van (the KKK still clinging to my consciousness—crosses, binoculars, rifles) . . . I wondered, I really wondered how I was going to live without them here: This beautiful farm with wild turkeys in the morning perched on the grape arbor where they're just starting to swell . . . where I plan to put 2 STEERS (not COWS, you eat steers) in the back fields, and Sally's taking me to the "feed store" to buy layers (chickens that lay eggs) and pullets (male chickens you eat). We've cleaned and whitewashed the barns, scraping old chicken shit (no joke) off everything—we had to cover our faces it was so bad, but we ended up singing "chicken shit songs" and cracking ourselves up. We even put some fake eggs in their straw to stimulate laying, which I'd read about, but Sally just laughed, "Hope it doesn't frustrate the poor critters." And so, here where I have my first real teaching job in the fall, my very own 8th grade class: This is where I live. NOW. Now. Now. But without these beautiful friends of mine, Virgen. . . .

Maybe some new friends—2 couples who I met in the Principal Impeachment trip (and what a trip), they came. One couple, Lynn and Danny (with their 2 boys, 6 and 8), is white and hippie-like—own their own farm on the back roads with 4 acres of apple orchards. Danny brought 2 gallons of fresh milk from his cow with a layer of real cream floating right on top—that milk disappeared so fast as the boys loved it. I was truly amazed, 2 gallons—and Danny says he'll drop it off every other day on his way to town for FREE if I want it, yes!! Now I'll have to figure something out to do for them, something special. . . .

The other couple lives about 5 country-long blocks from here, Raúl and Inez—Raúl is from Costa Rica and Inez is Mexican and Irish from Los Angeles. They went home for the night with their 6-month-old baby, but their 12-year-old son Shawn stayed the night in Theo's fort (with Wiley The Wolf). They have some chickens in their backyard and Inez grows most of their veges in their large garden, she tells me—Lynn and Danny also grow everything (they have chickens, 3 pigs, 2 steers, 2 cows). They've all offered to come and help me figure out the enormous field next to the house that's been plowed to plant—it could probably feed the entire populace of Sebastopol, so my mind boggles when I LOOK AT IT. Sally tells me this means canning, drying and freezing (and that she'll help me get started), but I went out and bought a 500 page book with whole chapters devoted to each process—one part of me is really excited about all of this, and another part of me wants to start crying like a wimp (whine whine). Like what if we grow everything and then I screw it up with all this "canning, drying, freezing" FREGADO. Wish me luck, Virgencita, cause I'm going to need it. (Luna La Farmer)

And so, on to the festivities (I'm not done yet)—an old neighbor from S.F. down the street from our Victorian Yellow Submarine (Anita, Jorge, me, 8 kids) named CHAN (real name Charlie, so the kids call him Charlie Chan too) ARRIVED. He calls himself just Chan—he's Chinese, Russian, Hawaiian, Portuguese, and he swears a sliver of Apache—that's what he rattles off as an introduction to his lineage. He's a poet, a longshoreman and gay, but keeps being gay a secret as he works on the docks with some pretty tough guys from the stories he's told me and the poems he writes. He looks tough, walks tough, talks tough (when he has to), but he's one of the most gentle men I've ever met. We used to swap poetry, reading new ones to each other over candlelight as it was slightly less embarrassing than 100 watt bulbs—plus candlelight is so nice of course. Peaceful. So, we always lit candles for our Poetry Swaps. Jorge and Anita thought he was just a little loco, but harmless and good at heart (which he is). My ex genuinely liked Chan, in fact they got drunk together a few times (I never told him Chan was gay, so I wonder if he ever figured it out)—but Chan made sure he was mellow by plying him with lots of Mary Juana. I don't smoke it very often, Virgen, since it just makes me hungry and jump at sudden noises, and that's all I need while viewing a cross burning—I might shoot my own fregado self, ha!

Anyway, old Chan was a SIGHT TO BEHOLD: He drives a huge Harley with black leather saddle bags, dresses like a Hell's Angel, entirely in black leather, tall black leather boots, has a very scraggly, longish, graying beard, a football helmet with the number 69, and around his neck are things you don't want to look at but are compelled to look at nonetheless (you just can't help it, it's like a car crash or something). On 2 thick chains he's affixed pens, small notebooks (I assume for sudden inspiration, directions to the farm), at least 10 keys, 2 bottle openers (for the quick beer since he likes bottles), pen knives, many ornaments—his name CHAN engraved in gold shone in the sun, the ying/yang symbol, his old army dog tags, a medical info tag stating he's a donor and "DO NOT chuck my body, recycle the sucker" written on it (I had to look), and more . . . his false teeth. Since I've never seen his false teeth dangling around his neck (I didn't even know he had false teeth), even I was stunned into silence.

Tania and her friends (the S.F. ones and the local ones) broke into fits of giggles so bad they had to throw themselves on the grass and just lay there helplessly convulsing—they did try to compose themselves, but it was useless. What could I say, "You're being rude!" I was a hair away myself from joining them—but what stopped me from collapsing into my own giggles was the gumball lights slowly turning and flashing as 2 police cars (and I think there's only 4 of them to begin with) crunched into the wide driveway where all the other cars were parked by the grape arbor and the redwoods where Theo's fort was. We were getting Top Priority, obviously.

"Shit," I muttered as I strolled up to the first scowling, yet astonished, cop who was getting his first look at Chan's adornment. Smiling too widely, I'm sure, I said, "Is anything wrong, officers?" (There were 3 of them taking it all in—one of them looked like he was trying not to crack up.) "We're having a party for my daughter's 13th birthday."

"Do you know this man?" one of them managed to say. They obviously wanted to tackle Chan, toss him into the squad car head first, false teeth on chain and all. Chan was just standing there smiling away, absolutely unselfconscious of his lack of teeth. He looked kind of like an aging baby, innocent even, except for the black leather get-up.

"Jesus F. Christ," I muttered as I walked toward them while trying to give Chan eye signals to SHUT UP DO NOT SAY ANYTHING! (You ever seen anything like this, Virgencita?) It'd been about a year since I'd seen Chan, so it was almost like a new experience even for me. And then Chan was walking toward the cops (one I recognized from the cross burning night), really smiling and about to say something—he tends to talk in poetry when he gets excited, and he had that glint in his eyes, so I knew that was coming. So I had to move <u>fast</u>. I ran, taking a deep breath, choosing the cop I'd seen before: "Officer, this man is an old friend of the family, he's a longshoreman from S.F. where I used to live. As you know, I just moved here and it's my daughter's 13th birthday. Mr. Chan is our guest." I smiled, but in fact I was starting to get pissed off—this is MY HOUSE, MY FARM, MY DAUGHTER'S BIRTHDAY PARTY—cross burners and cops, I silently seethed. I bet the KKK are getting a bang out of this up in the treetops (I couldn't stop myself—you know me, Virgencita).

On cue, Jason spotted Chan, yelling, "Kill it before it multiplies!"—and leaped on him trying to get him in a headlock, their usual greeting. When Jason saw, or rather got clunked by, the false teeth around Chan's neck, he yelled, "Put your damn teeth back in your mouth, Chan, that's so GROSS!" Finally, the cops started cracking up while Jason <u>made</u> Chan put them in. "Now you're starting to look like a regular human being, jeez Chan, what're you, nutsoid?" (Jason). Thank you, Jason, I mentally beamed him. I didn't even think of telling him to put them in his face—I was trying at that point to go with flow while trying not to look at his teeth, because they were so GROSS. I glanced around and caught Steve's look, eyes rolled back in his head for my benefit and enjoying himself no end, the asshole (sorry, Virgen, it's how I talk, or really just think nowadays since I've become a bona fide grown-up).

Teeth in, Chan walked up to one of the cops and <u>put his arm around him</u>—the mood changed. They definitely wanted to tackle, and probably club him, again. "You know Officer, I've done non-violence training, as in the evolution of our hairy ape species, with Joan Baez, that fairy godmother of our kind, and I can really and truly appreciate your most legally delicate position, believe me," he began. Jason, the ever astute 8 year old, perceived the deteriorating situation and said, "Come on, shut up, Chan," grabbing him by the hand. "Let's play some ping-pong, stupid." Chan yelled, "Thank you for everything, Officers!" as Jason dragged him to the ping-pong barn.

"Mrs. Villalobos"—they mangled my name of course, but then I realize they now know me by name—also, I forgot to tell you I changed my name back to my own, no more Mrs. you-know-who, Virgen—"considering your gathering here today," he swept his eyes over our wide assortment of guests (the Circus People, us), with a painful expression—"I'd keep an eye out for those guys you had a visit from the other night, and we'll patrol here tonight."

An offer of protection and a threat all at once, of course (seethe seethe). "I appreciate that, thank you," I replied in my most crisp teacher's voice. "I'll be teaching in Santa Rosa this fall, and I bought this farm, so I have no plans to leave. I appreciate any support you can give me as I have my 3 children to think of."

Then, one of the cops looked almost embarrassed for their thinly disguised disdain. "If anyone does come by tonight trying to burn another cross on your property, you call us right away and try to get their license plate." (Then I realized I'd have to tell everyone about the KKK as it was being publicly proclaimed, FRE GA DO! "Now, you have a good birthday party for your girl," the (cute) cop said, giving me a quick, sly smile—he has dark, curly hair, looks maybe Greek or Italian or both. (Stop me now, Virgencita!)

"Harold, John, Vincent! Are you pestering this woman? Good lord boys, she has enough on her hands for one day without you 3 here! And turn those damned lights off, they hurt my damned eyes!" It was Sally Oakley and she kept being right on their ASSES till they got in their squad cars (the cute one flashed me one last look, ay Virgencita . . .). Then they crunched back up the driveway, no gumball flashing lights. Gone.

She walked toward me carrying something in a bowl. "Here, I made some fresh guacamole just like my mama used to make, hope you like it, do you have any chips, well I'm sure you do, and where's that piñata, I want to take a good whack at it, it's been years since I've even seen one, I used to have one at my birthdays when I was a girl." Then she looked at my kind of surprised self and said, "My mama was part Mexican from her mama's side, and I even spoke some Spanish as a girl at home."

I wanted to grab her and hug her, but I can tell she's the kind of person who'd think I'd lost my marbles—she's the kind of person who never smiles when she's telling you something as though she's perpetually cranky, and then all of a sudden she does smile (or laugh), but only when she feels like it, I mean really feels like it, and I love that about her, Virgen. So instead of hugging her, I took a chance and touched her arm (a start), and said, "Guacamole's my absolute favorite, gracias, and you're going to get first whacks, come on." (And I almost said it, out loud, Sally Oakley, but now it'll be Sally La Oakley, right Virgencita?). Sally La Oakley is Mexican and had piñatas for her birthdays as a kid—you could've knocked me over con una pluma for sure. Now I have about a hundred questions to ask her, and I wonder if she keeps it a secret. . . .

"Oh heaven's no, maybe after all the children have a turn at it." La Oakley's eyes glittered with a child's delight. "Where is the piñata, dear, I wouldn't mind taking a look at it."

"I think Tania and her friends are still stuffing it in her room, so go on in, she won't mind, her room's to the right of the kitchen." I'd let Tania tell her she'd made it herself, drying it layer by layer for over a week—then papering it with an explosion of colors, rainbow streamers dangling from each point of the STAR PIÑATA. So, by the time it was ready I knew she was starting to dread the idea of it being smashed open—the fate of every birthday piñata. It hung in her room those last days, so beautiful with her gathering nightly dreams—I kept thinking this as I passed to admire her work, and I even thought of buying one so we could keep this perfect star piñata made by her perfect 13-year-old self—to me she's <u>perfect</u>, Virgencita.

"They don't want some nosey old lady pestering them. . . ."

"Tania!" I yelled. "Please come here!" And I tell La Oakley, "She'll love to show off her piñata. . . ."

Tania appeared looking slightly irritated, and I see it: The Witch Power Eyes. Just for a split second. They flash. In her 13-year-old perfect self. This girl-woman who started to bleed last year. The "coming of age" dress I made her with a multi-colored sun (pale yellows to bright golds) stitched to the high waistband just under her heart but centered in the solar plexus—my yoga teacher in S.F. said this is where the "SUN WILL CHAKRA" is, so as I stitched the rainbow sun I smiled and smiled. The dress that took me over a month to finish and the girls with the hand axes and knives had ripped in seconds (but sure enough, her sun will chakra had protected her when she knocked the girl in front of her down, breaking their circle and running for her life). Even as I made it for her I was aware that no one her age really dressed that way normally, and I smiled at the memory of Darling making me those pukola girlie dresses with bows that I dreaded wearing—but this wasn't a bow kind of dress, and Tania wasn't me. She likes being a girl, I reminded myself as I sewed. So I kept on sewing with the desire to see her in something more beautiful than the pattern I was following. I remember the first time she put it on, when it was finally complete, I cried. When it was ripped, I cried. I told her not to wear it to school and keep it for special times, but she was so proud of it—long, grown up and twirly with a SUN WILL CHAKRA glowing just below her "new breasts" (I imagined her staring at them in the mirror secretly, and hers are much larger than mine were—and as I've always seen, she's much more feminine than La Loca Tomboy me ever was). And so, Virgencita, there she was in the clothing of her own choice on her 13th birthday, flashing me The Witch Power Eyes. I've never seen them till that day and I wanted to cry, but I didn't. Sometimes I wonder if I'm turning into a fregado Cry Baby, kind of like I'm making up for lost time—all the years I refused to cry. And I think of my ugly scar tissue heart and the one tiniest red rose I can see vividly, and if I close my eyes I can actually see its yellow center, so perfect and soft. (The one part of me that's perfect.)

"Do you mind if Sally checks out the piñata?" My voice sounded strangled, far away, so I loudly cleared my throat. As I looked at her I looked at my own 13-year-old-girl-woman self, Witch Power Eyes and all—I thought of Sharon and Marta in her room, and I was so glad, so glad she could flash me those insolent eyes.

"Sure, come on in, we're putting in the goodies!" Tania jumped down the 6 wooden steps and, so at ease, put her arm around Sally, and Sally La Oakley let Tania help her up the steps though she didn't really need the help.

As the screen door closed behind them, it hit me—she reminds me of Darling, the directness of her manner, the rifle (Darling's gun), the bullshit detector voice. Darling. A very old Darling. And I wondered how she was now at about 58 or so, about Carmen's age (Carmen had me at 29, pretty old in those days she used to say). And then I wondered what I'll be like in my 80s with my trusty rifle at my side, and I wondered if my scar tissue heart would have more than one skinny (beautiful, red, perfect) rose by the time my grandkids start calling me Mamacita—you know me, Virgencita, I start thinking about something and old Plato takes over. . . . Anyway, I'm going to see if I can find La Darling, even if I have to drive over to La Mesa in Bolinas, so I'm thinking all this while slightly wondering if Chan still has his teeth in his mouth, if the KKK still have their binoculars trained on us, or their fregado rifles (right?), if I'll ever see the cute cop again (that's the truth, Virgen, I can't help it), if Jake and his gorgeous girlfriend are passed out in their tent or wandering somewhere talking to people and trees (so I'd better go check, of course), if a squadron of flies is landing on the food I tried to keep covered, and people keep going in and out of the kitchen for more hooch, and someone hands me a drink so I sip—one strong-ass margarita. "Perfecto," I say (said), and sip again—two more of these and I probably won't be a worrying little spic as Steve always calls me, which I am. . . .

THEN I heard a voice I hadn't heard in a century—Diana's. "Well, there you are, we couldn't find you, people here give directions that sound like—Turn at this bend and that fork by that oak—my God, Luna, where on earth have you moved, The Sticks? . . ." She's always had this very grown-up and elegant voice no matter what she says—that's just how she talks, which used to make me crack up till I got used to it, and now I love it, that voice. (Remember, we modeled together in S.F. at 18! and 19! when my ex was in Vietnam—in the meantime, she became an airline stewardess, sending me letters from places I've never been, and having boyfriends she had to hide one from the other.) And of course, she's still chingaso beautiful with her stylishly cut, very red hair soaking up the sun and beaming it right back, and those deep green eyes accented by green eyeshadow, long lashes, all the tricks we knew (and she reminded me of since I'd just scratched on some eyeliner, and it was probably smudged).

I screamed and ran over, hugging her. "I didn't think you'd make it, welcome, welcome, old buddy!" And then I was crying and laughing, and Steve walked over, handing us both a fresh strong-ass margarita—we all sipped.

"I wouldn't miss this for the world, Luna, and I've never seen so many cows gathered in one place in my entire life, everywhere you look there's a cow staring at you, my God, Luna." She actually looked disturbed about it. "Now, tell me why you moved here."

"Mooooo," I mooed to my own surprise (the margaritas were beginning to do their magic). We started cackling and then it felt like the old modeling days in S.F. when we'd tell each other about some pervo creep we had to deal with, and there were PLENTY of them. The guys who interviewed us for the jobs (like the old, extremely ugly guy who wanted me to take off my dress to model his furs, to which I told him, "I'm not that hungry" and left—for which I was not sent out on a job for a week after that as I'd been "rude" to a customer), the drunk guys at fashion luncheons lunging at us as we walked through the bar to get back to the dressing room, and the creepo guys who just wouldn't take no (or a fuck off) for an answer. I used to think, secretly, that if these pervs really saw me naked they'd run screaming because every bone in my body was visible to the eye—I used to think I looked more like a boy than a "grown woman" and that what fooled everyone was the high heels, floppy hats and all the makeup tricks I'd learned. In truth, I was a boy in drag. (Are you laughing, Virgencita?) And somehow Diana knew this about me, and without ever saying a word showed me how it was really done—The Woman Thing.

"Moooo yourself," Diana managed, still cackling, as we leaned on each other. "And now you have a passel (she talks this way, "passel" ha!) of kids and a farm, tell me you aren't going to have cows as well, please."

"Moooo," I answered just as a very handsome man dressed in an impeccable suit (hat and tie!) appeared. Obviously, he was lost, and just as I began to say, "May I help you?" . . . "Oh

Luna, this is my boyfriend, Frank" (Diana gave me a wicked look, her latest, and I suddenly felt like my old self, the boy in drag), "and Frank, this is Luna."

"Nice place, Luna, I like it, reminds me of the old country, Sicily, beautiful." And what a beautiful smile on his handsome dark face (Sicilian!), and his dark eyes that had no shame of just lingering where they wanted to linger. As Jason says, "Holy moly"—this guy is so handsome he's almost beautiful, those long dark eyelashes, ayyyy. . . . So, I mumbled thank you as a commotion drew our attention to the giant walnut tree in back by the creek.

Tania, her friends and all the combined, over-amped boys were trying to fling a rope over a high limb on the old giant tree, while La Oakley was standing in the middle of it giving directions in her loud, no-nonsense, know-everything voice. My brother Jake Jr. wanted to climb it, but he was obviously hallucinating (his girlfriend was lying on the grass blissed out). Pablo wanted to but felt he needed a ladder, then Theo (my 11-year-old son, that one) wanted to climb on Pablo's shoulders to get a boost to the limb, but Pablo still wanted a ladder. Suddenly, Frank just threw his hat, jacket, tie, shirt, shoes, and socks off (bare-chested, with his expensive looking trousers on) and started sprinting for the tree, and he was in very good shape. So I realized I was noting that for the first time in a chingado long-ass time, and that's the TRUTH, Virgen. So maybe I'm still ALIVE, you know, that way, just maybe—even that cop with the shy smile was kind of "cute"—okay, I'm alive. . . .

Then Diana said (BELIEVE IT OR NOT!!)—"He's a Mafia Hit Man, but he's gorgeous isn't he?"

"He's a what, come on, you're kidding, a what?" She said it again in her truth-telling voice, that Frank was a Mafia Hit Man. . . . She met him on one of her flights, oh-kay. . . . So, I watched Frank The Mafia Hit Man climb the giant walnut tree (muscles-a-rippling), fling the rope and tie it around a sturdy branch, joking and laughing with all the kids. "He's great with kids, but he kills people?" I blurt.

"That's his job, Luna," she told me, smiling as she watched Frank dangling from the branch and quickly becoming the most popular adult at the party—"but he really does love kids, he has 5 with his ex-wife and he provides for them entirely, they want for nothing, believe me. . . ."

I looked at Diana, her clear green cat-eyes enjoying the sight of bare-chested Frank (who wouldn't?), and then as I looked at bare-chested Frank, I had a flash of my ex (Theo Sr.) who I knew killed people in Vietnam, but it didn't stop me from loving him, making love to him, right Virgen? But it was WAR and he had to, I'd told myself—though I never told him I'd taken part in Vietnam protests, actually 2, the bodies of dead children and babies on posters I couldn't bear to look at. So, as I looked from Diana to Frank and back to Diana, I asked myself: Do I go over there and demand he leave my premises? I really sighed and tried to make Plato shut up. . . . Does he kill men with children, does he kill regular people for owing money to the Mob, does he kill families, does he put car bombs in cars that kill anyone who happens to be in them, does he put cement around the ankles of his jobs and toss them into the local waterways, and on and on and on. . . . And then I thought, I bet the only person the cops would think was a good citizen is Frank with his expensive looking suit, hat and tie—and then I began to kind of giggle to myself (and then I desperately wanted another strong-ass margarita). And so, I looked back at Frank The Hit Man, and what he looked like was a gorgeous Sicilian Santa Claus with well-defined muscles, legs dangling from the walnut tree, laughing and joking non-stop with the kids below. He had hold of the rope which would swing the piñata full of candy, 30 $1 bills, $10 worth of dimes and nickels I got at the bank, play $ and goofy plastic toys—he seemed completely happy, waiting to swing the piñata in wide taunting arcs over the heads of the would-be-whackers who would be armed with a formidable stick Theo found in one of the barns.

Raúl began to play some ranchero music (festive!) on his guitar, and Pablo ran to his car to get his. And it turned out that Danny (he has long silky hair past his shoulders and wears a beaded headband with an eagle on it) played the flute and also brought it just in case—and his wife Lynn (she has a thick blonde braid that hangs almost to her waist) could really sing, we found out later by the fire we kept going till past midnight. She can also play guitar, so she borrowed one for a few songs (as we sat close to the fire), and of course we sang The Yellow Submarine (twice), and Frank The Hit Man's voice rang out over everyone else's—and I had stopped counting the fresh margaritas being placed in my hand, each one perfecto, Steve's doing, and I had by then ceased being a worrying little spic.

Before the fire at midnight we sang HAPPY BIRTHDAY TO TANIA with guitars and flute, and though she tried to not look "too happy" she couldn't hide it. She just was. But before that we broke open the piñata and all its real and imagined gifts. I mean, even though I picked most of what it was filled with, it wouldn't have surprised me if Tinker Bell had come bursting out. I can't explain it, but piñatas are magical and absurd with HOPE and at a certain moment as it swings above your head, the blindfold on your eyes, someone spinning you in circles—at a certain moment you begin to believe what you really and truly desire will come crashing to the ground, and that you'll have to seize it before anyone else does, right Virgen? "That's the magic!" (Jefferino, remember . . . and don't start me on him, I wonder how he is, what he looks like, is he a father, does he love someone, does he still say it?)

So, the kids talked Sally La Oakley into being the first one to whack it—she kept saying, "No, no, the young people first." But finally she took the stick firmly in her hands, holding it like a weapon, and we had to also talk her into not wearing the blindfold. . . ."Well, if it makes you all feel better, bunch a scaredy cats." But she absolutely refused to not be turned in circles, and so I turned her twice, gently. She looked like a kid, about 12, except for the short gray hair. Then Chan started yelling, "Clobber that sucker, Big Mama!" And he kept yelling it at the top of his lungs (as I waited for La Oakley to clobber Chan). And Frank The Hit Man started swinging the piñata wider and wider, and for a moment I could see the KKK in the treetops with their binoculars and rifles, and the cops cruising by in their squad car probably hearing Chan yell, "Clobber that sucker, Big Mama, oh yeah!" And maybe they could even see Frank The Hit Man howling with laughter high in the walnut tree, rope in hand. It felt like

I was flying over everything and everyone, and I was seeing everything just as it was, just exactly how it was—the KKK, the cops, Frank The Hit Man, Diana The Beautiful, Sally La Oakley, Gay Hell's Angels Chan, Steve and his 4 kids with their so beautiful black skin, my brother Jake Jr. and his lovely girlfriend lying blissed out on the grass, holding onto each other, watching Frank and the piñata swing over their heads (and maybe seeing more than I could see, right?), Pablo with his thick "fro" doing the The Happy Skinny Kids Dance (though he's not skinny anymore), my sons (one blond, one dark-haired) and their friends mingling with all the other sons present, all dying to get their turn at the piñata and its mysteries—my old Guatemalan neighbors and friends from S.F., their 5 kids, my new (Latino and hippie) neighbors and their kids (one was breastfeeding her youngest), Tania's 2 best friends (black and Mexican) from S.F. and 2 new best friends (white and Mexican) from here—both raped by someone in their families (and as you know, Virgen, makes me want to KILL). And Tania, my perfect daughter at 13, the age I was when I lost you, Virgen. When I lost myself. When I forgot Jefferino's "That's the magic."

As La Oakley connected a good solid THUNK, I knew I was exactly where I was supposed to be. At that very moment. It felt like I had been dumped on the ground like a gift from Tania's Star Piñata. And I was full of so much absurd hope. And I knew—right then and there—I had to seize myself first and fast, even if I'm not perfect, I'm really all I've got, right? Luna La Mammal, me.

But I waited for Tania, her turn. Then everyone was blindfolded and twirled at least 4 times till they swayed a little hoochily, sometimes falling on the soft June earth, then up again to try, stick in hand, full of muy loca desire and muy loca hope, to break open the piñata that Frank kept swinging in wide, playful arcs. "NOW NOW NOW!!!" everyone screamed. 6 tries each and usually each person hit it at least twice. Finally, the once beautiful and perfect Star Piñata was becoming the now ripped and maimed blobby piñata—all the points of the Star were gone but one stubborn point that hung by a thread, barely. The honors were Tania's of course, so without a blindfold or being twirled, she grabbed the stick firmly with both hands (like a weapon a La

Oakley) and waited till it swung directly in front of her. No one screamed. There was absolute and sudden silence except for some breezes through the high branches of the walnut tree. Suddenly it felt like we were at a funeral, Virgen, a piñata funeral. Even Frank was quiet, but still smiling away (I guess he's used to funerals). Holy S. Fregado!

With one final incredible THUNK Tania split the piñata right in half and everything spilled to the ground—very little of it had leaked, so everything spilled at once. Without even thinking I raced for a handful of treasure (hope). Desire. My 13-year-old self I'd placed (without knowing it) in my daughter's handmade Star Piñata. Each night in dreams. (I'd dreamt myself flying for the first time since Tania was born, or before she was born.) The me with The Witch Eyes. The fearful yet fearless me. The Amazon me. Her. I unwrapped her sweetness and ate her. She was hard raspberry with a soft raspberry center so sweet it made me cry. Then laugh. Then cry again. Then I ate another one.

But nobody noticed. They were too busy claiming their share. Of the magic. Lying on the soft June earth. Waiting to be seized by all. If you're willing to seize it. The magic.

And I did, mi Virgen, I finally and truly did. Take my share.

Luna La Amazon (is this peace, Virgencita?)

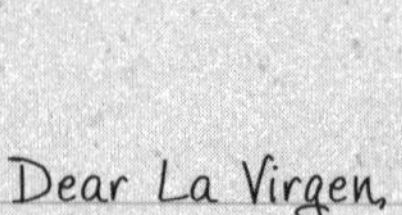

Dear La Virgen,

It's already almost 2 weeks into July and I haven't told you about what happened the night (morning) of the party—Tania came running into my room around 5 am, there was a truck in front, La Oakley had her rifle pointed through her front room window, and she was yelling curses and warnings, "You sons of bitches, you better get the hell outta here, I already called the goddam police. . . ." Tania had the license plate, she said—so I grabbed the rifle from over the door, ran for the bullets in my underwear drawer and loaded the rifle, but by the time I got outside the truck had sped away, doing a loud wheelie at the corner. As I'd snapped the bullets in I thought of La Oakley holding her ground and started to laugh even though I was scared shitless (why lie?), but when I ran out—my stomach in my throat, my eyes zipping all over the place—weirdly enough I actually felt <u>calm</u>.

Then I saw it, where they'd left it on the thick, green, summer grass. Another CROSS. Just two pieces of wood nailed together in a clumsy fashion (O see the poles are kissing as they cross . . . Dylan Thomas)—only I didn't think this as I wondered if these lame brains actually wanted to kill us, me and my kids. . . . So here's what happened.

"I called and the boys will be here soon!" Sally came out to her front porch.

"Tania got their license, holy shit!"

"I'd a blown their young asses away if they'd lit that thing, good lord in heaven!" Sally was still holding her rifle.

I picked up the cross. It was so light. Everyone in their tents slept through the whole thing—even Jason and Theo in their forts. Only Tania and her friends were up. I could hear them talking all at once. And it's funny, I was no longer afraid—I was PISSED OFF.

The next day they picked up the guys who did it (thanks to Tania's sharp eyes)—and they were <u>neighbors</u> and probably could see the fields and house. They were 18, 19 and 2 in their early 20s. I went down to the jail where they were holding them the next day—I was told they were going to be let out on bail soon. I talked the guy on duty into letting me talk to them, just for a minute, I promised. . . . I was so infuriated I figured my eyes were beyond The Witch Eyes, till I saw their faces—they were mostly boys, stupid boys, but boys. They were young, unamazing-looking white boy-men, no obvious evil here, just some teenage-looking guys. And the truth is, Virgen, I burst into tears (I just couldn't stop them) and said something like, "How would you like me to visit your home in the middle of the fucking night and burn a fucking cross on your front fucking lawn, how would you like your children to be scared shitless because someone obviously wants to kill them, have you thought any of this shit out, and do you really know what this burning a cross shit means, do you UNDERSTAND (I think I screamed this)—people have been lynched, men's and boy's genitals have been chopped right off and stuffed in their mouths, probably while they're still fucking alive, then they hanged them, whole families have been murdered while a fucking cross was burning, DO YOU UNDERSTAND THIS?" I looked at their faces and all but one were stunned—either by the impact of what I was saying or that they were witnessing a crazy woman lose her gourd, me La Loca. Then . . . I heard it . . . "I'm sorry." "Sorry." "I'm sorry, ma'am." The silent one glared at me.

My tears had stopped and I could hear the cop behind me saying, "Time's up, Mrs. Villalobos." He massacred my name and for once I didn't correct it. Instead, I looked at all of them very slowly, each one right into their eyes—including the one trying to give me his 2nd rate Witch Eyes. And I said, trying to keep my voice low and modulated so I wouldn't give in to just screaming at them, "I just want you all to know we're not going anywhere. This is our home and I won't allow any further bull-shit. Do you all know exactly what I mean by any further bullshit?"

Three Yes ma'ams.

"I believe you, for some insane reason I really do, so take care of your buddy here, I'd hate to see Sally blow his ass away, that is if I don't do it first."

Again, the three Yes ma'ams.

Then I looked at each face one more time, each face, and this thought just flashed across my overloaded mind: I bet these kids think Elvis Presley is The King and so chingaso cool, wouldn't it just blow their little pea-brains if they knew he was part dirty Indian. . . . I read that, Virgen, he's part Indian. But of course it would've been idiotic to say it at that point, plus I knew they wouldn't believe me, so I let it go . . . but their faces. They could be part Indian, part Mexican, part black—their great great grandfathers with their slave families. "Long live The King," I muttered.

When I got to the door that would open to the soft July sky, my hand pushing it open, one of the cops said, "You have a mouth like a sailor, ma'am."

I said, "Thank you," and walked out, and I swear for a second I could smell the ocean. The next day I went to the ocean, only about 20 minutes away. We took a picnic and spent the whole day, making a fire toward sunset. We stayed long after Venus appeared in the west, and even though it was dark and we were the only people left on the beach, I refused to be afraid. I am so sick of being afraid of violent men—I'm not afraid of violent women, dogs, cats, sparrows, seagulls, seals. And when I looked at my sons, their sweet boy selves, it made me sicker to imagine how boys lost this essence (and I think of Frank The Hit Man, that paradox). So, I just kept adding wood to the fire. . . . "You have a mouth like a sailor"—if I didn't I'd be locked up somewhere talking to myself, but I am so sick of it, mi Virgen. And I refuse to back down—like La Oakley—I asked her to come with us, but she said, "Looking at that ocean just makes me thirsty, but you go ahead and bring me back a good shell if you find one." And I did, a perfect sand dollar for her and a bunch of unperfect shells to take home for me.

And so, this is what I did with the cross (after I almost burned it myself)—I took it down by the creek and pushed it into the soft, damp earth—"We are the sons of flint and pitch, / O see the poles are kissing as they cross." I read the entire poem by Dylan Thomas and also some wonderful poems by Pablo Neruda—I needed to hear good things from MEN. . . . "I have slept with you / all night long while / the dark earth spins / with the living and the dead, / and on waking suddenly / in the midst of the shadow / my arm encircled your waist. / Neither night nor sleep/could separate us." (From "Captain's Verses," all poems of love to his wife Matilde Urrutia—and I like that she kept her own name—IF I ever get married in my life that's what I'd do.) And so, now I'm reading Neruda's love poems, and I try to imagine what it would be like to be loved like this. . . . "Neither night nor sleep could separate us." Because the truth is, I have NO IDEA—I know what it's like to love (my children) like this, but not to be loved like this (by un hombre). . . .

So as I sat there looking at the fregado cross by the now slow-running creek, letting the sun-filled water dazzle my eyes, I started stringing flowers together in a garland like Tania and I used to do in Golden Gate Park. I never did this as a kid, so Tania's the one who taught me how to do it, or even to want to do it. It takes a lot of patience and you have to really be with someone you like, kind of peaceful—and you can lie back once in a while to just watch some clouds, and you take turns finding animals and things in the clouds. (And I remember Tania used to see cats and dogs kissing a lot, and that's probably because she was a loved kid—and I used to tease her like "Dogs don't kiss," and she'd say, "They do so, they lick," and I'd say, "Got me there, kiddo," and she'd just crack up.) Then you sit up again to string the flowers together—Tania taught me this. I think because I was on such a lookout as a kid, you know, watching out for any sudden movements, pervs and psycho step-fathers, etc., I NEVER thought of stringing flowers together. (And now I realize that Tania taught me how to love my "girl self" —by watching her and loving her.) So finally, at 29, here I was by myself making flower garlands, Virgencita. Then I started decorating the cross with the flower garlands, the soft ferns that grow in the shade, and the bag of unperfect sea shells which I placed in a circle around the flower garland and soft green fern cross. . . . Is this peace, Virgen?

I decided to leave it there and keep decorating it from time to time—to keep making it beautiful. ("O see the poles are kissing as they cross.") And now it dawns on me, like Tania's dog and cat clouds kissing . . . that's the magic (like innocence). And right next to the now beautiful, garland and sea shell cross . . . the blackberries are ripening (fat, dark and warm with juice). A deal's been made—the boys are going to pick the blackberries, and Tania's promised to make blackberry cobblers and pies. Some mornings when she can't sleep she's up around 5 am baking cinnamon rolls and cinnamon twist bread from scratch (!)—she taught herself from a cookbook. And on those mornings I get a warm cinnamon treat and freshly brewed coffee IN BED (and I bring her a treat on other mornings, so we take turns). And I have vowed to make blackberry jam, so I went out and bought everything on the canning list, and got a recipe from La Oakley, so will call it "La Oakley Blackberry Jam" in her honor (I'll even write that on the label for the canning jars). Either she'll crack up or think I'm La Loca, maybe both, right Virgencita? Jason also likes to bake, though of course he'd never let his friends know this "sissy stuff"—when I call him he-boy sometimes (a joke between us), he puffs up his bony-ass chest and flexes his road-runner muscles for me. He cracks me up, skinny but strong like El Road Runner in my favorite cartoon (am I starting to miss cartoons?) . . . So, he often helps Tania with the baking, and she lets him do some all on his own. Of course, she ends up yelling at him because he eats half of what he bakes with—I just let them work it out and smile when I hear that authority in Tania's voice. And when I see Jason baking, his face tensed in concentration, then expanded in sudden joy, I think of the line from the now famous poem . . . "O see the poles of promise in the boys." Dylan Thomas, el poeta. And then I flash on the 4 boy-men sitting in the jail cell, their "promise"

. . . will they keep it, would I shoot if they didn't? Yes I would. Is this peace, Virgen?

And so, when I think of the "cross" now, I think of it out by the creek covered with wild flower garlands and ripening blackberries, curious hummingbirds, enormous gliding butterflies all around it (maybe at night the fox from the forest sleeps there, and I imagine that the fox gathers all of our dreams, at dawn taking them back with her for safe keeping, in case we ever forget our dreams, she'll know)—and the truth is I've stopped worrying like La Loca about the KKK all the time . . . cross burners, ignorant young men, their fathers, their friends. The parole officer says there's no KKK here, "Just boys playin' a bad joke, ma'am." And then I can't help it . . . I wonder if he's in the fregado KKK . . . but I refuse to think about selling this farm and moving back to S.F. And the rifle is still over the back door, so La Loca rides again and again. . . .

Diana sent me a book, "Women's Mysteries"—she wrote inside: "COWS are a symbol of the Goddess. Say hi to the Cows for me MOOO! Love, Diana The Huntress To Luna The Full Moooon." I'll have to tell her how "mooo" means "promise" to me—of course I'll have to explain why (the cows in Bolinas), remember Virgen?

I love this book, the Goddess, you La Virgen, Diosa. Mamacita would say it, "Ayyyy Diosa"—especially when she was tired, I remember her eyes, Ayyyy Diosa, La Virgen. But I'm not tired, in fact I feel like I'm 12 going on 13 half the time (weird but true). And guess what . . . the book says that the cross in ancient times (Goddess times) was a healing symbol—now I'm doubly glad I didn't break it up and burn it. That it's down by the creek (with the fox), getting more beautiful with each garland I make. Meanwhile, Theo and Jason have come up with some pretty terrible (but hilarious) Billy Bob Skits, where they pretend they're the KKK and live on the range "where men are men and the sheep know it"—also the chickens, cats, etc. . . . they make the appropriate animal sounds and each time the skit's different. Here I am, a teacher and laughing my ass off, but when they go too far (and they do), I make them stop, ayyyy Diosa! For example: "Hey Billy Bob, wheredjyou git that perty chicken, it shore do have some perty eyes on her, kin I borry her sometimes, fer the eggs I mean" (Jason). "Only if ya promise to marry this here chicken, boy, she ain't no dang floozie" (Theo). We're all sitting around the dinner table as Jason leaps up, making loud chicken-laying-an-egg sounds, arms fluttering, legs working, his face turning red with huge chicken effort—he reaches down between his legs and PROUDLY shows us his egg and says, "Why buy the chicken when ya can have the dang eggs fer free?" (Jason to Billy Bob Theo). "Yer startin ta look perty good ta me there, chicken boy." . . . Jason's chicken self has Tania and I wetting our calzones, but this is where I have to stop them. So with every weirdo skit we howl and heal, better than TV, and we wait (secretly) for Jason to get that look in his eyes at the table as the spirit of Billy Joe, that's him, takes over. . . .

The other day I was in Tania's room vacuuming and looking for stray laundry when I stopped to gaze around her room (which I love to do)—her dolls, her pillowcases which she stitches tiny flowers onto, her lacey curtains billowing in the breezes, her shelves where she keeps her treasures. And I saw it. THE SECRET CRYSTAL ROCK!! She'd found it at the bottom of the box with my diaries to you, but she didn't think it was "any big deal, it's only a rock"—I couldn't explain it to her then, but I asked her if I could have it. "Sure, Mom," she said in a patient voice like I'd lost it, you know, my noodle.

So I've been taking the Secret Crystal World Rock with me when I sleep outside on a flat, smooth spot by the creek, the cross (the fox). I just put netting over my sleeping bag, that way I can hear the mosquitos circling me, pissed off cause they can't get to my blood, and I can just lay there counting shooting stars till I finally pass out. Pretty soon it'll be September and Sally tells me the frost will keep me indoors—she says it gets to about 17 degrees in the winter. She cracks up when she sees me stumbling to the house with my sleeping bag in the early morning—and her pot of coffee is always fresh. And of course school will start, but I look forward to that, teaching. The children (Latino, Indian, black, white, Asian, they're all in Santa Rosa), all with their promise. And did I tell you one of the teachers there—in fact his classroom is 2 doors down from mine—told me to ask him for anything I needed, he's been there for 5 years he said (a muy cute Indian-looking guy, speaks Spanish, ayyyy Diosa) . . . I cannot remember his name.

THE NEWS: Virgencita, the other morning I found a huge spray of flowers on my front porch in a vase, with a flowery card signed by 2 of the guys I yelled at in jail (the cross burners). They wrote, "We hope you like these as there from our own garden." But a part of me waits for the other 2 (and maybe their friends) who didn't sign, right? However, the flowers, what they mean, makes me pretty happy. It's a start, the healing cross. . . .

And one of my poems is being published in a magazine at San Francisco State—my first published poem!! I sent a few off and actually forgot about them—I'd seen an ad for student submissions and picked 3 poems that seemed slightly promising (mooo). The one they picked is about growing up in S.F., being hungry and stealing food for me and Mamacita, and riding my bike to la mar—but I'll believe it when I SEE IT, Virgencita!

One night out by the creek I woke up to the sound of someone crunching through branches, so I shone my flashlight everywhere but couldn't see anyone. I almost ran back to the house, instead I stayed awake, shining my flashlight periodically to see if anyone was out there (walked back to the house to see if everything was okay, it was), went back to my sleeping bag, wide awake. I could go down my list as to who or what I imagined, or could be, out there, but I think you already know my list, right Virgen? So I ended up shining the flashlight on the Secret Crystal World Rock and remembering how fregado terrified I used to be of VAMPIRES as a kid (but I still won't exclude them from my list, ayyyy Diosa)—then this blazing STAR, maybe a comet because it didn't just shoot across the sky, it slowly blazed a trail, kind of slashing the dark night in half as it went, leaving a long line of light that very slowly faded away.

And then I heard this line like someone whispered it in my ear—not like I usually start a poem by trying so hard to write the first line. I found my grocery list notebook that I carry everywhere (with a pen clipped in it), turned on the flashlight and wrote down the first line I heard: "Stars dance their ancient tunes strung on light." And then I wrote this poem. . . .

NIGHT DANCE

Stars dance their ancient tunes
strung on light,
strung on light.

I get dizzy watching such acrobatics
as everything melts away
to light;

and the night has always played
such music
and the void has always sung
its hunger:

the wide expanse
the wide expanse

and I have always prayed for
daybreak, for Earth splitting
to sun;
fear, fear: listen:

love is the dance,
the spinning harp.

Every time I thought I was stuck or even maybe done, I'd hear the voice whispering inside my right ear again—if the California Poppies weren't all gone I'd swear it was them. Then I know you sent me this dream, Virgencita. . . .

I see the back field full of California Poppies, and they're all open because it's so sunny, sunny like early summer. There are so many poppies I can't move because I don't want to step on them, and they're a brilliant glowing pulsing orange like millions of suns all around me. They hurt my eyes to look at them, but I also love to look at them. I can hear shouting far away. I close my eyes to hear them better (in the dream).

"Red Rover, Red Rover," I hear more than one voice shout. I want to walk toward the voices, but I really don't want to step on the pulsing orange suns under my feet.

I hear them again. "Red Rover, Red Rover"—so I carefully, as carefully as I possibly can, walk toward the voices on my toes, trying my hardest not to step on the precious glowing suns.

I see 4 women holding hands, standing in a line. They're smiling at me. They know me. And suddenly I know. Who they are. Each woman is so beautiful in her own unique way . . . one is Yaqui Indian, dark-skinned with black, straight hair, one is Spanish with lighter skin like cinnamon and dark, wavy hair, one is English with even lighter skin and brown, curly hair, one is German with pale skin and straight blond hair. "Red Rover, Red Rover, send Luna right over, Red Rover, Red Rover, send Luna right over . . ." they shout over and over, laughing and waiting for me. Waiting for me. Luna. Luna the dirty Indian. Luna the wetback spic. Luna the chingada gringa. Luna la loca mestiza. Luna la mammal. Me.

And then I know I'm 13.

"RED ROVER, RED ROVER, SEND LUNA RIGHT OVER!" They're really yelling now.

I want to run toward them, I really do. More than anything in the world. But if I run I'll kill all the beautiful glowing suns, the ones that pulse between me and the 4 women. These women. Yaqui, Spanish, English, German. But I want to. I want to see if I can break through their hands. If I'm strong enough.

"RED ROVER, RED ROVER, SEND LUNA RIGHT OVER!"

"I'm sorry," I whisper to the beautiful, glowing-sun California Poppies.

"RED ROVER, RED ROVER, SEND LUNA RIGHT OVER!"

I run as fast as I can. I run with every ounce of my strength. And as I run I become mi Loba, running and running—I smell the earth, poppies, the sun, and so many smells for a moment, making me so fast. I push myself harder till I feel like an arrow, running, flying. Each woman's face becomes clearer. And clearer. When I reach their hands La Loba becomes me, and I aim for the middle, trying my utmost to break through, to be strong enough to break through their locked arms, but they catch me. They catch me. I'm held. We all fall in a heap, arms and legs entwining, we laugh. Then we stand, holding hands in a circle, and begin to sing, "Red Rover, Red Rover, send everyone on over. . . ." We begin to dance in a circle, singing these words, holding hands, till my hands, feet, heart, mouth, eyes are hot—I could feel it in the dream—hot with JOY. (I never thought I'd feel this kind of "me joy"—me, the whole shebang.) Until this dream, Virgencita.

I played this game so many times as a kid—my trick was to pick the 2 weakest kids and smash through their hands. And I always broke through. No one ever caught me. Till now (in the dream). All those times I yelled those words, that name, "Red Rover, Red Rover" . . . now I want to know, what does Red Rover look like, Virgen? (You don't have to answer that one, but I had to ask you anyway.) GRACIAS Virgencita, this dream will last me for the rest of my life, but send me more, many many more—and now I know Red Rover sent me over. And here I am on a farm with my <u>own</u> California Poppies. Me. My 4 mes. La Loca Mestiza me. The whole chingaso shebang. And I was caught (in the dream).

Late July Update

Dear La Virgencita,

This won't be long, but I'll get back to you next month (August). . . . I think Tania has her first boyfriend, Minnie's cousin Sam. When Tania and Sam went downtown to get a sundae she said they were stared at everywhere they went (of course)—that people actually stopped and stared. And that she heard some man say, as they walked by, "Nigger lover." Here we go, Virgen, and a part of me (sheer self-preservation and the starkest fear she'll be harmed by one of these nuts) wants to tell her to only see Sam here on the farm or when we go to the ocean for barbecues—but every time I start to say this I just can't. I look at her fearless face, her eyes, and I just can't. And Sam is sweet and gentle, bringing her little gifts he makes. He strung some seashells (from one of our outings) on a string, making a bracelet. He oiled the shells to make them shine with color, and she wears it every day. Ayyyy Diosa, Virgencita, send me a warning dream if you see danger, and watch over my daughter and her first boyfriend. La Oakley saw them together holding hands and her eyes grew soft for a moment. "The whole world's not going to agree with that." "I know," I said, on the verge of tears (tenderness and terror fighting it out in my brain). Then La Oakley changed the subject as we watched them walk, hand in hand, toward town.

And to top it all off my ex-husband called collect—I had to think about that, but out of sheer curiosity accepted. He wanted me to come back to him (!), bring the kids to where he's living in Oregon. We haven't heard from him in 2 years—he says he got my number from Chan and that he'd heard I was living on a farm—he never once asked about the kids. As he was talking, on my $, telling me about where he was and that he's logging now, I remembered one night during our last year together, that he raped me. At the time I didn't realize he'd raped me—since he was my husband—but I had wanted to kill him for weeks after, and though we fought about it I didn't let him touch me for over a month—and when he did it was never ever the same. When I was in a woman's group later and a woman talked about how her husband would beat her and rape her—her husband—finally I understood. And as I stood there listening to him, his voice so sure I was interested, I felt like I was being raped again, Virgen—and I very gently hung up on him, so maybe he kept talking till he heard the tone in his ear. So now when I think of him, I yell TIMBER to myself, and watch so serenely as the tree has an accident, and I feel so much better. And then I know even this will fail to amuse me, and I'll begin to forget what he looks like (again)—and I don't tell the kids that he called and never asked for them TIMBER!!!

Theo and Jason are playing baseball and their coaches asked them to cut off their fairly long hair. I talked to both coaches, both white guys with crew cuts—I could barely stand one of them (he was chewing tobacco, spitting it in an ugly brown stream as he talked to me), but I liked the other coach, who kept referring to Theo as "son" in a warm and fatherly way. As they massacred my name, Villalobos, I was sorry for a nanosecond that I didn't keep my name the same as my children's (as that also seemed to trouble them)—but after all those years of feeling like an imposter with a "good name" and people thinking I was French or something, and every time I'd explain to someone I was Mexican they'd look at me (most people) with the look of—And you're proud of this? (And of course I think of my mother Carmen's "good Irish name" from The Psycho—how does she stand saying that name every fregado day of her life?) . . . So, I pronounced my name for both coaches, and the one I liked gave it a good try—the other one smirked and wouldn't say it again, calling me ma'am. The boys were willing, so we compromised with a trim just below their ears, no crew cuts—almost every kid on the team has one. Theo and Jason said they were both teased in the beginning (fag, girlie, hey cutie . . .) but they both know how to take care of themselves, and a couple of guys on their teams seem to have longer crew cuts now. The evolution of Sebastopol or bust . . . should I write that on a giant chingadero rainbow banner and put it up on our front fence? . . . (Just kidding, Virgencita, but I would really LOVE to do it, can't you just see it?) Of course, I'd have to hire round the clock protection—I guess what we really need to do is "blend" yet still be who we really and truly are. And I would hardly call Tania and Sam holding hands and walking downtown as blending—so I'll just close my eyes once in a while and see the chingadero rainbow banner hanging on my front fence, I mean huge: THE EVOLUTION OF SEBASTOPOL OR BUST!!!! And I will smile to myself, secretly, and maybe sometimes I'll just break into a chingadero smile as I'm walking downtown and all the uptight White People (who look at me and secretly think "vermin") can just figure it out. And the "evolved" White People will just (maybe) see a human being mammal smiling—so far, I've seen a few of these . . . they have rainbows in their eyes. And I'm not kidding, I can really see this in people's eyes, more and more like I probably did as a kid, right Virgencita?

I finally called Carmen and I think she almost died of SHOCK when she heard my voice. I told her I was coming down to S.F. in a week and I asked her if she wanted to have lunch somewhere—so we're actually going to do it. I just hope she doesn't say something so mean and nasty I end up throwing her out the car door in traffic (just kidding). As you can see, I'm trying—what happened to her, Virgen? What's the big, terrible secret? I find it hard to believe she's happy this way—you know how she was with my kids, so they don't trust their own grandmother. But then I think of the woman who carried my baby self to the bus stop on that boiling hot summer day in Louisiana (where she was "no better than a nigger" as she heard from her husband's—my father's—family). So, I tell myself (repeatedly)—"I am the woman your mother was. We are the daughters of flint and pitch. O see the poles are kissing as they cross." The Most Arrested Man In Sonoma County will never know that his being hooched to the gills and screaming Dylan Thomas at the top of his lungs, in his beautiful Irish brogue voice, helps keep me sane, me La Loca. . . . The thing is, whenever Carmen's "nice" you know she's going to be mean in about one hour, flat—you can almost time it, which is why, of course, I haven't even talked to her in such a long fregado time. Anyway, when I asked her to go to lunch she started in with how The Colonel (her old boyfriend when I was a kid) used to take her to this Italian place on Fisherman's Wharf in S.F. by the Golden Gate (Sewerside) Bridge—thank La Diosa she didn't mention The Blood Sucker, I might've hung up, Virgen. So I just broke in on The Colonel Story and said, "We could go there." Maybe she'll be imagining I'm The Colonel—maybe that'll work, who knows. . . . I'll fill you in next month. Wish me luck, lots of luck, Virgencita . . . maybe when I see Carmen I'll think, "Red Rover, Red Rover, send Carmen right over. . . ." She'll be thinking of The Colonel and I'll be thinking of Red Rover, maybe it'll work and we can last 2 or 3 hours (fre ga do).

The other day the kind of cute cop, the nice one, came by to see how we're doing, and he ended up having a cup of coffee. It was pretty weird having a regular, friendly conversation with a guy in a cop uniform with a GUN in his holster—but then I remind myself about the RIFLE over my back door, ayyyy Diosa! Anyway, I can tell he's going to ask me out or something—he's dropping by soon again he said. I think he's a pretty nice guy, and like I said before he looks like he might be part Indian or Mexican (or both), but I didn't ask him yet. If I really get to know him I probably will, we'll see—because when Jason raced in for a snack, bumping into a chair and knocking it over (big deal), he said, "Boys need a man's hand." PUKOLA as my 13-year-old mammal self used to say. So he flunked that one, and to tell the truth I don't know if I ever want to LIVE with a man again (I can hear you laughing, Virgen)—but I'm serious. I guess the truth of the truths is . . . I know how to fight for my life, steal and lie (if I have to), and I know I cannot stand to hear things like "Boys need a man's hand"—my ugly, scar-tissue heart (with its one skinny red rose) has a bona fide heart attack, only I feel like attacking him. Maybe I've never learned how to be "a girl" or "a woman"—maybe I'll always be a boy in drag, because when it comes down to my beat-up, scar-tissue heart I cannot pretend everything's okey dokey if it's not. I wonder if Chula ever got married and if she ever got to fight the grown bulls, Chula, someone else I should try to find. I remember one time she actually said, "I'd rather face a bull than get married." Her father was always pestering her to get married, she was too old to be without a man, he'd say, I remember. Maybe I should start fighting bulls, Virgencita—more on this subject next month (if el cop returns). "I'd rather face a bull than get married" . . . sounds like the first line of a poem—I can just hear Chula's voice, her laughter, her GRITO. . . .

Finally, for this month—most of the chickens made it and I took them out of the brooder, their big, fake sun (Tania calls it their Chicken Universe, and it was), and put them, all 18 of them, into the scrubbed and whitewashed chicken coop with the small fake eggs in their straw nests that I read will coax them to lay (and that La Oakley says will only confuse the critters). We cleaned that coop for 2 days straight, scraping chicken poop with old knives (Jason and Theo pretending to eat it almost made Tania and I heave ho)—so pretty soon FRESH EGGS! Sally told me about a chicken called "Araucanas" that lay colored eggs, pastel colors of blue and green—I ordered 10 of those, figuring 7 or 8 will make it in the Chicken Universe gizmo. It turns out Araucanas are from South America and they still have a "wild streak" in them, La Oakley says, since they haven't been domesticated that long. So wild eggs it'll be EEEEHHAAA and hot doggy! Jason says "Hot doggy!" now when something's cool, as his friend Rocky Raccoon says it, so he caught it. Now I'm saying it . . . it's contagious.

And so, still no TV, and the kids are begging me to buy a new one. But I still like it. No TV. We talk and make a fire outside. We eat dinner and no one's rushing to get away from the table to see the fregado TV—and they're reading at night (Tania books, Theo books and comics, Jason comics). When winter really comes and we start making fires in the fireplace, I can just see them fighting for a place around the fire with a BOOK—I just bought "The Chronicles of Narnia" for everyone and plan to bring it out when school starts, those winter nights. I also bought an enormous paperback called "Bury My Heart at Wounded Knee," which I'm now reading—a true history of the Native People on this continent that breaks my heart page by page (I'll put this out by the fire as well). I also found some great books at the 2nd hand bookstore in Santa Rosa—"The Catcher in the Rye" (which still makes me laugh), "Demian" (the first novel I fell in love with), and "The Diary of Anne Frank" (the first book I fell in love with—well, not quite . . . "The Island Stallion" books in Bolinas were the first). And a couple of Steinbeck books that look promising, which I haven't read . . . what I plan to do is pile these "new books" close to the fireplace to tempt them in their weak moments of winter boredom. And so, the sound of morning cartoons (biff boff ouch yeow) continues to be replaced by Vivaldi and other wonderful music (flute, guitar, piano) . . . so we'll see if I can withstand their heart-felt pleas. (And if I can live without the Road Runner and the Coyote, the truth.) And I bet their grades would be even better, so I'd like to try this for at least one year. NO TV. Jason and Theo: "Do you really want us to turn into Billy Bob and Billy Joe, Mom?" Tania: "But you have to promise if we start going brain-dead in a year we get the new TV." So I promised MOOOOOO.

The first patch of corn we planted is coming up like little green fingers poking through the dark ground, like something being born fingers first. We planted in cycles, from early corn to late corn, which supposedly will keep coming up till Thanksgiving, and thanks, La Oakley says, to the warmth of the mulch she told me about (layered fertilizer, newspaper, hay). Also, the yellow squash, zucchinis, lemon cucumbers and chili plants are taking over their part of the garden—and the tomatoes, 2 kinds of lettuce, spinach, kale, carrots and green onions are in the small enclosed garden (so the birds can't get them)—and in this garden I've planted marigolds all around as I read they disgust all the plant chomping bugs, hot doggy!!! And so, all these PLANTS start yelling at me if I forget one day too long . . . "Water me, I'm dying of thirst over here, pendeja, WATER ME!!" I can really hear them, Virgencita—it starts kind of in my body, maybe my feet (where their roots are), then their voices rise through my legs on up to my ears, their words, their loud GREEN words that make me bring them clear liquid vida . . . it's funny, maybe I'm making all of this sound kind of ordinary, common place, regular—but the truth is I'm in the middle of a M I R A C L E and I know it, but I don't know how to say it, how to really say it (maybe that's what poetry is for).

Virgen, I see you (especially) in the so soft, tender, sun-green fingers of the corn being born and pushing through the beautiful, so fertile, dark earth. We've mulched everything as La Oakley advised and the earth looks so fertile now as though you could just drop the seeds and they'd grow because they felt like it—but I know this isn't entirely true. It takes a LOT of work, care, weeding (we don't want to spray with poisons), so the weeding is W O R K and I sometimes feel like a slave driver with a whip (Theo's version of me) as I make them do their share of weeding before they take off for the day. And Theo and Jason are learning to trap gophers, though it's pretty awful to find their dead bodies, and I wasn't prepared for those, I mean, huge gopher teeth (but I still felt sorry for them, you know me)—BUT you can actually see them pull a plant right into the earth, poof—but first they shake it and shake it. The first time I saw this early in the morning when everything is so still and quiet, I had to make myself not freak out and run, but to stand there and LOOK . . . shake shake shake wobble wobble POOF. It's actually kind of funny, like a Bugs Bunny cartoon where he steals all the carrots from his rabbit hole (What's up, doc?), except for the fact that they're eating our food—but we did plant a lot as we had (have) little faith in our farming skills. In the miracle.

Okay, here it is—even if the birds, bugs and gophers get to everything I'm still in the middle of a MIRACLE. . . . I look out my window and see it. I walk outside and see it. I look in my children's eyes and see it. I look in La Oakley's eyes and see it (she's starting to tell me some childhood stories, will save them for next month). I look in my own eyes and see it. I look in el cute cop's eyes and I see it. And here's the truth, even the cross burners' eyes, Frank The Hit Man's eyes, and of course Chan's eyes, Pablo's eyes, Jake's eyes, the eyes . . . and I wonder if at that moment that guy downtown said "nigger lover" to Tania, would I see it, and the girls with the hand axes and knives who ripped Tania's special dress, would I see it? The soldiers who killed the innocent in Vietnam, would I see it? The KKK, each face, would I see it? The slave owner's face who sold the children separate from the mother, would I see it? The Nazis who killed Anne Frank (and over 6 million people), would I see it? As I sit here writing in my notebook by the now slowly moving creek and the garland cross, Wiley The Wolf comes over and after turning in circles a couple of times he plops down next to me, putting his lobito face in my lap. As he begins to twitch his ears and paws I try to imagine his lobito dreams (which is probably getting his sharp puppy teeth on our chickens, right?) . . . All I can say is, Virgencita, is at this moment in late July (in 2 months I'll be 29)—I see the miracle. And maybe, just maybe that's enough in one vida.

And so, I'll place the first 2 ripe ears of corn on the outside altar here by the garland cross ("O see the poles are kissing as they cross")—and also 2 ripe ears of corn (La Oakley calls it "new corn" and she says they're tiny and sweet like candy, and you can eat the whole thing, can't wait!) on the inside altar I've moved to my bedroom by the picture window facing the fields. I've decorated the inside altar with flowers, seashells, candles and special objects, secret prayers, dreams; and my ongoing diary to you is hidden under the silky purple scarf that covers the altar, kind of like Darling's El Buddha altar, and Mamacita's Virgencita altars she made wherever she lived so she could hear you better (she always told me). Will you be La Diosa De La Maize, Virgen? Let me know in a dream—also, let me know if my crops are actually going to <u>survive</u> the birds, bugs, gophers, my stupidity, to the "new corn" stage, gracias. I've read that in the old beliefs and myths of Mamacita's Mexico, La Diosa De La Maize feeds the world and no one goes hungry—and also that dried corn can be cooked and eaten CENTURIES later. If my corn survives I'll dry some in the oven, that's what my Farm Bible says to do, just put the shucked corn, thinly layered, on a cookie sheet in a warming oven overnight, and then in a couple of centuries you have dinner. I know this is locita, but in my heart I imagine that this farm could feed the world, but the truth is it'll be a miracle if it feeds us—but if I could feed the world I would. I guess that's where La Diosa De La Maize comes in, Virgen, that's your job. . . . Red Rover, Red Rover, send La Virgen De La Maize right over! (Is this peace, Virgen?)

I'm sitting here holding The Secret Crystal World Rock Darling gave me when I was 12, and I realize, as I look around, that my Secret Crystal World sure has a lot of people in it now. As I pet Wiley's thick fur I feel his dog drool on my leg, so I gently put his head in the grass. I look out at the back fields and I already miss the California Poppies—the back fields look a little sad without them, but I know they'll be back next year. (Will I hear them next year, their singing, I wonder, I hope.) Next summer I'll sleep right in the middle of them . . . and then suddenly I thought of Whitey's ashes on the mantelpiece in the beautiful vase I keep them in kind of to the side, not right in the middle of the mantel (as the kids kept saying it creeped them out, though they loved him of course)—so I ran to the house and got them and then walked out to the fields where the poppies had been thickest (with Wiley awake now and excited about my running around). And I sprinkled Whitey's ashes, really more like crystals, secret world crystals from his bones. The secrets of his bones. Set free. To give the California Poppies their fiery sun and song, and I knew, as I scattered his crystals, next summer's poppies will be extra ordinary. And I know I'll hear them singing new songs. Always new songs, right Virgencita? And I wasn't sad as I sprinkled his crystals, I didn't cry like I always thought I would. When I set his crystals free. In fact, I was weirdly happy that his crystals will always be in this field, and then I felt like having champagne, but just me by myself (and a couple of gophers). So I stood there with the empty vase in my hand, looking up at a circling hawk which made me even weirdly happier. I imagined the hawk was Whitey's soul telling me, "About time, Pocahontas." And it was so quiet I could hear the hawk's wings move in the wind, I swear.

In my right ear, where I hear poems start now—the first line—I heard this. . . . "La Virgen is La Roja Rover." I fell on the ground laughing (and Wiley rushed over to lick me right in the face), and I could feel the other women (my 4 mes) in the dream, our arms and legs all in a heap, and we started to sing-yell, "La Roja Rover is here, yes, she's here, sending us here over and over, Madre, Diosa, Mestiza." And I realized this is part of a poem, so I tried to remember it as I watched the clouds gather and fly and gather. It smelled like rain. And rain will soak Whitey's crystals deep into this earth. Into the hard black seeds of my California Poppies.

"La Roja Rover is here, yes. . . ." I'll write this poem, Virgencita. More next month, August—maybe our chickens will lay their first eggs by then, and maybe we'll have the first new corn like candy, and maybe we'll get this beautiful gray mare that's for sale (and when I ride her I'll secretly pin a fake diamond necklace on her mane so I can see the zillion rainbows)—we voted on the mare and of course everyone wants her. And maybe I'll get to know el cute cop, maybe. Who doesn't want to be loved . . . I'm only a mammal, right Virgen? But to live with a man again in esta vida, I have to leave this to my scar-tissue, amazon, one skinny red rose heart . . . and then I think of the other poem I have to write . . . "I'd rather face a bull than get married!" (Chula). Then back to the field where I'd just scattered Whitey's secret world crystals from his bones. . . . I close my eyes (I feel a raindrop) and I can just see her—serious to smiling to serious—as she commands the beat-up red cape and the young bull, and everyone yelling "OLE!!" as the bull gallops by her. To her it's the most dangerous bull in the world, the largest and strongest bull in the world. And she has the cape moving like a dance in her one hand. "I'd rather face a bull than get married!" I say out loud, laughing. Then I do a loud-ass chingadero GRITO. And it starts to just pour with thunder coming closer—is this peace, Virgencita? And did I keep the promise mooooo to myself? (Let me know in a dream, gracias La Roja Rover.)

And one last cosa, I've been reading Pablo Neruda (found FULLY EMPOWERED in the second hand bookstore)—from the final poem on the final page . . . "So what there is of death surrounding me / opens in me a window out to living." I bet that's how Chula felt fighting her bulls, and so I have to find Chula (means Darling of course) and Darling in La Bolinas (tell me in a dream if I'm going to find them, gracias again). In the meantime, will write the Chula-bull poem. Also, say hi to God for me. . . . It's okay since I (now) imagine God as a beautiful young man, every race mixed into him, every human possibility—and he has no interest in smiting anyone. That's what people do to each other like pendejo-as, and I do not believe in El Diablo either, more pathetic mammal excuses, right Virgencita? So when I say to say hi to El Rojo Rover (or La Roja Rover) I'm definitely <u>not</u> talking about El Diablo, who's really the little red guy with a pointy tail dancing on the PHAM can, and who gave me the courage to steal some food for Mamacita and me when we lived in the projects in S.F. and we had no dinero. Nada. And so, ask God if he minds if I call him El Rojo Rover. . . . Who else can I talk to like this, ask these loca questions, be my Plato self? And say hi to El Buddha if you see him. But most of all say hi to God for me and tell him I'm watching him every chance I get (when I'm not watching you, Virgencita) here on Earth, not in heaven. This GRITO is for him, just in case he's forgotten what I even look like. More next month, Virgencita (send me the dreams, I'm waiting) . . .

Luna La Whole Chingadero Shebang (Por Vida)

Acknowledgments, continued

Excerpt from "I See the Boys of Summer" by Dylan Thomas, from *The Poems of Dylan Thomas*, copyright © 1939 by New Directions Publishing Corp. Reprinted by permission of New Directions Publishing Corp.

Excerpt from "Night on the Island" by Pablo Neruda, from *The Captain's Verses*, copyright © 1972 by Pablo Neruda and Donald D. Walsh. Reprinted by permission of New Directions Publishing Corp.

Excerpt from "Fully Empowered" by Pablo Neruda, translated by Alastair Reid, from *Fully Empowered*, © 1976, 2001. Reprinted by permission of Farrar, Straus & Giroux.

Excerpt from *Mosquito* (1999) by Gayl Jones. Reprinted by permission of Beacon Press.